Shawon

World of Eight Emblems

This book deals with subjects such as depression and abuse.
All depictions in this book are a fantasy. Any relation to a real-life circumstance is merely a coincidence. It should be regarded as fantasy fiction and nothing else.

ISBN 978-1-71690-824-8

Dedicated to
My caring friends

Below

Alex stood from his desk, brushing his fingers through his hair. Reaching forward, he wrapped his fingers gently around the handle of the door. Even after weeks of planning his escape, he wasn't sure he was ready. But there was no turning back, he had to do this, it was his destiny. Alex pulled the door toward himself forcefully, and after thinking through his plan one last time, he began to run.

The wind blew through Alex's hair as he rushed through the stone hallways of the castle. Not a care echoed through his mind as he weaved through the castle corridors. Suspicions grew as he passed by his servants, and it wasn't long before he heard his name. "Alexander Raider, your attendance is required this instant!" a chubby maid yelled through the echoing corridors, halting Alex.

Alex shook his head, peering behind her. He smirked, quickly pushing her aside as he rushed to escape the palace. "Sorry, but it's time I lived my own life, Pricilla"

"The king and queen will not be happy with this, your majesty!" she yelled as she caught her balance. Her small apron flew against the air as she attempted to catch him.

"Don't worry, I'll return eventually..." Alex rushed through the halls, finding the quickest path to lose the maid. She always found herself stuck behind a thin, yet quicker passage to the throne room. Slowing his pace, and turning to his side, Alex scooted through the thin passageway, his chest rubbing against the stone.

When the passage ended, Alex exited the small pathway and began to run through another large and tainted hallway. Glancing behind to see if the maid had caught up, he suddenly ran into another person. Backing away, he glanced at him. He was slightly taller than him and owned bright green eyes. His dark brown hair complemented his figure. "Where are you headed off to in such a hurry, young nephew? You'll be late for your studies."

"Forget it!" he yelled as he rushed past him and pushed the castle door open, flashing out of sight. As people were bustling through the thin roads, the air was filled with the sound of heavy gasps as Alex winded through their sweaty bodies, squishing through groups of people. He heard many gasps, and others aweing at the appearance of their prince, while confused as to why he was in such a rush.

Glancing behind him, he noticed the city guards chasing after him. He wouldn't let them catch him. The city gates were in sight and the hope of his own freedom had exceeded his expectations. Watching the guards begin to lower the gates, he doubled his speed and slid beneath the falling gates. Alex stood from his fall as the gates came to a close and laughed with great delight. His plan had worked, he was finally free.

As he left the grounds of the city, Alex slowed his pace knowing he could hide before the guards opened the gates again. With great delight, he gripped his shoulders and unclipped the beads holding his cape to his thin blue robe. He glanced behind him, watching it fly into the clear sky as he continued to walk away from his misery. He then reached for the silver-leafed crown which rested on his head. Alex grasped the crown and removed it from his figure. He stared at it for a moment recalling the memories, smiled, and then tossed it into the sand. Reaching toward his back, he felt for his sword and sheath, keeping hold of it as he knew the world had its own dangers.

As no other soul had followed him, he laughed, feeling free for the first time. He had not a care in the world, giving attention to nothing. In the near distance, a glittering pink juniperfall cascaded. With curiosity, he ran underneath the cool liquid, feeling the warm breeze in his hair.

Alex glanced to his left as the juniper pounded against his shoulders, noticing a large gap in the stone beside him. "A cave?" Alex curiously stepped toward the hole in the rock, peeking inside, and listening to the whispers of the wind. His soul glistened as it called his name. Curious to its call, for its beaconing sound, Alex stepped inside the cavern. As he stepped through the rocky entrance, he followed a small stone pathway inside the cavern. He ran his fingers ran against the rough, damp wall, searching through the nearly empty area.

Alex ceased his movement in the center of the cavern, lifting his head as he enjoyed the crystals and rocks emerging from the walls of the cave. He let out an awed breath. As the sound fell silent, he glanced behind him, noticing the light beginning to fade, shocked to see the entrance shrinking. "No, no, no!" He ran toward the entrance, crashing against a solid wall. He sighed in fear as the last shimmer of light escaped the room. "Help!" he cried, waiting for an answer to his foolishness, yet no one heard his fragile voice. He bashed his fists against the solid wall, yet his dreadful panic could not be found.

The darkness encased his lonesome body. He was freezing, his wet clothing adhering to his skin. He cried for his life, for a way out of the cave, but he knew that there was no hope. He knew that his mistake had foreshadowed his own death. His life was now a story left written only in the minds of those who were part of it.

Before he could fall to his knees in dread, a bright and warm glow lit behind him, torches igniting inside the cave along with many others before him. The light reflected off of the beauteous crystals, unlike anything he had seen. He observed the cave, now filled with an ominous violet light that led to a curious staircase. Wrapping his arms around his shivering shoulders, Alex stared into the glorious light. Unknowing to his future, he stepped toward the staircase and stared into the abyss beneath. It fell infinitely, the bottom invisible to his eyes. Without a moment of thought, he stepped onto the first crystal stair and began to follow it to the unknown bottom. Each step he took, another torch lit. Each stair he passed, the one before disappeared. He was left alone in the stone beneath the kingdom.

As he stepped, he found himself passing through a large pillar of light. It blinded him as he fell through its grasp. As he held his arm before his eyes, he felt a strange shaking feeling. He halted his movement for a moment, quickly placing the palm of his hand on the wall beside him for balance. As the light dimmed and he lifted his eyelids, the stairs before him rose and created a flat ground. He studied the small area, brightened by the luminous torches. It was a small, dirt area, only expanded by a small pathway which led to a mystery and a new life. He knew now that he would not have any say in his consequences.

Sighing for his idiocy, he continued. Alex bent down, dusted off his black pants and walked through the old and broken path, one which seemed to have been forgotten by the many souls who once lived. The torches burnt out as he passed by them, a feeling that could only be described as magic filling the hallway. When he glanced behind him, the pathway seemed to disappear too, flee from his vision. He squinted, his eyes peering toward a darkened door which blocked the exit of the hallway. It was shadowed, a void of smoke and sorrow surrounding the outlines. He began to walk quickly, hoping that it would lead him to the adventure he hoped for. He stopped and wrapped his fingers around the golden handle, the smoothness calming his fingers. He twisted the doorknob and pulled the door toward him.

A new terrain appearing before him, he stepped through the door, his eyes in awe at an unexpected evergreen forest. His clothing and hair suddenly became dry and soft, the wind gently blowing through. As he studied the area, letting go of the handle, the door slammed behind him. Startled by the sudden action, he glanced at the door he had come from, yet nothing was there, aside from a rocky cliffside. The large door which had once been placed there had dissipated like the path before. It was a mystery as to why any of it had happened. He was left confused in this strange fantasy of a world.

A startling snap played in the distance. Alarmed, he faced the forest, his mind breaking even more. A man that was no more than an inch shorter than Alex appeared in front of him, his eyelids shut. He looked slightly older than Alex. His hair was blonde, short, and slightly spiked up. A thin rope was tied around him, from his left shoulder to his right hip. His left hand was wrapped around the handle of a sword resting inside a large sheath on his back, the pommel of which was carved into a skull. As for his right hand, it was resting in his pocket.

The man opened his sagging eyelids, revealing empty sockets, filled with darkness. He seemed to stare into his soul as he crept closer to Alex. Alex stuttered in his steps as he slowly stepped backward, until his back pressed against the rough wall. “W-where am I?! Who are you?! I-I will draw my sword if you come any closer!” Alex reached for his valiant sword which rested on his back.

The eyeless man let go of the handle of his sword and held out his hand. They stared at each other for a moment. "Don't be afraid." he acknowledged as he wiggled his fingers. His voice was deep and calm, yet it felt uneasy, and unnatural. Alex lifted his hand cowardly, clutching the stranger's hand. Though covered in flesh, he could feel the thin, boney fingers of the being. "Hello." he released his strong grip and took a step backward, his uniform wrinkling. "I am Zorus." he paused and smiled. "I presume you have a name."

Alex stuttered in the sight of the being. "A-Alex." his blue eyes quivered. "Wh-what are you?" Alex asked anxiously.

"My apologies, my rec is quite rare. I'm a scelo rec, there are only two left in existence, my younger brother and me. He and I are sentries here in Treesy, always searching for the unnatural. And what rec are you?" he asked in return.

"Uhhh… a human...?"

Zorus quickly turned the opposite direction in distress. "A human? Th-that's impossible. How did you get here?" his playful expression shattered through his thoughts. He slowly stepped through the forest, pondering through his voice. "No, how could you have arrived without my noticing?"

"What are you talking about?"

Alex followed Zorus through the maze of trees. "Legend tells that a prophesied human would access the entrance and set us free. No one in this world has expected the prophecy to become a reality, it was always just a story." he stood very anxiously. "There is no way you could have come here." he faced Alex once again. "How did you get here?

"I...I…" he paused as he realized the sound of footsteps was nearing.

Before Alex could continue his speech, Zorus interrupted. "He's here..." he whispered ominously.

"Zorus, where have you been? Your attendance is required immediately." a raspier voice came from the midst of the trees.

"Heh, sorry Core, thought you weren't around."

"Of course, I am here, you know me. It is imperative that we leave with utmost urgency. The Sandern is lurking nearer each day." the pointy pines on the trees shook and out of the midst of the trees, another eyeless man stepped out of the darkness of the forest and stood before them. His figure looked similar to Zorus's, though he was much taller than him. His dark brown hair was curved at the top of his head. His skin seemed to be even thinner than the other, yet he seemed to have excellently crafted muscles. His rope led from his right shoulder to his left hip, carrying another strange skeleton sword within his leather sheath. "Zorus, who were you wasting your time talking to?"

"Why don't you come greet him yourself?" he questioned.

The second scelo stepped forward and let out his hand as he studied Alex. He grasped his hand and shook it before speaking. "Pleasured to meet you, I am Courier..." the being quickly dropped his hand in astonishment. "You found the human? Zorus, what were you doing? We can't let the Broken Souls..." Zorus shrugged his shoulders. "Why are you so rebellious toward your occupation? You tried out for it."

Zorus shrugged once again. "This job was your idea." Zorus reminded him.

The scelo shook his head, seeming more annoyed than anyone could imagine. "But you have to admit, you enjoy it as much as I do," he said as he wrapped his boney fingers around Alex's wrist, pulling them behind his back. He was surprisingly stronger than he seemed. "And, either way, we are both on this mission, and you failed to do the one thing we were sent to do." he spoke directly to his brother. "The Sandern can wait."

Alex looked into his empty eyes. "Hey, get your deficient hands off of me!"

The scelo looked into Alex's eyes and spoke again. "I would, but I have a very important assignment to complete. I would thank you for arriving, but I cannot make friends with the human. Instead, we will take you to the king in Krysal city, and there you will begin your quest in freeing our kind. You humans *were* the ones who imprisoned us here..."

Zorus chuckled. "Courier… what are you talking about?" he asked as he slouched backward.

"Well, according to the book *Pastime with Demons:* when we lost the war with the humans, they locked us in this dimension to punish us." Zorus shrugged his shoulders again. "Don't you remember the day when monsters and humans went to war? Our kind were not powerful enough, the humans pushed them back until they fell into their brilliant trap. Oh, and they sacrificed their own souls to seal the portal so any being trapped inside could never leave." He gritted his white teeth.

"How would I remember the day we were trapped in this dimension if we were not even alive?" Zorus inquired.

Ugh. Why is it you never choose to study? I know we were non-existent at that time, yet every Darlid has been told the story. I am disappointed in you." Courier admitted.

"Of course, I knew. I would hate to be *imprisoned* in this world any longer."

Wait, you said *this dimension.* Where am I?" Alex asked in an anxious shiver.

Well, you are in Shawon, the world of *monsters*." Courier grinned. As he spoke, he began to walk, pulling Alex along backward. His back bent awkwardly as his feet slipped further back. Zorus walked behind both of them, his hands kept inside his pockets. "Krysal palace is quite far though, so we mustn't begin to travel during the night. We will reside in the mansion tonight." With his free hand, he pulled a large pine branch away, revealing a large house, crafted of an oak-like wood.

Courier stepped through a small patch of trees and stood in front of the tall white door, leading to the entrance of the house. A detailed skull was carved into it. Courier pushed the handle down and opened the door. Letting him go, he gestured his hand inside for Alex to enter. Alex brushed his fingers through his light brown hair as he stepped inside. Courier pointed to another white door on the right. "Make yourself comfortable. I advise you to stay in that guest room. We will leave tomorrow morning." Alex uncomfortably began to step down the hallway. Stopping, he glanced back at Courier. "Oh, and the two rooms across the hallway are Zorus's and mine. Feel free to find us there if you truly need anything."

Alex twisted the handle on the door and stepped inside the room. He felt himself fall onto the comfortable white bed, resting his exhausted body and his anxious mind. Though he had freed himself from his prison, he found himself living in yet another.

His eyes beamed open, returning to the familiar sight of the old, broken-down cell. His blonde hair was ragged and crusted with specks of dirt. His clothing matched, tangled, ripped, the color so stained that no one could imagine the true hue. He was covered in cuts and bruises, heavy shackles crafted of a strange metal were wrapped neatly around his small wrists. He could not have been older than ten, but this was no place to raise children.

A small bed lay next to the wall on the opposite side of the room. The toddler was barely opening his shining hazel eyes, the drugs keeping him from crying in his hard times. He also wore shackles that held him to the wall. The boy cried for his younger brother, reaching for him, unable to comfort his sorrow.

The doorknob creaked and wiggled, the door peeking open. Light fled into the darkness. A tall, oozing creature stood in the doorway, his shadow draping over his body. He stepped closer to the boy, who covered his eyes in fear. He heard the click of the chains, and his arms were once again free. The tall creature tightened his grip around his wrist and pulled him out of the room, the large metal door slamming behind them. He was used to this, he had been there for as long as he could remember, but the fear still followed.

The Tall Being led the boy to a small room, a doctor's table standing in the center. He pointed to the table, the boy following his command, walking toward it. He laid him down, chaining more shackles to his limbs. He wanted to make sure that the boy could not change his *physical state* while in the process. "S, *every day I am one step closer to finding the pieces of Athreal.*" The Tall Being lifted a syringe from the counter, examining the needle for any fault. "*Your minds, S, are powerful, they can help the world in many ways. If I could just get the formula perfect, you can be* improved." his steps echoed as he stepped closer to him.

The needle pierced his skin as it was inserted into his mind. He felt himself fall into a dream... a nightmare as his memories and thoughts were sucked into the syringe. The tall creature pried the needle out of his mind, a swirling purple and yellow liquid bubbling inside. He placed the syringe on the counter and turned around, leaving the room.

The Tall Being left S alone for what felt like hours on the table, leaving him with only his thoughts to comfort him. The thoughts were horrific, the shadows on the walls seemed to create monsters, smiling freakishly at him. He could only imagine what Master was going to do to him… to his brother. Though it felt like an eternity, the Master returned only moments later with the small, drugged child in his arms.

He placed the small fragile body onto a clean counter and lifted an old, rusted knife from beside him. S watched in pain and fear as he began to cut into the child's skin, the drips of blood falling into a dented bucket. He lifted the syringe from the wooden counter and inserted it into the child's brain, the liquid leaked out of the container, the small child losing himself. "No!" the boy screamed, but nobody heard his cries.

Fight for Freedom

It stared at the human, gazing into his soul. *He* bent to his side, breathing moist air into his ear. "Wake," it whispered in a deep and disturbing voice. Alex's light blue eyes shined as his eyelids stretched open unpleasantly surprised to look upon a dripping, oozing creature. Finding himself unable to scream, he studied the being. It was a pure white, translucent, dripping thing. Through its clear, waving skin, he could see its bones and skull perfectly fitted underneath. It was standing upright on two legs, though no arms were visible on its figure. He held a disturbing grin, always growing larger. A scar laid over his empty right eye, his left, flushed with a bright green hue, almost shined. His dark clothing was draped with oozing white lines.

Alex, in shock, was unable to move from his frightened state. From the blade of its shoulder, a viscous arm was produced, flowing through the sleeveless cloak. An endless tentacle composed of its oozing flesh grew from its shoulder, lowering to his face. Its jaw and lips moved as he spoke, yet his disturbed emotion did not change. "You found your way to me, it was destiny. I need you, without you, I cannot succeed." His voice was deep and distorted, a million voices silently singing alongside its own. Yet he spoke slowly and calmly. Its arm hovered above his face.

"Ah, Let's find what breaks you." he lowered his tentacle to Alex's forehead, pressing his flesh against his skull. The arm began to phase into his head, entering his mind. Changing it, fixing it. Its arm began to glow, stealing the memories and feelings from his fragile mind. Alex's head went dizzy as his breathing slowed. "You will help me succeed..." his voice echoed. It suddenly halted its movement as a muffled voice played in the distance. The being's expression shifted to distress as it pulled its arm out of his head, allowing the tentacle to retract into his body. He lifted his broken face in the air and stared at the door in confusion and fear. He glanced at Alex once again before fading into the mist of the air, a white smoke disappearing into time and space.

Alex breathed heavily and placed his hands beneath his body. He heaved himself from the soft surface and glanced at the doorway, though his legs would not budge, they almost felt broken, unable to change their position. The handle on the wooden door shook. Alex quivered in fear, pulling at his legs with great force. The door swung open. Courier stood in the doorway, glancing behind himself irritatedly. He quickly looked forward and fixed his emotion.

"Today we will travel to the castle, where you will set us free of this prison. Do you understand?" Alex attempted to stand yet again, this time his legs falling off of the side of the bed. His fear had drifted. The being that had spoken to him had bound him to the surface. "Come, we have a long journey ahead of us." Courier let out his boney right hand and helped him stand.

Courier gripped his hand tightly as they stepped outside of the small bedroom. "You must be taken to the king, then the legend will surely commence. Your soul must be used to atone for your ancestors." Courier stated. "Do you have any objections?"

"Actually, I do. I don't want to be sacrificed. I want to go home. I am an important person where I come from." Alex declared.

Courier seemed absolutely shocked. "Really?" he asked in astonishment.

Yeah, I am the prince of my kingdom and a noble warrior in our army. I need to get back to Achnor." he attempted to sound as disconcerted as possible, yet he still sounded more irritated than so.

"I see, but as customary to law, if terms cannot be agreed upon, then a battle must take place."

"A battle, for what?" Alex asked in an annoyed tone.

Zorus's voice echoed through the corridor. "For your freedom. If you win, Courier and me will find a way to bring you home, but if he wins, we will bring you to the king to follow the prophecy."

"Actually, it is *'Courier and I.'*" his brother ranted. He turned toward the entrance door and before he took a step, he glanced at Alex. "We will battle in the forest." he added.

Courier opened the front door, leading them outside. He marched out of the mansion, Alex beginning to follow behind, Zorus keeping an eye on him. "Treesy woods will be a perfect battleground." Courier noted, studying the area before them. There was a large enough space between the evergreen trees to hold the battle.

Courier was wearing the same attire as the day before. He wore a white uniform, red stripes, cloth squares and patterns laid in the right corner, brown accents filling the blank spots. His pants matched his top, only there were not as many patterns and more blank space. He wore a crimson red cape falling from his broad shoulders. It was worn out, dirty and torn at the bottom. His brother too wore a similar outfit, there were only small differences, like the color of his uniform being dark blue and that his cape looked like it had just been retrieved from a tailor.

Courier drew his sword from his leather sling and lifted it. "Well, what are you waiting for? Draw your sword." Alex reached for his large silver sword and bore it from his leather sheath. Its handle was twined with a thick rope and was decorated with bright gold accents throughout the weapon. He fell into a battle stance as he faced his enemy. He was ready for this; he had been well trained in the arts of a swordsman and had enjoyed the skill more than any other.

Alex waited for his opponent to strike, but to his amazement, Courier waited. The scelo stood tall and began to suck in his already thin skin. His flesh began to decay, fade from his body. Other parts of his figure completely disappeared, like his ears, nose, and hair. His uniform shifted to meet the shape of his thinner body. The top cloth draped down and curled around his ribs, showing his spine. His now boney fingers curled around the sword. He smiled grimly through his skull. He was a skeleton knight, nearly indestructible.

"Oh, I almost forgot. Zorus will be joining me." Courier chuckled, aware of his advantage.

"What?" Zorus stared at his brother with a look of concern, pulling his hands out of his pockets.

You heard me brother, we can't lose this chance of returning to Achnor." Courier's lower jaw bounced as he spoke, his head balancing on his neck.

Alex glanced at Zorus before looking back to his opponent. "Now that's just unfair!" Alex stammered.

"You know I can't..."

"Zorus, we have no time for your apathy. You know well that this is all too fair. He is fighting for what he desires, while we are fighting for what we hope for."

Zorus sighed. "Fine." he dropped his hands to his sides and closed his eyelids. Taking in a deep, melodious breath, he reached toward the handle of his sword, his flesh diminishing. His uniform also shrank, the fabric tightening to his thin and short spine. His eyelids faded, showing the indents in his skull. Unsheathing his sword, he let out a longing sigh. He stood beside his brother and glared at Alex. He cracked his knuckles.

"Two against one? This should be easy."

"I wouldn't be so confident if I were you, Alex." Zorus admitted.

"Alex? Is that short for Alexander?" Alex, embarrassed at the notion, nodded. "I actually studied a theology on names for a good couple of months. It was quite intriguing."

"How come you're not a scholar?" Alex asked.

"Well, as much as I enjoy studying, I wanted to spend my career using my skill of swordsmanship, and... Agh, we're getting off-topic!" Alex breathed in deeply as Courier charged toward him and slashed his sword toward him. Courier twisted his hand, blocking the attack with his sword. He pulled his sword back and swung it forward. Alex jumped back, the blade barely missing his stomach. Courier bent his body and charged toward Alex, sword over his shoulder. Alex closed his eyes, lifting his sword, crafted of strong metal, in the air to block the pressure. He heard the materials ring, and opened his eyes, applying force against Courier. Zorus ran close behind them, standing by the fight.

Zorus swung his sword toward him. Alex struck back just in time. Courier swung his sword. Alex ducked, the sword an inch above his head. His sword flew to the side and struck a tree. As he was tugging against the handle, Alex swung his sword and hit Zorus's spine. He stumbled back and glanced at Courier in agony. Though he seemed to be bluffing, hiding some unknown abilities. "Zorus, this is not the time!" Courier complained.

Zorus leaned his back against a tree as his skin began to reform. "You have this, brother." he stated as he sheathed his sword. Courier glanced at Alex, who swung his sword toward his legs. Noticing the attack, he jumped over the blade and swung his sword. Alex struck his sword against the other, pushing it back. Alex ducked as he released pressure, allowing Courier's blade to skim the tip of his hair. Leaping from his crouched stance, Alex threw his sword toward his enemy's face, caught off guard when his attack was yet again blocked, as if he knew what was coming.

Alex's sword broke out of the stance, ripping Courier's ragged cape. They raised their swords, striking against each other again. But Alex was not strong enough, despite his father's excellent training. He had underestimated the ability of this being. Courier threw his sword against his weapon, dropping them both to the ground.

Aware of his mistake, Courier quickly grabbed Alex's shoulders and pushed him back. His feet slipped, the dirt flew from the ground, creating clouds of white dust. Courier applied more force. Out of strength, Alex fell to the ground in defeat. Courier placed his boot on top of Alex's chest as he lifted his sword and placed it underneath his elbow for balance. "I believe I, Courier, have won this battle." He lifted his heavy boot off of Alex's chest and let out a hand. Alex took it and stood from the ground. Zorus pushed himself from the ground and stood. "You put up a good fight Alex, if it weren't for my extreme training, you would have defeated me."

"You did have an *advantage,* Core."

"Zorus, remember, you yourself said that we should never speak of that." Courier redirected his attention toward Alex. "It is decided, we will go to the castle, but because of this glorious fight, I will allow you to wander around Treesy village, our home, before we leave." His flesh began to form again over his bones, his clothing stretching to fit his body as he spoke. Alex lifted his sword from the ground and placed it inside his small sling.

Zorus placed his hand on Courier's shoulder and jolted his head upward. Following his cue, they walked through the tall evergreen trees to their mansion and disappeared through their dusted doorway. Courier slammed the door behind them.

Alex turned around and looked between the trees. Ripped fabric and pieces of bark were laying on the ground, evidence of their battle. He looked into the lilac tinted sky above his head as he pulled the spiny branches away from his face. With uncertainty, he walked through the low roof of trees.

Trees were chopped down, and in place were wooden houses and small buildings. There was a restaurant in the center of the small road named *Mossery*, a shed standing by its side. His eyes peered to the left, an armory and blacksmith stood beside a market. He walked down the stone path in the small village. He shyly smiled at the indescribable creatures who stared at him in awe and fear. A small pink fluff ball waved his tiny arm at him, immediately running into its tiny house.

Alex walked to the edge of the town and followed the gravel path. Twisted trees were grown beside him, grinning faces carved into them. He only hoped that this would lead him home. He turned a corner, where an ominous white light shined in the distance. He walked forward, reaching his hand out toward it. It was beautiful, calling for him. "I wouldn't advise going that way." an echoed voice played in the distance. He turned around, seeing no one in sight. Confused, he turned back around. Zorus stood in front of him.

"How did you get..."

"We should really be heading out, Alex." Zorus placed his hand on his shoulder and turned him away from the light. "And plus, Courier would be unhappy if I lost you." He pushed him along the stone path laid beneath them and turned the corner. Courier stood at the end of the road. Alex noticed a chocolate-colored satchel resting against his side.

He dropped his hand from his hip as he glanced at Alex. "Ah, did you enjoy your time looking around?" Alex nodded. "Well then, are you finally ready to begin the journey?" Courier asked

"Yeah, but first we should stop by the Mossery, I planned for a celebration tonight."

"Have you gone awry?" Courier squinted and raised his arms in a questioning position. "You do know that this is urgent?"

Zorus straightened his back and stepped in front of them, walking down the long pathway. He stopped at the old fashion restaurant. "I thought we would celebrate the human's arrival. Everyone in this village ought to be there." The restaurant was wooden as well as all of the other buildings, but clear glass windows allowed light to flee from the building. Zorus walked to the glass doors, cracked his knuckles, and flung them open with his force. The bell rang violently.

Everyone at the many wooden tables ended their conversations and stared at him. Zorus walked inside, followed by Alex walking by Courier's side. Everyone continued to stare at them. Courier awkwardly smiled as Zorus walked casually to the marble counter in the back of the room. A small horned beast dropped his glass. As they passed by the wooden tables various creatures spoke. Some began to whisper questioningly, while others began to shout. "It's the one and only Zorus!" A black broomstick horse, with a red mane called out.

"Allo!" yelled a tiny toad.

"Hey, Zorus!" an eight-legged lemur greeted, taking a sip from his tiny glass.

Hey everyone. Good to see you." Zorus pointed finger guns and winked as various other monsters spoke at him.

Alex raised his eyebrow. Courier frowned and folded his arms. "Where's my recognition?" he huffed.

They stopped at the back counter. "Zorus, thanks for planning this party! Oh, hi Courier." the owner smiled. "And who's your friend?" asked the keeper, who was standing in front of a furnace, heated with a blazing fire. He was wearing a very neatly pressed and cleaned black tuxedo. A white handkerchief was poking out of the upper right pocket. But the strangest thing about this creature was the fact that his head was a bundle of plants growing out of his neck. A beak not unlike a toucan's grew beneath his owl-like eyes.

The three of them sat themselves down on the square stools in front of the counter. "This is Alex, a human." Zorus patted Alex's back and held his hand in place.

"And we are going to take him to the palace very soon." Courier added.

The plant nodded. "A human, like the prophecy?" they both nodded. "That's impossible!"

Zorus interrupted. "We thought so too before we met him."

"Then why are you wasting your time here? this seems urgent."

Courier gently glanced at Zorus in annoyance. “Zorus can answer that.”

The plant nodded. “Are you thirsty?”

“You know that our thirst is insatiable. I’ll take a bottle of natrin spider venom. Oh, and dactlaites glazed with crydge syrup to share.” Courier spat. He nodded, placing the towel down.

“Ha, spicy snart venom for me.” they looked at each other competitively. The plant rolled his eyes and bent down for a few seconds. He stood with two colorful bottles in between his fingers. He placed them on the counter and slid them across the smooth surface. He then turned around and walked to the tall shelves behind him. He picked up a small basket and placed it on the counter. It was filled with dried bugs, which looked to be winged centipedes, covered in a sweet syrup.

Zorus picked up the glowing blue bottle and twisted the lid off. Courier did the same with his orange bottle. They held the bottles in the air and clinked them against each other. “To finding a human!” Courier stated. Everyone in the diner cheered. They brought the bottles to their lips and chugged the liquids. After swallowing the liquids, they slammed the bottles onto the counter, splattering the poisons onto the surface. The colorful drinks swished inside the glass bottles calming from the pressure.

Alex looked away from them in disgust and stared straight at the leaf-headed man. The keeper stopped wiping the counter, turned, and looked at Alex. “Would you like something to drink?” he asked, leaning against the counter.

“Ugh, do you have juniper?” The keeper bent down once again. When he stood up, he placed a glass full of a lightly tinted pink liquid. He looked back at the brothers. Zorus picked up one of the glazed dactlaites and popped it into his mouth. Alex scrunched his nose.

“You are going to have to get used to our food while you are stuck down here.” Courier picked up a battered down bug and handed it to Alex. “It won’t kill you.” Alex was hesitant, but he placed the bug into his mouth and bit into it. Its texture was unusual, it was crunchy, yet soft. It was bitter, but at the same time, it was sweet. “What do you think?” Alex grabbed the glass that the keeper had just placed down and began to chug it. A familiar citrusy flavor dripped down his throat.

"Cleave, what do we owe you?" Zorus asked as the keeper was cleaning out a glass.

"It's on the house just for you two!"

"Thanks, we owe you!"

S opened his eyes, cradling his knees as he rocked side to side. The fear was substantial, and the sting of the cuts on his skin lingered. He was covered in cuts and burns, blood staining his skin and dirt crusting his hands. What had happened would never be forgotten, the fear would never subside. He and his brother would never be saved from the hands of their tormentor. They would always be locked in chains, kept from the outside world, enduring the torture until their bodies could no longer sustain their souls. Their fate was set, and no soul could save them from this Hell they called life.

This day was better than most he had lived through. He was left to nothing but his own thoughts, no torture, no gruesome images. Though, the lack of interaction was damaging to his mind, causing him pain irreversible. There was nothing to do but think to pass the time. Boredom leads to thinking, thinking leads to dementing thoughts, dementing thoughts lead to depression. He wished that he could see his brother. He wished that he could take off the chains and hold him close, comforting him.

Where was his brother? The last he had seen him was two days ago when he watched the Master cut into his fragile skin. He could only fear for what the Master was doing. He was only a child, and much younger than S was. For all he knew, his brother could be dead by now. "R, where are you?" he called, his voice echoing quietly as for no one else to hear his plea.

Far Away

The small bell rang as Courier opened the glass door. He ducked, his hair brushing across the doorway. He glanced behind him, making sure the others were following his lead. “Finally, it is time to travel to Krysal palace.” he took in a deep breath, continuing his march through the grass.

“Actually…”

“No Zorus, we are leaving now! End of story!” his voice was tense and annoyed. He clenched his fist and struck it into his hand.

Actually, the secret passage is left.” Zorus pointed behind them with his thumb up.

Ugh!” Courier stopped, turned around, and pushed his way in front of the others, walking the other way. Zorus grabbed Alex’s arm and pulled him along. Small bits of rocks caught in his shoe as he followed the scelos along the gravel road.

“Aren’t I older?” Zorus looked at Alex. “So, you look around eighteen.”

Wait how did you...?”

“Thought you didn’t look too much younger than Courier. He’s eighteen, and I’m, well, about six years older.” He pulled his boney fingers through his hair. As Courier led the way, Zorus kept Alex further behind him. Zorus wrapped his arm around Alex’s shoulder and pulled him closer. He began to speak quietly into his ear, as for Courier to not hear. “I know that you are probably overwhelmed with all of this. Hey, uh, just keep this charade up, and I’ll find a way to get you out of this mess.” he let go of him and gently pushed him to the side.

Courier stopped in front of several evergreen trees and turned toward the others. “As part of the Galaxy Knights, we were sent here on our own special mission, to guard this small village, to make it our home. We had to leave the main city by secret, and we are the only ones in this village that know about the portals." he turned around and slid his fingers in between each other. A swirling black portal formed into existence, waiting for someone to enter. "Portals are shortcuts, passages to get to specific places faster. But a moment inside a portal could translate to days in the world. This one will take us to Winter's Gorge." Courier stated as he stepped inside the black hole, disappearing from reality.

Zorus grabbed Alex's shoulder before he was able to wander inside and turned him toward himself. "Hey kid, there's something I want you to know." he looked into the swirling portal in front of him for any sight of Courier. "Before we came to Treesey village, we lived in Krysal city. Courier adored the sentries that walked by our house every day and yearned to become one himself. Of course, I wouldn't just let him go out on his own at a mere twelve, and I was worried because he only ever reads in his spare time. So, I went out with him, and let him fight in the city tournament.

"We were to perform our skills in front of the Knightmare, king, and seven Shadlas. Zidal, who at the time was a Shadla, pulled us aside, and let us know that we were the best warriors she had watched fight in the arena. She wanted us to be Shadlas so badly but was upset that the king thought that we were too dangerous to be in the higher ranks. Zidal was able to reason with him.

"He sent us as spies dressed as sentries to Treesey… he told us to watch over something. She, almost unwillingly, sent us to Treesey village in order to keep the promise with the king. Courier was not at all disappointed, he was very understanding, even at twelve, as he was not expecting to do so well."

Zorus sighed. "We have been protecting the village from a nearby ominous harm, the sandern. Now that we've found you, I don't know what will happen to that promise." Zorus took a breath. "We're more powerful than you think, more merciless. Don't think you can betray us, or you won't breathe another second. Do as you're told; I'll try to find a way to get you home. This is my exchange for your life." Zorus looked away from him and pointed into the portal.

"Where are you going?"

"Go on ahead, I'll meet up with you in a while. I've got to take care of that sandern." Alex watched as Zorus turned away from the portal and left his sight. He gave a shy smile and stared inside of the black void and forced himself to walk inside. His vision went dark as he curled his feet through the solid ground. He squinted, peering at the bright light. He followed it and felt the light burn him as he walked through the small passage.

The light faded into a dimmer setting. He grasped his arms as he shivered in the cold of the terrain. His boots were covered in snow, deepening to stone ground. Blurs of snowflakes covered his sight, coating his hair in cold flakes. Courier turned around and looked at him. The portal shrunk and disappeared. "It took you long enough. Hey, where's Zorus?"

"He said he had to *take care of something* first."

"The Sandern, I almost forgot!" Alex shrugged. Courier sighed. "It's alright, we can proceed. He can handle it himself." Courier exclaimed as he squinted past Alex's forehead, placing a hand above his sockets. His emotion grew with fear. "Broken Souls... draw your sword, we need to fend them off!"

Alarmed at his anxious words, Alex placed his right hand on his handle, and his left on the sheath. He pulled his sword out of his sheath and turned around. He looked at Courier, who had converted into his skeleton form, holding his sword valiantly. "Maybe it would have been better if Zorus joined us now." Courier exclaimed. Increasing amounts of the oozing creatures rose from the snow, forming a large army.

The two of them bent into a stance, ready to fight against the army of dripping black figures. The melting beings held every shape and size of creatures, huge teeth, and claws strong enough to break through rock. Their eyes were shining a bright emerald green through the snow. Many even resembled people. Their oozing skin dripped onto the white snow, staining it black.

Alex shook and shivered in the cold, icy terrain in fear, holding his sword as courageously as he could. He glanced at Courier, with anxiety, who stood with great impatience for the battle to commence. The leader of the strange, deformed monsters barked as it licked its lips. At the command of the beast, the Broken Souls charged toward them at full speed, unhesitant to destroy them.

Courier leaped into the air, holding the blade of his sword toward the snow. The blade pierced through the sagging body of one of the decaying beings. Its body melted into the snow as its soul faded. Alex closed his eyes, swinging his sword side to side, attempting to hit any Broken Soul he could. He knew that Courier was a more advanced and professional warrior than he, but his skill still counted. As he opened his eyes, he stared at the tiny blobs chewing on his stubby feet. He slashed his sword toward them, squishing them into puddles of blackness.

Searching through the crowd of monsters, Alex was unable to find Courier. The only creatures surrounding his body were the Broken Souls. As the Broken Souls neared him, they began to absorb him into their melting bodies, forcing him to become a part of them. His eyes quivered as he dropped his weapon into the ground, blanketed with snow. His breathing became heavy as his struggle to escape became more difficult. The Broken Souls would not let go of him; they only applied more pressure. Alex, in fear, attempted to make a sound, but was unable to comply with his circumstances.

He watched the world fade in front of his eyes before a blade impaled one of the Broken Souls that surrounded him. It fell to the ground lifeless, melting away. The others around him fell also, no life left within their darkened eyes.

Courier let out a hand, pulling Alex from his fall. "Hurry! We must leave this place at once!" He waded through the snow quickly, dragging Alex across. He peered to the left and pointed. "There, a cave!" Without hesitation, he rushed toward the cave, but was stopped suddenly by a Broken Soul. He let go of Alex's arm reaching to his sling and drawing his sword again. He thrusted his sword toward the Broken Soul, impaling it, allowing its skin to bleed into the snow.

After the Broken Soul had perished, another followed. Courier swung his sword, killing one after another, many more appearing out of the snow in their place. "There are too many, we will never have the ability to destroy them all." Courier spoke as he continued to fight off the army of Broken Souls.

Alex, left without his sword, lifted his arms in front of his face as the Broken Souls neared him. Without warning, the Broken Souls began to fall into the snow without a breath left in them. Each dropped into the snow, melting, and merging with it. Courier smiled as he continued to attack more courageously as his brother's skeletal figure appeared behind the hoard. "Zorus!" he yelled as he ripped into the skin of the beasts, many more staining the snow. As Zorus fought alongside his brother, many began to fall, and they began to flee from the battle. Courier turned his head toward Zorus. "You couldn't have arrived a moment earlier? There were too many, it was quite overwhelming. If you were here at the beginning, we wouldn't have been in that position." Courier spoke with a tone of anxiety.

"Sorry, I had to finish what was started." Skin began to reform around their jaws, a cushioning warmth for the freezing air.

I apologize, I wasn't expecting Broken Souls to follow us here." Zorus glanced to his left, his sword lying across his stomach. "We were only to *watch* the sandern, but you *took care of it* I suppose?" he questioned as Zorus nodded. "Well, I suppose it's better to protect than to learn every detail about the enemy." Courier turned toward the cave and began to walk toward it. The others followed toward the cavern's safety. Zorus, seeming incredibly weak, followed their footprints behind.

"You called those things *Broken Souls*, what are they?"

Courier sighed. "When a monster dies, Death guides their soul out of their body. But some souls will not follow his calming guidance and choose to return to their unstable body. The corpse melts as it should, while they allow their souls to decay with it. Most were created by experiments." Courier glanced at Zorus before looking back to Alex. "If one chooses that path there are two deaths, the first being guided by Death, and the second, their souls being shattered from existence. That is the only way to kill a Broken Soul. They will not die unless you break their soul." He folded his arms. "They need a human's soul and body in order to accomplish that which will destroy all our kind. Not only are you the hero of the prophecy, but you are also the cause of evil… if they get what they desire. They will not stop until pain is inflicted upon every soul."

Alex breathed in, shivering through the cold. "You know this dimension much better than I do. With your guidance, I will be sure that no Broken Soul will get their hands on me. I would rather follow you than those *monsters*."

He smiled. “That’s what we’re here for.” They stopped at the entrance of the cave and turned around, waiting for Zorus to catch up. Alex shivered as the light of the bright sun began to fall and the stars rose, a day well spent.

Zorus gave a weak smile. He held out his hand, Alex’s sword wrapped inside, and handed it to him. “I found this in the snow; it would be difficult to survive without it.”

Alex took it from him and slid it into his sheath. “Thank you.”

“Alex, you look cold. Here.” he unclipped his cape from his shoulders and handed it to Alex. “For someone with barely any nervous system, I don’t need warmth.” Alex wrapped the warm cloth around his upper body and smiled. Courier stepped inside of the cave and waited as the other two walked in behind him.

“I’ll get you out of here in no time, don’t worry.” Zorus remarked as he walked into the cave, nearing the opposite side that his brother was on. He sat on the cold stone floor, cold droplets of juniper dripping onto his head. He tilted his head back and shut his eyelids.

Alex walked inside the cold cave and stood beside Courier, leaning against the cracked wall. “You seem to be missing your home, yet also accept your place here.”

“Yeah, I do miss home.”

Courier stared at Alex in a query. “Alex, you are the first human to ever find your way here. I don’t get it, legend told that humans despised us, that they meant to destroy them all. Though I was not in the battle myself, because it was many centuries ago, I could feel human’s hatred from those stories. But you, you don’t seem to care, you seem to enjoy our company.” he shut his eyelids for a moment. “Tell me, why do you act this way when I'm forcing you into something you know so little about?”

Alex smiled at him. “You may be my captors, but you are also my protectors. All you want is to gain your freedom. Why should I fight against you when you don’t *really* want to destroy me?”

“You are starting to make me change my mind about this. No, I have waited too long for this opportunity.” he sighed. “We have quite a way to go to get to Krysal palace. If you stay down here for too long, the mind wavering will begin. Your mind will begin to change, it will begin to work like ours, and then you cannot leave, and the prophecy will not come to pass. You might even say that you have become a monster yourself." he tightened his fists and looked at him. "Ah, maybe my mind is shifting, I can't find a way for both of us to get what we desire."

Courier sat on the wet surface and breathed out. Alex touched the wall and sighed. "Well, if we can never come to an agreeable decision and I never get out, at least I know I will have someone to trust in this world."

Courier perked up. "Even after all the trouble I've made you go through?" Alex nodded. "Those are truly words of glory." he smiled. "Get some rest, we have a long journey tomorrow."

Alex yawned, his arms stretching against the air. The cave, now brightened with morning's light, displayed a damp, empty area. Zorus still lay fast asleep on the opposite side of the cavern, and Courier was nowhere in sight. Alex looked toward the entrance of the cave, where daylight swept in, and a dark grey smoke cluttered the view of the pure snow. He stood from the uncomfortable ground, tightening the cape around his shoulders, blocking the cold wind from embracing his skin. He ignored Zorus's lingering sleep and made his way out of the cave. Courier sat in front of a warming flame, burning meat on the blazing violet fire. The clear snow reflected the flame's light. "Morning, Alex. Thought you might be hungry." he took the blackened meat off of the flame and handed it to Alex. He accepted the meat because of his hunger, yet his stomach turned at the horrid sight and burnt smell of the creature.

As a crunch of snow sounded from behind them, they glanced at the cave entrance, Zorus slowly but surely growing nearer to them. He sleepily sat on the freezing ground next to his brother. Alex slipped the deep blue cape off of his shoulders and handed it to Zorus. He wrapped his boney fingers around the fabric and began to clip the golden beads onto his uniform. Alex tightened his robe around his back.

Courier plucked another burnt piece of meat off the bone and gave it to Zorus. "Thanks, Core. I'm starving."

Courier glanced at his brother. "This may be the last we get to eat for quite some time. Winter's Gorge is quite barren." Courier glared at him as he bit into the crispy meat.

Zorus gave a weak smile. "So, what is this anyway?" he asked, staring at the blackened skin of the creature.

"Hoswed, they say it is the best meat you can get in Winter's Gorge." he chuckled nervously as he took another bite.

"Hoswed? I have never heard of this creature." Alex claimed. He stared at the meat and began to pull a piece from the bone.

Zorus took a generous bite of the meat and spoke. "We were not the only ones imprisoned here, so too were our fauna."

"Darls, Zorus, Darls. All creatures with the ability to live after death. We *should* refer to ourselves as Darlids, monster being a bitter name that the humans of Achnor gave us." Courier faced Alex. "The difference between Darls and Darlids lies in our intelligence."

"While Darls must eat their prey quickly, cooking their meat ensures that their bodies will not return to the dust of Shawon, that way we can preserve the meat for later." Zorus interrupted.

Courier cleared his throat. "Anyway, Darlids have the ability to own any form, those are called recs. Recs each have their own special abilities, used for their own advantage in different environments." Courier took in a breath. "As you might have known, Zorus and I are the only remaining scelo recs."

Silence reigned as Alex took a bite of the bitter meat. He chewed slowly and forced himself to swallow. Zorus broke the echoing silence. "So, did you sleep okay?"

"With everything jumping through my mind at once, I couldn't get an hours' rest. This mission has kept me alert." Courier poked at the flame, as it slowly died. He stood from the ground, brushing the snow off of his attire and wandered to the edge of the mountain. Alex followed behind him. As he reached the rocky edge, Courier pointed to a mountain that seemed to be carved of vibrant crystals. It was reflecting gentle beams of blue, violet, and pink through the frosted forest. Its towers were held tightly in the air, surrounded by enormous shards of obsidian. The houses and buildings in front and behind the blazing castle were erected of various kinds of jewels. Fiery oranges, grassy greens, sweet pinks and more. It was unlike any other city he had seen, unlike any castle he could have dreamed of. "That is Krysal palace, that is our destination."

Zorus made his way to the view. He stood beside the others and straightened his back. Zorus placed his thin hand on his brother's shoulder. Alex stared at the castle of crystals in all awe. "I really do miss home." Zorus gave a slight smile, as he wiped a small fragile snowflake off of his cheek.

Courier placed his hand above his thin hip and breathed in the crisp air. "But seeing we are on the peak of Winter's Gorge; it will take quite some time. We cannot descend the face of this mountain in a single day."

Zorus glanced to the left, and smirked. "I have a couple of ideas." Alex and Courier stared at his gaze drifting beyond the snow.

"And what would those ideas be?" Courier asked with a curious desire.

"Well, one," he began as he held up his index finger, "Jump." he smiled at them.

Courier stared at him agitatedly and raised his voice. "Zorus! That is an utterly disturbing death." Alex smiled in a concerned way. Courier sighed and looked at him, softly smiling. "You well know I would rather die in battle, and we certainly cannot have the human die."

"Alright, I'll be serious now. Do you see those giant sheets of bark?" he asked as he pointed toward two large, flat pieces of bark peeking out of the snow. "We can use those to slide down the mountain." He explained as he rushed to the planks, digging through the snow around them. After a short moment of removing snow, he held the first sheet under his right arm and began to dig the other out of the snow. He tucked the second one under his left arm as they walked toward each other.

"As dangerous as that sounds, it could save us quite some time. Alright, fine, but if anything happens to the human…"

"I know." Zorus interrupted. "We'll be fine. Looks like we'll have to share one though."

Zorus placed both of the planks into the snow before them and sat on the larger one. Courier sat behind him and held tightly onto his shoulders. Alex glanced at them as he sat on the second plank. Zorus placed his hand into the snow and gently forced the plank off of the cliff. Their voices trailed off as their figures shrunk.

Alex grasped onto the taller edges of the bark, scooted forward and began to slide down the rocky cliff. He watched the others slide down as the wind drafted against his frail body. He watched as they leaned right to slide past a boulder. When he neared the boulder, he too leaned right, and followed them, the bottom of the gorge seeming further than it did before. He watched as their sled jumped over a pile of snow. Alex closed his eyes and held on tightly as he felt himself rise from the ground. He hit the rocky floor, bouncing off his sled. He quickly caught himself, scanning for his captors.

A large crystal branch fell from the cliff-side, blocking the path. He watched as they ducked under the stem and fled down a smooth path. When Alex came near the large branch, he leaned to his left, attempting to slide past. The sled began to spin out of control, pulling him right. "Ahhhhh!" he screamed. He was taken onto a rough path. It swayed his sled side to side, his vision blurred by the powdered snow flying into his eyes. All he could see was the darkness of a nearing cave.

The snow beneath him sunk deeper, and his sled began grinding across a rocky surface. His vision went dark as he entered the cave. His sled, increasingly slowing, continued to slide through the cavern. He squirmed as he felt thick and sticky strings snap across his body. He flew through the cave, each string which attached to him, the sled slowed more than the one before, until he fell into an enormous web where he stopped. He could not move, his limbs attached to the large web of strings.

Silence only played for a moment before the fast-tapping steps of something alive echoed through the cavern. A hideous hiss followed the ominous sound. A shadow passed by ten enormous legs stretching in front of him. In fear, Alex struggled to escape, the web continuously tightening to his skin. The enormous creature stood in front of him, staring into his soul with its many green eyes. It opened its mouth, its face splitting vertically in half, opening, and closing its jaw like scissors. Its large, sharp teeth pointed out from both sides of its mouth, a disgusting ink drooling from its mandibles. Its dark skin melted onto the cavern floor.

It stepped closer to him and stared into his eyes with its many glowing orbs. "Looks like you have fallen into my lair. I am Vennier, the answer to your death's call." a female voice traveled through the air. It was calmed yet echoed. It sounded as if two voices were trapped in one chord, one smooth and joyous, while the other coarse and rough. Her voice was quiet, almost beautiful, but it had a feeling that disgusted him. Alex studied her figure in fear. "I haven't feasted in so long. Your soul will sapor well." she fluttered her tongue.

Alex quivered at the thought of her desire. Afraid of what was to come, he silenced himself, but continued to wiggle, attempting to escape the trap, but the strings only tightened. Almost hopelessly, he tugged firmly, and his arms fell free from the webs. He reached toward his sword's handle. Noticing his intelligent move, the spider shot a large, sticky string from her eye, sticking his left arm to the web. She shot another to his right arm as for nothing to go wrong. Alex struggled.

"You don't seem to be afraid to question your decisions. What kind of *Darlid* are you?" she asked in a calming voice.

Knowing that the webs were impossible to escape from, Alex ceased to struggle. Yet he smirked, feeling that he could outwit the Broken Soul. "I am no Darlid!"

To his surprise, she gasped in joy. "So, you must be human. Ah, that's what they look like. Master will be so pleased with me; we have waited so long." she laughed in a freakish joy. She lifted her claw in the air, tightening the web around the rest of his body, encasing him in a cocoon of webs. It stuck furthermore with the help of its melting form. "Then we can finally accomplish what we have been wishing for." she giggled as she pried his webbed body off of the strings.

"Let me go!" he screamed, his voice echoing through the cave.

"I cannot let this opportunity pass me by, young human. It is worth all too much." She wrapped her front claws around his body, using her six remaining legs to crawl across the stone. "You can't stop me, you have no...Aghhh!"

The spider, shocked by a sudden blow, released him, and fell to the ground in pain. Alex hit the cold stone floor dizzy and in distress. He looked at her, watching as a scythe was drawn from her chest. A glaive grew from the top of the scythe, carved of a sharp, transparent crystal. Vennier, slowly lifting herself from the ground as blood drained from her chest, turned toward the weapon, and hissed.

A figure in a royal uniform, which was more refined than Zorus or Courier's, stood in the way holding its mystical weapon in the air. Its skin was formed of darkness and shadow, darkness vaporizing into the air. Its face was covered with a ballroom mask which seemed more demonic and demonized than gorgeous. It was painted silver, a crystal blue stripe vertically striping across the center of the mask, a shining purple stripe complementing it by its side. The stripes crawled up the center of the mask creating a horned crown. The pieces balancing across her ears were small blades, along with two large saber teeth falling from the bottom of the mask, covering its cheeks with white blades.

Vennier threw her arm to the side. The knight ducked and swung the sharp, rounded glaive toward Vennier's vulnerable legs. She screamed in pain as her front leg fell to the ground. "You will die for that!"

The knightly creature shook its head sarcastically as it swung its weapon to the right. The spider lifted its front leg and slammed it upon the knight, spraying her melting skin across the area. The hero leapt to the side before the sharp stub hit the ground, decay coating her uniform. It cawed in pain. "Speak you imbecile… I am impatient!" The being shook its head once again as it swayed side to side avoiding the spider's descending legs.

With a swift, unexpected movement, the scythe slid through its rightmost limb. The limb fell onto the stone, melting into a puddle of blood and tears. Vennier hissed as she wobbled on her nine remaining legs. She bent her neck and opened her mandibles, her sharp teeth spilling a red liquid onto the warrior. Her foul breath filled the entire cave.

The knight quivered as its body neared her mandibles, disturbed by such a fate. It lifted its weapon before its figure to protect itself. Vennier's mouth closed around the knight's body. Alex recoiled at the sight. "That wasn't so difficult, now…" she mumbled as she pressed her jaws against the knight's flesh. The knight ripped its arm out of the disturbing trap and lifted its scythe. With all of its remaining strength, the warrior plunged the blade into Vennier's brain. A terrorizing scream echoed through the cavern as the valiant beast fell through the dissipating jaws landing perfectly on the stone.

Alex closed his eyes as ooze splattered across the cavern, a soul shattering across space. When he looked upon Vennier, her body began to melt lifelessly into the ground. She stepped through the sticky mess, wiping the ooze from its uniform as it stepped toward Alex. The knight stood above Alex and stared at him for a moment. Without hesitation, it placed the scythe under the web. With force, it pulled the scythe toward itself, breaking the bonds. It held the majestic weapon by its side as it let out its hand and pulled Alex to his feet. He stared at the knight, formed of blackness and shadows. A somber feeling emitting from its soul. "Thank you…"

It placed its hand over his mouth. "I wouldn't thank me." it was now obvious that the knight was a female. Her voice was low and shadowed. It echoed through the room without bouncing off of the walls. Alex studied her uniform. It was silver, wrapping around her fragile body. Flashing hues of blue and purple, matching her mask, striped across her arms and legs. A blue cloth was wrapped around her waist. She wore two huge leather boots and a dead smile. She slid the glaived-scythe into a rope tied to the side of her waist. "We can't have the Broken Souls ruining our chances." she turned around, her hand wrapped around his as she walked out of the small cave. She pulled him through the snowy terrain with force. They only walked a short distance down the slippery slope until they hit a corner on which they turned.

"Alex, you're alright." Courier exclaimed, pulling his fingers through his hair. He looked at the knightly figure. He spoke with gratitude. "I still do not understand, Zidal. Why would you not allow us to accompany you to retrieve him?" he questioned. "You know we have skills unimaginable."

"Vennier was an Olk. I can't risk my best warriors against such a beast." Zidal spoke with a soft tone.

"You can take the human into your custody." Zorus demanded. "Now that you have what you want, will you let us depart?" he asked in an almost fearful voice. "You well know why."

"When the king learned that a human had arrived, and knew that you had him in your custody, he sent me on a mission to find and recruit you three to bring the prophecy to its beginning." She let go of Alex's hand and tensed her fist tightly.

"But the king specifically said..."

“He specifically wanted the both of you to take part in this mission, that’s an order. He is positive this mission will fail without both of your expertise, Courier.” she spoke with great force and authority. “By Death’s name we will take part in this mission and until it has succeeded, we will not give in.”

Zorus stared at Zidal in awe, struck by her words. “I refuse to take part in a mission this dangerous!”

Zidal shook her head. “I am the Knightmare, you need to cooperate. The king especially wants you to fight for this cause. He knows no other Darlid who has such skills.” she informed him.

“Fine, but when we fail, remember this conversation.” Zorus remarked strongly. Courier looked at him, his lips attempting to form a smile. “Come on Core.” Courier followed his brother as he stepped through the snow and led him out of sight.

Alex followed behind but stopped as a cold vapor-like hand rested on his shoulder. “Where do you think you’re going?”

Without a glance, he pointed around the bend. “We had better not lose them.” he pried her hand off of his shoulder and walked away from her. He listened to the crunching snow follow behind him as he walked behind the curb. He sat beside the others, in the snow, holding his freezing arms, shivering away the cold.

Zidal followed him to the side of the mountain and leaned her body against the cliff, staring at them in displeasure. Her arms draped across her chest as she knew what this mission had brought her into.

The young boy awoke in the same dungeon cell the following morning. Through his small crystal eyes, only shadows appeared. There was never a glimpse of light in his terrible life. The Tall Being stood by the small bed, staring at his brother. “Master...” he whimpered.

The tall creature stood taller, staring down at him. *“You need to comply with what is happening. S, I have finally created the recipe for this elixir, for your improvement. Soon you will understand.”* the doctor spoke before he left the room. He had disappeared for hours, only giving him and his brother a scrap of food for the day, as before. The pain endured inside him as he was forced to watch indescribable miseries every moment of his life. S rocked back and forth, as anxieties ran through his tortured mind.

With a mighty squeal, the door opened, interrupting his troubles. S stopped in his tracks, afraid of his own keeper. The Tall Being unlocked the chains and held his arm tightly, forcefully dragging him through the doorway, his shrieks echoing through the empty space. Once they had exited the room, the Tall Being shut the large metal door behind him with a whimpering slam. He led S to the medical room once again, he now crying in fear.

He lifted S onto the table and strapped him down with chains once again. He sought to escape, the shackles only feeling tighter with each pull. *"You see, this will only help us. When I took your thoughts, I was able to reserve your eyes. They will not melt away when I take them... as they should. Now hold still, this won't hurt... this will allow us to succeed."* the Tall Being spoke as he held a knife in the air. With a quick movement, it plunged into his right eye violently. The Tall Being carefully twisted the curved knife in circles, gauging S's eye out of his skull. When it was released, he carefully took the eye and grinned, placing it on the counter.

S whimpered in fear as the Tall Being began the same pattern around his left eye. Blood dripped out of the boy's eyes like tears as the Tall Being continued his experiment. After a moment, his second eye rose from his skull and was placed beside his other. *"These will do well for the elixir."*

The Keeper retrieved a bundle of cloth bandages from the counter. He stepped toward S, peeling the paper covers off of the cloth. He bent over S's frail body and draped the cloth in his eye sockets. They stuck to his skin, forcing his blood to cease its flow.

S lifted his eyelids. He was able to see through his eye sockets in his head as well as he could with eyes. The Keeper was cruel, he stole his eyes, but not his sight so that he could still witness the horrors of his experiments. He took his precious orbs away yet left his tear ducts so he could watch him cry, so he could watch his pain.

The Tall Being unchained the boy and walked him back to his cell. With blood like tears, he followed his footsteps. The Master led him into his room, and locked him in chains once again, where he was left to sit, alone with his brother. His cries echoed in the room as the day became darker.

"Help my brother..." he whispered. "Save him..." he looked to the rough bed, his brother sleeping soundly. "I know you are out there... I know there is someone that can set us free."

Darkness

Alex stood near his unusual acquaintances, waiting for anything to break the tension. Zorus, sitting beside his brother, stared at Zidal. He spoke in a calm yet passionate voice. “Why were you in the mountains anyway?” he questioned.

“Before I began my quest to recruit you, I noticed dozens of Broken Souls forming on top of this mountain, and I began to travel to the top to watch them. It is pretty unnatural for Broken Souls to do that. But by the time I was halfway up Winter’s Gorge, they disappeared." she remarked in a bothered tone.

"We fended them off and have reason to think that they knew Alex was human. I expect they were attempting to capture him." Courier remarked.

"They simply disappeared after we fled." Alex stated.

“That was quite noble of you." her voice was distraught, as if something laid underneath her tough attitude. Zidal positioned herself and fixed her gaze. “You protected the human, but you still left the human in immense danger!" Her emotions shifted. Courier stood from the snowy ground. Zidal stared at Zorus, returning to her disheartened sound, calming her voice.

“We were going to save him before you appeared.” Zorus explained.

“I know, I shouldn’t be so hard on you. You were doing what you were ordered to.” Zidal sighed. "I still believe that you both deserve higher positions. Why has the king kept you as high class spys for so long? Six years ago, I watched you fight like no one has before.” she spoke with great determination.

Courier glanced at his brother, unsure of how to respond. “The king knows the intentions of one’s soul better than any other being. It is his right to place us in these specific positions, Zidal.”

Zidal thought quickly, hiding her displeasure. "Both of you should be Shadlas. You hold the skill great enough to be the king's personal guards." She gave a shy smile and glimpsed at the scelos. Zorus folded his arms stiffly and stared at her with irritation.

"The Knightmare cannot make decisions for the Galaxy Knights. I assure you; the king knows what he is doing." Courier remarked powerfully.

"That's true, but finding the human, and fending off the Broken Souls from the kingdom, you deserve to be higher ranked. The king can't ignore the fact that you must be Shadlas." Zorus stood from the ground, balancing against the stone wall. "Now, let us make this official. Under the king's desire, I will now lead this unit. This will be your most glorious mission."

"Of any troop, why ours? He knows what lies behind our souls." Zorus questioned. "He knows that we are better off without a leader."

"He has informed me that you have the skills that are needed for this mission, he ordered me to have you take part, saying it is imperative that your skills are used." Lifting her hand from her pocket, Zidal held out a signed document. "Here is the proof if you so require it." Zorus ripped the document from her hands and paced himself back and forth as he read each word. Zidal sighed. "The human must be part of our unit too. Without him, this mission cannot be completed." Her emotions drifted as she lifted her body off of the crooked cliff.

Zorus halted in the center of his track and tore the paper, letting each piece fall into the snow. "I refuse," he declared.

"Zorus, please, let us comply with this." Courier begged.

"Agh." with a grunt of pain, suddenly, Alex fell to his knees, holding his head.

"The mind wavering, it has begun, we haven't much time until he is no longer *human.*" Courier stated, pulling Alex from the ground.

"No longer human? What is happening to me?" Alex asked in pain.

"You'll be alright, don't think of it, we will get you home. But to do so, we must continue in this mission." Courier frowned, pulling Alex off of the ground. Alex covered his frail arms with his hands, shivering away the freezing air along with the unbearable pain of the mind wavering.

"What is *this mission?*" Alex asked, a little afraid.

"I have been instructed to keep details classified until necessary." As leadership entered her heart, confidence followed.

"I know that you're the Knightmare, but you can't control us." Zorus stated bitterly. "I demand to know what I must take part in!"

"Zorus, we follow orders, it will be for our benefit." Courier asserted.

"We must return to Krysal palace immediately, we must inform the king that the human has been acquired. Courier, lead the way." Zidal remarked, pointing down the slope.

"Really? Even Shadlas do not lead when the Knightmare is present." He carried on his knowledgeable thought.

"You know this mountain better than any other soul. I need you to lead us to Krysal."

He smiled, pointing down the slope. "This path leads to Krysal city and the Krysal palace." He stepped away from the others, who followed in a close distance.

Alex followed closely behind Courier as Zorus and Zidal fell slightly behind. Zorus began to whisper in a bitter tone. "Why in the Abyss would you agree? The king never wanted us as Shadlas, *you* know that. We are too dangerous to be held that close to the castle. Knowing this could mean our own self-destruction." He grabbed her shoulder and stared into her violet eyes. "I have been my brother's protector for all I can remember, if any harm comes to him, I will blame it fully on you. Why? Why did you agree to recruit us for this mission? He and I should be hiding..." he asked before pushing her gently to the side.

Zidal breathed deeply. "When I questioned the king, he told me that he saw deeper into your history, you could be Darlids that attract attention from unwanted Broken Souls. But he knew the risk was worth the skill you would bring. I didn't argue with him because I am under his command. You know that I wanted you and him to be in higher ranks when I first saw your war and defense tryouts, I know your skill, I trust the king when he says you are needed."

"You know I can see right through you; you've never liked me. But I must say, that was a good attempt at a lie." he spoke sarcastically as he folded his arms.

Zidal took a breath. "Fine, you're right, I didn't like you, but both of you are strong enough to be Shadlas, and both of your skills are needed in this mission more than any other Galaxy Knight. You must complete this mission, even secretly."

"I will follow your command, but only because I must. You can't comprehend how difficult it is to allow you to put my brother and me into more danger than you could imagine through this mission. *I know that we are not just taking the human to the king.*"

"None should fret for this fateful world. You will always be by his side. I will not allow anything to get in the way, not death, not war, not this mission." she promised.

Zorus stared at her in annoyance. "My sight will always follow your actions."

Embarrassed, she blushed as she began to speed through the snow. "Let's catch up." Zorus nodded as they rushed to walk beside Alex.

As they slowed their speed and followed Alex, he glanced to the side of the mountain. A frozen juniperfall, as shattered as a diamond, shimmered its glorious glow through the snowy plain. Icicles hung from the branches of frozen crystal trees. The pure white snow reflected a lilac light, almost blinding them from the magnificent wonders in front of their eyes. Darkness was forbidden from the path of beauty.

Alex gazed into the sky, which was sparkling with its morning star. He smiled, his jaw-dropping in the beauty of the unusual place. He felt a cold hand land on his shoulder. "It is beautiful, isn't it?" Alex dropped his head and looked into Zidal's somber eyes through her mask. "The entire city is just the definition of beauty, the mountain and her frozen juniperfall as its base." She seemed to smile, her eyes glowing a peaceful glimmer.

They glanced forward, Courier and Zorus side by side, proudly walking down the steep path. Courier stopped with suddenness. They stared at the wall of snow that had fallen onto the path the night before. The wall of fallen snow had frozen into large blocks of ice that could not be easily removed. "The way to the castle is blocked." he announced. Courier sighed and turned to the others, thinking of another way.

Zidal drew her gloved hand over her shoulder and pointed back. When in lead, she was much more confident, fearless, and tough. "I noticed a passageway not too far back." She pushed through their bodies and began to walk up the hill. Courier stopped her, tugging at her uniform. She folded her arms and turned around tapping her foot. "What?"

"I wouldn't advise you to follow that path, that is the way to Olkned. Are you crazy?!"

She froze, clamping her fingers around her weapon. Alex stared at them confused and afraid. "What *is* Olkned?"

Zorus stared into his soul. "Olkned has been told to keep the most determined of the Broken Souls..."

"...The most feared Broken Souls in Shawon. Their souls are unable to be completely destroyed without magic. They are the ones that *he* is saving for the destruction of Achnor, also known as Olks. They have a soul that is so powerful that they will destroy any soul that crosses their view." Courier finished.

"Destroy... they will shatter your soul across the boundaries of the universe, where you would be lost forever," Zorus added in a powerfully concerned voice.

Courier stepped closer. "Fear not Alex, a Broken Soul would never kill a human, rather capture and torture you until their task is completed." Zidal shook her head in his boat of facts. "But you should still prepare yourself for battle." he acknowledged concernedly.

"Olks will not end their urge to kill until there is nothing left." Zidal remarked. When not distraught, she was brutal. "This place is the definition of war." She leaned against the rock wall beside her. Snow fell from the slope, cloaking her body. She placed her hand onto her mask and sighed. "Look, we must do what we have to. We must find a way to complete this mission no matter what it takes, the entire world is at risk." Gasping her glaived scythe, Zidal walked toward the mystery of darkness without second thought.

Courier wrapped his fingers around the handle of his sword. "We best listen to her, she is the Knightmare after all." Zorus reached for his sword, waiting for the worse to commence as he walked toward the forbidden pathway. Alex shivered worryingly as he stepped through the snow.

Zorus stepped near him. "Don't worry, we will get through this... alive. I promise. Stay close." The glowing crystal blue ice faded into a darker and more fearing coloration. Darkness was dripping from the cliffs of snow, shadows crawling against the scenery. Courier drew his sword in fear of the movement within the city of broken ways. Zorus too unsheathed his sword watching the walls crumble. Their skin began to fade away, they better protected from harm. Zidal held her glaived scythe by her side ready for an attack.

Alex attempted to stay calm, wandering through the ghostly place, but his breathing was heavy, it was strong and anxious as the others were quietly stepping in the snow, so as to not startle any Olks. He slowly drew his sword from his leather sling. The cliffs above were beginning to widen, creating a dim shadow above them. The thin canopy of rocks could break off at any moment, causing disaster. The melted skin of reincarnated Darlids dripped into the snow.

A fearful chill fell through the air. A freakish presence looming near them, a breath, unlike any other. Zidal halted, the others following, becoming silent. A dark shadow flew past their eyes from the roof of snow above. Chills fell down their backs as they felt the breeze follow them. Another shadow ran closer, a high-pitched growl following the presentation. Zidal raised her weapon as a small being fell from the roof in front of them. It growled.

Clinging to the icy roof with its broken claws, it tilted its head. It was short, hanging on two legs, an enormous cat eye for its head. No arms were present on the being. It blinked at them and dropped to the ground, now facing right side up. It wobbled back and forth as its skin dripped onto the thick snow. Alex held his sword, ready to attack along with the rest of the troop.

The small creature tilted its head and purred before it began to grow larger and taller than the rest of them, its eyeball head stretching and morphing into a deer's head. Sharp teeth stuck out of the sides of its tainted mouth. "The broken Nidaret!" Zidal screamed, striking its enormous leg with her weapon. With the beast indifferent to the blow, Zidal pried her weapon from its slick body. Its mouth opened widely, roaring out an unpleasant sound that pierced their ears. It was deep and undesirable. Zidal, knowing that their only chance to escape was to fight, rushed behind the being and jumped onto its melting back, swinging her glaived scythe toward its neck.

Courier and Zorus stood by its feet striking its legs and claws, though no damage was taken. "You are too weak; our Master will get his hands on that human." he roared. Courier's sword split through its skin, its black blood dripping from the wound. The Broken Soul did not whimper or scream from its injury but reacted with a smile. "I can taste our victory." his screeching voice echoed through the rocks. Courier fell back as he forced the sword out of its bone.

Alex charged toward the Nidaret; his sword held over his chest. Courier stood from his fall and glanced quickly at Alex. A sudden strategy entered his mind. "Bounce off my shoulders!" Alex nodded before taking a step back. He ran toward Courier as he bent forward with a powerful sprint and jumped onto his shoulder bones. He bounced off his bones as Courier straightened his body, reaching the creature's body. As he landed, he struck his sword into the Nidaret's shoulder. It wobbled as the sword stuck inside its malleable body. Alex held onto the grip of his sword, holding strong so he would not fall.

Even with all of their power and experience combined, Courier knew that they hadn't a chance of victory against such a beast. Yet, with such a hopelessness encased in his heart, Courier urged the battle forward. He raised his sword in the air and began to chase after the beast. Glancing to both of his sides, Courier noticed rocky ledges on the cliffs on either of the right or left walls positioned perfectly to jump between. Leaping onto the lowest ledge, Courier jumped between the rocks, each one becoming slightly taller and further away. After the third faithful jump, landing on the rock, his left foot slipped, causing him to fall off of the ledge. His fragile bone bent as he hit the snow. He dropped his sword as his skin began to reform, his body becoming more vulnerable. Alex, stabbing the beast's neck, watched in agony as its large claw ripped through his chest, blood staining his white uniform.

"Courier!" he heard a scream from the distance. Zorus stopped his action, dropping his sword to the ground, running back to his brother. He bent by his side and placed his hands under his body. "Don't leave me like this!" he lifted his brother from the ground and looked at Zidal displeased.

"Go, he needs your aid." Zidal smiled. "We can take care of this." Zorus nodded and as he stepped into the distance, he faded away with his brother in his arms.

Alex tugged against the sword he had stuck inside its neck. It raged in pain, creeping backward. The Nidaret laughed as Alex stared at its sharp teeth. "You left yourselves to me, without *their* assistance, I can control you. You never stood a chance before, but now, there is even less of one." Its tangled horns stretched out and began to coil fiercely through the air. Alex pulled his sword out of its thick skin and swung it against the advancing horns. Without warning, one of its horns curled around his weapon, pulling it away from his grip, another stealing Zidal's. His heart filled with greed, his twisted horns reached the ground and stole the skeleton swords from the snow.

"Alex, jump off, we can't win without weapons!" Zidal yelled across the Nidaret, as she bent down and closed her eyes, flying off the Broken Soul. "Ugh!" she was pulled back as a twisted horn wrapped around her body before she could land. Another antler braided around Alex's waist and arms holding him to the Broken Soul. He struggled in his chains of oozing horns. They tightened around him, he felt stiff as his stomach was pushed inward.

"Let us go to the dungeon. Believe me when I say I would kill you both but Lade would most desire to do the honor." A sinking feeling pulsed through the air as the Nidaret merged through the stone ground. Alex closed his eyes as he felt the rocky mountain pass his structure. He felt an emptiness surrounding him, a cold breeze through the area.

As they reached the bottom, the horns let go of their bodies, allowing them to fall onto a cold, stone floor. Alex opened his eyes to a small, crooked space. The room was made of stone and had no doors, and aside from themselves, the room was empty. Zidal sat beside him, looking at the Nidaret. It smiled at them menacingly. "Won't he be excited to finally find the pieces of Athreal?!"

Zidal gasped as the Nidaret laughed, floating through the ceiling of the cell with their weapons. "The pieces of Athreal?" Alex asked.

Zidal glanced at him, sorrowfully. "Athreal was the leader of the twenty-three living demons. After the war against humans, all of the demons were killed, but his souls lived and flowed into Shawon. Legend tells that his soul can be found in many pieces. If he is put back together, his ambitions will grow stronger, he will torture Darlids for all of eternity, he will break souls that are impossible to reach." She dragged her knees to her chest and wrapped her arms around them. "Only a human can find the pieces. You will be the successor to their victory."

Alex took a deep breath. "I will not let that happen. I will stay strong until the end, even until my very last breath." He leaned against the mossy stone wall thinking of everything this had come to.

Zidal placed her hands on her mask and tightened her finger around its loose edges. It fell into her hands as they drifted away from her face. Her dark cheeks were cracked, her expression lost. Her hair conjured by darkness fell in front of her broken sentiment. She dropped her mask onto the ground and gazed at him, the white cracks in her skin bleeding through. Tears fell from her vibrant eyes.

"Zidal?" She glanced at Alex. "Are… are you okay?"

She attempted to smile as she spoke. "If you will listen, I am willing to speak. It is a sorrowful tale to tell."

"Please, tell me."

Zidal took a deep breath and spoke slowly. "Before I became the Knightmare of Shawon, my true love was. He was the noblest creature I could name in a split second. He encouraged me to join the Galaxy Knights, and I admit I was hesitant at first being young and careless. I decided that I would train, stay near him, and support him as a sentry in the main city. After a month or two, the king found me a spot as a Shadla expressing how well I fought. And I was extremely grateful." She leaned against the wall. Alex bent closer to her, listening carefully to every word she spoke. "Not too long after I converted into that position, the Broken Souls attacked the castle, looking for the same answers we desired. Kyron was valiant in battle, but alas, he was not powerful enough. He *changed* that day, he *died* that day..."

Zidal closed her eyes in despair. "I killed three hundred and eighty-seven Broken Souls that day in anger and vengeance for his life. The only reason that I am the Knightmare now is because I did not know the power I held was stronger than even Kyron's. After he left, I was the worthiest Darlid to become the Knightmare, dubbed to protect Shawon from the Broken Souls and be sure that they would never succeed." She frowned. "Ever since his death, I haven't been the same. I can't control my emotions the way I used to, yet I choose to continue the path that he took."

"Zidal, I…"

"Don't speak, I need some time to think over my actions Alex." she lifted her mask from the rough ground, fitting it onto her face. She scrunched up; her head buried in her knees. Alex closed his eyes listening to the sorrowful song of her tears.

"Core? Courier!" Zorus's voice pierced the silence.

"Huh, wha…" Courier jolted slightly from his rest, clenching his stomach. "Ow," he groaned in a voice questioning the pain.

"Calm down Core, you need to sit back." Zorus grasped his head and shoulders and helped him lie back onto the surface below him. He turned to a small counter on the left, retrieving a metal spoon and a small bottle with a liquid swishing inside it. He balanced the spoon between his fingers as he poured the liquid into it. After placing the bottle onto the counter, he brought the spoon to Courier's lips and poured it into his mouth. He swallowed as Zorus placed the spoon onto the cluttered counter.

Courier lifted his hand to his face. "Whose blood is this?" He moaned, staring at his hand, covered in his own dripping blood. He shifted his head to the side, looking about the strange area. It was familiar to him, his memories screamed at the unusual room, unable to remember fully where he was. Aside from the bed he laid on, which was stiff and uncomfortable, and the counter beside him, the room was nothing but an abyss of whiteness, his sheath, boots, empty satchel, and cape laid neatly on the floor behind his brother. He calmed his voice. "Where are we?" he used less breath and energy to speak.

"You're somewhere safe." Zorus, holding a small bottle in his hand, punctured the cork with his boney finger. He forcefully pried it from the bottle. With a clean motion, the green liquid bubbled. He placed the cork onto the counter and looked at his brother. "Courier, you need to rest and heal.

"What?" he asked as he lifted his left leg. "Ow." he groaned. "I haven't been in this much pain for almost a decade. What happened?"

"You were severely injured in battle." he returned in a calm and notorious voice.

"Zorus, please tell me, what *really* happened?"

"The nightmares of our past are coming back to life, I thought *he* was eradicated." He bent and pulled Courier's shirt off of his skin revealing the deep wound in his body. He poured the green liquid onto the wound and blood. It sealed the gap in his flesh.

"Ah, ow." he groaned as it sizzled on his flesh. "You mean *he* is back, that *he* is creating all of this nonsense, that *he* has been sending the Broken Souls for Alex? impossible!" He stiffened his posture and laid his head onto the pillow. Zorus stayed silent as he pulled Courier's shirt over his ribs. Zorus reached over his shoulder. He tugged at his cape. It began to rip off of the golden beads. "He *is* eradicated, I watched him die!"

"*He* should be *dead.*" Zorus shook his head. "But still, somehow, the nightmares are coming back."

"This is terrible, he shouldn't exist. With his return, we are all doomed. Please, let me know, where are the others?" Zorus hovered over his brother's leg as he wrapped the cape underneath his brother's ankle, tightening it to his foot.

"That's for us to find out, they were taken by an old friend as you were wounded." He let out his hand and helped his brother to his feet.

"Well, why did you not aid them?" Courier lifted his cape from the ground and tightened it to the clips on his shoulders.

"They were fine on their own, you were on the verge of dying!" he raised his voice in care. "There is no one else that I would choose to save, Courier, don't you see, we might be too late..."

Courier stiffly turned toward his brother. "No, I will not give up on them, we must find them, Zorus! All hope will be lost if the Broken Souls kill Alex!" he grasped his empty sheath and ducked as he pulled the ropes over his head.

"I know, but you can't throw yourself into a situation like this, doing this could kill us, doing this could destroy more than us! The outcome would be better if we just stayed out of this. You can't do this just for honor." He began to become impatient with his brother's reluctant hope.

Courier lifted the empty satchel by the strap and pulled it over his head. He then bent down and pulled his left foot into a boot, stiffening his leg as it tightened around his ankle. The blue fabric of his brother's cape folded slightly over the rim of the boot. "Honor or not, Alex and Zidal are in danger. You must know where they are, you must!" he raged as he pulled his right boot over his foot.

"You have become too attached to these irrelevant beings!"

Courier huffed. "I am starting to believe that you are attached to someone irrelevant too. Now, everything will be fine if we can just get a hold of them again. Zorus, you are the only one who can help me find them, your abilities, knowledge, for me."

Zorus took a deep breath. "Fine, I'll try my best to find them, but you have to promise that you will stay behind me, I can't let you die Core." He nodded as he took his hand and stood. "Come on, we don't have much time. Follow me." Courier, knowing not to let go of his brother's hand, followed him through the fading doorway. He followed his brother, a feeling of fear running through the empty hallway. Zorus stopped, breaking through the walls with his own unknown power. They sighed, a wall of stone resting in front of them... "Well, here we are."

"But where are the others?"

Zorus took in a deep breath as he searched the area. "I don't know, but I know they are here."

S wrapped his thin arms around his knees and began to rock back and forth. Anxiety was a problem that was beginning to take place in his mind. Along with that, the experiments had caused him to become agoraphobic. His fears followed him every moment that he could spare.

The door gave a familiar creak as the tall figure stepped into the room. S covered his empty eyes, which had now healed from the experiment. He gazed upon the tall figure, fearfully, as he looked much more horrifying than before, his left socket empty. His right eye seemed to glow much brighter than before, lighting the almost pitch-black room.

His brother groaned, yearning for something to fill his stomach. The tall figure stepped toward the child. "No, R… R." he struggled to speak.

He was starving along with his brother, ill and thin. "Don't hurt him." he spoke, taking a deep breath afterwards. The Tall Being placed a small plate in front of R, who gladly ate. It stroked his brown hair before letting go of the child.

He then walked toward S, reaching his fourth arm from behind his back, dropping yet another plate of dry food onto the ground, followed by a cup of dirty juniper. "*Eat, for you will need your strength.*"

The aliment was more plentiful than usual, but the taste was awful. S would only eat this food if he was starving. He lifted the fork and stabbed a flimsy piece of raw meat, the sound of his clanking shackles disturbing the silence. He carefully brought the fork to his mouth and bit the meat off, chewing slowly. It was gamey, disgusting, and harmful for his insides, but he did as his Master asked for worse consequences to flee. He lifted the drink to his mouth. It was tasteless, grainy, and freezing.

The Tall Being kept his eye on him, making sure that he followed his command. As someone as awful as him, he did not care about the mental health of experimental beings. Saying nothing, he took one last look at S and left his sight, slamming the door behind.

S looked at his younger brother, R, who was once again asleep, drugged by the medicine hiding inside his food. It was a terrible sight. He could bear no longer the things he had to witness. He knew that they would never forget these sights as long as they were there. He continued to eat his meal, at low comfort, pleading for his escape. "I know you are out there, my saviors, the ones who will save us from this laboratory, this prison."

Mission

They felt a disturbance, as a strange oozing void of sound filled the small area. Alex opened his eyes, looking upon a familiar being, one dressed in a black cloak, his bubbling skin white as the snow, dripping onto the ground. Its grin filled Alex with fear and anxiety. He placed his viscous tentacle on Zidal's shoulder, slowly waking her. She blinked and looked in terror at his sight.

"Who are you?" she cried in despair.

The being's black robe draped onto the ground as he removed his tentacle. "Ah, it is I, *Lade, the first Broken Soul*. We have no time for this. No room for these... cries. I could easily modify you, force you to follow my every command. I did create them after all."

"You don't mean…"

"Ah, yes, you know well that I have found a way to drive Darlids to become broken inside, aside from the mere craving to breathe for eternity. It can be very, very torturing to the mind." his green eye, glowing from the right side of his face, twitched ominously. "I could manipulate your mind in ways you could not imagine, that is the kind of power you acquire when you turn to me." he turned away from them. "And are you not one who craves power? Your mind is not enlightened, not yet. You would become much stronger than you could ever imagine. You could protect so many more souls with this power."

"You wouldn't dare!" Zidal placed her hand beneath her, standing from the rough ground. Lade uncoiled his arm from his insides, grasping her body, holding her against the ground.

"We will have none of that. Besides, that is not what I am here for, of course, I have other things to take care of that may be quite... ruinous." he turned his skull toward Alex, his disturbing smile widening.

Alex shook, opening his mouth slowly and sacredly. "What are you going to do to me?" his voice was raspy, tortured by the disorder in the room.

“Ah, I will manipulate your mind in such a way that you will almost willingly show me the places in which Athreal’s eight pieces lay. Transform you into a Broken Soul in some way. May we call it perception shattering?” he stepped closer to Alex, his right arm extending. “I know how to shatter the minds and change the ambitions of every single creature that lay beneath the rocks. But a human, now that twists *my* mind. I must search your mind and thoughts before I find your soul’s weakness. I will have my way, for you will follow.”

“You shall not do such a thing; you cannot release the souls of the emblems!” Zidal raged. She struggled through his grip, raising her arm, her fist clenched tightly.

He looked back at her. “Ah, you *would* be a perfect Broken Soul, an Olk even. You would fit in, and I know one being who has been *dying* to see you again.” he laughed.

“Kyron is a disgrace to Darlid kind, you cannot make me follow your rule! I follow my own!” her fearless compassion rang.

“Ah, Zidal, you twist my swaying mind, you fracture my melting heart, you tempt my Broken Soul. You are the strongest Darlid in Shawon aside from Death himself.” he tightened his extra limb around her waist and lifted her off of the ground. She squirmed through the tentacle, though she could not escape. It held onto her waist tightly so she would not slip through. “With this power, you would become even more powerful than he. You deserve to have what you want; you can succeed furthermore when you become broken inside. Just imagine how many more souls you can save with power like mine.”

“I will never give my soul to the monsters who killed Kyron!” he smiled as he wrapped another tentacle around Alex’s waist.

“You truly do not understand, Kyron is living, breathing, craving to be with you again.” he lifted Alex off of the ground. Two more oozing tentacles began to grow out of his shoulders. He used them to reach to the once far ceiling, gripping the solid ground above them. They phased through the coarse stone and flew within the dense air as they merged through the ground. Alex could feel the stone brush across his face and body as he broke through the ground.

They landed on the snow-laced ground. Lade’s extra limbs retracted into his body leaving them floating in the air. Alex bounced through the air, his nose barely missing the freezing snow. He felt the movement, new footprints appearing in the snow as they walked further from the dungeon. He heard Zidal's grunts as they passed by the many structures housing more Broken Souls, many glowing green eyes shining through the darkness.

Lade halted before a stone wall, crooked and rigid. It shook, the rocks breaking open, falling onto the ground, opening into a strange room. He stepped inside, forcing his prisoners to follow, the rocks reversing their fall and covering the hole as they entered. The room was huge, filled with equipment and traps, weapons, and deadly poisons. A doctor's table stood near the front of the room; a counter cluttered with medical equipment set by its side. There was a large cage set near the entrance, and beside it stood their stolen weapons.

Lade placed Alex in the large golden birdcage, shutting it before he could even move. Immediately, it locked, and Alex was forced to watch this treacherous sight. Lade's arm retracted into his body using less energy to function as he stepped toward the doctor's table. Zidal struggled to release herself from his tense grip, yet his melting flesh gripped onto her tighter, forcing her to follow his movement.

As he reached the table, he forcefully laid Zidal on the platform, tightening a rope around her waist to keep her from moving as he worked on her mind. "Zidal no!" Alex screamed. Lade sent one of his tentacles toward Alex, covering his mouth in a white slime, sealing it shut. He then encased Alex's arms in his own skin, holding them back. Alex mumbled, attempting to scream through the strange substance, but to no avail. His arms were weak and held back from breaking the cage open or even attempting to save this untrustworthy creature from a fate worse than death.

"This work, this practice will not break your soul as is told, it will improve it, strengthen it. You will become strong enough for vengeance, to take care of the ones who destroyed your life. Your poor soul needs this fixing, this knowledge, this power to survive. If you just listen to my voice and follow it, your pre-death will be painless." he walked around the platform in dizzying circles as he spoke. "You see, when you become a Broken Soul, you gain a second chance to live, you die once, but your body chooses to claim its soul. After you are broken, you can only die if someone kills you, not of old age or of illness. There is no harm or pain as this new creature. It is true power."

"Get out of my head!" she yelled through the empty space.

"Ah, I haven't even begun the fun. I haven't even scratched the surface."

Lade smiled dimly at Zidal. She tightened her eyes shut, attempting to forget about her past. "You have a powerful soul, one that is too powerful for the taking, and that is why we are here. I have invented a formula to permanently sink a being's soul into their body. One that I have been working on for sixteen years. Then I can forcefully kill that being to bring them to my side."

"Courier and Zorus will come, they will save us. I will stay strong long enough. I will not let Shawon lose me." she squirmed through the ropes that held her to the surface.

"Do not rely on your allies to save you, for they know of the power I hold, the way I control other's lives." Zidal's breath became heavy. He paused as an echoing knock hit the door.

He faced the stone wall and watched the shattered door. As he waited, pieces of the door began to break from the wall and fall to the floor. He quivered as he witnessed the sight before him. Two figures, covered in shadow, stood in the doorway, menacingly searching the area. Seeing as he had no chance against the figures, he vaporized into the thin atmosphere before their sight laid on him. The figures stepped into the cavern.

"Courier, Zorus, thank goodness you are here!" Zidal cried, noticing the blue cape wrapped around Courier's leg, his wounds slowly healing. Zorus, seeming out of strength, and Courier, stepped toward the golden cage and took their weapons from its side. Zorus walked to the platform in the center of the small space and slid his sword underneath the rope. As he lifted it, the strings broke, setting Zidal free. Courier unlocked the cage with a key left beside it and opened the small enclosure. He peeled the strange oozing substance off of Alex's skin before he left the cage. Alex retrieved and sheathed his sword, raising it over his back.

Zorus looked at Zidal in displeasure. He grasped her armored wrist and pulled her to the entrance of the cave. "What? It was not my fault, Courier was harmed by his own doing.`` As they neared the entrance,

Zorus let go of her wrist and Zidal took her glaived scythe from the ground, placing it in her ropes.

"You know that I have the power to destroy you..." Zorus whispered powerfully.

"I have learned not to mess with those I cannot handle Zorus." They waited in front of the others. Alex wiped the remaining ooze off of his mouth as he stared at them.

"I was gone for less than a day and you guys got into this much trouble? How could this possibly have happened? You are both too excellent of warriors to have failed." Courier pondered.

Zidal dusted off her uniform. "Courier, the Nidaret was an Olk, we were destined to fail from the beginning. It was considered much more impossible when you disappeared." Zidal remarked. "We are glad that you are okay, you were considerably wounded back there."

"Well, if it were not for Zorus, none of us would be safe. He knew where you were taken." Courier disclosed.

Zorus stared at Alex and Zidal intensely as he spoke. "I know that you interacted with the leader of the Broken Souls through this conundrum, what did you learn of his plans?"

Zidal stared at the ground silently, attempting to keep her treacherous history from spilling. Alex spoke. "He is searching for the eight pieces of Athreal."

Zidal sighed in relief, glancing at Zorus. "This mission, the one you unwilfully entered, was to find these emblems. The only way for the prophecy to proceed is if the human finds *all* of them, and each are destroyed." her somber voice flowed.

Courier interrupted. "Even if we are able to destroy one of them, recreating Athreal would be impossible. But we mustn't let *him,* or his followers reclaim a single piece. Even one would give the Broken Souls the advantage, they are far too powerful. It is better if we all are stuck down here for the rest of time than if the pieces of Athreal are shattered. If they are found by the Broken Souls, hurt will enter all hearts." Courier sighed.

"The eight pieces have been described as emblems. The emblem of death, the emblem of destruction, the emblem of magic, the emblem of life, the emblem of greed, the emblem of strength, the emblem of knowledge and the emblem of love." Zidal finished.

"But remember, the emblem of knowledge and the emblem of love have never been found." Courier added.

"The Broken Souls have been searching for far too long, at some point they will find them... well, at least if we don't first." Zorus remarked.

"There is a map in the library of Sinsto of their foretold locations." Zidal placed her hand on her mask. "It might be necessary."

"Alex has the power to sense where the emblems are because he is human, he does not need a map. This is one of the reasons that the Broken Souls want him... alive." Courier remarked.

"But if we split up, we can find each piece faster. We must retrieve the map." Zidal added in command. "Alex, I now declare you free from our hostage, and you are granted an apprenticeship as a Galaxy Knight."

"Seeing that I can't go home, I accept." the others smiled. Courier nodded diligently.

"Alex, you should choose who goes with you for the emblem of death, as for the two others, they will go to the library of Sinsto for the map." Zidal finished.

Alex nodded, glancing at the Darlids, but before he could answer, he fell to the ground in indescribable pain. "It's happening again... the mind wavering... I can feel myself drifting away." the Darlids stared at him in silence for a moment as he coughed violently and held his head.

Zidal let out her hand. As he took it, she pulled him from the ground. "I'll go with Alex." Zidal spoke up. She was confident in her decision, and willing to put herself into danger. "He needs someone that can protect him, especially during moments of the mind wavering."

"If anything happens to that kid while we are split, you're dead." Zorus expressed intensely.

Courier placed his hand on his brother's shoulder. "Do not fret dear brother, all will be well. We will stay in the library of Sinsto until they have found the emblem of death. Then they will meet us there safely."

"Agreed." Zidal sated before staring into Alex's eyes, closely into his soul. She spoke sorely. "Now, picture in your mind, whether physical or spiritual, death. Search the air for all signs of departure and sadness. See if you can find a way to the emblem death."

Darkness flowing through his mind, he spoke. "I… I can see it, it is all darkness and sorrow, captured in a dark sword locked away in a darkened area. I can feel the direction in which we should head."

"A dark sword? I know where that is. Come Alex, we must begin our journey." she commanded.

"But be wary, you should know that the Broken Souls will be searching for the emblems as well. They know that Alex can find the pieces. You must find the emblem, but you must also protect the emblem." Courier added.

"Understood." Zidal wrapped her frozen hand around Alex's and pulled him around the corner.

"We will be waiting for you two at Sinsto library!" Zorus called.

"Farewell Zidal, until the morrow Alex!" Courier yelled, waving his thin hand in the air. He took a deep breath. "I suppose that we should begin our trek to Sinsto, we must find that map." Courier turned his head to the right, noticing that his brother was already halfway down the snowy path.

Zorus stopped for a moment and looked at his brother. "Well then, come on, Core." Courier stuttered in his step as he ran down the snowy slope to the distant path. As he neared his brother, his foot slid against the icy hill. He let out his hand and grasped Zorus's shoulder to regain his balance. "Whoa there, careful, you could slip."

"Well, wouldn't you know?" he uttered sarcastically as he let go of his shoulder. Courier and Zorus began to walk down the path, laced with ice and snow. They walked in silence, searching for anything to spark a conversation. Courier lifted his hand to his chin, drawing his finger across the large scar on his lip before finally deciding to speak up. "You are afraid, Zorus, you are remembering our past, and because of you have, you have only reminded me of *him*. Why must you encourage these troubled thoughts? We don't even know if *he* is still actually alive."

"Courier, our past is a difficult memory that should be forgotten. We should never speak of it, even to each other."

"I was there, I remember the pain, the sorrow, the horrors."

“Every moment in that place was torture, there never was peace. Even the shadows betrayed us. Every second was pain.”

“Is that not the reason we decided to become spies, to fight against those like *him?*”

“I joined to remind myself of my past, to save others from torture.”

“Zorus, you cannot let your mind live in the past. With those thoughts following you, this mission will be impossible.”

“This mission is causing my mind to flow more freely, recalling the pains of our past.”

“But it is not worth your life to distract yourself in an obsolete past life.”

“Don’t you remember, *he* was a corrupt being, every memory of that place has stained my mind.”

“I understand, Zorus, I was there too, but I have yearned to forget about it, to keep myself sane. I fear that the constant reminder of your past is causing your mind to falter.”

Zorus spoke powerfully. “Don’t you get it? We killed *him, yet he* has returned, *he* is the one causing this misery, and if we don’t succeed, if the legend fails, the horrors of our past will return and curse the world.”

“Silence your thoughts Zorus.”

“But they will always return, they will never subside from my memory.” Zorus let out a deep breath.

Courier stared intently at him. “Everything will be fine, dear brother, we will put an end to this misery.” They stopped in mid-track. Courier glanced behind them at their never-ending trail of footprints.

Zorus sighed in sorrow. "Let's just go find this map of emblems." he remarked before beginning his step through the mountain again. Courier followed him closely, afraid of what was to come. The air became silent aside from their feet crunching the snow and the whispers of a Broken Soul following their tracks.

S stood from the ground, free from the shackles that weighed his wrists down. The door was too heavy for his frail arms to open, so still, he waited in the cell for the worst to happen. He stood by the bed, gazing at his brother, still chained to the wall. For the first time in months, He reached for him and gave him a loving embrace. “It’s okay, we will get out. I know there is someone out there that can save us. They might not be like us, but I know there is someone who will save us.”

He brought his brother close to his chest, wrapping the small blanket around his thin body. He gave a faint smile as he stared into its dark hazel eyes. He let go of him, his brother lying down for the night. The child fell asleep, accompanied by the creaks of the bed and the soft breaths of his older brother.

Once R was soundly asleep, S laid down on the stone floor beside the bed and closed his eyes. He slept soundly, knowing that all would turn right, and they would be saved.

The wind blew through the cell, a disturbance flowing through the air. Though it was dark and frightening, the boy opened his eyelids. He glanced at the small bed. The thin blanket fluttered against the wind, his brother nowhere in his sight. He stood slowly, afraid, checking the blankets once again to prove the facts to his mind. He looked toward the door, a crack of light shining through the metal door, which was still barely open.

Despite his thoughts, he crept to the door and grasped the thick handle. With all of his strength, he pulled slowly and carefully so as to not make a sound. Light fled into the room, the hallway sending in a chill. A soft sound of screams played in the near distance, sending fearful thoughts into his mind. The young boy wrapped his arms around his shoulders sneaking out of his cell. He followed the source of the light to the experimental room that he had known too well.

He cracked open the door, taking a peek inside. Screeches of pain filled his mind, the sound of a knife drawing out flesh following its tone. His empty eyes filled with salted tears that drove down his cheek as he watched in fear, and sadness as the Tall Being ripped out his brother's shining eyes, just as his. One by the other, each were placed beside his own crystal blue eyes and the caretaker's own green eye.

The Tall Being glanced at the door, but he could only see shadows, as the boy had fled from the scene. Crying, he closed the large metal door behind him and sat on the floor, cradling his legs as he rocked back and forth. He fell asleep to the sound of his dripping tears.

The large metal door creaked open early in the morning. The Tall Being stepped inside, the child held weak in his arms. He wore bandages in his eyes as blood stained his cheeks. As he struggled, the knife had cut his lip, leaving a scar only to remember the awful experience. "*It is done, I must now create an elixir, one that will allow me to accomplish what I am destined to become.*" The Tall Being turned from the bed and walked through the door. "*You will be the reason for my success. I can see it in you. You will give your life for me, for Athreal.*" he slammed the door behind him.

The young boy had a hard time believing him. After all he had been through, all he could imagine was the opposite. He would be the reason the tall figure would perish.

S ran to his brother's side, he was once again asleep, drugged by the caretaker's doing. He lifted him from the bed holding him in his arms, keeping him from the harmful ways of the being, and of the world. "I will not let any more harm come to you, even if it causes my death." he whispered into his ear. He held his brother tightly, slowly calming down from the treachery he had witnessed.

Melting Heart

Alex and Zidal walked, the soft, dry ground rolling beneath their feet, followed by a pebble or two. The noticeable pebbles became slightly larger every few steps they took. The snow was beginning to melt, a new terrain emerging. The scenery was more pleasant than it had been before, flowers were blooming, and grass was growing. Flowers of all kinds, never seen by the eye of man, were blooming, flying creatures singing their sorrowful tunes, the desolate world becoming colorful. Alex stared at the unique colors twisting through the terrain as they neared ground level.

The snowy mountains were beginning to become warm, feeling more like a hilltop in the spring than a freezing glacier drifting miles away. Alex ceased to shiver as the daylight warmed his body, his robe emitting a comforting warmth. Alex glanced at Zidal, startled by her sudden words. "Look out!" Before he could react, his hands hit the muddy grass. He lifted his foot off of the large stone caught beneath it and looked at Zidal, lifting himself from his fallen state.

"Ugh! You're slowing us down! Who knows where a Broken Soul could be hiding!" Anger entered her empty heart. Alex swallowed his fears as he listened for any disturbances. Zidal pulled her weapon out of the rope holding it to her hip and crouched behind him. He could feel her warm breaths falling down his spine as she placed the blade of her scythe across his neck. "With one quick pull, I could slide this blade through your neck, immediately leaving you lifeless." her vice disturbed the silent air.

Alex swallowed his fear. "Am I not needed for this mission?"

"Of course, we need you *alive* to succeed. Trust me when I say that I would kill you if you were not so important to this mission. You are making this mission all the more difficult." Zidal licked her dry lips. "We cannot let the Broken Souls collect a single emblem, they cannot recreate Athreal!" standing from the damp grass, Zidal placed her weapon in her ropes. "Get up, we cannot waste any more time." Zidal let out her hand, allowing him to take it as he stood. Alex let out an anxious breath as he let go and followed her behind at a safer distance. Watching from a distance, he noticed Zidal's mask fall from her face. Catching it in her fragile hands, she quickly returned it to its original position.

"You said that you know where this emblem, this sword of death, is. How do you know?"

Zidal spoke in a regal tone, confidence engulfing her previously sorrowful emotion. "I grew up in the small town of Grandts. An old monastery erected by our ancestors, which displays a corrupted sword in a glass casket, is the most recognized building. Kyron and I used to visit it all of the time, I mean, before he moved to Krysal city to become a member of the Galaxy Knights."

"How are we supposed to steal this famed sword, and then destroy it altogether without being caught, and even killed?"

"Destroying it, well, that's for us to find out. Stealing the sword is a different story. We will have to be prepared to fight for it. This mission cannot be as simple as it seems." Zidal glanced at Alex. "Come on, you can trust me, I wouldn't dare lay a finger on a being with such a glorious burden." she spoke somberly. Zidal halted at the edge of the mountain, staring at what was to come. Alex stood beside her, gazing at the beauty of the greenery. "There." she pointed downward. "That is where Grandts lays, we have quite a long slope to trek." Alex searched through the large canopies of the leafy trees, hoping to see a glimpse of her village rather than the way to his undoing, yet all he could see were the bright teal canopies below, reminding him of his home.

He felt the ground beneath them fall steeper each step that they took. He had many questions in mind, yet he was unwilling to open his mouth to break the comforting silence. Zidal glanced at him, her mask falling onto the bridge of her nose. "So, kid, you must have come from somewhere. What is your story?"

Alex looked into her unique violet eyes. "What's the point of telling my story? I ran away from my life on Achnor. I had no freedom, and the only excitement I had was battling with the warriors of Gaoly. I was forced to follow every command I was given by my father." he sighed. "I was too curious, I followed the calming voices into the cave, and locked myself into this new life. I have no reason to regret my mistakes, I brought this unto myself."

"You ran away from home?"

Alex sighed, a clear memory echoing through his mind. "I could have stayed, lived life as royalty, but I have a feeling that this is where I am meant to be. I can't drop that feeling, I know that I am important to this world."

"How sentimental." Zidal answered before stopping in her tracks, staring at a rock wall. She held out her hand, gesturing for Alex to halt. "Just what I was searching for."

"Huh?" Alex studied the wall in front of him in a confused stutter. Zidal lifted her hands and intertwined her fingers. The rock began to fade, and swirl into a darkness unlike any other. Zidal glanced at Alex, assuring him to follow as she stepped toward the portal. "We will arrive in Grandts faster this way." she assured before she disappeared from sight walking into the darkness.

Alex followed her, having stepped through the strange substance before. He felt himself fade from existence for only a moment. When he opened his eyes, he looked upon a beautiful village. The dark portal disappeared before any other soul could notice it.

His eyes followed the majesty of the small town. The buildings were tall, growing miles above the ground and reaching to the sky. They came in all shapes and sizes, the foundations sometimes being much thinner than their heavy tops. The mixture of colors was unlike any he had ever seen. Whites, blacks, reds, and yellows draping each building with a dramatic look. Dragons were carved into the sides of each estate, even more swirls and patterns following their tails. Statues which stood at the front of each building represented the same symbol.

He was in awe of the craft of each building. "Wow." he managed to say as he let out a breath. "I have never seen this much majesty in the craftsmanship of simple buildings like these."

"Do humans decide to disregard all beauty and build with speed rather than diligence?" Zidal asked, curious to Alex's awe of her small village.

Alex dropped his head and glanced at Zidal. "The most beautiful building that I can recall in Gaoly has been in ruins for longer than I have lived. At least compared to these." He opened his arms, collecting all of the buildings in his sight. "I... I'm beginning to forget Achnor, the mind wavering is making me forget what I have lost." falling to the ground, he breathed deeply, taking in the pain. "The pain only worsens as I try to remind myself." Alex stuttered, holding his head.

"Come on kid, we can't waste time. The pain will subside eventually" Zidal pulled Alex from the smooth floor and began to walk down the road erected of red crystals and dark stone. The pain continuing to linger, Alex followed her constant steps. Her boots clattered as they hit the hard ground. They turned through the twisted roads of the town, finding their way to the monastery.

Many other Darlids walked across the stone pathways in the beautiful lilac light. All of the beings were tall, thin, and quiet. Most were as colorful as the buildings surrounding them, others as bland as the white dirt blanketing the surface. Some looked similar to familiar animals on Achnor that Alex could remember and even more of them seeming close to human form.

Zidal stopped in front of a strange building, it seemed to be a worshiped monastery of some sort. It was painted with reds, golds, and greens, standing out from all of the other buildings in sight. The dragons were shown more proudly than all of the others, bringing joy to the Darlids that claimed that place as home. "Here it is. The sword should be the first thing you see when you enter the building." Zidal claimed.

Zidal lifted her hand in front of her, stretching her arm further out to open the black doors. She wrapped her tainted fingers around the pure gold handles and pulled the lightweight doors toward her. Heavy air brushed across their heads, swishing Zidal's smokey hair aside. Staring into the room, they glanced at each other and stepped inside, their footsteps echoing.

The glass case laid in the center of the first area, shining brightly, yet it was empty. Zidal touched the crystal glass, staring intensely inside. "I don't understand. The sword *was* here. What happened to it?" an echoed tap sounded from behind as she finished her phrase. Alex and Zidal looked toward a darkened hallway. A Tall Being stood in the midst of the shadows. He wore a white robe, his arms folded neatly across his chest. His silver hair falling from his head was so long that you could barely see his chocolate eyes.

"Recently we found that the honored sword was much more dangerous and powerful than we could imagine. If one Darlid got their hands on the sword, they would curse the world with death. That power alone should belong to Death." his echoing voice was low and raspy.

"So, what happened to it?" Alex asked curiously.

"I made sure that it was hidden where no one would go. No one will ever find it, and no one should ever go looking for it." the strange creature stepped away from them and disappeared from sight. His joyful voice echoed as he turned the corner. "Be aware of the danger you are in…"

"Huh? Danger? The only danger we are in is if the Broken Souls get their hands on the sword! How are we supposed to find this sword if it is nowhere to be found?!" Zidal raged.

"Zidal..."

"Silence, let me think."

"But Zidal,"

"I said *let me think!*"

Persistent to say his mind Alex raised his voice. "Zidal, I can find the sword!" Zidal turned her distress expression toward Alex. "I can sense where it is. Remember, that's why you *need me.*" she placed her head in her cushioned hands, relieved. She took a deep breath and gazed at him with excitement.

"How could I forget? Thank goodness, I almost believed that we had lost for good. Come on Alex, lead the way." Alex turned toward the large doors and walked toward the entrance of the building. He pushed the heavy wooden door open, stepping into the warming sunlight. Alex closed his eyes, breathing in the fresh air deeply. His light brown hair swayed in the gentle wind. He allowed the thought of death to take over, finding the way toward the emblem. After a silent moment of thought, he opened his eyes pointing in a northwest direction.

"There, if we keep walking straight, we should arrive at its location promptly." Alex began to walk into the distance, avoiding anything that stood in his way. He glanced behind him frequently to ensure that Zidal was following behind him. Though he would rightfully lead his troops on Achnor, he was unsure of his ability toward Darlids.

The tall tilting buildings began to shrink in size, each one they passed seeming more usual to his eyes. The foundations seemed to become larger than the tops, or the same size now that they were outside of the town. The trail of his echoing footsteps faded as the crystal roadways drifted into white dirt.

The sound of crashing juniper began to echo through the open space, the trickling of streams following their dubious steps. The pounding of waves deafened the sounds yearning to enter their ears. Zidal continued to follow Alex, despite the feeling that he would fail, that they could be finding themselves lost in an unexplored part of her world. The sound of crashing juniper in the distance became louder as they continued their trek. Zidal lifted her head, searching for the source of the sound. “It must be just behind the cliff.” Alex assured, speaking louder so that the crashing juniper would not override his voice. Zidal nodded, agreeing to his assumption as she had faith that he would find it.

Zidal glanced behind her, the buildings in the distance fading from her sight like an old memory. The scenery was now laced with a sego hue, the grass smoothly laid in the ground. The dirt beneath her feet was soft, damp, filled with juniper.

The rushing sound became clear now. The pounding of juniper echoed through the area; the only sound heard as they witnessed the river rushing through the valley. Alex bent toward the river and stared deeply into the rushing juniper. Fish, blazing a violet flame as they swam through the liquid, followed the uncontrollable current. Alex dipped his fingers into the river, questioning his understanding. “The sword should be here.” he pointed into the juniper.

“In Felou river, The deepest and most dangerous river in Shawon?” Alex nodded with confidence. “Tell me, how long can you hold your breath?”

“No more than a minute.”

“Ugh, must I do everything?” Zidal sat beside Alex and stared into the river. She placed her hand onto her mask, peeling it off of her face. The gentle scars plastered across her face revealed a sorrowful story that words could not tell. She sighed as she handed the royal mask to Alex, along with her scythe. Alex took her belongings and stood from the side of the river, waiting. He glanced upon her frail cracked face, her wispy hair flying along the gust of wind. She gazed into the river and opened her mouth. Taking a deep breath, she dove into the river.

Zidal pulled her weight through the juniper, reaching the bottom of the river. Her eyes were burning, the liquid staining her eyes. Her chest grew painful cramps, her heart pumping heavily against her ribs. Not even halfway down the depth of the river, and her lungs were begging her to breathe. She ignored the urge to take a breath, kicking her legs and folding her arms as slowly as she could.

The rocky surface of the river's bottom came into her sight, light from the firefish barely reflecting off of the crystals. Her eyes surfed the bottom of the river for the emblem of death, searching for the shape of a sword. The river was dark, the sword's symbol nowhere to be found. She dragged her hand across the sandy surface, feeling for the handle, though she could not find it.

Her chest aching, she allowed herself to float to the surface of the river. Using the last of her energy, she begged her arms to pull her to dry ground. She reached for the surface and held to the ledge of the river, lifting her head out of the water. She gasped, her lungs craving the taste of the sweet air. Alex looked at her. "Where's the sword?"

Taking in deep, laborious breaths, Zidal spoke. "I couldn't reach it in time. I'm going to dive again, it's too important.`` Before Alex could say a word, she held her breath, diving into the depths of the pounding waters once again. She pressured herself to reach the bottom once more, this time, much more prepared. Her lungs slowly bled her breath she hoped to hold.

Her eyes scanned the surface once again. Finally, she spotted it, its violet glow begging her to grasp its handle. She stretched her arm toward it, her mind falling short of thought, wrapping her fingers around the smooth grip.

She looked above her, swishing her arms and legs, rising from the deep end. Air fell from her mouth and nose as her chest could not hold onto the pain of breath. She swam with more determination than could be described, hoping to taste the sweet air above. Reaching toward the light in the near distance, she grasped the edge of the cliff, lifting herself to the surface. She threw the sword onto the ground, breathing heavily, coughing, releasing the pain from her body.

She stood from the ground, her uniform drenched in juniper, dripping like a Broken Soul's skin. The dark sword gleamed brightly in her hand, emitting a powerful feeling through the air. Alex returned Zidal's mask and scythe, which she gracefully placed in their original positions as she handed forth the sword of death. "Take it, the elder was right in saying that no Darlid should wield this weapon." she took another deep breath as the sword fell from her grip. Her breathing slowed to a normal, yet desperate pace.

They both stared at the sword of death, admiring its majesty. "This sword holds all the power of death?"

Zidal nodded. "But the only being that should control it is Death." she turned away from the river, beginning to walk, the sound of shifting cloth following along. Alex followed her toward a new destination.

"Each emblem holds a power Athreal once held. If the powers combine once again, he will be recreated. He will first overthrow the leader of the Broken Souls, and soon after, the king of Darlids. Finally, he will use you to escape Shawon and destroy Achnor, ruling overall. That is why we must destroy them, we don't have the power to release the souls, they will be lost forever." she remarked. "We must bring each emblem to the king to destroy them."

"Why must the king destroy them? Can we not destroy it now before Broken Souls do?"

"No Darlid is strong enough, save he. And we know not the spell to destroy it rightly. If we destroy it improperly, the soul will find its way to a new host." she glanced at Alex, halting as he stopped mid-track. He unwillingly dropped the sword with a large clatter, kneeling to the ground as he held his hands over his mouth. A sickening feeling entered his soul, a terrible control taking over his body.

Zidal bent to his side, looking into his eyes. He coughed, his mouth beginning to taste of medicine as it filled with a dark black liquid. It spilled from his mouth like a waterfall as he gagged. Zidal carefully retrieved the sword of death and grasped Alex's hand. She lifted him from the ground. He was still gagging the liquid as his mind raged in pain. They waited as fear loomed over them. "You have spoken wrongly,

Zidal. The emblem must be destroyed by *my* hand." an ominous voice rang.

Zidal stared into the oozing black puddle, frozen with fear. Without turning toward the sound of the shadowed voice, she spoke as if she had been betrayed. "You!" The strange liquid dripping from Alex's mouth suddenly ceased to fall.

"It is so wonderful to see you again." a deep and intimidating voice sang from behind.

"I could recognize your magic anywhere." Zidal held the sword tighter while turning toward the source of the voice.

There he stood, a majestic being, tortured and fearless. He seemed to have a human figure, yet his features changed his identity. His dark hair was dripping from its roots, covering his left eye completely. His uncovered right eye allowed tears of dark decay to fall across his lightly toned skin, which also seemed to be melting off of his bones. His ears were pointed as the horns of a demon. They too were seeping into the dirt. He carried two large dragon wings on his back as a cape. They were ripped, gently swaying against the breeze, the layers dripping a familiar black slime to the ground. His arms stretched and moved as if there were no bones holding his body together. Behind his valiant uniform, large ropes held two giant scythes to his back. "Kyron." Zidal raged.

He placed an arm in front of his stomach and bowed. "But what a pleasure it is." his voice sounded as if it echoed from behind him, yet his mouth was opening clearly, his fangs allowing the same dark liquid to drip out.

"You *died,* Kyron. You became the very thing you swore to destroy." Zidal spoke with an anxious breath.

Kyron leered, lifting his crooked head, chuckling. "No, you don't understand. I'm not the villain here… you are. Now, hand over the sword and things won't have to get messy." he sounded aggressive, willing to harm anything in his way to succeed.

"I won't give in." Zidal raged.

"Then come, let us be together again like we were before." Kyron let out his free hand, waiting for it to be taken.

"I don't know you anymore." she spoke with a tone of calmness, yet rage followed.

"Care to dance then? Remember the grasp of our hearts?" Zidal, pulled towards his words, dropped the sword, indifferent to his voice. Alex swiftly took the sword from the grass, keeping it from the being's grasp.

Zidal stepped toward the Broken Soul willfully, taking his melting hand carelessly. "It would be bliss."

Kyron slowly stepped toward Zidal before placing his soft hand on her waist, his other on her shoulder. She copied his actions, gently holding him. Kyron smiled as he began to step through the grass. Zidal copied his movement, returning to the joy of her past, forgetting about the things that held her back. She followed his steps, keeping herself from sorrow. Kyron stopped suddenly, letting go of her shoulder, allowing her to spin around his hand, then taking her back, returning to the dance.

Zidal felt herself fly into the air, quickly being caught by his slick grasp. After her feet touched the ground, they continued to waltz. Zidal danced with an empty emotion, taking in the feeling of sweet nostalgia. They danced in bliss for what seemed like an eternity until it ended with Zidal bent over his arm.

While holding her still, caressing the joyous memory, Kyron swiftly drew one of his scythes from his back, holding the blade against her neck. As the blade rested across her throat, he whispered cunningly. "Join me."

Zidal drew her glaived scythe and returned his motion with a hard blow. "Never!" Kyron caught himself and retrieved his second scythe, swinging them toward her. She lifted her weapon against the air, catching her weapon between his.

"I've taught you well." He licked his lips.

"And so, let this battle commence." Zidal commanded. Kyron crossed his weapons against his chest, swinging each one toward Zidal. She ducked, the weapons falling short of her wispy hair. "Your heart is nothing but a melted mess! You don't remember who you were."

"Oh, I remember who I was. I was incompetent, I had no idea how much I could gain being like this. You *should* join me." He placed a scythe against her neck again, the other behind. His wings bent and flapped against the thin gusts of wind.

"I said never!" Zidal struck the weapon away and ducked before he swung another blow. She then shoved the glaive toward his open stomach but was caught by his quick reaction.

Kyron laughed. "Weak, feeble, incompetent. You cannot harm me. I am an Olk." As she increased her force against his scythe, Kyron threw another blow to hers. With the force of the blow overpowering, Zidal fell to the ground, yet she did not hesitate to stand from her fall, to continue her battle. Their weapons clashed once again. "It seems as if we are at a match, you cannot defeat me, and clearly, you know all of my moves. We would just lose our perfectly beating breaths." They stood for a moment, weapon held against weapon, staring at each other, until, suddenly, Kyron spun and knocked Zidal to the ground once again. He bent to her side and held her against the cold grass. He smirked as he stared into the near distance.

Zidal lifted her head and looked at Alex. "Alex, run as far as you can, I can take care of this! I'll catch up with you." At her command, Alex began to run, the heavy weight of the sword of death capturing his movement.

Kyron stood, dropping one of his scythes beside Zidal. He reached into the distance and clenched his fist, pulling his hand toward himself. Alex, unable to control his movement, was dragged against the ground by Kyron's force. Filled with weakness, Alex dropped the emblem onto the ground, pulling against Kyron's powerful force. Zidal stood from her fallen state, glanced at Alex, before returning her sight to the sword. She bit her lip as she ran to the sword of death, swiping it from the ground.

As Alex reached his destination, the dark liquid began to spill from his mouth once again, an uncontrollable sickness in his heart. Kyron latched his viscous skin onto Alex's back. He lifted his silver scythe and held the blade against Alex's neck. "I have no problem killing this human, it will be to our benefit, Athreal having arisen or not. Now, hand over the emblem, I won't hesitate to decapitate your friend." His dark eye leaked down his face, dripping onto Alex's head.

"I don't care for his life; I care about the lives of Darlids! Athreal cannot rise again!" Zidal screamed. Alex began to breathe heavier, the blade inching ever closer to his skin.

“Just watch, I’ll make it slow and painful for both of you. I won’t ask again, give me the sword!” the blade rested against Alex’s skin, breaking the bonds slowly. Alex swallowed deeply.

Zidal clutched the sword tightly against her palm, her senses getting to her. “I can’t let you win. I will not let Athreal Arise once again." She spoke as if she had no energy.

Kyron pulled the blade against Alex’s neck, the bonds holding his skin together beginning to rip. Dark blood poured down his neck, staining his skin. The pain was too unbearable for him to make a sound, his breathing was loud and slow. As the scythe dug in deeper, the pain strengthened, blood trickling across his skin.

“Stop!” Zidal commanded. Kyron slid the scythe out of his neck, blood seeping into a small puddle in the grass. “I will let you take the emblem of death.” Kyron retrieved a white handkerchief from his pocket and rubbed it against the mark of blood on his weapon.

“Hand it over, I am becoming impatient.” he demanded as he tucked the bloody cloth into his pocket and dropped his scythe onto the ground. He held out his hand, the other still keeping Alex captive.

“Not until you promise to heal his wound.” Zidal pulled the sword further from his reach.

“You cannot trust a promise from a damenor.” Zidal did not flinch. Kyron chuckled. “You do remember that even the smallest amount of Darlid blood only makes me stronger? Who knows what power a human’s would grant me?” she swallowed and nodded. “I like where this is going. Now, hand over the sword or he dies!” He carelessly shoved Alex onto the ground with a heavy force. Alex grunted in immense pain, holding his hand to his neck. Zidal took a deep breath as she stepped closer to Kyron. She held out the emblem of death, which he graciously took from her fragile hand. He bent to Alex’s side and pried his hand off of his wound. His unusually long and thick tongue slid out of his mouth, covered in dark saliva. He pressed it against the wound and slid it across the length of the slit. As he drank his blood, the wound sealed. “Quite delicious…”

As his task was complete, he stood, the sword in hand. He looked closely at the dark sword, holding the blade in one hand, the handle resting in the other. “Thank you, I will remember this moment for eternity." He smiled. "For the reincarnation of Athreal, your soul is free!" As he ended his chant, Kyron applied pressure against each side of the sword with all of his might. The strong metal began to crack, a light shining from the middle. The force too strong, the emblem snapped in half, a dark violet explosion reaching across the plains. Violet light rose from the remains of the sword, floating into the distance, returning to that which would become Athreal. "The first piece of Athreal has been released. My task is complete." He tossed the pieces of the sword into the river, freakishly smirking at Zidal.

"You're pure evil!"

"Zidal, some of us are just born to be evil." He reached to the ground, grasping the sticks of the scythes that laid in the grass. He slid them into his ropes and disappeared into the air. "Ahahahahaha..." he laughed maniacally. Not one laugh could top his bitterly stricken heart. Not one could create such a sound that would make the mighty fall.

Alex stood from the ground, rubbing his neck. Zidal sighed, melancholy and disappointed. "He wouldn't have killed you. He knows well what would happen to him if he disobeyed his Master. But he also knows all of my weaknesses. His manipulation was too great."

"Don't worry Zidal, we can find the other emblems, make sure that they will not claim all of the pieces. Let's head to Sinsto. They are waiting for us." Zidal nodded, though bitterly, as if she missed something from her past, and quietly followed Alex in his silent footsteps.

"*Allow me to teach you of these strong wills, S. The way to an ignited life. This elixir will allow... changes to occur in your body. Things that you may not even be able to imagine.*" the tall figure held the child's hand, leading him to an unfamiliar room. He watched his brother sleeping in the being's cradled arm as he walked. He attempted to keep in his sorrowful thoughts, trading his soul for this awful creature.

The Tall Being stood at the mouth of a freakish room, leading the children into the room. S stood at the front of the room. The tall figure slammed a large door behind him, his prisoners unable to leave the room.

The room was unlike the one S had seen so often. It was much larger and was filled with much more technical equipment. A large counter covered with bottles of strange liquids, containers of odd ingredients and sheets of paper stood on the side of a wall. A small cauldron stood over a pile of wood in the center of the room and a small bookshelf was held on the back wall.

"What is this place? Why are we here?" his voice shivered as he spoke.

"This is where I will create the elixir. I know that this will help me get places I couldn't before. It will enable me to find the emblems to recreate Athreal, and you are the perfect first attempt. As the other elixirs have not done what I need, I feel that this one will... that I will finally succeed." S shivered as he listened to R's whimpering. *"Here, hold your redundant brother while you witness the creation of this elixir."*

The Tall Being placed R on the floor. He stood slowly, rubbing his eyes. He took his brother's hand and held it tightly as he looked at him. "What's happening?" He asked sleepily.

"Shhhh... we will get free." S whispered to him.

The Tall Being ignored their strange speech as he continued his experiment. It stepped to the counter while the children stood helplessly in the corner. He retrieved a bottle filled with a magenta liquid. He turned toward the cauldron and reached toward it. The wood began to burn ominously as he stared intensely at it. He ripped the cork from the glass bottle and poured the entire liquid into the large cauldron. Smiling, he let the glass bottle crash onto the ground.

He returned to the table and took a handful of dried leaves. Their shriveled pieces were at loss of color. They were a dull brown, crumbling into tiny pieces. The tall being held the leaves over the pot and crumpled them further into the boiling liquid. His eye reflected the burning terror of the elixir.

He once again looked at the counter. He hovered over the ingredients until he reached a small bottle filled with a familiar yellow and blue liquid. Returning to the pot, he unscrewed the top of the bottle and allowed a drop to fall from its small mass. The liquid sizzled as it fell into the cauldron.

The Tall Being then reached to a pouch which was held on his thin belt. He opened the leather hatch and reached into the space. He pulled out five separate eyes and laid them on the table's empty space. The child stared at them in fury, his sockets reflecting the blazing fire. The eyes were once those of him and his brother. The third left over from the Tall Being- their Master. It was a memory which was too fragile, too sore to remember.

The Tall Being lifted a mallet from the ground and swung it onto the table many times. The pounding sound echoed through the room as he watched his precious eyes turn into dust. The pounding of the mallet matched the beating of his heart, the particles lifting into the air with an intent of evil.

Grinning, the Tall Being held the mallet in the air, and allowed it to drop onto the stone ground with a mighty clang. He took the dust, glowing blue, green, and hazel, and mixed it into the elixir. The Liquid shifted colors and texture as it was mixed. It became a dark, bubbling liquid. It was thick and viscous. He watched as it shifted into the perfect mixture. He took a ladle from the counter and a glass bottle. He dipped the ladle into the pot and scooped the liquid into the bowl. He poured the elixir into the glass bottle and closed it with a cork. He repeated the process with a second bottle

He placed the bottles onto the counter and allowed the elixir to cool. The fire underneath the cauldron ceased to burn. The tall creature stared at the children. "*See what you have learned here. I have the power, and soon you will too. The next time we meet, I will give you, and your brother, this elixir to help my cause.*" S stared at his brother's chubby face and gulped. "*You fear for your kin, yet not your own life, how curious. What makes you tick?*"

"You wouldn't know how it feels to care for someone. All you do is take, torture, and kill. I could not live without him."

"*I see, and yet, you don't seem to remember your life before me. You were brought to me by fate, unknowing of the dangers. You and your brother are mine. If it were not for fate, you may not be living at all. Your kin can be harmful to you, unlike my elixir.*" he opened the door and pointed outward. "*Return to your cell, have your brother sleep, and watch over him.*"

S left his sight, dragging his brother along. Following his plans would be for the better, for if he did not, he would surely die. Though he never knew his life before this misery, the stories that he had been told only made him wish for R to be safe in his care. He spoke to his brother as he walked. “I will watch over you, no matter what happens. I am the only family you need. We will escape.”

Sinsto

"We have arrived." Courier remarked, pointing at a tall wooden sign that read *Sinsto*. Buildings crafted from fine marble stood about them, reaching the clouds above. The city was pure, and humble. Courier gently smiled as he stepped through the marble city, in awe of its unwitnessed beauty.

Zorus followed his brother through the streets of Sinsto, weaving through the maze of the marble buildings, searching for the legendary library. Each building seemed a reflection of the one before, mimicking the structure over and over again, the only difference, the signs resting above each of the glass doors.

They searched through the beautiful city, until Courier ceased his movement. "Have we found it?" Zorus asked as he scanned the stone roadway. Veering his vision, he noticed streaks of dark stains draping across the stone, smeared out as if a large slug had passed through the city. It wreaked as strongly as a rotting corpse.

Courier's stomach turned at the sight. "What happened here?" he asked, confused, and afraid. Hopeful that the map was still intact, he quickly glanced at his brother and nodded before they began to follow the path, created by darkness. Soon it was obvious that the stain led to the library they were seeking. The white tower was covered with blackness, it was corrupted, broken, its beauty and purity captured from it and thrown into oblivion. Courier glanced at Zorus, seeking assurance. Zorus reached for his sword hiding inside his sheath gently wrapping his fingers about the handle. Courier, too unsheathed his weapon, holding his sword by his right side. He took in a deep breath as they stepped to the doorway.

"One of *his* creations I presume." Zorus uttered quietly.

Courier bent to his feet and retrieved the cape which was tied around his ankle. He held his hand toward his brother, the cloth strewn across his fingers. "I am healed enough; this will only slow me down." Zorus took the cloth from his hand and once again tied the fabric around the buckles on his shoulder, the familiar cloth brushing against his legs.

They stood for a moment, waiting for something to happen, before Zorus reached for the golden handle of the door. He wrapped his fingers around the sticky handle and pulled the door toward himself. The door opened, revealing a disastrous room, books scattered across the floor, papers ripped and crumpled. Bookcases were splintered, many laying across the ground, bare of books. The room was coated in a dark inky liquid, puddles upon puddles strewn across the room, a pungent scent filling the area.

Zorus, his skin fading from his bones, stepped inside the library. His brother followed his lead, he too shifted his form. Zorus peered at the front desk, the librarian hiding beneath the barricade in fear, holding her arms in front of her face for cover. As they listened, rustling sounds, books hitting the ground, hissing, and a low groaning sound twisted in their ears. "Looks like we'll have to fight for it." Zorus observed.

Zorus crept, almost silently, around the corner of a bookshelf, nearing himself to the sound of destruction. Courier followed behind his slow movements, holding his sword tightly. A pile of books laid on the ground, covered in the dark liquid. They were shaking, almost trembling. Zorus placed his hand on the book and lifted it from the ground. A small Broken Soul hid inside, munching at the corners of each page. It barked and hissed at the bright light falling into its hiding place as Zorus tossed the book aside. Alarmed, it clawed at Zorus, leaving a large scratch on his boney hand. Zorus recoiled, groaning.

Zorus swung his sword toward the pile of books. The small creature ran from the blade's grasp before it struck the ground, leaving an inky trail behind. He ripped his sword out of the now dented books and searched for the being through the huge library. The Broken Soul began scurrying around the room, avoiding their huge boots and weapons.

Courier began to chase after the Broken Soul. He swung his sword in intricate circles, barely missing the tiny blob many times as it bounced and scurried swiftly. The Broken Soul leapt across the room as swiftly as a rabbit, landing on various books, tables, desks, and the librarian. "Ahhhhhhhh!" the librarian screamed, the slimy being running up her stomach. She closed her eyes as she dusted her chest violently. As the tiny creature flung off of her body, it began to scurry in front of her. She kicked against it with her maroon high heels, yet the tiny creature dodged each attack, sprinting about her court.

"Zorus, veer left, I'll go right!" Zorus nodded, changing his direction instantly. The stubby Broken Soul sprinted back and forth, distancing itself between the blades. It became anxious as it cornered itself between two walls, Courier, and Zorus. It shivered and hissed, slashing its claws against the air to deter its enemy.

Zorus chuckled and glanced at his brother. "You want to do the honors, Core?" Courier smirked playfully. He raised his sword into the air and slammed it against the Broken Soul. The librarian squeezed her eyes shut as he impaled the creature. The skin and body of the Broken Soul melted into the floor, its soul shattered and lost forever.

Courier and Zorus slid their swords into their sheaths, their bodies reforming as they walked to the front desk. Zorus let out his hand and pulled the young woman from the ground. "Thank you." she exclaimed. They studied her appearance as their skin reformed. Dark red seaweed grew from her head like hair, bundled in a messy bun. She wore a white cardigan over a dark shirt. A badge, which read *Amy Seaway, Sinsto Library,* was pinned to her coat. Of all her features, her eyes stood out. Like a squid's, they were large, cloudy blue eyes. A pair of rounded glasses, which seemed slightly too big for her, rested around her eyes. She pushed them upon the bridge of her nose as she looked around her library, which was in ruins, and sighed. "Believe it or not, it has been worse." They stood before her awkwardly. She gave a quick and simple cough.

"What was that Broken Soul doing here?" Zorus queried.

"I have not the faintest idea," she remarked in a sweet, subtle accent.

Courier glanced at his brother in fear and whispered. "It must have been searching for the *Book of Emblems.*" he returned his gaze to the librarian.

“So, what can I help y’all with?” she asked kindly as she turned the wooden desk right-side up and stepped behind it. She leaned against the ink-laden desk.

“We were hoping that you could show us the whereabouts of the map of emblems.” Courier remarked.

“Heh heh, you boys look like a couple of sentries, funny I’ve never seen you around Sinsto. I’m afraid I can’t show that book to you.” She poked her round glasses onto the bridge of her tiny nose.

“This mission is extremely important.” Courier explained in a more confident tone.

“And we just saved your life, can’t you make an exception?” Zorus asked.

“I’m afraid not. I have been instructed to show that book strictly to the king, the Knightmare, and the seven Shadlas.” She shook her head.

Courier glanced at his brother and sighed. Zorus nodded slowly, in assurance, as if he knew exactly what his brother was thinking, returning his sight to the librarian. Courier rested his arm against the desk as he spoke. “Fine, we’ll explain. We’re willing to let you in on this secret. My brother and I are top class spies for the king, sent from Krysal.”

“In order to hide our identities, we had to dress like low class sentries.” Zorus added. Which was altogether true, but still a little unbelievable.

“We were sent on this mission to retrieve the map without a trace and return it to the king for its destruction.”

“Look, we're just doing what we were ordered to do, I’m not afraid to draw my sword.” Zorus added as he reached toward his back.

“Zorus, there will be no need for that. Zidal will arrive soon.” Courier remarked, reaching toward his brother’s arm. Zorus let his arm drop to his side.

“Y’all seem like you're making a stretch, I can’t risk having you take the map from this library, who knows what could happen to it if you take it. You could have stolen those uniforms for all I know. If Zidal does show up, you can have the book, but if not, it’ll be a lost cause. ”

“Then it is a good thing that she is on her way right now.” Zorus whispered frustratedly. Courier turned away from the wooden desk and began to walk toward the front of the building. Zorus followed in his footsteps.

"I'll be cleaning the library. Oh, you are welcome to stay until Zidal shows up." the librarian mocked. She walked in front of her small desk, moving toward the back of her library. She began to pick up the tainted books from the ripped carpet. She looked closely at the labels on the side and began to organize them in the tall wooden shelves, ignoring the broken bookcases.

Knowing that they could be waiting for hours, Courier shuffled through a pile of tainted books on the ground. "Sinsto library, it has been said that it holds the most rare books in Shawon."

"Courier, I'd nerd out with you, but I've got more pressing matters to deal with." he acknowledged, anxious for what could happen at any moment. All could be lost after one simple mistake. Courier shrugged as he watched his brother find his way to one of the wooden chairs near the front of the library. After searching through a nearby pile of books, he lifted one off of the ground, titled *Determined to Survive,* and sat on a chair near Zorus, opening the book to the first page. Zorus glanced at the cover and chuckled. "*Determined to survive?* Haven't you read that before?"

"Three times, actually. It's quite crucial to know how Broken Souls live." he remarked, as he scanned the page.

"I thought that you said that this library has the most rare books in Shawon." Zorus noted.

"Zorus, this *is* one of the rarest books in Shawon. I just happen to own one of the four copies." Courier remarked as he flipped the page. Zorus leaned against the back of the chair as anxieties ran through his mind. Thoughts that followed him like a nightmare, though unreal, they made him fear greatly. Terrors in which he never imagined to be true were coming to life, haunting his every memory.

Courier and Zorus waited for hours. As Courier continued to read through chapter thirty-six of his book, waiting for something to happen, Zorus dully watched the librarian fix the mess that he and his brother had helped the Broken Soul create. He glanced at the glass doors intensely waiting for both Zidal and Alex to appear safely with the emblem of death in hand. They were only accompanied by the sound of books hitting shelves and the slow anxious breathing of each other.

Zorus closed his eyes and began to drift away in silence but was startled by the sound of the crashing doors. Zidal and Alex stood in the shadows. Courier stood from his seat, dropping the book onto the chair, Zorus standing beside him. Zorus dusted his uniform as he stepped toward the others. They stared at each other in silence. Zorus examined Zidal and Alex's figure, searching for a change. "Where is the sword?" Zidal looked at her feet. Alex shook his head.

"A Broken Soul stole it from us. He was too strong to fight against as he was an Olk. He released the soul from the sword before we could take it back." Zidal sighed. "Luckily, we still have seven other pieces to find." she recalled.

"What about you, do you have the map?" Alex asked. Zorus shook his head. "Oh, don't tell me a Broken Soul got that too."

"No, the librarian will only let the king, Zidal, or a Shadla see it."

"Oh, I'm so stupid, I forgot about that rule. I should have gone to Sinsto." Zidal remarked.

"It's alright Zidal, at least we were here to save the library." Courier looked toward the young lady, who was continuing to clean the library. "Ms. Seaway, Zidal has arrived." At the sound of his voice, she stopped what she was doing and looked up.

"Hello Amy, are you busy?"

"Oh, no, I'm just cleaning, but if you need something I can take a break." She dropped the books in her arms and wandered to the backside of her desk. Zidal followed her while the others waited.

"I sent those two to retrieve the *Book of Emblems*, but they seem to have been unsuccessful." She glanced at Courier and Zorus. "It was imperative that they collected the book."

"Sorry your honor, I don't know why I had such a hard time believing those guys. Let me grab that for ya." Ms. Seaway bent out of their sight for a moment. The sound of a dial twisting, and a click played below the desk, followed by the sound of rustling paper and then a slam of a metal door. When she stood again, she held a black book in her arms. She handed it to Zidal. "Is that all?"

"Yes, thank you, Ms. Seaway. Now, you mustn't tell a single soul about what happened this evening."

"Yes, of course, your honor."

"Best of luck to you." Zidal said as she stepped toward the entrance.

"Bye honey." She waved as Zidal followed the others through the library entrance. "Good luck y'all." Zidal smiled, taking her last step out of the room, shutting the door behind her.

Zorus sat on a nearby bench on the side of the road. Courier sat beside him while Alex and Zidal decided to stand before them. Zidal held the book slightly above her waist as she opened it. There the map laid in its glorious state, showing the entire mass of land that occupied the dimension. It was much larger than Alex could have imagined. The huge mountains they had scaled were drawn as thinly as a paperclip, much more land surrounding it. The castle was small in size but stood out from the dull-colored areas. The map was part way faded and torn on the edges. The emblems were drawn onto the page as symbols, carefully labeled.

They silently studied the page, locating the remainder of the emblems. "I understand why the emblems of love and knowledge are not present, but where are the emblems of destruction and living?" Courier asked in shock.

"I… I don't know, it seems to have faded from the map. But Alex can still find them. We'll still need to split up." Zidal bent to the ground and wrapped her fingers around the edges of the map. She tugged at the page, ripping it from the book. She stood, holding the book in her fragile hands.

Courier reached for the book and took it from her delicate hands. He drew his fingers across the smooth cover as he studied its appearance. Unbuckling the strap on his leather satchel, he placed the book neatly inside. "Though we haven't the time to study it now, this book might come in handy." He shyly smiled as he dropped the cover of his satchel over the book and buckled it again.

Zidal studied the map as she searched for a convenient emblem to travel to. "The emblem of magic and power is the nearest to Sinsto. Who would like to travel with me?"

Courier and Zorus exchanged looks. Zorus sighed in brief agony as his brother spoke. "It would be my pleasure to locate the emblem of magic. It is said to be hidden beyond ancient runes." Zorus stood from the bench, staring into Zidal's eyes knowingly. Zidal shyly smiled and acknowledged his wonderment. "Now, Zidal, where in Shawon will we be heading to?"

"The emblem of magic and power is in Ticoal, the tropical dry forest." she somberly replied.

"But where in Ticoal?" Courier asked.

"Blue River Volcano." she gasped, studying the map carefully.

"This will require great sacrifice." Courier glanced at his brother. "Zorus, I believe this time you should use your ability to find us again." Zorus nodded at his brother's acknowledgement. Zidal began to step across the stone pathway, urging Courier to follow her command. Zorus sighed, somberly watching his beloved brother fade into the distance.

"Don't die, okay?!" Zorus yelled through the large, clustered buildings.

"Until the morrow brother!" he replied, his voice echoing through the wind.

"Until the morrow…" Zorus whispered in response.

"What does that mean?" Alex questioned.

"It's a saying my brother and I use to remind each other that only the future knows what will happen to us." Zorus searched the area for his brother, though they were now fully out of their sight. "I taught him that very saying from the first moments that he could speak, knowing that it could motivate us during times of turmoil." He shook his head. "What the future will hold is out of our control." he chuckled distraughtly. "We'd better go find this emblem. Where is this emblem of destruction?" he asked in such a way that made Alex freeze. He closed his eyes and envisioned destruction of all kinds. Natural disasters, explosions, breakage, and more. A picture filled his mind, its essence pulling him toward the emblem.

"North." he declared.

"You're going to have to skip the directions and just point." Alex pointed to his left. "Alright, kid, let's head off."

S woke, once again in chains, glancing at his brother, who, too, was carrying shackles too heavy for his small wrists. He watched as R woke and looked into his empty eyes. "Why are we chained again?" R's thought was interrupted by the sound of an unlocking door. The Tall Being stepped into the room.

He spoke, disturbing the silence. *"Ah, you own insignificant minds. You don't know what my mind seeks. You don't seem to realize, but you are more dangerous than what meets the eye. You must be held back as my elixir has not been committed to your blood."* he took an unnatural breath. *"We must experiment with this elixir."* the tall figure stepped closer to S, holding a rusted key. The key interlocked with the hole in the chain and screeched as it twisted. The shackles fell cleanly off of his wrists.

S felt his dry wrists as he watched the tall figure release his right wrist. He stood, waiting for something to happen. The Tall Being stepped toward his brother and began to release him. S listened to the fall and crash of the chains, followed by his brother's small footsteps. R wrapped his arms tightly around his brother's waist. S returned a loving embrace to his brother's sorrowful tears.

"Come now, we must determine your traits. We must use this elixir." unwilling, R and S followed their Master through the creaking door, nightmares filling their minds. They did what they were told, for there was no escape. They followed the rules, for they knew the consequences. Aside from their Master's interest in finding the pieces of Athreal, he enjoyed harming those who could not defend themselves. They were his *test subjects.*

"What's happening?" R asked in a whisper to his brother.

"We are becoming the successors of Athreal." his lip trembled as he spoke back to his brother. "Master is corrupting us." he spoke as quietly as he could, yet the Keeper still heard.

"You will not only be the successors of Athreal, but the head of the battle. This elixir is not only to help me create him, but also to create overbearingly strong forces." R whimpered. *"Do not fret R, this will*

make you powerful, you will overcome the world. You will be unstoppable in battle and strong in your words. You will fight with the beings which will be victorious."

The Tall Being opened the metal door, letting his subjects in. They knew well what was going to happen. From the wooden counter, the Master took the two small vials, both filled with the elixir they had watched him create. They had fermented overnight, the magic taking full effect. The Tall Being pulled the cork out of the first bottle, handing it to S.

R looked at his brother in fear, tears falling from his empty eyes. S, disgusted with the thought of drinking the elixir, brought the bottle to his lip and smelled the strong flavor of the potion. He lifted it to his soft lips and began to pour it into his mouth. The liquid drained down his throat, an indescribable flavor caressing his tongue. At a loss of words, and a dizzy expression, S hit the floor in a deep sleep.

Call of the Charmer

Silence swept the city as Courier and Zidal began their journey to the forest of Ticoal. Their shallow breaths were followed by the sound of the whispering wind and the quiet bickering of creatures. Zidal glanced at Courier, holding the map to her chest. "This emblem will be difficult to discover. We have been given hints as to where it is, but not its exact location." Zidal acknowledged, more somberly than before. She folded the map into a neat square before placing it inside of her pocket.

"Do not fret, Zidal, it shan't be too hard to find." Courier remarked. "If I have learned anything, knowing a little of something makes a task easier than knowing nothing at all."

"Danger still lies in the depths of Ticoal, and Blue River is nonetheless a cavern filled with pain."

"We have trained for years in order to accomplish tasks as difficult as this. I don't understand why you worry."

"You're right, I shouldn't be afraid, we are ready for this, and if we die, it would be for a remarkable cause." she sighed. "But the world still sets aside the heroic actions we partake in."

Courier glanced at Zidal, a deep mystery in his glare. "Zidal, you haven't seemed like yourself recently."

"What?" Zidal asked in a confused manner, knowing all too well what he was speaking of; determining something she tried to hide.

"Your emotions, Zidal, the longer you devote yourself to this mission, the more your emotions fall."

"Fall? I don't understand." she indicated.

"Your confidence has dissipated as you recall your past. You seem to be missing a piece of your heart." He pulled his thin fingers through his hair as he waited for her answer.

Zidal stared at the soft glow reflecting from Courier's face. His empty eyes seeped into her soul, his curious words echoing in her heart. His words stuck to her soul, her heart pounding at the thought of the words. Though she was afraid to speak again, words fell from her soft lips, ignorant of her own emotions. "I don't understand, I feel the same as I have always felt."

"Allow me to speak more blatantly. Zidal, you are distancing yourself from the world in such a way that you don't acknowledge your own emotions. Do you wish harm upon yourself?"

Zidal placed her shadowy hand on her chest and spoke briefly, though, without all of the feelings in her heart. An innocent lie which easily fell from her lips. "No."

"Remember, you are required more than any Darlid. This mission would be impossible without a Darlid such as you."

His words fell through her skin. "I... I really needed that." she walked silently for a moment, recalling his words. "How could you read my emotions so easily, like a page of a book?"

Courier sighed, knowing to be careful of what he spoke. "I hold power unknown to the eyes of most Darlids. I have the ability to understand the needs of the soul, what they desire." he remarked, though he knew that he had not explained his secrets thoroughly, nor did he give any hints as to his true ability. He dragged his finger across the scar on his lip as he glanced at Zidal. "Zorus too holds his own unique traits. I remark, you should not underestimate his abilities, he chooses to hide more than he should. Though he seems apathetic, he is tenacious and coercive. If he is determined, nothing will defeat him, he will get what he desires."

"What?"

"I shouldn't speak further, but you must understand, we were not meant to be this way, Zidal. We were taken away from a *normal* way of living, forced into a life of pain, into unnatural traits. I'll warn you now, demons escape from our souls as we rest, we are not to be toyed with." Zidal quivered as she stared at his chilling smile. "But worry not, you are an ally, a hero."

Zidal smiled shyly. "I'm no hero." she whispered, though too quietly for Courier to respond. The pearl city of Sinsto had shifted into a large grassy plain, filled with dying flowers. The grass was grey, signifying that it had dried. There was not enough rain in the plains and too much sun for the grasses to handle. As they walked, a constant crunch of the grass followed. "Where are we? Or more importantly, how close are we to the emblem?" Courier asked.

Zidal pulled the map from her pocket and unfolded it carefully. She studied the drawings with ease. Before she could find their place, Courier's voice entered the silent plains. "Hoqer grassland. Ticaol should be around eighteen miles from here." Courier remarked before she looked up. "We best be moving forward." Courier stated as he began to walk through the dry grass.

Zidal folded the map again, placing it inside her pocket. She followed Courier through the empty plains, listening to the sound of her heartbeat. A sudden aching feeling entered her bloodstream, weakening her leg. "Agh." Zidal agonized as she fell to the ground, a stinging pain resting in her ankle, as if something had bit her. She wrapped her hands around the wound, groaning as the pain rose through her leg. She glanced at Courier, who let his hand out for her. Resisting the urge to take care of her wound, she took his hand, raising herself from the dry grass.

She felt her imperfect breaths beat as she stood in the grass. Courier let her hand fall from his as he stared into the distance, the sun lowering into the horizon. Courier smoothed his finger over the scar on his lip. "Come on, time is of the essence." he reminded her as they began to trek through Hoqer again. The pain was bearable, yet her step was wobbly. Zidal glanced to her side, alarmed when she noticed that Courier had disappeared. Halting, she glanced into the distance behind her, shocked to see that he was uncontrollably being dragged through the tall dry grass.

Courier, his flesh in pain, looked at his leg, a long, slithering stick covered in pink, blue and lilac feathers pulling him through the painful grass. It was an enormous serpent, powerful and determined. Its sharp fangs dug deeply into his skin. "Agh!" he winced in pain. He reached for his ankle and pried against the jaws of the beast, attempting to release himself from its tight grip.

"A feathered boa constrictor!" Zidal screamed, her emotion shifting again. Without hesitation, she began to chase after him, the tall grasses covering his thin body. She searched the area, the grass too tall to notice another creature, the colors too dark to find other hues shining through. "Where did you go?" she asked, frantically searching for him.

"Zidal!" she heard him scream in the distance, using her ears to follow the constrictor's evil snare. The dry grass crunched underneath her feet as she ran with a determination stuck in her heart. She listened to the sound of the being slithering through the terrain, rustling through the grass. She crept, following its sound, covering its tracks. "I would be most grateful if you got me out of its painful grip!" Courier remarked as he pried against the snake's bite. The constrictor would not let go of his ankle; it fused its fangs into his skin. Blood leaked from his wound. He was unable to change form, the pain keeping his skin where it needed to be.

"I know, I just have to find you." Zidal declared as she ran. Panting, nearly out of breath, she stopped for a moment and searched the grass. Finally, she spotted the colors of the snake, the grass moving along with its movement. Zidal, though tired, ran through the grass, reaching toward the snake. Zidal carefully laid her hand on the constrictor and pulled against it as forcefully as she could. Alarmed, the snake sprung, and pulled Courier away from her sight. She ran once again, the sun beating on her dark skin. As she ran, she pulled her fingers through her shadowed hair, pulling it away from her face. She sprinted with a steadfastness unmatched, determined to save Courier from danger, as if without him she would be unsuccessful in her mission, though she knew that she held the map.

Caught off guard, she halted, realizing that before her stood a ghastly being, saving herself from crashing into it. She studied its figure as she caught her breath. It was tall, reflecting the features of a human, yet it was covered in delicately dripping feathers. Its expression was covered by a frightful leather mask, its bright green eyes shining through the windows. Its long beak grinning as it oozed. On the left side of the beast, there grew one more arm than its right at the back of its shoulder. Its melting talons wrapped gently around Courier's neck as the feathered boa constrictor slithered upon its body. "I am Merchel, the enchantress of snakes." her beak opened widely as she spoke. Her voice was raspy, sounding as if she had been choking on a branch for years. Her dark cloak draped onto the ground as she lifted a talon-like finger. "Master wanted me to find the emblem of power, you know the means of its hiding spot. Take me there, and you shall live."

Zidal drew her weapon from the rope resting on her side, aiming the glaive toward the beast. "Let him go." she charged aggressively.

"I have no agreements to make until you agree to mine." she spoke, unfazed by the weapon. her melting insides dripped from her beak, her talons tightening around Courier's neck.

Courier reached to her talons, pulling against her tight grip, yet they would not loosen. The pain inside his body was too great for him to change form, stuck until he could heal. "Agree with her. I would rather not *fall* from her grip." he choked.

Despite her fear, Zidal spoke, replacing her weapon. "We cannot let the Broken Souls have any more of the emblems."

"That's okay, Lade will take prisoners in its stead. Who knows what he'll try to do? At the least, killing you would be mercy." Merchel cackled.

"I beg of you, agree…" Courier again pleaded, knowing much better than Zidal could ever imagine. "I have a plan."

"Fine, let him go, we will lead you to the emblem of magic." Zidal stated somberly.

As her talons loosened, Courier fell to the ground. He stood, unbalanced, shaking off the melted skin from his bones. He nodded gratefully. "That's what I like to hear… now, let us find this emblem of magic."

"We would head off immediately," Courier stated deceivingly. "But my leg is far too injured for travel. Your serpent has a strong grip." he used his words cunningly as he needed to protect himself.

"Fine, take this." Merchel reached into her pocket and pulled out a small rock. "Eat, it is medicine." Courier graciously took the pebble and placed it in his mouth. It was bitter, spice coating his tongue. He quickly swallowed, and his limp was immediately cured, the bite healed completely.

"Thank you." he remarked as he finally transformed himself, his skin merging into his bones.

Zidal began to walk past Merchel. Courier, who stood in his protective state, followed behind her for a moment before he was able to walk in the lead. The enchantress took kindly to their step and followed farther behind them. Zidal glanced at Courier. "Where are you going, why aren't we in battle? This is strictly against my orders. What's your plan?"

Courier coughed as he stared at the trees in the distance. "We would surely die in a battle against a charmer, especially because she is an Olk. I know better ways to distract her. Patience Zidal, we need to set camp in the trees of Ticoal in order to proceed." she nodded, unsure if she trusted his words. Before this mission had commenced, Zidal had only known that he was a warrior. She never knew of his strategic Mastery. Courier looked toward the Broken Soul following their tracks. "I sense that you crave freedom, yet you adore what you do. You adore your Master. You are grateful for a second chance in life, being more powerful than before."

The enchantress perked up, her snake curling around her neck. "How could you know that?" the enchantress pondered. "There is no possible way you could know so much about me when I have barely even met you." She declared in a raspy voice.

"I am no *normal* Darlid after all." the enchantress grimaced at his words, knowing too well where he had come from.

"Well, even if you do know my story, you are still taking *us* to the emblem of magic." she reminded them as her snake hissed. "It will belong to me, and I will have accomplished what many have yearned to."

"Of course, we are showing you the way." Courier smiled. "You are the kindest Olk I have ever encountered, you only threatened us. I'm sure we would be fighting you otherwise. Maybe, we could both get what we want." Courier knew his words buried under her skin; an insult taken lightly.

"You mean you want to be allies?" Courier allowed his skin to grow over his bones, showing that he was serious. As his hair grew back, it bounced into his perfect style.

"Well, of course we do. What's the point of causing turmoil in a time like this? The emblem on the other hand, we'll just have to agree on what to use it for… Athreal or salvation." Zidal gave Courier a dirty look.

He leaned over and whispered to her. "It all has to do with the plan, we will defeat her eventually."

"But I don't understand why we cannot fight her."

"She is far too powerful for us to handle, *she is an Olk.*"

"Shouldn't I be leading? I have the map. I am the…"

"...The Knightmare, I know, but you don't understand why I must lead at the moment. I'll explain everything later, we mustn't let her get suspicious."

The trees of Ticoal came into view, a canopy of darkness arising over their heads. Merchel quivered as the leaves brushed near her. The sun was dimming, the night stars creating a blanket over their heads. The moonlight bled through the leaves, and for a moment, Zidal noticed a smirk fall over Courier's shadow, but it soon dissipated. "How do I know that I can trust you? Zor... no, Courier." Merchel asked.

Courier spoke. "Ah, see we do have something in common. You know who I am without a proper introduction."

"I have been told about you, you and your brother are both great enemies to *us*." Merchel noted.

"Was *he* the one who told you this?" Courier asked with great intention.

"Indeed, but I have yet to see otherwise, you make great conversation." Merchel remarked as a branch brushed across her shoulder.

"I am glad you think so, I was beginning to think you had forgotten our deal." Courier reminisced.

"I won't break it, just don't let *him* know." Merchel promised.

"I haven't encountered him in eight years. Merchel, you see, I am no Broken Soul after all, even I can't be trusted." Merchel nodded as Zidal stopped under many trees.

"Here, night is falling, we should rest here. Merchel, take all the rest you need, Courier and I will take turns guarding the area." Zidal ordered.

"I am grateful for your offer, but I may be able to stay awake for longer periods of time without an effect." Merchel declared.

"That's not an offer, it's an order. We need to know that we can trust you, and for that, you need to follow my orders." Zidal harshly depicted in her words.

"Very well, but shouldn't we make camp first?" the enchantress asked in a kind manner.

"Of course, that way beasts are less likely to find us here and ruin our chances. We better not split up." Courier declared. He smiled at them as they followed his lead. They nodded in agreement and began to head forward into the dark forest. The sound of their dry footsteps filled the night air with joy.

Courier stepped through the forest, without perfect silence, a chattering of voices surrounded his steps as he followed a trail of small creatures. He shook his leg, letting something alive fall from his knee. Now feeling uncomfortable, he unknowingly changed his physical form, and held onto his sword's handle, barely drawing his sword from his leather sheath. "Night locks." he whispered to himself, knowing all too well what was happening.

"Did you say something?" Merchel asked, holding a freakish emotion.

"Huh? Oh, nothing, worry not." he dropped his hand from his sheath.

"Merchel, would you please take that log?" Zidal asked, pointing to a dry piece of wood. Merchel nodded, lifting it from the dry ground without difficulty. "Courier, I'm concerned. You're in your protective state. Are you sure that there's nothing wrong?"

Courier looked at his boney hands. "Am I? I barely noticed." he spoke softly, knowing he couldn't hide his fear as leaves crunched under his feet.

Zidal stepped closer to Courier and quietly spoke to him. "Well then, what exactly are you doing?" Zidal asked, annoyed.

"There is nothing to fear…" a loud bang fluttered from behind their backs, interrupting his speech. Courier kept quiet, stopping in his tracks. Glancing behind, he realized Merchel was left further behind, the log far from her reach.

"I can't move my legs." she cried. "Please, help me…" she called as Courier hurried toward her.

Zidal rushed after him. "Why are we saving her? This is the perfect time to leave her behind. We should be moving forward."

"Let's just say, an old friend has sent me a terrible gift." questioning her trust, she continued to follow her ally. Courier bent toward Merchel's feet, staring at the black sludge which held her legs to the soft grass. Merchel's snake slithered down her body, biting against the liquid. Its fangs phased through, puncturing her leg.

"Ahhh…" she screamed as she pulled the snake off of her leg. It slithered to her shoulder, seeming afraid. "Tellibous, it is not… alive… it can't be killed." she began to breathe heavily. "It feels as if it is corroding me without a stomach." it surrounded her lower legs, beginning to reach her thighs. Zidal pulled her scythe from the thick rope on her side.

Courier held his hand in front of her. "Do not use your weapon Zidal. Please, be calm, stay completely still. Night locks only consume moving things, and even more interesting, they devour things that are decaying. Now, the only way to rid of them is fire. I thought that you could possess it…"

"I am a master of pyro, but I need something to fuel it." She studied the area as the oozing pulse of fluid began to drag her arms into its mass. She pulled against it, yet still stuck to it. "Zidal, is it? Give me that stick." Zidal glanced to her left, the direction in which Merchel was peering. She ran, lifting the torch-like stick from the ground, rushing back to the creature. Courier continued to stay calm, reaching through his knowledge of the past.

Zidal returned with the branch, allowing Merchel to take it with her leathery beak. Thinking of heat, embers and light, she caused the branch to ignite. Unexpectedly, the night locks began to scream and melt into the ground. As it fled their sight, Merchel held the branch in her cold talons. Her breath fell and her impatient heart beat calmed. "Thank you. Maybe I *should* trust you." as Courier's skin began to renew, a faint, mischievous smile returned to his expression.

"We should make camp here." Courier stated as the others nodded in agreement. "I will retrieve that log."

"Be careful." Zidal added.

"I needn't any luck." he affirmed. Courier stepped only a few feet into the distance and collected the huge log. As he returned to the scene, he dropped it onto the dry ground. Merchel placed the burning branch onto the log and allowed it to envelop the flame. She then searched through her cloak and pulled out a decaying creature. "I always keep something edible with me." she stabbed it with a nearby stick and held it over the log.

A warm purple blaze arose from the borders of the wood, the unusual meat roasting over it. It was cut into three sections, barely keeping together on the stick. Merchel removed the darkened meat from the flame and pulled off each piece, giving one to each of them. "Thank you again, for earlier." Merchel acknowledged.

"You didn't have to mention it." Courier acknowledged. Zidal pried a thin piece of meat off the bone and began to chew on the sweet fat of the creature. Courier stood, still holding the meat. "I should get to my post; we don't want the night locks to find us." He took a branch from the ground and set it against the fire. As it ignited, he looked away from the others and began to walk into the distance.

"Wait!" Zidal yelled as she ran toward him. "What's your plan? To make friends with the Olk and ultimately get the emblem?" she whispered as he glanced at him.

"In Death's name, no! Have you ever encountered a charmer rec? They are very cunning yet are fooled by kindness. Betrayal is the easiest way to defeat her. Also, her greatest physical weakness happens to be trailbite leaves. Charmers lose all strength when it is on or surrounding them. Luckily, these trees grow those leaves. I am going to create a layout of these leaves and leave her before she awakens. A perfect, destructive betrayal." he chuckled. His voice was soft, yet confident.

"Wait, how do you know all of these things about recs, I thought that you could only sense emotions." she reminded him. Courier unbuckled his satchel, placing the remains of meat beside the *Book of Emblems*. After which, he tightened the strap against the golden ring.

"Have you forgotten the very purpose of my being? Have you forgotten that I have read basically every history book that has ever existed in Shawon? Learning comes from pure determination, not power. Merchel is a snake charmer rec, of course her weakness is trailbite leaves." Zidal stared at him, confused yet left in awe of his immense knowledge.

"Why wouldn't you tell me earlier?"

"Let's just say, it's a way to distract her from being suspicious." she nodded, though without understanding. "Go, Merchel might get suspicious." Zidal nodded. "We'll switch in two hours." she nodded again as she left his sight.

S's eyelids opened, his vision blurry, and his mind ringing. He did not feel like the same Darlid he was before. Something had happened, something that he could not remember. His mind was in pain, but not in the way a headache would cause pain. His vision was cluttered with hurt and memories. His arms carried a heavy weight, they were even stronger than the chains before. His body ached, it reacted to the chains in a strange way, as if he could not control himself the way he used to.

He tilted his weak head, staring at R, sitting in chains just as he. He sat in peace, waiting for his life to be the same, yet he whimpered in pain, lacking the warmth of his brother's care. He attempted to speak but was caught by his tongue. S watched as his brother reached for him, unable to touch him, nor could he act the way he wanted to.

S weakly pulled against the chains, a bright, shocking pain filling his bloodstream. At the shock, he stopped, panting, worrying, it was never like that before. "What has Master done?" he asked his brother in fear, though R could not respond to his calls.

He listened as footsteps grew nearer to their cell. A shadow casted inside from the bars resting at the top of the doorway. The handle shook, though it felt like the entire room rumbled as the door began to open. The tall figure stood at their feet, grinning, leering, his evil mind running through their thoughts. S began to breathe heavily, as his echoing footsteps grew nearer.

The tall figure spoke, their ears blaring with the unnatural sounds he created for them. *"Keeler stone, a very rare substance in Shawon, only found in the deepest, darkest caves. Only found where sorrow weeps freely and filth is the only cleanliness. I see you have realized that your chains act differently. That means my elixir worked, you are filled with power that those chains can eliminate for a short time. You might feel in pain..."* he stepped closer to them, giving their bodies a shaking feeling, a warning to his dangerous form.

"What did you do to us? Why am I in pain? Why is my heart beating faster than it has before?" S asked, frightened by his appearance. He stared at his gleaming green eye, his thick skin oozing around it. His heart collapsed as he felt his Master touch him.

"Have you not remembered what this is all for? This is for my benefit. This is for the recreation of Athreal, the recreation of death and pain and suffering. The only way to be brought back to Achnor with a purpose, to destroy those who have kept us here. S, you, and your brother are the entrance to our victory. With your new properties, you will succeed as Broken Souls." his thick, dripping skin fell onto S's cheek.

"You're going to kill us?" S asked in fear, taunted by his words.

"Ah, but not yet, you don't understand your souls yet. Your newfound magic must be trained, you must be ready to serve me. You see, I can't kill you until you choose to be this way. And I know you won't." He stared at them gleefully. *"I am still working on an elixir that will force your soul to connect with your decaying body. With my other experiments, I will prepare it. And by the time your magic is fully trained, you will obey me."*

They watched as the Keeper left the room, listening to his freakish laughs and melancholy breaths. Tears fled from R's eyes, as he sat in the corner. Barely able to speak, he opened his mouth. "S, when can we go home? Haven't we gone through enough?"

He looked at his brother's sorrowful tears, searching for an answer. "There is someone out their R, the one I have told in those stories. They will come here to save us. It only takes time until they'll come. They're battling other evils at the moment, saving other Darlids that cannot protect themselves. I just know they'll come; I just know it…" He finished as a tear fell from his eye.

Extinction

Zorus and Alex walked along the rim of the pearl city. Nearing the edge, Zorus followed Alex through an ominous trail toward a beautiful oak wood forest. The trees began to canopy over their heads, casting shadows of darkness overhead. The magnificent light of the sun peeked through the leaves. "So, this emblem of destruction, what exactly are we searching for?" Zorus asked in a cheerful query, as he drew his fingers through his hair.

"From what I can tell, it is some sort of drinking horn." Alex described.

"Quite the strange object to encase the emblem of destruction." Zorus stated. He turned away from his lost thought and looked at Alex. "We have a long way ahead of us and knowing what happened when you attempted to obtain the emblem of death, we should expect to fight for the emblem of destruction."

Alex chuckled nervously. "Olks are undefeatable."

"Oh, come on Alex, all creatures have a weakness. *I should know that.*"

"They must, but their weaknesses are hidden deeply. I don't know much about Darlids anyway. How am I supposed to fight against creatures I know nothing about?"

"If Courier were here, he would be able to give perfect explanations of their weaknesses. I am better at fighting than knowing." Zorus spoke with understanding.

Alex sighed. "I was an excellent warrior in Achnor, but even Zidal expressed my weakness." he added.

"I would never trust any of that ungrateful Knightmare's words!" he spat. Alex ignored his arrogant thought. The air went silent for a moment, leaves rustling and their footsteps thumping. The area was dark as night, the wind ever so slightly blowing against Alex's broad chest. He felt alone, not a breath following his own.

Without a second's notice, an almost unnoticed blade rested against his chest. His body did not lose movement until he felt the sharp edge of the sword resting against his chest. "Well then, it seems that you still have some sort of skill in battle. Why don't we have a little practice?" Zorus pulled his sword away from Alex's chest and pointed it toward his sheath. "Well, draw your sword…" he commanded. Alex reached behind his head for his sword, yet he did not feel the thick, leather-laced handle resting in the ropes. He returned his gaze to Zorus, confused. "Of course, one always has to be aware. You must be prepared for the worst and most unexplainable things to happen." He handed the glorified sword back to Alex's possession and drew his own sword from his back.

"How… how did you do that?" Alex queried.

"I've got my ways." Zorus smirked before his skin and organs began to melt, deform, and sink into his bones for his own protection. "Come on Alex, I'm serious about this." Alex lifted his sword into the air and aimed it at Zorus. "That's right, ease into it. When you land a blow on me, we'll be done. Go ahead, don't be afraid to hit me."

Alex threw his sword toward Zorus's ribs. His attack was easily blocked with the swift movement of his sword. Zorus returned his attack with a powerful blow, Alex ducking before it clipped his hair. "Agh…" Alex thrusted his weapon forward. The sword clashed mid-attack against Zorus's weapon.

"Good, kid." he encouraged just before dropping his sword at Alex's legs. Alex swung his sword to his side, barely blocking the sword from hitting his fragile body. He then swung his sword toward Zorus's unguarded spine. His strike was powerful and quick. Despite his accurate swing, his sword beat against the air, cutting through with ease, much too well. Alex lowered his sword searching the area with immense confusion. Zorus had disappeared, fallen from his sight.

“Zorus?” Alex asked in fear, confused by his sudden disappearance. “Reveal yourself!” he demanded, afraid of what might come next. He felt an ominous gleam staring at him in the distance. The fearful gaze caused him to feel uncomfortable as if he was a helpless victim. As if his sword was as useless as a blade of grass. He turned toward the figure, facing Zorus once again. He swallowed nervously, his Adam's apple bobbing in his throat.

As he began to back away, knowing he was no match for a being as powerful as he, Zorus followed his every move. After only a few swift steps, his back rubbed against the bark of a tall tree. He was now trapped, unable to flee from Zorus’s grasp. He licked his dry lips, his hand brushing against the rough bark. Sweat ran down his cheeks, anxieties running through his mind. *Would Zorus really kill him?* he asked himself.

Alex held his sword before his face in attempt to protect himself. He watched as the skeleton knight crept toward him, freakishly preying on him. Before another word could fall from his lips, he threw one last attack. He felt his blade strike something other than the strong metal of Zorus’s sword. He opened his eyes, his sword resting on the blade of Zorus’s shoulder. He stared at him unbelieving. “You let me strike you.” he admitted in disappointment.

“But I can’t help but say, you fought wonderfully.” Zorus slid his sword into his leather sheath. Alex copied his movement, sheathing his sword as he stepped away from the tree. Zorus’s skin began to coat his bare bones once again. His clothing expanded as he returned to his original state.

“I would have never expected you to be such an amazing warrior, Zorus. You never seemed to have owned such talent.”

“There is a difference between having a talent, and wanting to use that talent, there is a time and a place to use it. Who do you think trained Courier?” Alex stared into his empty eyes, they made him feel trapped. There was something about them that wasn’t natural.

Night began to blanket their bodies, light fading from the world around them. The dark forest filled with the shadow of night, the light of the moon and stars their only company. Alex felt a familiar pain in his mind as he stared at the leaves, the mind wavering corroding his every thought. "It's getting dark, should we take a break?" he asked, the hope to cure his suffering echoing through his mind.

"Come on, kid, we can travel in the dark. The faster we get the emblem, the faster we can destroy the Broken Souls' chances." Alex followed his sense toward the emblem, attempting to ignore the constant pain. Zorus followed closely, knowing that he would find the emblem of destruction, that he would aid them in completing a long-awaited success.

Zorus lifted his hand into the teal leaves of a tree and plucked two round fruits from a branch as he walked. He handed one to Alex. "You're going to need to eat, we have a long journey ahead and I don't know where we will find food again."

Alex stared at the strange fruit. It was colored orange, green and purple. Many small warts and lumps popped out of its skin. Though he worried, his hunger was too great. Alex took a bite of the fruit. It was crunchy and sweet, a sticky syrup leaking from its core. "What is this?" he asked, continuing to chew.

"This is cryddge fruit, the best fruit in all the land." Alex stayed silent, continuing to eat the sweet fruit, his hunger slowly subsiding.

Alex ducked beneath an oncoming tree branch before he spoke. "I have been wondering, how is Shawon so similar to my world?"

Zorus swallowed and then began to speak. "That is an interesting thought. You asked the wrong Darlid, kid. Courier would have a much more accurate answer, but I'll try my best to explain it." he admitted. "When you entered that portal, you were transported to this dimension. A world sister to Achnor, following the same rules. This world is locked in the universe. It acts as a prison to us, one which we are unable to escape. The only way to escape is if a human willingly opens the portal to set us free."

"Is that why Darlids and Broken Souls need me so much?"

He nodded and took another bite of the sweet fruit. "Athreal initiated attacks on Achnor, beginning a war against Darls and mortals. Humans, fabled grends, sorna, and other beings fought against them until the Shaens could create a sister dimension, our prison. The Shaens finally destroyed each of the demons and imprisoned all of the Darls in Shawon in case we decided to attack once again. If we ever return to

Achnor, we want to finally make peace with your people." he acknowledged. "So anyway, the reason that Shawon is so similar to Achnor, is because of our past. When the Shaens created this dimension, Shawon modeled itself into our very own parallel world, introducing new species of plants, strange substances, and even keeping many attributes from Achnor."

"This world is amazing, why do you Darlids want to leave so badly?"

"The Achnoreans would have been better off only trapping the demons and Broken Souls here. As much as Shawon is beautiful, the Broken Souls are a threat to us." he frowned. "If we could just get back to Achnor, we could all be free from their grasp. They would no longer be a danger to us, and any Darlid that chooses to become one would promptly be banished to Shawon.

"We cannot let the Broken Souls escape before us. Every species would be in danger if they got free. We would be stuck in Shawon, tortured by their wrath. The creatures of Achnor would also suffer their torment if they escaped. Do you see our reasoning?" Alex nodded. "That's not the problem right now though. We must focus on destroying the emblems so Athreal cannot return." Alex stopped in his tracks. Zorus Stopped along with him. "What's wrong, kid?" A chill fell down his spine. "I see, we're being followed. Good call. Now, as long as we don't make any sound, we can *vanish*." Zorus held out his hand. Alex looked at him confused. "Where to kid?"

"The emblem seems to be about eight miles forward, from what I can tell."

"Alright, hold on, kid." Zorus grasped Alex's hand. He held on tightly in great worry as he felt his body fade and break into pieces as Zorus concentrated. The area was silent, nothing disturbed their doing. He watched the trees and grass fade into a dark Abyss. It was much different from the portals he had trekked before, for this was real magic. He was walking through a long empty hallway, a dark light shining into his eyes as he followed Zorus, who was leading him to their destination. Alex watched him as he followed him through the Abyss. Zorus's body seemed to be breaking into pieces of blackness, the dark pieces floating and surrounding him before they returned. He felt his own body drifting out of existence too.

The hallway seemed to warp, shadows crawling in the empty space, yet he could still see fine. It felt unbearably dark and evil, though Zorus seemed unaffected by the feeling. He took a deep breath, breaking his anxiety away from what was in front of him. The feeling drifted away as Zorus stopped in mid-step. He let go of Alex's hand, and they drifted into reality. Tall trees still stood in the area around them, only they were miles away from where they first began.

Zorus was out of breath, and even seemed to be in pain. "Now, where would this emblem be Alex?" Zorus asked in a charming voice.

"It seems close, but it is moving."

"It's moving? How is that possible?" Zorus searched the area of trees and small bushes. "A Broken Soul could not have gotten here before us." an unnatural breeze blew through the trees. The small needle-like leaves brushed against each other.

"It is still moving." Alex claimed. The vibrant leaves of a small bushel shuffled. "What was that?" he stuttered.

"Oh, Death."

"What?!"

The leaves brushed against each other again, a creature leaping out from the branches. It seemed to be a deer throughout its long and slender body, but its neck grew into a hound's head. It was marked with a devilish smile across its fur, torturing the soul. A horn grew upon its head, in the shape and size of a rhino's. It was pure white, covered with golden patterns. A tail of vines covered in the most radiant of flowers grew from its hind. Its underbelly grew many more plants of vibrant colors. "Oh, Death!"

"What is that thing?!" Alex wailed.

"That is the hiccertaden, a legendary beast with indescribable power, and its horn *is* the emblem. We'll die before we take it from him." Zorus clumsily reached toward his back and drew his sword. Alex slowly grasped his weapon, yet a little more confidently than Zorus.

"To retrieve the emblem, we'll have to kill it!"

"Kill it and we will be sentenced to death! It's the last remaining of its kind, and it is well known across this world!" it glanced at them, grinning with pleasure. Despite Zorus's warning, Alex charged after the beast. To his surprise, it growled and bucked in a more powerful way than imagined. Zorus ran after them, his skin beginning to fade from his bones. The hiccertaden dropped its large jaw, which vertically split into two lower jaws coated in small yet sharp teeth.

"Ahhh!" startled by its action, Alex dropped to the ground, his sword held tightly in hand. Zorus bent down and gave out his free hand. Alex graciously took it and stood from his fall, facing his hideous opponent. The hiccertaden immediately swung his head to the left, the tip of his destructive horn cutting through Alex's vulnerable skin. "Ugh!" he placed his hand over his wound in agony, blood staining his skin.

"Don't give up Alex, you're right, we need this emblem more than anything!" Zorus swung his sword at the hiccertaden. The sharp blade nearly missed, only slicing off a bundle of its fur. Blood dripped from its small wound. It roared in pain, swinging its large vine-like tail about the forested area. The vine whipped against trees, bushes, and the soft ground, allowing dents to form. Alex struck forth his weapon, but he missed as the hiccertaden dropped underneath his attack.

"This thing is impossible to strike!" Alex claimed as he and Zorus swung their weapons another five or six times, the hiccertaden jumping, ducking, and deflecting each and every blow. Its tail swung toward Zorus, the large vine wrapping around his weapon. It forcefully stole his sword.

"It has my weapon!" Zorus hollered as he ducked from his own sword. Seeing no other option, Zorus fled. Alex swung his sword against the hiccertaden's stolen weapon. Sweat ran down his cheeks as he followed its movement. "Aim for its chest!" Zorus commanded. Listening to his advice, Alex aimed his attacks at the beast's open chest. The tactics of this beast were unlike any he had seen before, he had never had to fight like this before. After all of the training he had acquired over his lifetime, his skill as commander of the warriors of Gaoly had come to this. He was fighting unlike any other person in his world.

With frustration unmatched, he closed his eyes and struck again. Unexpectedly, he felt something break off of the being. He opened his eyes, noticing its shriveled tail lying across the ground. Zorus ran to the scene and grasped his weapon from the grass, joining the battle once again. The hiccertaden did not scream, rather it grinned, glancing at its blank back. It closed its snake-like eyes and stood completely still. Alex and Zorus stared at it, confused by its action, unable to determine whether they should attack. As they waited, it stretched out as two long and dangerous vines grew from where the other was before.

Finding its battle stance, it began to violently whip its tails through the air. The thick vines flew inches above their heads, barely flying above them. "Ahg!" Avoiding the vines, Zorus jumped off of the ground and aimed his sword toward the hiccertaden's back. Landing on its body, his sword plunged into its spine. Blood began pouring from its back as the sword ran through. It howled in pain but would not easily give up its life. Its tails shot back and began to wrap tightly around Zorus's waist, holding him captive. The force of the grip was so tight that his skin and organs began to form again. The pain immediately became unbearable as his body reformed. The strength was so immense that he was unable to draw in a breath.

Noticing Zorus's pleading expression, Alex faced the beast and held his blade before him as he began to charge. He closed his eyes, and with all his might he struck the beast. The blade slid easily through its chest and stuck into its heart. It whimpered in pain and fell to the ground in agony. Soon its breaths shortened, and its eyes glazed over, the beast now left lifeless.

Its body began to decay, its tails shriveling and loosening. Zorus, close to suffocation, ripped the vines off of his chest and began to breathe heavily. Alex uncomfortably pulled his sword from the being's lifeless corpse and stood. Zorus unmounted the hiccertaden and ripped his sword from its back. Puddles of dark blood stained the sego-colored grass, as well as their clothing, as they caught their breath. Zorus placed his hand on Alex's shoulder and sighed deeply. "Good... fight!" he spoke through heavy breaths. Alex slid his bloody sword into his sheath.

Zorus bent beside the hiccertaden's cold head and took hold of the horn. Lifting its head from the ground, he sliced the horn off the hiccertaden's head with one heavy blow. He held it proudly in the air and smiled as its body lay dead in the grass, ever so slightly melting. He sheathed his stained weapon and stared at Alex. "We have the emblem. Now we must return it to the king for its destruction." Zorus took another breath. "Here, *I* should not be holding this." he held out the large white horn before Alex and waited for him to take it from his grasp.

"Why? Why can't Darlids hold these… these emblems?" Alex asked as he held the horn in his arms. Now cut from the hiccertaden's head, the resemblance of a drinking horn seemed to take form.

"Well, only Darlids and Broken Souls can activate an emblem, if that happens, destruction will end all." he glanced at his uniform, stained with blood. Alex too glanced at his clothing, noticing that his expensive robe was stained with the hiccertaden's blood. Zorus closed his eyes for a moment, pondering. "Well, I can sense that my brother is… safe, we should return to them."

"You and your brother must have a close relationship, I… I never have felt that close to my family."

"Well, I was the only kin he had. We've bonded over the years. Come now, we best be going." the light of the violet sun began to peak between the trees. Zorus held out his hand, which was laced in dirt and blood. Alex took it, ready to get back to the others, to show them what they had accomplished. Taking Zorus's hand, the horn in his other hand, he felt himself begin to fade from reality again.

The silence of the emptiness calmed his jumping mind. They were safe now, and after the emblem was destroyed, there was no possibility for Athreal to rise once again. Everything suddenly felt strange. As they continued their silent trek, Alex's leg began to feel irritated, as if something was attached to it. He halted for a moment, shaking his leg as if something would fall from his clothing. Without warning, he was pulled back into reality by the twisted thing. Zorus, aware of his disappearance, jumped back into reality and began to chase after Alex, the dripping limb dragging him toward an awful fate.

The dark limb pulled Alex to an abrupt stop. Zorus stumbled, grasping his sword, and rising from the ground. His bones were showing, and he was ready to fight anything in his path. The being stepped out of the shadows revealing itself. It smiled. "It's so nice to see you again." it did not let go of Alex's leg but entangled its horns across the entirety of his body. "Zorus, is your brother alright? Because I would love to kill him again."

"Let go of my friend, Nidaret!"

"Isn't this delicious? A careless being wishing for the human's wellbeing. I'd love to help you, but I have a Master to obey." it chuckled. Zorus charged toward the beast, colliding with a wall of horns which forcefully pushed him away from his destination. The entanglement of horns began to wrap around his limbs. It used another of its unused antlers to take a hold of the drinking horn. "I must thank you for killing that hiccertaden for me. You saved me the trouble." he pulled at the horn and ripped it from Alex's weakened hands. Zorus's breath became heavy as he struggled, unable to escape. "I would have killed you for it, but your soul is not worth my time. I only came for the emblem."

Zorus continued to struggle through the Nidaret's grip, determined to return the emblem to his possession. "I won't let it be released!"

"You have already failed then." the beast mocked. "For the reincarnation of Athreal, your soul is free!" he cried as he smashed the horn against the ground. A blinding orange glow arose from the broken pieces of the emblem. It squirmed as it flew, reuniting with the soul of the emblem of death, beginning to recreate Athreal.

S lifted his eyelids, staring into the empty abyss of a room. He stared at his hands, boney and frail. The shackles were still heavy, but in a way that drained his mind rather than in weight. He sighed, staring at his brother, who too was bound with chains. He was reading one of the few books that the Master had left for them to study. It was something that R enjoyed much more than S could imagine. R glanced at S as he flipped the page. “Why does Master do this to us?” he asked, his childish inquiry flowing through his brain.

“So, we will never forget what pain feels like. Master’s mind is ill, he doesn’t know how much evil he’s spreading. Soon there will be nothing left of the world.” His sorrow seeped into his thoughts.

“S, when will we go home?” his small and insecure voice rang through the empty room.

S attempted to keep a smile as he spoke to his younger brother. “When we see the stars. When our heroes bash through the doors, R. When we see their smiling faces as they destroy Master.” His bones shook. “It’s only a matter of time, you’ll see.” he sniffed as he began to lose belief in his own words. He could hear his brother crying, again, softly.

R’s shackles shook in the silence of the room. “What do the stars look like?”

“The stars are the most beautiful light in the world, they light Shawon even when the sun’s out of sight. The stars sparkle in the dark sky, their light traveling further than the moons’.” he sighed, longing to be free of the dark prison, of the home that was so fraudulent to him, the torture that left a mark in his mind. His brother was too young to understand, too young to comprehend the horrors that were happening in front of him.

He watched his brother wrap himself in the thin blanket, warming himself from the cold. He dropped the book onto the ground. As he laid onto the bed, he quietly spoke. “S...?”

“Yes?”

“Until the morrow…” his soft voice rang as he returned to his studies.

Blue River

Dawn had broken through the skyline, the lavender sun rising above the grass. "Zidal..." Courier whispered as he shook her fragile body, rousing her from her tender sleep. "We best be going." Zidal removed her mask for a moment, rubbing her eyes. The fire had ceased to burn, trailbite leaves surrounded the entire camp, piles holding guard to Merchel. The ominous trap of leaves flowed for at least five hundred feet in every direction. There was no escape from Merchel's weakness.

"Huh? Did I sleep the entire night?" Zidal asked sleepily, as she stared at the leaves on the ground.

Courier didn't respond to her query as he turned toward the forest. "Hurry, she'll notice us leaving." Zidal nodded as she began to run behind his pace, rushing across the ground layered in leaves. The shriveled leaves bounced from the ground as their feet clashed against them, falling back to the ground slowly. A large mountain became clearer to their blurry vision as the trees parted from its view.

Zidal began to breathe heavily, her footsteps falling behind, yet with her determination, she did not fall short of step. Courier quickly glanced at her and realizing that his long legs gave him a greater stride, slowed his pace slightly so that she would not be left behind. The trees rushed beside them, their branches swaying in the wind, the leaves blowing across the skyline as they sprinted across the dry ground. The leaves beneath their feet began to dissipate as they had run across the entire length of the trap, realizing that it was finite.

Sweat running down his cheeks and heavy breaths slipping from his mouth, Courier's physical form shifted. The sound of his panting disappeared, yet the air was only silent for a moment. "Noooooo!" they heard a raspy cry following them from the distance. “You will pay *dearly*, Lade will get what he desires!” her voice followed.

“Is she stuck here forever?” Zidal asked dully through her beating breaths, hoping it to be true.

“Her soul will slowly, but surely shatter if she interacts with those leaves, but there is still a chance for another Broken Soul to release her. Now, let us head for the emblem of magic.” Courier paused. “We must reach a safe distance though.” he chuckled.

“Why?” Zidal asked, catching her breath.

“She still has a chance to find a way out. We can't have her catch up.” After running for what seemed like forever, they had traveled an entire mile. Zidal’s chest ached as she took in air, her lungs tired and her heart beating heavily. Courier stood unphased as he allowed his body to take form again. His lungs filling with air, he began to pant. His skin began to form over his bones, his more human-like figure returning. Zidal peeked around the trees, beginning to realize there was no danger near them.

She looked at Courier and took a deep breath in before speaking. “We're close to Blue River. We need that emblem just as much as any other. Especially if Alex and Zorus can’t get their hands on the emblem of destruction.” They began to walk through the maze of trees. “The king sent me on this mission for a reason. I cannot fail.”

“Nor shall I. I know better than any other being in Shawon the consequences that will come if we do not succeed in destroying even one of these emblems.” Courier listened to the beat of their footsteps, waiting for a response. His lips moved before Zidal could speak. “Let’s just hope that nothing goes wrong.”

Her somber voice followed. “There is always something lurking near us. We are always being followed, we are always being stalked, we are never alone. That’s one of the quirks of being a member of the Galaxy Knights. There is always a Broken Soul lurking in the shadows, waiting to kill…” she stopped, realizing that Courier stood much further behind her, standing completely still. “...Us? Courier, we have a mission to complete. There is no time to waste.”

“I sense an ominous presence nearby. A very powerful one at that.”

Zidal backtracked her steps, finding her way to Courier's stance. "Merchel, has she escaped?" she asked fearfully, her violet eyes quivering.

"No, we are surrounded by trailbite leaves, she couldn't come near us.

"Then what is it? We have to get to Blue River." she draped her hand across his broad shoulder, beaconing him to leave.

Zidal turned around and began to leave his presence once again, her hand falling by her side. Despite her movement, Courier waited calmly in his spot. "I feel *Zorus's* presence." Zidal stopped and waited for something, anything to happen.

"They've completed their task already? That was quick." she again walked toward Courier.

Heavy breathing sounded behind them. "On our way, are we?" a low voice spoke. Courier turned toward the voice. Zorus and Alex stood behind them, waiting for a response.

"Zorus, Alex, you've returned." Courier opened his arms and gave Zorus a long-awaited brotherly hug. "It's wonderful to see you again." they let go of each other. Courier studied their blood-covered appearances. "What did you get yourselves into? You're drenched in blood."

"The emblem was attached to the hiccertaden. After a mighty battle, we finally achieved victory. It was quite the bloody mess." Alex indicated.

"Unfortunately, the broken Nidaret stole our reward. Leaving us behind in the forest to escape." Zorus explained. Zidal stared at him. "Luckily, we still have more chances." he gritted.

"But those chances won't last forever." Alex interrupted. "If I can recall correctly, there are only six emblems left, assuming that Zidal and Courier haven't found the emblem of magic yet."

Courier shook his head. "Two of which can only be found by you," he added.

"Though your task is complete, we are still on our way to the emblem of magic, we had a little delay last night. You should head on to the emblem of greed." Zidal noted as she stepped into the small circle of beings they had created.

"I was thinking maybe having more in our troop will allow us to win this battle." Alex noted. He dusted his crusty blood-covered shirt. "Usually, two of us against one Olk ends in our loss, but if they are not expecting four, we could overwhelm them."

"Olks are unusual creatures." Zorus responded.

"Why not have four in our troop? It may slow us down, but we have a better chance of succeeding." Zidal added. Everyone nodded in agreement.

There was a short silence, which Zorus quickly interrupted. "Of course, we should search for it as soon as possible, but I'm starving. Alex and I haven't had anything since those crydge fruits yesterday evening."

Courier reached into his satchel, pulling a slice of thin, roasted meat from its contents. "Here, the Olk provided some sustenance for us last night. I have a little left if that abates your hunger." Zorus took it from his grasp, biting a piece off of the bone. Alex too took a slice and began to eat.

"May we rest for a while?" Alex asked, chewing on the sweet meat. "I can't say I have enough energy either."

Zidal nodded. "The Olk is quite far behind. I suppose I need a break too. Let's stop at that river up ahead." she pointed to a rushing river of juniper. Without hesitation, they followed her to its flow. As they reached the mass of juniper, Zorus leaned against a tree, taking another bite of the meat. Courier stood by his brother, pulling the *Book of Emblems* out of his open satchel and began to read. Zidal sat on the leaf-covered ground, taking in a deep breath, her legs resting against her chest.

Alex walked to the shining river and knelt, splashing the liquid over his face. He began to rub away the dirt and blood stained on his skin. He then cupped his hands and dipped them into the juniper, drinking the juniper from them. Zidal spoke. "So, you killed the last remaining hiccertaden?" she acknowledged uncomfortably.

Taking another bite, Zorus responded. "It was part of our mission, don't put it on my record." he urged.

"Of course not, it will be confined to the Galaxy Knights. We'll tell the public that it died of natural causes." she sighed. "There's no need for you to lose your job, or Courier for that matter."

"Why would Courier lose his job?" Alex asked, standing from the muddy ground. Zorus threw the thin bone onto the ground.

"Because I would be related to the cause of the disaster. If you or a family member has caused a crime, you will not be permitted into the Galaxy Knights. It is for safety." Courier spoke as he turned the page. He studied the page for a moment before speaking. "Look at this." Courier exclaimed in awe.

"What is it?" Alex asked as he stepped closer to Courier.

Courier pointed to a line in the book as he spoke. "*Though the emblems are crucial for the recreation of Athreal, a derx potion is needed to activate his powers. The main and most rare ingredient, an oru, is hidden in the tower of Sel.* " Courier skimmed down the page. *"The tower of Sel is well hidden in the Careless Meadows. Not a soul has found it since its creation."* Courier closed the *Book of Emblems,* returning it to his satchel. "We best find the emblems, but if we cannot destroy even one of them, we might still have a chance."

"We..." Zorus's speech was interrupted, Alex dropping to the ground in pain. He held his head in pain, succumbing to his illness. "Death! Courier, the mind wavering, it's getting worse. We still have so many emblems to collect, and the oru if we fail each time!"

Coughing, Alex spoke. "What... What should I do? The pain is unbearable. It's like having a thousand knives stuck through my head."

Pulling Alex from the ground, Courier spoke. "I… I don't know, but Zorus is right, we have to destroy the emblems and you still have a time limit. We should be advancing. The faster we get these emblems, the better chance we *all* have to get back to Achnor, including Alex as a whole."

Zorus broke down in agony. "Time limit?! Are you saying that we may never be able to accomplish this mission, that we're better off quitting?!"

"Are you forgetting the purpose of this mission? This is so we can get him home! His memories are strong, but without all of the emblems being destroyed, whether by Broken Souls or Darlid hands, he only has a small chance to survive destroying the barrier. If you just trust me on this, we will defeat the Broken Souls and if necessary, wait for another human to open the portal!" Zidal fought back.

"That is true, but Alex may never have a chance to get back to his home through this mission." Courier stated.

"You're treating this human like a toy, like he is just another one of your weapons! Zidal, he has a life too." Zorus looked at him. "Kid, what's your view on this?"

Easing through the long-lasting pain of the mind wavering, he spoke. "I… I don't know, okay." Alex spoke with passion. "It was a mistake; I shouldn't even have found my way here. I should never have left. As much as I want to go home, I can't remember what it's like entirely. It's like I've been in a long-lasting unthinking dream the entire time I've been here. There is just too much weight on my shoulders." he took a deep breath and calmed his voice.

"I see, I have been totally ignorant of your pain and suffering. I should know better. Alex, it's your choice whether you continue to take part in this battle or not." Zidal remarked, fear draining from her voice.

Coughing, he managed to speak. He sighed. "Zidal had a point, I could not only never go home, but also die without the destruction of the emblems." he shyly smiled. "And it seems important to this world that I find the rest of the emblems, saving it and mine from a worse disaster."

Courier stared at him. "You know well that doing this, you may never be able to go home?" wiping a tear from his eye, he nodded. "I will gladly support you in your decision, I may even begin to call you my brother." he reassured. Alex stood from the ground, the pain of the mind wavering subsiding. "No one knows what you have been through, but everyone has their own pains to remember. Zorus and I, too, have been through more than we thought we could ever handle."

"Courier, I ask you to refrain from acknowledging our past." Zorus commanded bitterly.

"Sorry Zorus, but we shouldn't hide from our past. It did happen, and I can't ignore that."

Zorus looked toward Zidal and spoke. "Should we move onward?"

"Forward it is. We have a long way to go and be ready for an Olk to meet us there. She will be angry." Zidal began to walk through the wall of trees, the others following behind her shallow steps. The light breeze draped across their sweating bodies.

Courier took a deep breath. "Can't you take us to the volcano Zorus? You know that it would give us a great advantage." Courier swiftly acknowledged.

"You know well enough that even transporting once on my own drains my energy. I fear that I am at the brink of my usage at this moment." he glared at him knowingly, panting.

"Indeed, my apologies, I forgot to search your being first."

"Not everyone can do what we can, brother." he reminded him, smirking. He nodded in exchange. The lavender sun beat against their brawny muscles. Their weapons clanked against their backs as they walked through the forest. "How close are we to the Blue River Volcano anyway?" Zorus asked, almost in an anxious way.

"We shouldn't be too far; I can smell the ashes from here." Zidal stated.

"Yeah, the sulfur is bleeding through the air." Courier agreed. "I hope that it won't take us too long, it can be damaging to your insides." he added, pointing at Alex.

"Why me specifically?" Alex asked.

"If you couldn't tell already, Courier and I can adapt to our surroundings in order to keep ourselves alive. We are the last living scelo recs. We have to be able to take care of ourselves." Alex nodded, remembering their abilities.

"Our bodies have adapted to the dangers of this cruel and precarious world." Courier finished.

"And I am an ash rec, I can take a little heat and smoke." Zidal mentioned.

"How am I supposed to survive in the volcano then? Wouldn't I die in the first moments of entering?"

"Um, I haven't thought of that." Courier stated.

"Well, you better think quickly then." Zidal let her arm in front of the others. Her breath was anxious, her heart beating to the wind's song. They all stopped, waiting for her command. She pointed in the short distance, a mountain waiting for them. "There it is, Blue River Volcano." the blazing heat began to rush against their bodies. Before they could blink, Zorus and Courier fixed their form into a much more protected one.

"Courier, do you know of anything that could help him breathe, survive in the volcano for the amount of time it will take to retrieve it?" Zidal asked as she stepped in front of them.

Courier sighed deeply. "There is something for everything in this world. Unfortunately, I do not have a quarry rock on me, and they are far too difficult to find. If you couldn't remember, we are on a strict schedule, as long as we are quick enough, he will be able to survive without it."

"It's okay, I will be able to last." Alex assured.

Zorus sighed. "Fine, let's go, the faster we get the emblem, the faster we can destroy it without Broken Souls getting in our way." he said in a bothered tone. "What exactly are we looking for anyway?"

Alex closed his eyes for a moment, feeling the magic of the world surrounding him. He looked into the distance of a bright, burning void, seeing the emblem take form. He opened his eyes and looked at them, almost in fear. "The emblem, it's a book, which is eternally burning with a sweltering blaze."

"So, what, Courier or Zorus can handle it, right?" Zidal asked as she walked through the tall trees, hiding the sun's glorious light.

Zorus shook his head. "We can't stay in this form forever, the magic ceases to work when we are physically damaged. I fear that the flame would burn our bones, and we would return to our normal state, leading ourselves toward Death's grasp."

Courier, recalling the facts, spoke. "There are only three recs of Darlids that can wield fire without consequences. Charmer recs, blazer recs, and damenor recs. *That's* why Merchel was sent on this mission, they knew it would cost a blaze."

"Well, there's no point in not trying." Zidal added, pointing at the volcano. "Plus, we are this far, why quit now?"

"We should really get going, a Broken Soul could still beat us to it." Alex reminded them.

Zidal nodded. "Onward it is." she commanded as she began to walk toward the heated mountain, the other's tracking her footsteps.

S awoke to the dreadful creak of the door. Light cast in creating shadows, darkness resting in his soul. The Tall Being walked toward him ominously, a knife in hand. S shivered, as he stared at the cuts left on his mortal body. He shut his eyelids and listened to the sound. He felt it, the strike of the knife rattling against the chains. He peeked at the chains laying on the floor, whilst his arm held the shackle and nothing else. "*Oh S, your insignificant mind just can't comprehend.*"

S shook his head as the Tall Being stepped to his right side and forcefully struck the chains off of the shackle. "What are you doing?" he asked as he stared at the being's four, elastically dripping arms. His green eye rested on his figure as he grabbed his hand and lifted him from the ground.

"S, your weapon training begins today, as you are of age. Your brother will follow in your footsteps as he grows older. Follow me." S shivered, holding the Tall Being's oozing arm as he walked through the empty hallways, distant screams playing through the air. *"As for your magic, your gifted power, your brother and you will train together, when the magic takes heed in your bodies."* S took in a deep, sorrowful, breath as he thought of his brother, sleeping on the uncomfortable bedding of the mattress, whimpering for him to comfort him. *"In here."*

The Tall Being turned to the left and opened a large metal door, similar to the one that he was kept behind for his entire life. He walked inside behind his Master. It was much lighter in the room than the one he was kept in, torches emitting a bright lilac light through the cold walls. The only thing that broke the room from emptiness was a large weapon rack, filled with weapons of many types.

The Tall Being glanced at S. "*Well, choose your weapon...*" S stepped closer to the wooden weapon rack, and studied the various weapons which lay inside. His small hand was drawn to the handle of a simple sword. The long blade shined a silver light as he drew the sword from its place in the rack and stared at his reflection in the blade. The grip was coarse and dark. The crossguard bent upward at each end, lined with silver. The pommel was a silver sphere, a dark crystal fused in the center. *"A sword? So few know the ways of swordsmanship like I do. This will bring your soul ultimate power. Hold it uprightly."* S held the weight of the sword in his fragile grip, listening to the powerful instruction that the Tall Being spoke. *"Good..."*

"Master, why must I learn to wield a weapon? Won't that only cause harm to the innocent, to Darlids like me?"

His ominous voice rang after his speech. *"You will soon not be like them S, soon you will understand. Soon..."*

Heart Broken

They stood at the foot of the mountain; the heat of the content lava encased in their hearts. It was a miracle that the Blue River volcano hadn't erupted in hundreds of years, that not one single leaf had caught fire. The volcano was highly stable and could even be called home for some Darls. Yet nothing dared to enter, for their lives cost more than an exploration through its catacombs.

Zidal let out a strong breath as she stared into the opening of a cave which led to the emblem. Darkness emitted from the hole, darker than the scarce light which seeped into the forest. Above the opening, various symbols were written. Zidal looked over her shoulder. "These symbols are from the Darlids of the past. Courier, can you decipher them?" she asked in a remorseful voice.

"Indeed, these symbols are quite ancient." he remarked, walking toward the tunnel entrance. He stared at the strange carvings in the wall and studied the carvings carefully. Recalling the meaning of each, he spoke slowly. "You who enter the depths of the beast, be wary, for it allows its lava to flow relentlessly through its endless tunnels. Stay clear of its fury." he turned to the others, retelling the story written in the walls. "It seems as if some paths inside the volcano will be filled with lava."

Zidal turned her fragile head and gazed at the others. "We only have one chance to collect the emblem. We must search for that book." Though defiant, she sounded much too somber in her words. She began to walk toward the opening. "Alex, you know the whereabouts of this emblem. Please, lead the way." Alex nervously nodded as he stepped in front of her.

As the four of them began to walk into the shadowed tunnel, a roaring cry followed their trail. With a shift of movement, Courier and Zorus's skin cracked and decayed, hiding beneath their structured bones as they entered the cavern. Alex shivered, knowing that something did not feel right, his anxious breaths filling the empty hallway. He felt uncontrollably warm and only continued with the desperation to become a hero.

The walls were dry and brown, like a desert rock waiting to crumble. The ends of the hallways were dark- Alex did not have a sense of where they were. He could not see whcre he came from, nor could he find where he was going. He continued to pull the others down the depths of the never-ending tunnel, continuing to skip the various paths beside it, trusting his instincts to find the emblem. He began to feel as if they were drifting further from the emblem rather than closer, yet he did not interfere with the directions his mind gave him. His mind continuously pulled him toward the emblem's ominous power.

Alex's footsteps echoed along the others, his leather boots paddling against the dirt. He shuddered as another terrifying growl echoed through the cavern. He glanced at the others, who seemed unphased by the sound and continued to walk forward. He watched them, Zidal the furthest behind, Courier and Zorus standing side by side, whispering things he could not hear or understand. Their thin skeletons bounced and rattled as they stepped through the unknown. He attempted to remain calm as the others did not seem affected by the sound.

Alex finally found a left turn that caught his attention. He stopped for a moment, admiring the lilac crystals that hung from the opening. The crystals shined a bright light, illuminating the once darkened tunnels. "She's a beauty, is she not?" Zidal asked in an almost unidentified voice. She was becoming more troubled as time flew by.

Almost startled by her shadowed voice, Alex responded to her call. "Yeah... this way." the volcano rumbled, cutting his shallow voice off. He began to walk down the crystal hallway, his eyes distracted by the sight of the gems. His feet continued to move through the empty depths of the tunnel.

The silence only lasted for a moment, as Courier mumbled. "*You who enter the depths of the beast...*" he repeated. Concerned, Alex turned his head, staring at Courier. "I'm beginning to think that there's more to this volcano than lava."

"Like what?" Zorus asked. "What more could there be?"

"A beast, Zorus, a beast. There's something here, I know it." He shivered at the thought as another roar burst through the cavern. "It's interesting, Blue River has never erupted. That only gets me thinking. There must be a reason that this volcano is a *beast*." Courier followed Alex's right turn through another tunnel filled with light blue crystals.

"Core, it's probably just referring to the rumble of the volcano." Zorus assured.

"No, Blue River has *never* erupted. The rumble mustn't be the volcano... there's something wrong." his voice echoed as they turned down another hallway, this time, orange crystals hanging from the delicate walls. Each turn the crystals grew larger, making it much harder to squeeze through the elaborate tunnels. Anxiety began to fill the halls as roars blasted through the catacombs. "There must be…" Alex lifted his hand, covered in beads of sweat, stopping Courier's speech. He attempted to back away, yet they stood still, stuck to the rocky wall.

Alex stared at the end of the tunnel. Three glorious golden eyes beaming at them. There it waited, its glowing snake-like body resting at the end of the hallway. Its pink tongue flickered, sensing their presence. Its body tumbled against itself, molded of thick, molten lava. It tilted its head, its fraudulent blue scales slipping into its body. "Oh, Death… that is *not* lava." Zorus stated fearfully. The serpent lowered its jaw and sang a mighty roar. "Alex... run!"

Alex glanced to his left; an opening stood only a few inches away. He began to run, the others chasing after. They quickly turned down the hallway, dimly lit with crystals, and sprinted with heavy breaths. They could feel the tunnels shake as the serpent slithered behind them, so closely that it could instantly swallow each of them whole.

Anxiety filled the hallways as the beast inched closer. Tears began to fly from Zidal's eyes as she attempted to stay near the others. Alex continued to follow his thoughts, which would lead them to the emblem of magic. Right turn. Straight. Another right turn, then a left. The hallways passed by as crystals changed colors, the serpent roaring through the cavern. "It would be helpful… if you… could find a hiding place!" Courier yelled in a cold pant.

"Does it look like I'm not?!" Alex returned. He turned his head for a moment, staring at the beast which was clenching its jaw. He saw it in its eyes, its only purpose was to destroy any being that entered the catacombs, its only instinct, to kill. Its screams trembled through their ears. Alex's mind felt faint, the heat blanketing him, his energy dissipating, yet he still continued his step. Sweat ran through Alex's light hair, glimmering on his smooth forehead. He wiped it off of his head as he turned left again.

He slowed to a stop, the others falling behind him. They stood hopeless in a large cylindrical room. There were many openings surrounding them, yet many of the tunnels were blocked by the body of the colossal serpent, whilst mountains of rocks laid in front of the others. "It's circling in on us. This would be quite a clever move if we weren't the ones in its center." Courier stammered.

"Now what?!" Zorus screamed. Alex drew his sword, followed by Zorus and Courier. Zidal pulled her glaived scythe from her sling and faced the tunnel which they had exited moments before. She waited for something to happen, anything, for the beast to swerve into the cavern. Watching the others, she cluelessly followed Alex's plan.

They each ran toward a separate tunnel, throwing their weapons at the impassable skin of the beast. They ripped through its liquid-like skin, creating enormous scars which mended themselves immediately. Their attempts did nothing. Their weapons did nothing but become sweltering arms. The beast did not scream, nor did it seem phased, but their attacks did not go unnoticed. They turned to face the monstrous beast. "Have we failed?" Alex asked. "Was this all for our own undoings?"

"No!" Zidal raged. "We mustn't lose! We must destroy this beast!" she screamed in an unmatched determination. "*I* must destroy this beast." she regarded, in a much softer tone. The serpent drove its large head through the last open tunnel. Its molten jaw creaked open as it screeched, its venomous fangs waiting to clutch its next victim. Its hunger would never subside. It hissed. Swallowing her fear, Zidal led her troop toward the head of the serpent. She lifted her scythe in the air and plummeted it into the serpent's lower jaw. Her blade broke through its skin and drove into the dirt beneath. She clamped its jaw to the soft ground and nodded at her allies.

Courier sneered, plunging his sword's point into its right eye. A sweltering liquid poured from its golden iris as it roared. Venomous saliva shot from its mouth, drenching Courier's uniform in a disgusting liquid. Zorus chased after the beast, ramming his sword into its leftmost eye. It screamed in pain as he ripped the point out of its socket, the same golden liquid spilling from its socket. Alex lifted his illustrious sword in the air, aiming for its center eye. He held his breath as it descended into the gooey mass.

The beast, now blind, roared, knowing that it could still be successful in its task. Ripping her scythe from the beast, Zidal smirked. She looked at the others and spoke. "Stay back, I don't need you guys risking your lives." Confused, her warriors stepped away from the beast and watched as Zidal rushed toward the beast, ripping into the rocky scales on its head. It screamed, inching forward. She let out a deep breath, and ran breathlessly into the beast, her figure disappearing as its mouth snapped shut.

Zorus looked to the ground in disgust. He choked. "Oh, Death..." he managed to leak from his jaws. Courier placed his free hand on his boney chest. Alex looked at the scelos, concerned. He lifted his sword before his face and waited. The serpent opened its mouth once again, this time roaring, screeching, in pain. They watched in disgust, yet with delight, as a glaive ripped through the beat's skin. Zidal's scythe sliced through its neck, severing its head from its spine.

The serpent fell, lifeless, its body darkening and seeping into the crusty ground. Zidal stepped from its inside, caked in its decay, and threw her scythe into its rightful place joyously. The others stared at her in complete shock as they slid their swords into their sheaths. Alex opened his mouth "That was…"

"Complete idiocy." Zidal finished. Alex raised an eyebrow. "Come on, take us to this emblem." The pathways were clear, aside from the dark, melted body of the beast, a feeling of peace and security passing over the scene. Alex looked through the hallway parallel to them, a strong feeling of magic pulsing through. He pointed into the darkness and disappeared as he walked into it.

Dirt scattered beneath his feet as they walked toward the tunnel. A feeling of excitement and hope filled the emptiness. Finally, light. Alex stepped into the area, the scelos and the ash recs followed him into the blazing room. Though the serpent was dead, boiling lava- emitting a bright blue light- surrounded a dark quartzite pillar where a burning book laid. Stones, which were large enough to step on, surrounded the pillar- each pillar slightly further from the one before- creating an imagined staircase.

Their sight peeled away from the glorious relief of the emblem, stretching across the vat of lava, where two beings stood on the opposing side of the room- emerging from a nearby tunnel. Their viscous skin peeled away from their bodies and leaked into the lava. It was obvious that they were Broken Souls. "The charmer?" Courier questioned, studying the figures. "And who is leading her?"

"Kyron…" Zidal whispered in a voice barely loud enough for the others to hear.

"A charmer rec and a damenor rec, of course *he* sent them." Courier stammered.

It wasn't but a moment before the Olks noticed them. "Zidal, it's a pleasure to see you again, but I believe that you're too late. The soul of the emblem will be set free. Join me Zidal or choose to suffer your desperate loss." Zidal didn't respond. Her mouth sealed shut as her voice was captured inside a broken heart. The heartache was too painful to bear. A silent tear dropped behind her mask, her eyes glossy and sorrowful. "Don't shed a tear, I'm still here, I still care." his soothing voice broke through her skin. She stared at his slender, melting body, his glorious, melting wings, missing something long gone.

"She's not reacting." the charmer cackled as her snake slithered upon her shoulder. "You may have the *advantage*, Kyron." Zidal's mind rolled at the sound of his name. It caused her heart to swell, knowing that she cared so deeply for the Darlid which once owned that name. The charmer coughed, her raspy voice cawing. "We may gain a new soul along with this emblem."

Kyron glanced at the emblem but resisted his calling. He stepped forward, his charming footsteps echoing as he walked around the rim of the chamber. The charmer followed him closely. "Zidal, I would steal a broken heart to have you back. You know I can't live without the taste of your *sweet blood.* You refused once, but I see that your heart is full of fury." His thick tongue caressed his lips.

"With both of them here, we don't stand a chance." Alex remarked, holding his sword in the air.

"But we still have a duty to fight for it." Zorus acknowledged. They nodded, all drawing their weapons once again, except for Zidal. She, instead fell to the ground, her hands covering her tear-filled eyes, overwhelmed with sorrow. "Zidal, we don't have time for this!" the sound of his words stung her open wound.

"Ah, but she does, we won't attack, not yet I *promise*." the charmer sang.

"Wait here." Kyron demanded. The Olks stood far from her, but just within her reach. Tears streamed from Zidal's eyes as she looked at them, she had no control over her thoughts. "All you need is to release your fury, allow anger to settle in your mind. Kill if you must, then your soul can attach, and we can be together again."

The final words echoed inside her mind, it was her greatest desire, one that she could not resist. Zidal swallowed, and glanced at Alex, fear in her eyes. "Zidal, don't listen to them, please." Courier spoke softly.

Zidal ignored his speech as she stood and stepped toward Alex, who began to back away, his sword held before him. Kyron leered as he watched her hunt. There was no hope for Alex, Zidal was much faster and stronger than he. More experienced. More determined…

She reached toward him, tearing his arm away from his chest, violently grasping his neck and ramming him against the nearest wall. His sword clattered against the ground. Zorus ran toward Zidal in fear but was held back from them by an unidentifiable force, one which could not be explained. As if there was an invisible wall standing between him and the others. "Zidal, let him go!" he yelled, in an anger stronger for Alex's life than for his own. "The damenor is getting in your head!" Zorus drew his sword and beat against the invisible force.

"Zidal, if you have any sense of what is good in this world, let him free! We will get through this!" Courier yelled.

Alex struggled against her grip but was too shocked to defend himself. He could feel his breath leaking from his lungs. "Destruction is the only way to happiness; death is the only way to everlasting life." She listened to Kyron's soft, craving voice. "You know that I can't be with you again, not like this." His voice tortured her, it was filled with passion, and pressure, an angry calmness flowing through her ears.

"Let him go!" Finally, with a strong enough force, Zorus broke through the invisible barrier, powerfully gliding through the air and slicing through her arm in the process. Her violet eyes sheeted with a layer of tears, as she let go of Alex. Alex began to breathe heavily, fear stricken in his heart. Zidal held her arm in agony as teal blood dripped from her wound.

The pain of the past unbearable, the need to kill, she raised her tired voice. "Kill me now!" she screamed. "I am of no use to this world!" scorching tears flowed down her cheeks as she forcefully drew her scythe. "I will only fail!" Zorus rushed to her side, pulling the scythe away from her grasp, though she continued to force the blade toward her stomach. Kyron smirked, knowing well of his intentions. His dark eyes leaked onto his apparel. Zidal pulled the scythe toward her vulnerable stomach, but Zorus would not let her win.

"Courier?!" Zorus yelled.

"She has immense feelings of depression, worthlessness, and incompetence. So much so that if she kills herself, she will become a Broken Soul!" Courier blurted. "I see what is happening. The damenor is attempting to gain her advantage, and he's winning!"

Courier ran to his brother's side, breaking the scythe from her grasp. "Kill me!" she screamed once again. "I cannot win!"

"Zorus, if you would, take her somewhere safe. Alex and I will retrieve the emblem!"

"Courier, you know I…"

"Take her, she needs help desperately, and you are the only one who has that ability!" he enraged.

Zorus's mind quickly agreed. "Yes brother, then go to the emblem of living, and when Zidal has healed, we will travel to the emblem of greed, she has the map." Courier nodded in agreement. "'Till the morrow brother." Zorus placed his sword in his sheath, grabbed Zidal's scythe and lifted her- though she kicked and screamed- disappearing from sight in an instant.

Kyron spoke in a vat of fury. "You blazing devils! You can't imagine what you've done! You might have saved her *now*, but soon she'll see the truth. You won't get your hands on the emblem!" he raged. His voice cackled through the empty space. "Merchel, retrieve the book. I'll take care of the scelo, he's an old friend of mine." he commanded.

"After her Alex, I'll take care of the damenor!" Alex nodded, running toward the pool of lava. He jumped onto a stone, wobbling, careful not to fall into the molten liquid. He watched as the three-armed Olk climbed the stairs easily, reaching toward the book. Determined, he rushed up the rocks, following her every move.

For a moment, he glanced at Courier. His sword clashed against the scythes of the damenor. Once he let go of the push, he ducked, allowing the scythes to scrape past his skull. He then threw his sword at its tapered wing, ripping through its dripping skin. Kyron screamed in agony, shoving him to the ground.

He quickly removed his gaze from the battle below, jumping to the next stone. Two steps left, and he would retrieve the burning book, no matter how much pain he endured. One step, Merchel was close on the opposite set of stairs. He reached the top pillar facing his worst nightmare. A disgusting three armed being, a beak as nightmarish as the night. She cackled. "Too late boy…"

Alex swung his sword toward her. She swerved, her foot nearly slipping from the crumbling platform. She stared at him, annoyed, yet she did not fight back. Merchel pointed at him. "Tellibous, do your worst." The snake trailed off of her slimy body and wrapped around Alex's limbs, binding them to his body. He was unable to move, and if he struggled the bind only tightened. He could only watch, helplessly watch.

He looked at Courier once again, who was held against the ground. Kyron held his weight on his ribcage, a scythe balanced on his neck, as he stared into his eye sockets. "I would kill you, but it's not the task at hand. And Master would be disappointed if he didn't have the chance." he applied pressure to his chest, Courier's form forcefully shifting. He began to breathe heavily as they looked at the platform. "Merchel, you must do the honor."

"Alex!" Courier screamed. "Set yourself free, the Broken Souls mustn't win!" Though he struggled, the snake continued to squeeze tighter.

Merchel glanced at him, and then the blazing book. She reached toward the emblem and took the fiery book from the pillar. She lifted it into the air. "No!" Alex yelled, struggling through the feathers of the constrictor.

Merchel raised her crooked voice for all to hear. "For the recreation of Athreal, your soul is free!" She took her two free hands and began to rip the books into pieces and pages of all sizes. A vibrant white light climbed through the smokey air, returning to the other various pieces.

"Ahahahahaha!" Kyron laughed as he disappeared. Courier pushed himself from the ground. Merchel cawed, her snake loosening its grip and returning to her. She gracefully walked down the pillar of stairs, vanishing from their sight.

Alex, sweat coating his forehead, carefully climbed down the stairs, reaching Courier. "I'm sorry, I couldn't get it in time. She was…"

Courier placed his boney hand on his shoulder. "It's okay Alex, we still have our chance with the emblem of living, greed, strength, and especially the emblems of love and knowledge. We must be prepared." Alex slid his sword into his sheath. Courier, too, sheathed his weapon, letting out his hand. Alex took his hand as they walked toward the entrance of the tunnel.

The sound of clanking metal echoed through the room as S threw his sword against one similar. His attack was weak and simple, but it was nonetheless an upgrade from the last three trainings. "*Good S, fix your form.*"

S spread his legs out and held his sword uprightly as the Tall Being slowly walked around him, holding his weapon. Though he was only training, his Master was careless, and would not act bitterly of S's injuries. "*Strike again!*" The master screamed.

Fast to his command, S threw his sword at the tall figure who blocked it with his sword. He quickly dodged another attack as his master carelessly threw one toward him.

Balls of sweat fell from his ragged hair as he followed the toughening commands of his Master. His breath became heavy as he struck the sword again, the calls of his Master filling his mind with anxious blows as sharp as his sword. He could only think of his improvement as the Tall Being stared at him with his deceiving eye, a glare that no other soul could attempt to show, a corrupt smile that no other face could form. A looming shadow of pressure lay overhead as he followed his Master's words.

S listened to the soft movement of his feet. He watched closely as his Master threw an attack toward his legs. He dropped his sword to the ground, blocking the blade's wrath. Unable to process his Master's next move, the sword's blade cut into his arm. Blood spilled from his wound as he fell to the ground in pain. He dropped his sword, holding his hand against the bloodied wound.

"You have got to be aware. You never know when something like that will happen. Now get up and strike me!" He followed the order, knowing that training would only end when he struck him. Reaching for his sword, he stood. Though in pain, he ignored his wound- which only added to the many others he owned. A mighty clang followed his weakening attack. S jumped from the stiff floor as the Tall Being threw his untangling arm toward him. His limb ran through the air as S landed on the stone floor. "*Good, I see that you are able to avoid unsuspected attacks."*

Without command, S swung his sword. The Tall Being dropped his sword, catching the attack before it could harm him. S's hands, covered in blood, trembled as he pulled his sword away from the Tall Being. He knew that he was too young, too weak to defeat a monster such as he, but he had to strike his body. His determination to rest, to see his brother again rested in his mind as he raised his sword toward his Master. The Tall Being raised his arm, the sword impaling his waving flesh.

S dropped to the ground, relieved as his sword fell from the Tall Being's soft flesh. His anxious breaths shrank as the Tall Being took his sword, returning it to the weapon rack along with his own. He let out his arm, S taking the sticky stub to stand himself upright. He heard the door creak before he felt the soft light land on his skin. He took in a slow breath before following his Master to the cells.

"*Well done S, soon you will have skill unrecognizable to the eyes of any Darlid. You will be able to fight against the mighty, even defeat them if you choose."*

The light of the hallway disappeared as the Tall Being led him into his cell. S sat against the wall and waited for his Master to link the chains to his shackles. *"You are ready."* Those words stuck in his mind, lingering as the echoed slam of the door followed.

Memories

Zidal's eyes opened, aside from the feathery cushion underneath her soft skin, and a small desk beside her, the room was empty, dark, and eerie. She felt as if she ceased to exist, yet she knew that she was not dead. She knew that her wish did not come true. Nothing but a shock of fear entered her heart. She was alone, not a single soul to set her free. Not a single sound to calm her heart.

Chains, she noticed the shackles wrapped around her wrists and ankles, begging her to hold to her place. She couldn't move, her body bound to the soft surface. She opened her mouth to speak, but was caught by her own tongue, unable to create any sounds except for her own breath. Footsteps, she listened to the pounding footsteps that neared her figure. She began to breathe heavily as the sound dissipated, and the handle on the door began to shake.

The rattle of the handle shook through her ears, the unfamiliar sound echoing in the empty space. The door swiftly opened, a dark figure standing in the shadows. She stared at its ominous figure, its body fading, warping in the shadows. Its footsteps continued as it stepped closer to her. A calm, yet deep voice flowed through her ears, echoing through the blank space. "You've awakened." The blur in Zidal's eyes began to fade as she stared at his shadowed figure. "Those elixirs should be wearing off soon. It may feel strange to speak." She squinted her eyes and took a deep breath. "Go ahead, don't be afraid." his voice resonated in her mind, though she was unable to recognize it.

Zidal trusted his unfamiliar words and opened her mouth again. To her surprise, words flowed through her throat easier than she would ever expect. "What happened?" she asked, attempting to sit up straight. Her body was held still by the heft of the chains. "I can't remember where I am, or why I am here."

His mouth opened into an empty abyss. "There are some things that are better left forgotten. There are some things that should not be told. There are some things that would *kill* you if you knew Zidal."

The figure knew who she was, yet she couldn't recognize his voice. She squinted, unable to recognize his figure- dark and shadowed. "Who are you?" her shallow voice rang. She watched as his lips formed a thin smile, breaking through her fragile soul. "Answer me." her voice droned through the empty space. His lips stayed still, his shadowed figure waiting for her to beg again.

His voice did not follow her command, yet it strayed to another thought. "Coldness flows through the heart, emptiness through the soul. Not one Darlid has found a weakness to faith, not one to the untold..."

"Answer me!" she wailed.

"To which you know may not be fact, to which you understand may not be the truth..."

"Answer me!!" her voice trailed into the emptiness.

"As your mind creates lies, your eyes create truth. Watch and listen, see and find, hear and understand." the shape of a smirk draped across his shadowed face. "You have hidden from your demons for far too long, now you must control them."

Zidal looked at his broad skull, his words made no sense to her fragile mind. "Who are you?" she asked again, more calmly, curious to his voice.

He stepped closer to her. She heard his voice before she could recognize his face. "You already know who I am." She stared at his lean figure, his bones sticking out of his skin. His empty eyes stared into her soul, asking her for sweet relief. His light blonde hair flickered through the meager amount of light that shone. His complexion rang through the void, filling her with calmness.

"Zorus?" He nodded at her query.

"Good, you still have control over your memories." his voice sounded mysterious, as if he was hiding something from her. Something that she was so ignorant of. She looked to the desk by the bedside, where Zorus retrieved a small bottle. He poked the cork and ripped it out of the glass. "Lift your right arm... please." Zidal followed his command, questioning his intentions. He held her arm and poured the liquid over her wound, in which a blade had sliced through.

She whimpered as the green liquid sizzled on her blood and sealed the hole in her skin. "What's happening?" she asked again, staring at his ominous figure. "Why am I held in shackles?"

Zorus placed her arm onto the soft surface and returned the cork to the open bottle. After he placed the vial onto the desk, he reached into his pocket, pulling a strange key from its contents. "I brought you here, somewhere where you are safe from your own hands." He lifted her soft hand from the bed and began to unlock the shackles. They fell off of her wrists, one by the other. She rubbed her wrists with her smooth fingers. He continued unlocking the chains at her feet. They fell, and Zorus placed the key in his pocket.

"Are you reminding me that I tried to… to kill myself?" To this, he did not answer. She felt sickened at the thought of her own impurity, the wish to destroy her vessel and join the Broken Souls. He let out his boney hand and lifted her from the cushion. She stood, yet he did not let go. "Why are you acting so strange?"

Zidal watched as his playful smile bent over his lips. He chuckled. "You should realize quickly. I was only trying to protect you… from yourself."

"I understand. My life was in serious danger." Zorus bent down and conjured her weapon. He lifted her scythe from the ground and handed it to her. She did not question where he had placed it but slid it into her ropes. He led her toward the doorway, the only way light could enter the room. "Where are we going?"

"To the emblem of greed Zidal. My vitality is weakening though, we must *exit* here." He stepped through the doorway, never-ending light filling their eyes. He let go of her hand, the world around her fading into a divergent one. It was frozen, snow collapsing underneath their feet. It was barren and rocky. They could see for miles under the dim light of the sun. She stared at Zorus, who was unphased by the cold, his skin hiding beneath his skeletal disguise. His bones shook to the beat of the wind. He seemed weak, almost in pain, though he acted perfectly. Zidal wrapped her arms around her shoulders, warming her dark body. "You have the map; you know the way to the emblem of greed." Zorus remarked calmly.

Memories flowed into her mind, things she felt like she had forgotten years ago followed her thoughts. "Did we succeed? Did we earn the emblem of magic?" she asked as she reached her freezing hand into her fuzzy pocket. She found the thin edges of the map and pulled it out of her pocket.

"That's for us to find out. We left before the battle even began. Only Courier and Alex know that answer." questioning his words, she unfolded the map, and scanned its surface.

"Where are Alex and Courier now?" Zidal asked, unable to remove her gaze from his hardened jaw.

He spoke broadly, though partially upset. "As we are finding the emblem of greed, they are following the pathway to the emblem of life. Though I worry for him, we must find the emblem." he sighed and glanced back at Zidal. "Well, where are we headed?" Zorus asked.

Zidal stared at the worn map. The golden glow of the drawing emitted from an empty white space. "The emblem of greed is located in the caves of Noul. Seeing that we are in the middle of a tundra, it may not be a bad guess that the caves are nearby." She looked around her, almost fearfully, as she folded the map into her pocket.

"Good, then my prediction was accurate."

"Prediction? Zorus, what's going on?"

Zorus sighed, staring into the distance. "There are some things about me that I would rather keep to myself. Though my brother may be idiotically recognizing his abilities, you should not know what power our souls hold." He left broken footprints in the snow as his feet left the surface.

Zidal shook her head and rushed toward him, placing her hand on his shoulder. He stopped at the tug of his fabricated uniform, waiting for her spoken response. She swallowed her fear and spoke. "Of all the places the king has sent me, not once has he wished for me to walk these plains, not once to understand its mysteries. I know that there are Broken Souls here that are as powerful as Olks. I know that those beings crave for every soul to taste death."

"You should be prepared, Zidal, you are the *Knightmare*. He sent you on this mission. Were you not the one to bring me along so forcefully? Danger is the only part of this mission we *can* predict." He began to walk through the open plain of snow.

"Zorus, you don't understand. We will die here!" Zidal screamed. "You can't even defeat the demons of your past!" Zidal covered her mouth, realizing that she had spoken what was forbidden.

Zorus stopped at the sound of her voice. He did not turn to look at her. "What did you say?" His coarse voice rang through the empty air. "Am I not powerful? Did you not once say that I exceed your own strength?"

"Zorus... I…" Zidal watched his left hand as it touched the handle of his sword, and gently pulled it from the leather sheath. She knew that he had the advantage. His resting anger for her, finally released. He once saved her pathetic soul from her own harm but would not waste a second to kill her himself. Zidal had always known of the hatred he pointed toward her, yet he wouldn't dare show it in front of his innocent brother. "What are you doing?" she asked, her voice full of fear.

Zorus turned toward her. "I bet Courier has told you not to mess with me." she recoiled at his words, wondering how much he knew. He let silence ring through the air. "But you have broken through the thoughts of a demonic soul, and I wouldn't waste a second taking a breath. You are the Knightmare, you should be prepared for anything. I won't be hesitant to kill you before an Olk can. You can fight against me, or you can wait here and die." his intimidating voice rang through her head as she reached for her glaived scythe.

"I'll let you know now that my hands won't tremble when I watch your blood trickle into the snow." He said freakishly. She slowly pulled her scythe from her ropes as she stared into Zorus's empty soul. His bare bones embraced the fear. "Come on, I know that you wish to release your anger, your wish to harm someone, to kill someone... *like yourself.*" His taunting enraged her soul. She lifted her scythe and charged toward Zorus.

Zidal gracefully swung her scythe toward Zorus's open spine. She tripped over her own feet as only a mist of snow resided where Zorus had stood. Confused, she ducked, and flipped forward as she heard the swing of a sword slip behind her head. Turning around, she faced Zorus, wiping the glaive toward his head. To her surprise, he lifted the sword in front of his vulnerable skull, blocking her favorite attack. He quickly followed his block, kicking toward Zidal violently. She jumped backward, the edge of the boot scraping against her stomach.

Zidal threw her sword toward Zorus's cloth-covered ribs. He blocked with a swish of his sword's movement. Zorus returned her feeble attack with a powerful blow, Zidal ducking before it brushed across her head. Zidal rammed her scythe forward. Her scythe clashed mid-attack against Zorus's weapon.

"Why are you doing this?!" Zidal asked as his empty eyes smiled. To this, he did not answer. She raised her scythe as Zorus's sword swung toward her. Their weapons collided with a strong ring. "I fail to see why you want to fight. This does nothing for the mission." Zorus, again, did not answer, yet continued to apply force against her weapon. Zidal pulled her scythe away and ducked as Zorus's sword swung toward her. Zidal swung her scythe, finding herself breaking through the cold air once again. It was less than a second before she felt his fierce emotions rise behind her again.

She swung around and clashed her weapon against Zorus's. Zidal quickly released her push and swung her scythe behind Zorus's legs. He allowed the scythe to break his stance, falling into the snow. She stared into Zorus's empty sockets, falling into his stiff skull. Tears began crystallizing in the frozen air as she swung her scythe towards Zorus's boney neck. He reacted more quickly than the body could allow, holding his sword's strength against Zidal's weapon.

Knowing her strength would be overwhelming, Zorus vanished from her sight. "Zorus?" she held the stick of the scythe, searching the area around her. A white void of snow and sunlight waited around her. She could only listen to the sound of the rough wind as it rushed through her hair. Her breaths became heavy as she listened for his footsteps, as she felt for his ominous presence. Her throat bobbed as she swallowed her fear, her thoughts rising, asking why he wanted to kill her.

The sound of the wind shifted it rounded and stormed. Something began to fall from above her, but before Zidal could look into the sky, she fell to the ground, Zorus's heaving weight pushing her into the soft snow. His power was exceedingly unbearable, he was too difficult to fight off, he was much more determined and even more experienced than she. She struggled against his powerful grip; his boney fingers wrapped around her shoulders. Tears formed in her eyes as Zorus lifted his sword, placing the blade directly above her chest.

His intimidating, empty sockets stared into her violet eyes as she dropped her scythe into the snow, surrendering to his blade. He sighed as he lifted his sword, standing from the snow. "You're not worth the energy. And I couldn't bear Courier's reaction." he spoke morosely as he stepped off of Zidal's stomach and let out his hand. Though his words bore the same weight as an excuse. There was something else, another reason he had held back... She took his hand as she stood from the freezing snow. "Come, we have an emblem to find."

S awoke to the feeling of painful rips in his skin. He could feel his blood trickling down his arms and legs, warming his cold skin. Soft, yet horrific breaths rose and fell over his body as the blade dug deeper. His eyelids slowly lifted, his vision clearing ever so slightly. He knew exactly where he was, *the doctor's room.* The familiar fabric of the table brushed under his soft skin as chains fell from his limbs.

He listened to his small drops of blood as they collapsed against the bottom of the empty bucket. All he could feel was pain and a brief coldness which swept over his chained body. He stared into his Master's gleaming eye as he smiled with evil intent. He was barely able to speak with the indescribable pain rushing through his veins. "Wh-what's happening?"

His Master stared at him with a looming grin. *"Ah S, the vile you drank was successful in giving you and your brother power beyond words, beyond thought. But without activation, you will amount to nothing.`` The* tall figure held S's cuts together with the excess of his skin as he placed the blade onto the counter. He reached for a syringe and began to fill it with a blue liquid. *"Your swordsmanship is astounding, your form is perfect, and your observation is ever growing, you can* *defeat the undefeatable. Yes, you have magic that is unique to your rec, but with this, you will be invincible."*

S's mind became anxious as the syringe plunged into his skin. *"I have acquired snart venom, found only in the deepest caverns. It will activate your power, and soon you will be unstoppable. If this experiment is successful, your brother will go through the same procedure, his activator being natrin spider venom, in order for your skills to vary.`` The* liquid inside of the syringe leaked into his blood, a sizzling pain residing. All he could hear were his own terrible screams before the syringe departed from his vessels.

His Master placed the syringe on the counter, and quickly retrieved a key. After each cuff was unlocked, S's body became overwhelmed by magic and pain. His body was so incredibly weakened, that the tall figure had to carry him to his cell, screaming in misery. His brother awoke to the sound of his cries as he was chained against the walls. The overwhelming feeling drifted away as the chains restrained his newfound power. His screams ceased, yet his empty eyes still strained with tears.

"Tomorrow, we will see." The door locked behind the tall figure as light fled the scene.

Pathway

Alex took in a deep breath of the crisp morning's air as they exited the tunnel. His body openly accepted the coolness of the forest as the volcano's heat lingered in his bones. The trees were covered in bright teal leaves, reflecting the light of the sun. The grass felt soft on his aching feet as he stepped through the forest. He stopped as Courier sighed, pulling his thin fingers through his hair. "Alex, find the emblem of life, I have a feeling that we will succeed this time." he encouraged.

Alex closed his eyes feeling life flow through his mind, the breeze allowing the leaves to blow through the air. He felt the grass under his feet, the flowers growing within the forest along with bushes and vines. The sounds of Darls singing, buzzing and barking flowed through his mind. Small creatures scurrying across the plains ran through his thoughts. An image began to grow in his mind, a ceramic pot, black paintings of plants and Darls draped across its rough, brown surface.

Alex let go of his breath and opened his eyes. "West, the emblem of life is to the west, surrounded by the most beautiful garden."

Courier nodded. "West it is. We will travel until we succeed, we will fight until the Broken Souls parish." he smiled as Alex began to lead him toward the unknown. The forest of trailbite trees loomed above them, a shadow cast from the forest's canopy as the sun warmed the tops of the trees. The grass beneath their feet waved as the short shocks of wind blew past. The dry dirt underneath the plants powdered their boots as they walked through the trees, Courier's worn cape drifting through the breeze.

Alex glanced at Courier, his confident expression exceeding his own. Alex's thoughts drifted as he opened his mouth to speak. "Why… why did *she* do that? Was it the fault of one of us?"

Courier understood what he asked, the mention of her fury, her desire to kill herself, any way that she could, froze his thoughts. "No Alex, it would never be. She cares for us more than she shows. Her mind is ill, and this mission has been putting plenty of pressure on her. The words which the damenor spoke only triggered her upsetting thoughts." his voice chilled as he spoke of her, keeping the air still. He swallowed his sorrow for her. "Best we don't acknowledge Zidal, her spirit needs space." Alex swiftly agreed, as he watched the trees roll by.

Alex stared at the leafy tops of the trees as he walked through the cluttered space. His thoughts traveled as he led Courier through the maze of trees. He knew that he may never see his parents again, that he would never feel the soft fur of his scal again or the thin points of his crown. He wondered of his parents' reaction when they found his belongings, but never even his body to bury. His cape torn, and his crown shrouded in dirt, silky memories draped in the wind.

As Alex searched for an exit in the forest walking toward the open skies, Courier followed keenly toward a better future for all of them. But a presence lurked behind them, one he was all too familiar with. He knew that *it* was no normal Broken Soul, nor a usual Olk. His fear lingered as Alex spoke. "Do you hear that, the rustling in the trees?" Alex stopped for a moment, looking into the forest, yet he was surprised to see a dense fog rising into the trees.

Courier's empty eyes lingered on the smoke-like vapor but reminisced on Zorus's warning before speaking. "I suppose that you must only be imagining things." he looked into the trees where Alex had peered, searching for any threat in the air. The trees were beginning to shrink in size as they walked closer to the edge of Ticoal's forest. Courier drew his finger over the cut on his lip. "Besides, we are exiting Ticoal, so there shall be no threat in the trees…"

"It's not just the trees, I can feel a presence that holds my mind clear of thought, that even eliminates the presence of the mind wavering. Courier, what are you trying to hide from me?" Alex asked as he stopped at the edge of the forest.

Courier sighed as he stood beside him. "I know how much your mind questions this world, but you have to trust that you know who *he* is. *I know that you have seen him*. Let's just move on." his voice rang with a tip of urgency and sternness as he spoke. The rustle through the trees began to catch up with the swift pace of their footsteps. Courier began to step faster, even passing Alex.

"Courier, what's going on?!" Alex asked as he began to rush his movements.

Courier glanced at the leaves, quickly returning his gaze to the path. "Run, Alex! I promise you that I will explain later!" Alex followed his instructions, quickening his steps as the rustle in the trees followed them closely.

"What in the name of Death is after us?!" Alex screamed. He glanced at Courier, who's form was shifting, his skin disappearing as he ran. Alex then knew that they were in mortal danger.

"Your worst nightmare!" his voice rang through the air as Alex's breaths trailed behind. "And even if we run, I fear *he* will still find us." Alex stumbled in his fragile steps as he attempted to stay caught up with Courier, breathless, yet alive. He was agile and steadfast as he ran from a fear so unknown to the rest of the world. His bones rattled and shook as the wind rushed by his thin body.

Alex glanced at the trees, a fog traveling through the leaves. The presence never slowed yet continued to follow at a faster pace as they began to slow. The fog grew nearer, and then faded into the darkness. He watched as their bodies came closer to a stone wall, Courier's fingers intertwining. A dark portal opened as they ran toward the wall. Alex felt his body phase through the substance as darkness began to surround him. Courier soon followed behind him, the portal closing, none to enter again.

Their footsteps slowed as they walked through the darkened area. It was only a few moments until the Abyss faded into a beautiful forest unlike the one which they had exited. Courier stopped, turning his skull toward Alex. He was panting, holding tightly to his knees. He watched as Courier did not change form. "What…"

"*He* is still here; *he* will never leave my presence. Not until I give up. Come Alex, we still have an emblem to find." Alex began to walk into the depth of the forest, his mind leading him to the emblem of life. Though his fear still lingered, he showed confidence through his expression.

The trees swayed through the song of the wind as the sounds of life added a harmony. Shawon's beauty seeped into his heart as he walked through the beautiful forest. There seemed to be more plants and mosses growing the further they stepped through the trees. The forest around them seemed so different, yet they knew that they were still within the forest of Ticoal. Alex reached toward a bundle of vines, removing them from their pathway. He ceased his movement as he stared at a stone wall covered in rusted red markings. "I don't get it, the emblem should be just beyond this wall. There must be another way to it." he exclaimed as the vines fell from his fingertips.

"Wait," Courier pleaded before Alex turned around. "Let me see those markings." Alex stepped aside as Courier stepped through the dangling vines. He followed him, staring at the darkened wall. As his skin formed over his bones, Courier stared at the dull red markings for a moment, attempting to find meaning in their faded words. "This is in the writings of our ancestors."

"Can't you translate them?" Alex asked patiently. Courier nodded as he laid his long finger on the wall.

"It speaks of the prophecy, and It tells of *Gehalla*, the war against humans."

"The prophecy?"

"Yes, the story of the war." Courier glanced at Alex, beams of joy in his expression. "No book written by our *ancestors* has words of our past, we have only had legends, and books of historians to learn our origins."

Alex stared at the pictures and symbols peeling off of the walls. "What do the writings teach?"

Courier cleared his voice before he spoke. "*Humans and Darlids once lived peacefully together for a time. Centuries of peace had passed, yet Athreal and the twenty-three living demons rebelled against the rule of the humans, wishing death upon each so they may acquire the throne. They attacked the humans, with a power unknown to a point that the humans did not trust even Darlids anymore. And thus, the war began.*" Courier paused as he continued to translate.

Alex stood silently as he watched Courier read the ancient writings, words that could never be understood by his eyes. Symbols that were left to those who were willing to understand their terrible past.

Courier continued the tale. "*The Darlids were forced to join in Gehalla, the fabled war, or face certain death. Though the humans were powerless, they were well trained in battle, and they had Shaens by their side. The demons stood at the head of the battle, their powerful vessels falling one by one. Though they won, the humans feared Darlids, and each was forced into a new dimension, to Shawon. They killed Athreal and used his soul to seal the portal. His body melted into Shawon, and thus his soul. Death broke his soul into eight pieces and gave them each an attribute to keep them safe from Darlid hands. He then hid them across Shawon, never to recreate Athreal.*"

"What does the war have to do with the emblem of life?" Alex queried. Courier bent over as he deciphered the markings at the bottom.

"*Though some wish death on others, some wish life upon their own dead souls. What lies ahead flourishes, only after the tests of life lie. No soul should dare open the door, none should know how.*" Courier shifted his gaze. "We're at the right place Alex, we just have to understand the riddle, find a way to open the hidden door. Look for something, anything to open the door."

Alex immediately left his place, searching for any unusual pieces on the length of the wall. Courier too placed his long, dry fingers on the base of the wall, feeling for something to release the hidden door. The wall was made of stone, rough and brittle. Alex pressed his fingers against the small lumps and unusual bumps on the wall's surface, searching for the answer to fate's puzzle.

The wall was covered in light teal leaves and vines of every shade. Courier's hand wrapped around the stem of a vine, slowly moving the leaves from his view. A marking, which remained darker than the others, rested on the stone. Courier translated and whispered the words to himself. "*The last demon still lives…* no." he whispered.

"I found it!" Alex's voice broke the tense silence as Courier dropped the vines, covering the markings. He turned, following the thin trail of dirt to where Alex stood. Alex glanced at Courier and pointed at a golden bulge in the stone. A carved image of a trailbite tree popped out of the still image. "At least, I think I found it. What do you think, Courier?" he asked as he trusted Courier's thoughts more than his own, which he was still losing rapidly.

"Applying pressure to the marking is worth a shot." Courier reached out his long, thin finger and pushed the golden knob into the stone. He released his finger from the small image. The wall began to shake, vines falling from its edges, dust spilling from each crack. The hidden door rolled into an unseen opening to the left. They stared into the open abyss of the cavern as the shaking feeling subsided.

S awoke at the sound of the crashing door. His sight led immediately to the tall figure; a grin plastered across his face. *"Success."* he cawed as he stepped toward his chains. *"The snart venom has activated your abilities, you now have untold powers fused within your body. I know not the power in which you wield, but its possibilities are endless."* his Master's grin widened as a tentacle began to grow from his left side. *"Your brother will go through the same initiation, and you will witness the glory of my success."*

"What are you going to do to my brother?" S asked as his Master retrieved a key from his pocket. The Tall Being unlocked his chains, a never-ending fear emanating through the small space. Though S's arms were free from the stone wall, his wrists were kept inside keeler stone cuffs. He stretched his arms out as he stood from the ground.

"He will experience the same things that I did to you, all which is necessary for his powers to activate." his Master explained as he stepped toward R. S followed him, though fearing greatly for his brother's survival. *"You and he will accompany Athreal in his return, as his personal guards because of your infinite power."* S shivered in the thought of guiding evil to victory, he was at risk of death.

S watched as another tentacle fell from the Tall Being's right side. He slid his arms underneath R's body as he lifted the sleeping child. He was heavily drugged, a waking moment scarce in these difficult times. Yet another arm formed on his right side, able to open the large metal door. S followed him through the doorway. He was always one to follow commands, even those that were unspoken. He walked behind every step through the endless hallway until they reached the experiment room.

The tall figure wrapped his tentacle around the handle of the door and used his force to pull the door open. After stepping inside the room, The Tall Being gently placed R on the surgery table, attaching the four cuffs to his limbs. S watched as he stepped to the side table, reaching for an unwashed knife. He lifted it from the counter, returning to R, who lay unconscious. As the Tall Being began to rip into his skin, S noticed the rusty bucket beneath the table, where his brother's fragile blood would spill.

The Tall Being began at R's left shoulder, creating a shrieking, wet sound as he dug into his skin, followed by his right. S covered his eyes with his small hands yet continued to watch through the cracks of his fingers. The knife fell toward his left leg, creating a deep cut in his skin. The torture only stopped when the blade was lifted from his right thigh. S watched carefully, tears leaking from his sockets, as his brother slept in pain. His blood trickled down his arms in thin streams, each leading to the rusty bucket. The room was only filled with S's cries and the sound of dripping blood.

The Master balanced the sharp knife on the edge of the counter before returning to his experiment. He let his translucent skin drip over each of the wounds, sealing R's skin back together. Though his wounds were mended, his blood still fell. S dropped his hands from his face, witnessing the horrors that monster he called Master had committed. But his devious, corrupt smile lasted in his unforgettable memories, waiting to haunt him in his future.

"Now S, the time has come, your brother will gain magic. His power will be activated by natrin spider venom." The Tall Being reached to the counter for a syringe filled with a glowing orange substance. His tentacle wrapped around its circumference, pushing it closer to R. The Master pushed the needle into his skin, forcing the liquid to reside in his system, to give him *something* that was never meant to be received.

S watched his brother scream in silent pain.

Heart of Ice

The sorrow wisp of the sky's clouds reflected the dulling sunlight. The light of the stars shined through the thin gaps in the clouds, the violet reflection brightening the dull night. Zorus and Zidal's feet fell into the deep snow, the cold flakes reaching their knees. Each step they took, the snow left mysteries to their survival. The snow crunched under their thick boots leaving a mark of their story behind.

Zorus's cape flew silently through the air as a short gust of wind fell against their bodies. Their lonesome figures stepped through the empty terrain, no other soul lurking near them, none to calm the laborious tension between each other. Zidal's fearful thoughts calmed the storm of wind cooling the air. She silently winced as Zorus glared at her, his empty eyes following the rise and fall of her anxious breaths. There was something about his stare that made her heart sink. An unrecognizable emotion followed her.

Zidal couldn't help but gaze at him, his golden hair covered in the night's frost. His empty soul torturing her mind. But her eyes didn't dare to loom over Zorus's figure, his distraught emotion filling the chilled air. His anger oppressing the situation. As her mind traveled to unknown places, she followed his movement.

Placing her foot into the soft snow, Zidal's foot fell deeper into the ground than expected. "Ahhhh!" her voice rang as she fell through the seemingly endless pit. She landed on a hard stone surface, wincing in pain. Shortly after, she heard another thud, Zorus landing by her side. Snow fell from the surface, covering their bodies in a layer of soft ice.

"Ah, Death!" Zorus yelled as he punched the stone ground. His voice was bitter, strongly resisting peace. He stood from the cold ground, staring into the cloudy sky. His energy left insufficient, knowing that he could not use his magic, he leapt from the ground, and reached toward the edge, yet it was far from his grasp. Zidal rubbed her head as she pushed herself from the ground. She glanced at Zorus, who again jumped, and failed to catch the edge. He grunted as his feet met the ground. With all of his strength, he slammed his foot against the wall. "Ugh!"

"Zorus, it's no use. We're trapped here." Zidal's morose voice fell through the silence.

"No use? No use?! You would rather wait here for eternity than try to escape this silent grave?! There is no other soul in this terrain to save us!" his raging voice echoed through the silent air.

"Zorus, we're trapped!" Zidal lifted her hand and silently placed it on Zorus's shoulder. Shivers rolled up her body as she made contact. "We are trapped." her voice calmed as she spoke. "There's no use in reaching for the top when the edge is never going to reach for us." she felt her hand fall from his shoulder as he balanced his arm against the wall. His skull rested against the cold stone as he clenched his fists. Furious breaths fell from his lips.

"Because of your *mission*, we are stuck here. Because you wouldn't let Courier and I hide, we are stuck here. We are suffering because of *you*." Zorus's quiet, yet powerful voice rang through the silence. "I am weak. My body hungers, and my mind follows. You're right. Without something, anything, we will never escape. *And it's all your fault.*"

"This place was never meant for a Darlid to set foot in. But now we must accept the consequences of our actions and rest here for eternity." Zidal spoke through a teary voice.

"Rest… Why won't *he* let me rest?" Zorus mumbled into the stone. "Why do my bones ache when bruises aren't there?" Zorus turned his head and watched as Zidal fell to the ground, peeling her crystal mask off of her cheeks. So little had seen the white scars clinging to her cheeks. So little had witnessed the horrors of a true hero. Holding her knees to her chest, she wept.

A soft song of tears played through the empty space. "Why must I suffer? Why won't my thoughts let me rest? Why do I feel pain when I am loved?" Zidal questioned, the walls caving in. She closed her eyes, wondering of her fate. "Why can't I win when I try so hard? Why won't my soul wither away?" she felt a coldness cover her hand, Zorus's soft touch resting over her own. She opened her eyes, glancing at Zorus's sorrowful smile.

Zorus's emotion calmed as he realized something he never thought before. Zorus crouched beside her, staring into her violet eyes. "Zidal… I didn't know…"

"The world was meant to torture us. We will never be free from this *prison.*" Zidal smiled weakly, a fragile tear falling down her cheek, freezing in the cold air. Zorus gently squeezed her hand as he looked into the sky, snow falling from the cotton clouds. He let go, his gaze resting on her. "I shouldn't have brought you into this. I owe you an apology."

"I didn't know…" he repeated, as he dropped his hands toward hers, lifting them from her sides. Her soft palms balanced on his, he stared into her sorrowful eyes.]

"You don't deserve this pain, not by me, only I do."

Zorus's breaths became anxious. His mouth opened, words struggling to fall from his lips. "Zidal I… I'm sorry."

"You shouldn't need to apologize. I should be *dead.*" her voice shook as she spoke, tears gently dripping onto her uniform. "I should be *gone.*"

"Zidal," Zorus's throat bobbed as he swallowed his fear. He held her hands as he stood from the ground, Zidal's weak legs coping as he pulled her to her feet. Zorus pulled her closer, her sorrow emotion resting in his mind. "I was wrong…"

He wrapped his hand around her head, pulling her lips toward his. He was almost alarmed as she did not pull away, but rather deepened the kiss, asking the same question he was. *Was the anger they held for one another only because they loved each other more deeply than emotions could explain?* Zidal's warm arms wrapped around his neck, holding him closer to her as she submitted into his kiss. Her heavy breaths fell against his skin as she surrendered to his warmth.

Zidal fell from him, her arms wrapped around his shoulders. She cried bitterly as she rested her head on his chest. Zorus stroked her hair, holding her close to him, all of his fears slipping from his mind. "I love you." she whispered as her tears froze on his uniforms. With a few shuddering breaths, they fell to the ground, falling asleep to the sound of the whispering wind.

Zorus awoke to the chime of the wind, the numbness of snow keeping him still. His eyelids peeled from his lethargic slumber; the sights set in front of him leaving him confused. Trees, stricken of leaves and fruit, knots in their twisted bark surrounded him. The knots of the ugly trees caught his eyes, each pattern creating a foreign face. Each arrangement disturbing him.

It was then that he realized that he was laid against the bark of a knotted tree too, the bark unfurled beneath his back. Searching the area, he realized that he was abandoned, no other soul in sight. As he attempted to stand, the chime of shackles entered the wind's song, his wrists burdened with the heft of the shackles. He shivered, feeling the absence of power in his heart. A flood of harrowing memories repleted his empty mind as his wrists fell.

Shadows over-casted his body, lurking nearer as his breaths grew shorter. "Oh, Death." Zorus whispered as a figure emerged from the shadows. A woman stepped into the icy heart of the forest. She stood tall, appearing to be beautiful from a distance, yet her features described her differently. She wore a crown of branches, blossoms of flowers as white as the snow and leaves reflecting a vibrant teal hue growing from the twigs. Her dark hair draped onto her shoulders, thinly dripping onto her ice-blue dress. She wore a fur shawl of a slightly darker hue, and held a staff crafted from a large branch, topped with a small ice globe. Her bright green eyes stood out from her white face, along with the left half of her lip, which was melting into the snow. Zidal laid unconscious, the brim of her uniform stretched between the woman's fingers.

A pack of four fox-like Broken Souls stood by her feet, each one melting more than the last. The bottoms of their legs were left as stubs, as if their feet had been cut off before death. Their ears were those of a bat's, large and pointed. One of the four stood out from the rest, seeming smaller and more confident. "Fones." Zorus whispered in fear.

He returned his gaze toward the woman. She spoke as Zorus's breath raged. "It is I, Willow, queen of the ugly trees. Queen of this forest." she spoke with the softness of freshly fallen snow.

"Get your hands off of her, you dirty demon!" Zorus yelled, pulling against the chains.

The queen frowned. "You should think twice before speaking to royalty." she spat, raising her scepter.

"If you're a queen, where is your kingdom?"

"The trees are my kingdom. The Darls and Darlids which once lived here obey me, some even more powerful as they are now broken inside. I'll let you know that I took this kingdom with force. I don't choose to hide my violent methods beneath my beauty."

"Beauty? Who lied to you?" Zorus questioned, disrespectfully.

Willow ignored his taunt and leered. "If I didn't choose to continue my rule, I would surely be living with the Olks."

"So, you admit that you're not powerful enough to be one."

"I *am* one, but not living among them!" Zorus opened his mouth to speak, but tired of Zorus's mocking words, Willow lifted her staff, placing it before Zidal's neck. Zorus flinched. "Ah, so you do care. Now, listen, or may both your lives be cut short." Zorus settled down as Willow dropped her staff to her side.

"What do you want?" his voice bellowed.

"I want to make a deal, one I'm sure you won't refuse."

"I'll listen, but not until you let her go."

"Fine." Willow stammered as she shoved Zidal's cold body into the snow. Willow aimed her staff at Zidal's unconscious body. Zorus took in a deep breath as he stared at Zidal's silver hair. Her bare cheeks, cloaked with cracks and scars that told her story, sunk into his soul.

"No!" Zorus screamed. The fones barked as flakes of snow emitted from the bulb, falling upon Zidal's body. Zidal disappeared with nothing, but a pile of snow left where her body once laid. Zorus quivered.

"Oh, do not fret, I only transported her to my dungeon." the queen cackled. "I'll treat her well, give her comfort, and aliment." she promised, pointing her staff at Zorus. Zorus closed his eyes as snow fell from the icy sphere. He felt magic run through his body as the sound of chains hitting the snow cackled. He held his bare wrists. "Now come, join me for a banquet, for my quest, and I may release her. You'll need the energy."

Zorus opened his empty eyes, standing from the ground as the queen stood, facing away from him. She stepped forward and took hold of the dry branches of a tree. Zorus followed the five Broken Souls, watching her gentle movement as their stubs left marks in the snow.

She removed the branches from their sight, showing him a castle, or what used to be one. It was covered in dry, twisted branches, forming faces and disgusting shapes of all sorts. Everything was covered in growth, except for the entrance doors and a single stone tower. Snow had fallen gently across the surface of the castle, hiding it from plain sight.

As the queen walked forward, Zorus stepping behind, the trees seemed to part, allowing her to enter her domain. The fones followed her movement, waiting for her commands. She reached toward the handles of the doors, pulling them toward her. The door opened into an empty abyss, scarce of any light but of a few candles. The floors seemed to be crafted of stone and ice, presentably beautiful to the naked eye. The walls were painted dimly, and almost bare of decor aside from the finely crafted candles.

Glancing at Zorus, Willow stepped into the endless corridor, doors opening into unknown areas, Willow's sparkling green eyes lighting the shadowed halls. She pointed forward, the fones immediately running into the darkness of the hallways as she began to walk in another direction. Zorus followed her soft footsteps as she walked down the hallway. Neither of them spoke, the only sounds: their breaths. The queen turned left into an open door, where light scarcely bled into the hall. Her hand gestured toward the room, and though he was skeptical, he stepped inside the dining room.

The queen of the ugly trees followed him closely, allowing him to sit on a chair of ice. She sat on an identical chair facing opposite of him. The frozen table, which sat in front of them, held meals fit for royalty, gorgeous candles set in the center of the ice. The queen lifted her fork, stabbing a piece of meat. "Go ahead, eat, and then we'll talk."

Zorus, almost reluctant to follow her command, lifted his fork and took a piece of the meat. "What do you want… demon?" the queen recoiled in his words.

"All of this must be kept from Zidal's knowledge." she smiled. "I will allow you safe passage through Noul and reunite you with the

Knightmare if you grant me the emblem of greed." she smirked. "You see, I know the exact location of the emblem, but the guardian is unbearably dangerous, and my soul would shatter almost immediately."

"I don't make deals with decaying usurpers!" Zorus taunted, slamming his fork on the table. A shard of ice broke from the surface.

"I thought you might say that. What if I told you that Zidal's *life* is on the line?" she watched as Zorus's emotion fell, as his thoughts traveled to places unknown. He took a bite of the sustenance, filling his weak body. "Such a difficult decision... her life, or the loss of another emblem? What to choose, what to choose?" Willow tapped her melting lip. As he pondered, Zorus frowned. "Without a Knightmare like her, who's to *save* Shawon from Broken Souls?"

Zorus's bones shook as he stared into her devious eyes. His thoughts traveled as Willow's frozen smile remained. His anxious breaths rose as dark memories flowed into his mind. Looking at the queen, he spoke. "I'll... I'll accept your quest." his cold whispers drained him. The queen reached her arm across the length of the table, unfolding her hand. Zorus reached out his hand and took it. Their hands shook, binding the deal.

Willow drew her arm back to her plate. "Oh," she tapped her lip, "I almost forgot. She will be my prisoner until the task is complete. You break your promise, I break mine."

"You dirty demon! You never..."

"It's too late Zorus, you shook on it, now the task must be completed. I promise that you will be reunited with her when you return it to me." the queen cackled as Zorus slouched in his seat.

S awoke in chains once again, his body feeling weak, but full of power along with it. His eyes were drawn to his brother, who was laying against the stone wall, reading through one of the few books that were given to them. He too seemed to be in immense pain, but with the help of the keeler stone chains, their newfound power was not overwhelming. "I have failed you R." S uttered as R flipped the page.

"What do you mean?" asked his brother.

"I promised to protect you, I promised that I wouldn't let any harm come to you. But look at us, we have been cut to the bone, and turned into monsters with unknown magic hidden inside us… demons hidden in our shadows."

"Do not fret brother, I feel fine now, weak, and helpless, but still fine." At the age of five now, R's vocabulary had increased immensely. "S, when will we understand this new power?"

"I… I don't know. Master has his ways. He has told me that soon, we will discover our invincibility, our strengths. The power that will help him succeed in his quest to recreate Athreal." S spoke with an unmatched bitterness as he stretched forth his weakened arms.

"What do you suppose our magic will do?" R questioned.

"I don't know. Whatever happens though, we must train it highly, and find a way to overpower our Master. We must find a way to rid him of this world, and escape." S punched the palm of his right hand before sighing and falling against the hard wall. "Our power might not be enough though. We should train it along with swordsmanship, that way, we may be able to overpower him."

"But I won't even begin learning how to wield a sword for another five years, S."

"Then focus on your magic, when we discover it, and I will teach you the basics in my free time… without a sword, of course." S shyly added.

R nodded, agreeing with his opinion. "Then we will attempt in five years' time brother, maybe we will be our own saviors." he mentioned as he began to read once again.

Tests of Life

Courier stared into the open darkness as he stepped forward. Alex followed his nervous steps as they neared the entrance of the cave. "This cavern should allegedly lead us to the garden." Courier remarked as he glanced at Alex. "But how could there be soil with enough nutrients to sustain a garden inside of a cavern? And without sun or water?" he asked as the darkness overcame his body.

"Maybe it doesn't have to do with the nutrients Courier, maybe it's the emblem itself. Maybe the emblem creates the garden." Alex depicted. He squinted in the darkness and followed a small and rocky pathway. "What I'm worried about are the tests of life." shy light bled into the darkness as they grew nearer to an opening.

"Fear not Alex, the tests mustn't be too difficult. I suppose that they are testing our worth in life, our worthiness to wield the emblem." as Courier stepped through a small opening in the cavern, light spread through the area. Torches were lined around the barriers of the cylindrical walls, bringing light to the first challenge. Courier held his arm in front of Alex's chest as he stopped at the first test. He swallowed in fear as his skin sank into his bones.

The room was nearly empty, nothing but two ropes and an endless pit stood in the center of the room. Courier and Alex stood at the edge of the cliff, the brightness of the torches fading into the endless pit. Not one soul knew what lay at the bottom of the darkness but the bones of the ones who came before. Courier lowered his arm as small crumbs of rocks slipped into the abyss. Across from them stood another opening, and above the entrance, ancient letters were written. Alex pointed at the lettering. "There, what's written?" Alex shivered in fear as he stared toward the bottom of the pit.

Courier stared at the ancient sandstone walls for a moment translating the markings. After waiting in silence, he spoke. "The first of the tests of life: only if you survive can you move on." he glanced at the dangling ropes, waving in the shallow breeze. "To pass the tests, you must *be alive*."

"What do you suppose we must do?" Alex asked as the coldness of the abyss rose.

"I suppose we must take a leap of faith and take hold of those ropes." Courier glanced at Alex. "How's your arm strength?" Alex gave him a nervous shrug as Courier bent his knees. He watched Courier as he jumped from the edge of the cliff. His body slowly fell from the solid ground as his arms reached toward the dangling rope. His fingers clutched the twines of the ropes, gripping to his life. Using all of his strength, Courier scaled the rope, bringing himself closer to the ceiling of the cavern, staring at the second rope.

Courier fell into deep thought before he began to swing with the rope. Each kick of his legs, he came closer to the second rope, and then the cliff. Again, the rope neared before he swung back to Alex and the cliff. Finally, as his boots were able to reach the cliff, he kicked off of it, and as soon as he neared the second rope, he jumped. Alex sighed as Courier's boney hands clasped to the second roped, the bottom of the endless pit only seeming farther from his feet.

Again, he began to swing the rope from front to back, nearing the second edge. He had lost the advantage of the first cliff, only the nearing one to give him hope. As he swung himself back and forth, he prepared himself to reach the other side of the chamber. At the top of his swing, he let go, flying through the air, reaching toward the rocky edge. His fingers latched onto the edge of the cliff before he could fall to his doom. He used the last of his strength to lift his legs over the edge and pull himself to safety.

Courier looked at Alex and cupped his hand around his jaw. "You must reach this side!" he yelled as Alex cowered. Alex took in a deep and laborious breath as he stared into the endless abyss of the pit. He then glanced at Courier followed by the rope. It seemed much further from him than it did moments before. He looked into the empty hallway behind him before he took a leap of faith. He felt himself fly for a moment, the wind brushing through his hair. But quickly, soaring became falling before he caught the end of the rope and pulled himself higher, where there was more rope to hang on to.

Alex looked across the emptiness. The second rope moved further from his sight as his anxious mind played tricks on him. As bulbs of sweat ran down his forehead, he began to recall what Courier had done. He began to kick his legs back and forth until a steady swing commenced. Back, then forth. Back again, then forth until he could feel the heel of his boot touch the previous edge. He flew forward, and when he returned to the edge, he pushed himself off and jumped toward the second rope. As soon as he felt the rough material between his fingers, he clutched the rope with all his might.

His hands now in treacherous pain, burnt from the rope, he stared at the ledge. Courier's encouraging expression beaconed him to continue onward. "One last jump Alex. I know you can make it." his arms feeling much weaker, Alex climbed up the rope and stared at the ledge before him. He began to swing once again, until the rope was the nearest to the edge it could be. He let go. At first, he could see the ledge near to him, but as he came closer, he only continued to fall. He reached for the rocks; his fingers barely able to clutch the rough ledge.

Alex's left arm hung below him as his right held on tightly. He swung himself upward, but he could not reach the cliff. He felt the weakness in his arm give in as he felt his fingers slip. He fell for only a second before he felt Courier's stiff joints wrap around his hand. "I won't let you die today, dear *brother.*" with his unseen strength, Courier pulled Alex onto the rough ledge before he collapsed.

"Thank you." Alex wiped the sweat off his forehead, letting out a deep and anxious breath. He stared at his hands, tortured, and scared from the test, blisters forming in his skin. He glanced at Courier, who let out his hand. He took it and stood, staring into the entrance of the next test. "Well, one test is complete." he stated as he ran his fingers through his knotted hair. "How many do you suppose there are?"

Courier shrugged as he stepped through the passage. "I don't know. There could be a hundred for all I know." Alex followed Courier's shallow footsteps through the doorway, but his steps were abruptly stopped as Courier let out his arm once again. "Wait." he pointed at a thin string that rested slightly above the ground. "If I know anything, this must trigger something awful." Courier imparted.

Alex lifted his sight, studying the room to come. Strings stretched across the room endlessly, and each set to a different, unthinkable trap. Yet another line of symbols rested above a closed door on the opposite side of the room. "Look, another inscription." Alex pointed at the doorway.

Courier scanned the markings, reading each in their native tongue before translating it. "This door shall remain locked until the correct button is pressed. Each incorrect button will set off a trap, and each string will trigger one as well. Nothing is as it seems, agility is key." Courier searched the area of strings. He noticed the large stone buttons, each with a different picture, carved on different sections of the sand-colored wall. One was of a lock, another depicting a fire, another illustrated a book, and the last showing a tree. He glanced at Alex before looking at the maze of wires. "Alex, you must go first."

"What?! How am I supposed to know which button is correct?" he asked fearfully.

"You *won't* have to press any buttons. I want you to get to the door safely, to ensure that I won't trigger any traps before you reach the other side." he sighed. "Meanwhile, I will study the buttons, detect which ones will be our doom, and which will open the door. Be careful." Alex nodded as he stared at the maze of wires.

Alex stepped over the string beneath his feet as he stared at the puzzle to come. He ducked underneath the wire that was stretched above him as he lifted his right leg over another which was held slightly above the ground. He lifted his left leg higher to step over another string while he bent over backward to avoid the wires above him. He carefully maneuvered his step to ensure that the pommel of his sword would not catch on the thin threads. He quickly glanced at Courier, who was still pondering, pacing side to side, as he continued to step through the maze of wires. Though he had stepped through half of the length of the room, his target fell farther from his sight, as if he had not moved at all.

Alex continued his trek through the maze of wires as he crawled under a thin space, soon after fitting his body through the thin opening of wires above and beneath him. As he stood, he was careful to miss a wire hanging above him, while fitting the left side of his body through a thin passage. He took in a deep breath as he stepped over one last wire and held onto the handle of the door. Looking at Courier, he spoke. "I made it! Now it's your turn. Have you found the correct button?"

"Nothing is as it seems." Courier whispered. "It doesn't make sense. They want us to choose the tree, yet, since it is obvious, it could only lead to our doom. The lock implies that the door should open, but it will instead seal the entrance for eternity. The book has nothing to do with the emblem of life, only of knowledge, and the fire consumes all, only death shall win." Courier paused. "Alex, it's a trick, they wanted us to push a button, but all should lead to our demise."

"What are you talking about?" Alex asked in confusion.

"Alex… you are going to have to break the string in front of you." Courier spoke confidently.

"What?!"

"I know that it sounds insane, but you're going to have to trust me." Alex wrapped his fingers around the thin wire. "Trust me." Alex's breaths became anxious as the thread stretched between his fingers. He closed his eyes as the snap of the string echoed. He felt the rocky ground rumble as a scraping sound emitted from behind him. As he opened his eyes, he watched the door rise from the sandy ground, revealing another test.

A sharp grin stretched across Alex's face. "I can't believe that it actually worked." Courier smiled as he lifted his leg over the first wire. He continued by ducking under the second wire, followed by lifting his leg over one slightly above the ground. As he lifted his legs again, his heart froze as he felt the pommel of his sword catch and break the string behind him. "Run Alex!" he yelled as the room began to rumble.

"But…"

"Just go, I'll make it out!" Alex turned toward the entrance and fled as Courier fell behind. As Courier began to run through the maze, he watched spikes fly across the room, breaking another wire. Fire began to erupt from the ground, snapping many more threads. He, himself broke more strings than could be counted as he rushed through the maze. Arrows and spikes flew as pieces of the ground fell into oblivion. Fire warmed the room as poison leaked into the air. Rocks fell from the ceiling as sentient vines erupted from the walls.

Within the chaos of the room, Courier watched as the door began to close. His bones shook as his motivation to cross the room exceeded his thoughts. He no longer worried if he cut another string as long as he could get out alive. He ducked as various spikes flew past his skull and jumped as the ground beneath him fell. He ripped vines out of walls, throwing them into the endless pit below until he finally reached the door. As the entrance reached its final height, Courier quickly slid under, the traps never to be seen again.

"Ahhhh!" Courier's voice ragged as his bones cracked. The stone door pushed against and crushed his right hand. His bones broke as tears slipped from his skull. With all of his strength, he ripped his hand from underneath as his skin began to reform. The door slammed shut. Bruised and broken, Courier remorsed in pain.

"Courier, are..."

"Do not fret Alex, we have a mightier task at hand."

R looked up from his book as deep echoing footsteps neared the room. He slammed the book shut before the door creaked open. As light fled into the room, the tall creature stood in the doorway, grinning, excitement filling the room. He first stepped toward S, breaking his chains off of his shackles, but keeping his wrists cuffed. S stood from the ground and watched as he did the same to his brother. *"I will release you from your shackles, but not yet, we must go to a safe room. Follow me."*

The Tall Being stepped through the doorway, and after giving a long-awaited hug, S and R followed him through the hallway. Their plan was finally coming into action. Leaving the doorway, for once, they turned right instead of left. They found their way to a room blocked by an unusually small door. Releasing a tentacle from his body, their Master pulled the door toward himself and guided them inside. They walked into the room like slaves.

This room was much different than the ones they were used to. It was much smaller than the others and was completely empty aside from themselves. After the Tall Being stepped inside, he slammed the door shut, and grinned. *"The walls of this room are embedded with keeler stone, and because it is difficult to find, this room is much smaller than most. When I release you from your shackles, your power will also be released. But, because the walls are lined with keeler, your power will not allow you to escape."* as he explained the magic of the room, he pulled a rusted key out of his pocket. *"R, you must be the first to explore your new abilities."*

As his shackles were unlocked, each of them fell to the floor, his body aching with new and old abilities, some which could not be performed because of his injuries. Looking at his Master, he spoke. "I can sense something, Master, I can sense your excitement, your every thought. And S's too. He is afraid, and sorrowful, but also excited for what is to come."

"Interesting." the Tall Being stated as he held his skull up with his tentacle. *"Not what I was expecting, but interesting nonetheless."* After replacing, and locking the shackles around R's wrists again, he removed the ones around S's. S was filled with an overwhelming power, discovering his newfound traits. Time seemed to stop as he closed his eyes, but the moment after, he found himself in a void. He began to step through the empty space, but soon found a barrier, the keeler lining.

S felt himself drop from the emptiness, returning to the room, but in a different position. Though he did not have control over his power yet, he understood what he could do, and how helpful it could be. *"Teleportation, what a fine art S, what a perfect trait to own. We will continue to train these powers soon, as for now, return to your cell, you are free to roam tonight, I am proud."* he instructed as he latched the second shackle over S's arm. S immediately felt the loss of his ability but took his brother's hand as they journeyed to their room.

Lair of the Snowic

Zorus stood from his seat, full of drink and aliment. The queen of the ugly trees stood as well, turning her body toward the door. As her footsteps echoed, Zorus followed her path. They walked through the dimly lit hallways, filled with the light of the dying flames, with nothing but the whisper of the wind following them. The numbing air rushed through their skin as they walked, the only warmth, the torches.

The queen halted at the front entrance, facing Zorus as he ceased his movement. "You poor soul Zorus, you must feel awful. I could only imagine the pain you've been through; it must be so difficult to have to go through more." Zorus could feel her simper. "You mustn't go on this journey alone; I wouldn't want you to die unknowingly. One of my fones will accompany you."

"I wouldn't trust those fones, even if they weren't broken." Zorus spoke with a voice of confidence, yet fear leaked from each word.

"True, fones can be sly, intellectual, and determined, but under my command, their skills can be used for my benefit." she smiled crookedly. "Yes, I chose to remain in my kingdom instead of giving up my rule to reside in Olkned, therefore I am no Olk, but if I chose to, the fones would be my strength." she finished before whistling an eerie tune, a song that could shatter the souls of the weak, a tune that could beckon hearts to still.

The smallest of the four fones scampered into the entrance room. Its green eyes shined through its dark, dripping fur. It stretched forward and bowed to his queen, displaying a bare bone in his back right thigh. "Arise." Willow commanded. The fone balanced himself on his legs, obeying his queen. "This is my most trusted fone. The most intelligent, and the strongest of all I've known." she described. The queen of the ugly trees gestured toward Zorus before she spoke again. "Alder, I trust you to guide Zorus on his journey to the emblem of greed. Take him and retrieve it, then bring it to me, and we will have appeased our lord."

"Yes, your eminence." Alder spoke in a deep, rough voice. "I will not fail you."

"Good, now go, and do not return until it is in your possession." she smirked before she turned toward the darkened hallway and walked into the abyss of Ice.

Zorus and Alder's eyes met quickly and sternly. Alder smiled through its eyes as if he knew something that he did not. The fone turned his back toward him and stepped through the open entrance of the palace. He cocked his head before he spoke. "Come on, we have a job to do." Zorus, though nervous to follow his command, followed his shallow steps. His form shifted before he entered the frosted forest.

The ugly trees stood proudly, their ghastly faces leaving a mark of terror in the woods. A layer of freshly fallen snow was draped across each of the light brown branches, each with a story to tell. A scurry of motion filled the forest as Broken Souls ran across the ground. Alder barked forcefully, frightening the small dripping beings away. Wind gusts blew huge clouds through the air. A winter storm was swirling above them as they stepped through the snow. Zorus's voice entered the shallow sound. "What's so dangerous about the emblem of greed? Why won't the queen go herself?"

Alder spoke as he trudged easily through the snow. "The emblem of greed is hidden inside a snowic's lair. If one is to get inside, they would need to have good skill in battle, or a way to disappear in plain sight." he growled as Zorus recoiled in fear. "Willow, though she fought for her kingdom, cannot win against the snowic." Alder smirked. "She has been told that you have both of those abilities. *He* is still aware of your existence. Tell me, why are you fighting for the emblems when you should be hiding?" asked the fone.

"It is my duty to fight against evil. Even if I must give up this emblem, I will fight harder for the others. I would never allow Broken Souls to reincarnate Athreal." Zorus spoke with a voice of passion, and confidence.

Alder lifted his head, staring into his soul. "How are you sure that you are fighting for the right side? It's just as obvious to us to bring him back from the dead. He is our savior." he spoke in a cunning voice, in a knowledge that so few could ever realize.

"I… I…"

"...Don't know? I thought so, you were meant to fight on *this* side Zorus." Alder cackled with a rusty sound as he trekked through the deep snow. "Do tell me, why do you care for the Knightmare? She is a worthless being to you seeing that her soul is breaking, and the emblem of greed would give you the advantage."

Zorus remorsed at the mention of Zidal. "A life is worth more than an emblem, no matter who's it is. One more becoming a Broken Soul, especially one with her power, would be a terrible loss to all Darlid kind." he spoke with a sternness in his voice.

"I see, you wouldn't dare express your feelings to anyone, not even a beast like me. The queen knew all along, but I only needed to know for myself." he grinned through his emerald eyes.

"Let's just get this over with." as they exited the forest of the ugly trees, what seemed like an hour later, the sky became void of light, and flakes of snow began to fall from the heavens. The strong gusts of wind continued to blow, filling their eyes with icy tears. One by one, each unique flake found its way toward the ground as they fell from above. Only a couple of minutes had passed before the sky was covered in a layer of snowflakes, blocking the horizon. The snow beneath their feet only deepened as they continued their treacherous journey through Noul.

The snow beneath them crept to their knees, slowing them down greatly. The mountain of ice was held from their reach, a long walk ahead of them. Though the air was frozen, and their bones were stiff with ice, they continued to march through the icy terrain. A song of chimes flowed through the wind as they continued to journey.

As they waded through the lake of snow, Zorus's anxieties wandered. His mind was covered in thoughts thicker than the snow they were stepping through, not a moment could his thoughts calm. His thoughts only traveled between the emblem of greed and Zidal. He longed for her to be in his arms once again, for her warmth to calm him of his anxieties. But he knew that the task at hand was just as important, for if he did not appease the queen of the ugly trees, then he would likely never see her again. His mind wept at the thought, but he was more determined than ever before, he would not fail.

Zorus stared through the snow with his empty sockets, imagining only what was to come, never what was left behind. The crisp scent of the midnight air filled the freezing terrain as the star's light bled through the brightening clouds. A sense of peace drifted over the tundra, though the skies knew the misfortunes to come.

The snowstorm had lightened, but the short and powerful gusts of wind continued to flow. "Halt." Alder commanded in a firm, yet quiet voice. Zorus immediately followed his direction before gazing into a huge cavern, resting in the mountainside.

The snow was resting inside the darkness of the cavern, sending light fumes of juniper into the sky. The snowic resembled an enormous dragon, its leathery wings draping over its scaly legs. As its frozen tail wrapped around its body, it thinned, until a huge icicle, shaped as a mace, grew from its tip. Its head was bare of flesh, its skull smiling dimly as it was crowned with majestic antlers, glimmering like diamonds. Its scales were coated in an icy blue hue which lightened until it was the purest of whites. Huge claws grew from its feet and wing tips, and its teeth were more powerful than could be described.

"It is asleep, guarding its treasures with its dreams." sated Alder as he silently stepped through the snow. "Best we retrieve the emblem before he awakens. Now, how does one disappear in plain sight?" he asked, staring straight into Zorus's soul. "How does one take what is not theirs? Please, do tell." Alder pleaded as he stepped away from the magnificent beast.

"Take my hand, and I will show you." Zorus answered as he crouched into the snow. He let out his bony left hand, waiting for his foe to take it. The fone licked his dry lips before placing his pawless leg into Zorus's empty palm. Zorus closed his fingers around its viscous limb before entering his own created void. "Don't speak." he commanded.

Alder whimpered and faltered in his steps as he attempted to walk on three stubs. He trembled as he followed Zorus through the Abyss, void of color or hope. Zorus seemed much less afraid, as if he had done this for his entire life. But it was over only after a few steps, as they had entered the lair of the snowic. As Zorus let go, and returned to reality, the void revealed the cavern hidden behind. Alder stood in awe as they had found their way into the cavern untraced.

The cavern was filled with golden light, treasures piled to the ceiling. Sparkling crystals and radiant gems filled the empty space with glory, and a beauty indescribable. The snowic laid asleep behind them, an ominous roar sounding from his breaths. "How should we be able to find the emblem of greed, when everything is treasure?" pondered Alder. "The queen was right to know that it would be here, but she never told us of its shape. How will we know when we find it?"

"The emblems have a certain feeling when you hold one. A feeling that can only be recreated by another emblem. You will know if you are wielding it." Zorus stared at the piles of valuables as he spoke. "We best begin searching… quietly." Alder quickly agreed as he trotted toward one of the many piles of relics.

Zorus, his hands cold and fleshless, reached toward the treasures, carefully and silently lifting a gem. As a strong pulse of power ceased to strengthen, he carefully set it aside, so the snowic could peacefully sleep. Then after he set it away, he lifted a golden chalice and felt for the powerful feeling before putting it beside the gem. Again, Zorus reached for a valuable and took it from the pile before ultimately placing it into the one he had created, his only wish, to save Zidal.

Alder, too, searched with care for the emblem of greed, taking a treasure from the pile, holding it in his jaw for a moment, and finally placing it by his side. As he had never felt the power and security of an emblem, he was often unsure if one did have the ability, and he was much less efficient than Zorus was. He suspected that his mind would be filled with greediness as he held it, but still he was unsure. He continued to search through the piles undetected, his only wish, to appease his Master.

This went on for a time, taking a treasure from one of the piles, waiting for the feeling of greed, and then placing it into a new pile for safe keeping. Each of them were left unsuccessful more times than could be imagined, the piles growing and shrinking continually. Treasure after treasure was filled with an empty feeling, not one held the soul of greed, not one was considered a possibility. It was considered a miracle that the snowic continued his slumber as they rummaged through its possessions.

As memories flashed through Zorus's head, he found a better determination to find the emblem. As he knew what would happen if they had Zidal on their side, he continued to reach toward further treasures. But as he remembered the being he was giving this to, his mind cowered, and his soul flinched. He knew that in either scenario, whether he gifted the emblem to the Broken Souls, or let Zidal perish, there would be an unforgivable loss.

Time had passed, pile after pile relocated, valuable after valuable checked for the soul, it had seemed as if they were at a loss, as if they would never find what was hiding. Zorus, though hesitant, lifted a dull grey rock from the open ground. Almost immediately, his mind was filled with greed, and he craved the treasures around him. But what he craved more dearly was the warmth of Zidal's arms. He resisted the treasures around him as he peaked around the piles. "Alder." he whispered as he gestured for him to come.

"Have you found it?" he asked, excited to be finished with the laborious task.

"Indeed, I have." Zorus held out the rock, allowing him to touch it. Alder was skeptical at first, glancing at all of the more radiant treasures in the cavern, but at that moment, he knew that it was the emblem. He let go of the rock before his mind went too far. "Let's get out of here."

S swung a large branch against another, in which his brother held. Though their wrists were kept in shackles, they were set free from the walls, experimenting with their skills. Their plan was only beginning to take action, yet their Master was unaware of their progress. They had to train in secret, only when they knew that they were alone, for if the Master found out, they would find great consequences. R swung his branch swiftly, but S was quick to duck under the attack.

He swung his stick quickly toward his brother's neck but was surprised when he slid to the side. Swiftly, R moved himself to the side as he blocked one of his brother's attacks. It was becoming easy for him to block attacks, and even easier for him to assume what attacks were to come. R watched as his brother swung his branch toward the ground, and in response, he jumped over the harmless weapon.

He smiled as he thrusted his branch toward his brother's chest. S lifted his branch in front of his chest perfectly in sync with the attack, applying pressure to the forceful move. R pushed back, attempting to reach his brother's heart, but could only hold onto the attack for a few moments until his feet slipped back. He caught himself before ducking from another swift movement of S's stick.

"Good form R but continue to work on your leg position." S exclaimed as he struck forth his weapon. R quickly lifted his stick and blocked the attack, pushing against the pressure. As S shifted to the right, his brother stumbled. "See, if you continue to stand that way, you'll slip. Move your left leg out a little." R nodded, copying his words through actions. He swung his stick again toward S twice, both blocked by the quick and swift movement of S's hands. "See, much better. But don't let yourself down. Remember, I've had more practice."

Though a little disappointed in his own skill, R was determined to learn the art of swordsmanship. After the first strike of his weapon, he knew that it was a skill that he would use his entire lifetime, and he enjoyed it. His mind was quick to adapt to every scenario and he learned quicker than his brother had expected. Only after one lesson was, he as skilled as S was with three. S only had to train harder in order to keep up with his brother's wish to fight. Quickly ducking underneath an attack, R struck his branch against S's legs. "Good, the enemy would no longer be able to walk. Perfect choice of attack. What move would you go for next R?" S asked as he kneeled onto the ground.

"Since the enemy could still use their arms, I would quickly rush behind them and stab them from behind." R stated confidently.

"Even better than what I had in mind. Now show me what you would do." R nodded, lifting his stick into the crisp air. As he rushed to S's side, he swung his branch against the simple attacks which his brother gave. As the attacks followed his urgent rush, he frantically hid himself from harm. Quickly enough, he was able to thrust his stick into S's back, leaving a small prick in his skin. S smiled as he stood from the stone ground. "R, I'm proud of you. You're learning so fast."

S let his branch fall to the ground as he opened his arms widely. R placed his stick on the floor before he embraced his brother. "Soon S, our plan will take action, and we will finish what started years ago, and then, we can help those that cannot fight for themselves."

The Garden

Courier stood from the hardened ground, holding his hand carefully. He let out a painful groan before staring at the room ahead. A strange, looming fear encased the room, but there was no turning back. Five feet in the distance, the ground was covered in tiles marked with ancient characters. Behind the strange puzzle another door stood, markings surrounding the frame. Alex stepped toward the tiles, but afraid of the consequences, he did not further his step. "What are we to do?" he asked, glancing at Courier.

Courier let his hand fall to his side as he studied the words. "Step through the maze of tiles carefully, one wrong step, and the floor will crumble beneath you." Courier pondered as he walked toward the tiles. He stared at the lettering and read. "Dai, delta, ter, and ite." though the characters were drawn indescribably, Courier read each with ease. "It's the same four words repeated on the tiles. Dia, delta, ter and ite. What a strange selection."

"What do they mean?" Alex, standing beside him, questioned. "Maybe it would make more sense if you translate it to sendran."

"Dai is an ancient name for Death, delta translates to Broken Soul, ter means Darlid, and ite roughly translates to Darl."

"I don't understand, what's the difference between them? Each word is so similar, any one could be correct. Which ones could lead to our doom?" Alex anxiously asked. "This entire maze of puzzles has made no sense. Nothing has had to do with life, only fighting our way out of deadly traps."

"There is some sense to this Alex. Fret not, we will get through this." Courier paced across the safe area for a moment, pondering the puzzle. Carrying his hand gently, he spoke his thoughts. "Darls and Darlids barley have a difference, they each can bind their soul to their bodies and can choose to become broken. Broken Souls will cease to exist after their soul is shattered. Death is a living being, but controls something that no other being can… guiding souls." Courier lifted his unblemished hand. "That's it! Death is not only a being, but also a force. It must be the answer. This maze of traps has been hiding life behind its walls, but of course it has been attempting to test us in our ability to defy death."

Alex glanced at Courier; a nervous expression plastered across his face. "Are you completely sure Courier? Who knows what could happen if we don't select the correct tile?"

"Was I incorrect with the answers to the previous two puzzles? Have I not spent my entire life studying logic, and every perplexing thing about this ambiguous dimension? Have I not shown my intellect clearly? You'll just have to trust me with this Alex, there is no way to move through this maze except forward now. Allow me to begin, then, if nothing goes awry, you may choose to follow."

Courier stepped closer to the tiles embedded in the sandstone floor. Staring carefully at the tiles, he chose one, and delicately set his foot against the tile. As nothing happened, he applied his entire weight to the tile, and began to search for the next one. He held his hand uprightly as he studied the area, only slightly easing the terrible pain. Finding the next tile, Courier stretched his leg out diagonally, balancing himself on the plate.

Alex watched him with pure anxiety, fearing for his life as the mind wavering continued to flow within his complicated mind. He noticed Courier's gentle movements as he stepped from tile to tile, completing a maze that seemed more simple than it was. The thought process was challenging, without Courier alongside him, Alex would have already died. He took in a deep and anxious breath, licking his dry lips in fear.

Courier stepped onto a platform of sandstone set on the opposite side of the room. He turned and glanced at Alex before speaking. "Haven't you begun the maze?" he asked as Alex's cheeks fumed crimson. "That's alright. The tiles you must step on are marked with two triangles, a vertical line slicing down each of their centers. Come now, I promise that nothing will go wrong."

Alex, though still skeptical, the mind wavering, torturing his confidence, stepped to the edge of the tile maze. There were four symbols which repeated themselves throughout the maze, confusing anyone who was blind to it's true meaning. For every row, each symbol was drawn twice, but even choosing one correct symbol could lead to a dead end. Alex lifted his foot, and gently placed it on the first tile, the same in which he had watched Courier step onto. He studied the area beyond his step, realizing now that the faded symbols would be much harder to differentiate as he furthered himself through the maze.

Carefully, Alex followed a seemingly simple pattern. One step to the right, two steps to the left, another to the right. His confidence was uplifted as he continued to follow the symbols. A diagonal step to the right, one step to the left, another to the right. But his confidence didn't last forever, soon he was confounded as it was harder to discern the markings on each tile. His courage depleted, his mind falling back into the mind wavering, his legs trembling and his lips dry, Alex placed his foot on the left tile in front of him. With a sudden shock of movement, he trailed his leg back to the former tile.

The maze shook for only a moment before the incorrect tile slipped into an endless pit of darkness, followed by every other tile set in the three rows in front of him, leaving a large open space between him and Courier. The tiles on either side of him too began to collapse, each second, a chance for him to follow. With quick breaths, Alex glanced at Courier. "Alex, jump!" Courier exclaimed as he was unable to assist him in any other way.

With sudden anxious thoughts, Alex licked his dry lips and leaped from the tile beneath him as he felt it fall. The soft breeze fell across his face as he flew over the abyss. He fell for a moment before he caught the rough edge of the maze. Alex took Courier's reliable hand, and with all of his strength, he lifted his leg over the edge, and pulled himself to safety. He let out a shallow breath. "Are you alright? That must have been terribly alarming."

"I'm fine… sometimes I need a little scare." Alex took another breath. "My training was definitely worth it." Alex, his heart filled with determination, looked into the doorway. "Come on Courier, we must not give up. We have made it this far, there shouldn't be many more puzzles." Courier and Alex walked into the following room. Courier stared at the writing above the doorway and began to translate.

"You have reached the final test. Avoid the..."

"Watch out!" Alex yelled as he pushed Courier out of the way, an arrow slicing through his cheek. A shock of pain filled his face as he placed his hand on his wound, crimson blood staining his skin. He ducked as another passed by his head, clipping through his light brown hair.

"Alex, thank..."

"Courier, there's no time for small talk, just run!" Courier quickly agreed as they rushed through the seemingly empty room. Arrows rushed across the room, flying past their bodies. They continued to search for paths through the flying arrows as they dodged ones nearer. The air was filled with their heavy breaths as they rushed through the deadly maze. Soon enough, the room grew short, and less arrows appeared. Out of breath, they slowed their pace as they reached the doorway.

Courier and Alex stepped through the entrance, a veil lifted, they were filled with peace, an unrecognizable sense of elation overwhelming them. The smell of sweet grass and dew drops filled the tranquil garden as the sound of rushing juniper flowed through the air. Soft sego grass rested beneath their feet, as glorious trees and vines rose above their heads. A river flowed through the center of the garden, beside a bed of golden flowers. The garden, lush with flowers of all species, was the most beautiful and fruitful of any garden seen before, but they were drawn to the center of the garden where a pillar of flowers rose, displaying a ceramic pot, the emblem of life.

Alex and Courier, both in awe, stepped toward the pillar. A warm springy wind blew against Courier's tattered cape as they stood in front of the emblem. "I can't believe it. The emblem is right in front of us." Alex exclaimed, glancing at Courier. "We've done it, we have completed the tests of life." Alex reached toward the emblem before worryingly pulling back. He glanced at Courier for confirmation.

"I believe you will have to carry the emblem, Alex; I am in no condition of holding something so fragile."

Alex reached for the emblem, wrapping his fingers around the fragile arched handles of the emblem. Almost immediately, his pain dripped away, the blisters on his hands dissipated and the scar on his cheek sealed, leaving no mark. Carefully, he brushed his hand against his cheek and stared at his fingers, not a drop of blood staining his skin. "The emblem of life… it healed me."

Courier drew his finger over the cut on his lip, thinking deeply. "This is ponderous. I almost cannot believe something so against the rules of this world could occur." Courier remarked as he studied Alex's bare face. Courier reached toward the pot and held his shattered hand against the smooth surface of the emblem and waited. He watched curiously as his curled bones straightened, as they connected and healed, as all of his pain was drawn from his body making him whole once again. "It is almost sorrowful that such a powerful item must be destroyed by the king's hand."

Courier's hand slid from the pot, his emotions drained, and his mind filled with a sense of fear before a viscous white tentacle wrapped around his arm. He immediately tugged against the substance but was alarmed as it only gripped his wrist tighter. It continued to wrap around his thin body as his skin contracted, but he was unable to transform as it caused him pain. He glanced at Alex and was struck with abhorrence as he knew it was too late, as he too was encased within a dripping arm. A third tentacle flowed past and wrapped around the handle of the pot, stealing it from Alex's hands. "Ah, did you miss me?" a freakish voice played behind them.

Courier turned his head toward the being, staring into his shining green eye. He spoke without thought. "Eight years and you've finally chosen to show yourself, old friend. I thought we *killed* you, but alas, we were deceived. Yet, after what we did to you, I never thought that you would return. I didn't even think you would remember who I was." though in pain, Alex did not choose to struggle, he knew that he hadn't a chance.

"I have to admit, I didn't recognize you at first *R*, but how could I ever forget you? You never were one to hide from a fight. You always strived to be in the spotlight." He grinned through his melting skull. "You tried to defeat me, but I have my own ways of hiding. And now you have led me to things that are more important than you could ever imagine."

"We will not let Athreal be recreated... you monster! Haven't you realized the pain and suffering this will cause if he returns?!"

"I have, again and again. But you don't realize the advantages, as long as you are broken, tortured, yet alive, he will spare you."

"I will never return to your fatuous faith! I will never call you Master again. I will fight against you for eternity if I have to, as long as Athreal hasn't risen!" Courier bantered, tugging against the sticky tentacle, reaching for his weapon. But to no avail, he was trapped. "You will never succeed; you will never find the remaining emblems. You will perish knowing that I have avenged the life I once lived."

"Your berating will do nothing against my plot, it will only delay it. And unlike my inconspicuous followers, *I* will not set you free after I take the emblem's soul, ah, the troubles you have caused me will be silenced forever, dear friend. I will not allow you to stand in the way of my plan one more day…" Courier swallowed in fear as he glanced at Alex. Lade lifted the ceramic pot above him, speaking in a clear tone. "For the recreation of Athreal, your soul is free!" fear shadowed the garden as the pot shattered against the ground. Once beautiful, the life inside the garden faded, the flowers dying, its beauty lightening to brown, the world dying once again.

A bright green soul rose from the remains of the pot, reclaimed, reunited with its brethren, Athreal was one more step to recreation.

S's heart jumped as the metal door opened with a clatter, and his younger brother slid across the floor. R coughed as he pushed himself off of the ground, wiping the blood off of his cheeks. Loving arms wrapped around him gently, calming him from his tortures. "R, what did Master do to you?" S asked in fear.

"He said that he was testing my magic. Master used his methods to see how much I could be pushed, to see how immortal we are with this newfound magic." R drew his finger over the scar on his lip. "Don't you see S; we are nothing but one of his experiments. He may want to use us for his benefit in the future, but we are just a *science project*. S, we don't even have names, just tags." R remarked as tears fell from his sockets.

"Names? R, what are you talking about?" S asked.

"S, I read the plate above our door. It read *experiment R-41 and S-41.* We are identified by a tag." R smiled weakly. "I want a name S, I want something to be identified with. I don't want to be known as an experiment number, especially when we escape. S, from now on, I want you to call me *Courier.*"

"I don't read as much as you, but isn't a courier someone who delivers things?" S questioned. R nodded in response. "Why do you want to use that for your name?"

"I've come to like the sound of the word, and it's something that I would like to be associated with. I will *deliver* us out of bondage." R declared, smiling. "S, I don't want you to go by an experimental number either, what do you want me to call you?"

"That's easy, *Zorus*... I saw it in a book once. He was the hero of the story. Isn't it a cool name?" R nodded. "R... I mean Courier, we can't let Master know that we have names now. Who knows what he will do to us."

"Of course, let's just stick to the plan, just five more years Zorus, five more."

Mind of Greed

Zorus, holding the emblem, smoothed his finger over the stone before placing it securely inside his pocket. Only a little while longer, and he would be reunited with the Darlids he cared for. Drawing his fingers over his damp skull, Zorus spoke. "Are you ready? Should we return to Willow?"

Alder's ears perked at the sound of his voice. "Yes, her majesty will be pleased with our accomplishment, and you will surely be rewarded with what you were promised." Alder licked his dry lips.

"I never *said* that I would trade the emblem for her life." he stammered. "I never *said* that I care for her."

"But you do. I can sense it, though it will cost you regret and pain and one step closer to eternal darkness, you will provide. All this is, is a distraction, a way to keep you from the things that really matter..."

"What are you talking about, demon?!"

Alder laughed with a coarse and freakish voice. "Can't you feel it in your soul, something is going to go wrong, and you still can't help but to save the Knightmare."

"Stop with your riddles this instant, what are you talking about?!" Zorus questioned again, angered with his impatience.

"Let's just say, an old friend will be visiting someone..." Alder let out his leg, wishing to leave the cavern. Zorus took his thin, leaking limb and brought himself into the void, accompanied by his enemy. The void, colorless and cold, spun and laughed, bounced, and tripped, like the thoughts spinning in Zorus's mind, torturing him, keeping him from peace and joy. His thoughts overtook him, he could feel that something was wrong, though he was unable to understand what was. With the unbearable feeling of wrongness, with great pain enveloping inside his soul, and his mind screaming at him, Zorus fell from the void, unable to journey to the castle secretly.

Zorus fell into the deepened snow, coughing and hacking as his skin and muscles grew over his bones. Alder stepped closer to him, smirking through his emerald eyes. "You can feel it now, can't you? Something isn't right."

Recovering from his curious illness, a blackness dripping from his mouth, Zorus spoke. "What is it?! Why are you torturing me?!" he spoke with a sickening rage. The wind blew ice cold, and the blizzard had dissipated.

"I have nothing to do with the matter Zorus, you know who is causing your pain." Zorus glanced at him as the blackness continued to drip from his lips. "Come now, we haven't much time." the fone pushed himself under Zorus's chest and heaved him upward. As Zorus began to stand from his sickening fall, a deafening roar blasted from behind them, shards of ice soaring above them.

Zorus turned his head, staring at the raging snowic, insightful of their terrible deed. Zorus reached to his pocket, his fingers brushing across the stone before reaching toward his back for his elegant sword. In pain, unable to save his flesh from the ripping claws of the beast, Zorus held his weapon against the powerful icicles. The snowic screeched an eerie tone as it stretched out its sharp wings.

Zorus ducked as a fleet of icicles flew across the sky. His sword raised in the air, many shattered against the metal. "It knows that we took it, it knows that we have relocated its treasures!" the fone yelled as he charged toward the beast, his jaw closing around its scaly leg. Drops of cold blood slipped from its wound as it shook Alder off of his ice-cold leg. With a powerful strike of the snowic's claw, he collapsed into the snow, whimpering in pain. He was wounded, covered in blood, yet he still stood, continuing with all of his strength. "We mustn't let the snowic take back what was rightfully his, nor shall we allow ourselves to perish." he trotted forth, balancing all but his back right leg.

In his own defense, Zorus rushed toward the snowic, sticking his sword into its frozen skin. "And how do you suppose that we can destroy it?" Zorus asked as he ducked underneath the snowic's tail, drawing the tip of his sword across its scales. "It's a snowic for Death's sake!" he enraged as he jumped to the side, the snowic's foot landing where he was once positioned. The snowic roared in pain, icicles drifting across the silent wind. It swung its tail violently, the icy mace crashing into Zorus's stomach. "Agh!" Zorus yelled, holding his stomach as the blackness continued to spill from his mouth.

The fone scoffed, careless toward his injury. "I understand, it's undefeatable… all we need to do is distract it long enough, just until you can use your magic again!" Alder implied, clawing against the beast's leg. "Focus on your mind." Zorus coughed again, the black liquid dying the snow. His sight went blurry as he watched the snowic near him again. Following the sounds of the snowic's roars, he swiftly bent underneath its body. With confidence, Zorus plunged his sword into the snowic's chest, nearing its heart. The snowic screeched as it beat its wings against the air. Zorus's sword slid out of its body as it took into the skies.

Alder scampered away from the snowic as its powerful wings blasted freezing air against him. Covered in blood, he stared into the clouded sky. As Zorus's vision cleared, he watched staggering icicles fall from the sky. He glanced at Alder, and nodded, before running through the snow. With heavy breaths and weak legs, they fit themselves in between the plunging icicles. The snowic flew close behind them, creating endless weapons to fight against them as they fled.

Zorus sheathed his sword and reached out his hand, grasping Alder's front leg quickly. Finally, with his mind strong enough, they entered the void. Their breaths lightened as they stepped through the empty space, the faint roar of the snowic sounded from the distance. An unknown coldness followed them through the void, a dreary thought encased in their minds, never to be known by another living being. Their slow movement through the void was only accompanied by the soft sounds of their steps, nearing the castle of the ugly trees as they continually faded from reality.

Zorus reached into his left pocket, his fingers wrapping around the smooth stone. He looked to the ground as he walked, his heart filled with greed. But his greed was not of gold or of treasures, only of his wish to save the Darlids that he cared for, the things that kept him going. But he knew that his duty required sacrifice.

He glanced at the fone as it whimpered, limping on his weakened legs, his scarlet blood staining the fictitious ground. He coughed, wiping the dark stream off of his mouth, continuing through the vast void of time and space. He stopped and let go of the fone's stubby paw as they returned to reality, surrounded by the forest. "The time is at hand; we must bring the emblem to the queen."

"Let's just get this over with… demon." Zorus spoke under his breath. Alder, lifting his back leg, stepped through the snow, returning to the castle. He glanced behind, watching as Zorus followed slowly, holding his stomach tightly. He stopped at the entrance of the castle, allowing Zorus to enter before he followed inside, shutting the large door behind him. "Where are you, you decaying bride?" he asked as the sound of footsteps filled the castle with life.

"Zorus, Alder, you have returned. I wasn't expecting you to succeed so soon." her silky voice sang as she revealed herself. Alder bent forward, appeasing his queen. "Very well, Alder. Go and rest, you must heal from your wounds." the fone nodded at her command before he trotted into the hallway behind her, disappearing from their sight. The queen returned her gaze to Zorus before speaking. "I expect you found it?"

Zorus reached into his pocket, clutching the emblem tightly. As he pulled his hand out of his pocket, he tossed the rock into the air, catching it as it fell. "I did what you wanted, now release Zidal." he commanded, coughing up darkness.

Willow smiled, letting out her hand. "Not until you show that you have kept your promise. Give me the emblem of greed… I have never broken a promise." Zorus stepped forward, taking in a deep breath. His hand hovered over hers for a moment, waiting to release the emblem. He reminded himself of what he was doing this for, then he released his grip. Willow caught the emblem, immediately filled with power, she smiled.

"Now let Zidal go, you dirty demon!" Zorus commanded again, staring into her emerald eyes. "I demand you free her this instant!"

"You'll get what I promised you, Zorus. Be patient." the queen raised the emblem above her and spoke. "For the recreation of Athreal, your soul is free!" she cackled as the emblem fell from her hand and shattered across the floor like glass. Zorus stared at the pile of rubble, fearful, knowing that what he had done could never be reversed. A bright golden soul lifted from the remains, and drifted across the sky, reuniting with the remains of Athreal. The queen ran her fingers through her black hair as she turned her back toward him. She waved him closer as she walked through the dimly lit hallway. "This way, you will gain your reward."

Zorus willingly followed, finding his way back to the things he loved. Knowing that this was the only way to get what he wanted. The stone walls brushed by him as doors passed him, a familiar sense filling his soul. The queen reached into her pocket and retrieved an obsidian key as they neared the end of the dark hallway. She halted at the final door, placing the key into the lock. She turned the key, pulling the door open. As she gestured inside, Zorus entered.

Zorus let out a breath of relief as Zidal slept, waiting for his return. He bent to her side and shook her, her eyes slowly opening. "Zorus?" she asked as he stood her upright. His only answer was an embrace. Tears fell from her eyes as she wrapped her arms around him. "You came for me."

Darkness encased the room as a loud slam played behind them, followed by the click of the key. Zorus's arms fell from Zidal, as he turned toward the door. The queen of the ugly trees peered through the barred window of the door. Zorus stepped toward the door and clasped the bars as he stared at the queen. "You broke your promise, demon!"

"Oh, but I didn't. I promised that you would be *reunited* with Zidal, and now you are." she smirked. "I am only doing what I was ordered to do. *He* would surely be grateful that I have you in possession."

"Death…" he murmured angrily under his breath as he glanced beneath him. "You will pay for this; *he* will never succeed!" Zorus spoke with a deadly tone.

"Will I? No. You are nothing but a mere hoswed trapped inside an inescapable cage." she smiled. "Good luck getting your *happy* ending." she remarked before walking away with an echoing cackle.

"Death! we're trapped again… I'm so sorry Zorus." Zidal cried.

"No, I'm sorry." Zidal looked at him, afraid and confused. Zorus sighed before he spoke. "I traded the emblem of greed to free you. I was such an idiot. I could have taken it and used my magic to save you, but I was thoughtless… greedy." he sighed.

Zidal smiled weakly, taking Zorus's hands in hers. "I forgive you." her voice softly rang as she wrapped him into a warming embrace. Zorus pulled her into a gentle kiss- claiming her as his own.

Zorus pulled away. His weak voice played as Zidal's fragile tears stained his uniform. "We can escape, but the queen doesn't know that… she doesn't know we can get out of… oh Death… oh Death!" Zorus stammered frantically.

"Is everything alright?" Zidal asked, falling from the embrace.

"The devilish fone knew the plan all along… I wasn't there to protect him. I took hold of the distraction. *He* took him, *he* took Courier! The tortures of my past are coming back to life, I am in pain because… he is." Zorus spoke in a painful rage. He coughed for a moment before continuing. "We must depart at once; we must save him before it's too late." Zorus let out his hand and waited for Zidal to take it before fading from reality.

S awoke in his cell, his back sore, his fingers bruised, and his bones aching. It was colder than he was used to, and his thin grey jacket did nothing against the cool air in the dungeon. His brother slept across the room, shivering the cold away as a breeze fell through the cracks in the damp walls. Through the bars on the large metal door, light fled into the cell, but it was scarce, and dull. S pushed himself up from the ground, the cuffs wrapped neatly around his tattered wrists, and stepped toward the door. Standing on his toes, and clutching the bars tightly, he was just tall enough to peer through the window.

He listened to the footsteps that neared the door, his Master walked along the hallway with a second being beside him, covered by his dripping body. They stopped at the door across from his cell, and S ever so carefully watched them. His Master's cackling voice played through the hallway, and he was joyful in his words as he spoke to the unknown creature. S listened to their conversation as they stood across the hall.

"Ah, you are such a brave soul to commit to such an experimental task. But, I promise, when I have completed the process, you will no longer be ill, better yet, immortal for all of time."

He listened to an unrecognizable voice that flowed from behind his Master's dark cloak. It was slow and sickly. "But why must you experiment on Darlids, why not something more disposable?"

"You see, Darlids are much easier to manipulate. This isn't just a game of trial and error; this has to do with logic. Believe in the power, and you will own it, young friend." His Master smiled, his light skin dripping onto the floor.

"But what about Death? Won't he take my soul? Won't my soul stray from my body before I have the chance to live?" it asked, anxiously waiting for an answer.

"That's what I am experimenting. If your soul can be bound to your body, you will never die. But you will have to serve him who gifts you this power, for he is not forgiving, he will not allow you mercy for your disobedience."

The being began to shiver, wondering in fear of his life, knowing that this was an impossible feat. "Doctor, I have little understanding of this experiment. How could one complete a process that makes one immortal? It's simply preposterous." The being coughed, reaching its arm out in front of itself.

"You see, our souls can be bound to our bodies in a way. When the mind is sealed to the soul, the soul can live eternally inside the body. Furthermore, you will have entitled yourself to infinite power- more than any Darlid could imagine. Trust me." his Master spoke calmly as he reached for the door handle.

"How experimental is this? Have you been able to accomplish this feat before? Doctor, I have so many questions." the being coughed.

"So many questions, indeed, I will answer them all in time, but we mustn't waste time, you're not the only one I will be experimenting on today." His Master cackled as he pulled the door toward himself, leading the sickly being into a laboratory of nightmares, a dream that would be impossible to escape from without knowing the twists and turns of the maze well enough.

S fell from the bars, letting go of the bitterly cold metal and quietly stepped back to his spot in the cell. He leaned against the wall and stared into the distance, fearing for the lives of the many Darlids who would perish. He could feel it in his soul, a warming feeling, one which made him weep on the inside. S fell onto the floor, staring at his brother, who slept peacefully, dreaming of the day when they could finally escape their prison and be reunited with a life of happiness.

S smiled before falling into a deep sleep, void of hope, void of courage, yet filled with fear.

Newfound Knowledge

Courier awoke in a familiar room, shackles wrapped around his wrists, chains leading to the walls, and his magic consumed. The dry-stone walls encased the darkness around him, only a shy amount of light bleeding through the cracks in the huge metal door. He couldn't remember anything past the emblem of life being destroyed and couldn't recall how he had arrived in that dreadful place.

He pulled against the chains for a moment, struck with the understanding that he would be unable to escape. He took in a deep breath as he reminisced in the mere thought of his past life. He glanced to his right, Alex slumped over, drugged into a deep sleep as he also was.

Courier grasped Alex's shoulder and shook him, the sound of clashing chains interrupting the silence. Alex's head bobbed, and his eyes opened. After a moment, he realized that he was not where he thought he was, and he quietly gasped as he searched his new surroundings, fearful of what was to come. "Wh-where are we?" he asked anxiously, a whisper of breaths following his voice. He examined the curious shackles wrapped around his wrists.

"The most dreadful place. I can only imagine what *he* is going to do to us. Whatever happens, you won't be the same person you were before." Courier remarked, drawing his finger over the cut on his lip. "He takes what you think you are and replaces it with the unknown."

"We must get out of here; we have to warn the others. There aren't many emblems left!" Alex remarked in a panic.

"Silence." Courier commanded as he glanced at the door. Clanking metal sounded from the hallway, a shadow looming over the scarce light. The shadow of the figure paused in front of the door, and the clicking lock turned before the door opened. The damenor stood in the shadows, spinning the key ring around his tattered finger as he stretched out his dripping wings. He ran his fingers through his slick dark hair, his fingers brushing against his horns.

"Your fate awaits you; *he* is ready when you are… wait, you never will be. Ahahahaha!" he cackled.

"I will not allow him to destroy my life once again, damenor!"

"How shameful, you don't recognize me, Courier." The damenor spoke smoothly as he stepped into the cell. "And of all the Darlids, you should."

"I remember who you *were, Kyron.* Who stands in front of me now is an entirely different being." Kyron leered as he stepped closer to the back wall, dangling the keys between his fingers. "Are you here to do *his* dirty work?"

"Unfortunately, *he* is stealing all the fun for himself, he especially ordered us to keep you alive, else I would have killed you in Blue River. But alas, I will still taste victory today." Kyron licked his lips as he stuck the key into the chains, loosening them from the wall. Courier stood from the ground as he remained in cuffs. Alex too stood, waiting for the worse to commence. The chains fell to the floor after Kyron let go. "I trust that you will follow my lead...? You always did." he recalled as he stepped through the doorway.

Courier and Alex unwilfully followed his steps through the broken hallway, following his lead. "I fought by your side for four years, and now here we are, against each other." Kyron stated. "It's too bad that the *heroes* are never powerful enough is it not? I should know… I used to be one."

"But then you fell, you betrayed us, you could have let your soul rest peacefully, but you turned away instead, joining the very beings that killed you." Courier stated.

Kyron chuckled. "I was naive at the time; I didn't realize the power that I could hold. I was only greedy, I wanted a second chance… for Zidal, but it is obvious now that I cannot be with her again until she chooses to follow. But now, you are the one that must choose."

"I will never join *his* side; you were foolish Kyron!"

"And you won't have to…" Reaching an unrecognizable area, a wooden door stood in front of them, one that was old and splintered, yet never seen before. Kyron wrapped his fingers around the metal knob as he twisted it, opening the door. He bowed as he gestured into the room. "Your destiny awaits you." Courier- Alex following behind- stepped into the large room before the damenor smirked and locked the door shut.

"Ah, so you have awoken. How pleasant this is." a shadowy voice played from the darkness. Lade stepped out of the shadows, grinning, tentacles emerging from his slender body. He took hold of their cuffs, reeling them closer to him.

"You can't make me broken, monster! I will stand in my right for all eternity."

"Ah, but that was never my intention, R." he stated. "After I'm done, you will be entirely unable to become broken."

"What are you demonstrating, you demon?!" Courier questioned as Lade attached Alex's cuffs to a string of chains falling from the wall. After tightening the chains to the wall, he slid his tentacle over Alex's dry lips, covering his mouth with his own viscous skin, disallowing him to speak. He glanced at his back, and unsheathed his sword, tossing it into the darkness, before moving to the side. Alex stood in panic, a dreadful feeling crossing his thoughts as Lade pulled Courier nearer to a large wooden post in the center of the nearly empty room.

"Ah, Courier, I thought you knew, but I admit, I didn't realize it until I had set you free." The dripping being forced Courier to bend on his knees as he connected his cuffs to a chain held to the post. He held him down with his forceful weight. Courier's breaths became irregular as he sat on his knees, staring into the Tall Being's eye. His empty eyes questioned all that he knew.

"Explain yourself, monster! I demand to *know*!"

"But you always have *known*... I thought it would be obvious. The way you've learned so quickly, your superior will to understand and to read, your immense knowledge of this world's history and facts of every rec and Darl in Shawon! Your soul is incredibly powerful, but not in the way I imagined. Encased inside your heart is the very emblem of knowledge!" Courier gasped, clutching his chest, an unbearable pain raging in his heart as it beat against his ribs. "And now, I must grasp your heart- the heart of all knowledge- and claim it as my own." He was speechless, nothing but a stream of tears falling from his empty eyes as he realized his mistake.

"But… how? None of this makes any sense. It can't be… it isn't possible. The emblem… it shouldn't… I can't..." he somberly stumbled in his words as he stared into the darkness, unable to understand his own meaning.

"It was prophesied that a human would find the emblems, and he led me to what I needed, even if he was unaware. I always expected that you and your brother would come to my use, but not like this. Now, dear friend, though I never thought that it would come to this, I must bask in your demise." he remarked as he studied Courier's anguish.

Courier spoke through his fearful tears. "After all my life, after every second I fought against you... I have failed. I never could outwit you, I never could. And now it has come to this…" he took in a shuddering breath. "Zorus.... What will he think? He has always protected me; he has always been by my side. I… I can't imagine..." Courier glanced at Alex, who stared at him in fear, wishing to speak, but unable to emit a sound.

Courier focused on Lade once again. His body trembled, he chose not to struggle, he knew that there was no way to escape. Lade bent to his side, placing the end of his tentacle against his shoulder. "Any last words, old friend?" he asked in a coarse voice, staring into his soul.

"I… I don't know. I never thought it would come to this after all of my training, after all I have learned. I know that I cannot win now, I am powerless and obscured. My heart is beating like a thousand together, screaming to know what will happen when I'm... *dead.*" he shuddered. "Let my brother know that I loved him, that my life was lived for him, that everything will turn right. Let him know that my life was not lost for an unknown reason, but that I served nobly, and that I did not forget him." Courier swallowed his tears. "Tell him to move forward, and to not let my death get in the way of their triumph. Oh Death… I cannot fathom… I cannot fathom being obscured from life… I am filled with anguish for those that need me."

Lade smiled with a joy of all that which was evil. "Then we shall commence in his honor…" A white tentacle drew forth from Lade's body and slowly merged into Courier's chest. He gagged with an aching feeling as the viscous skin wrapped around his heart, squeezing it. He bled through his mouth as his body was filled with unimaginable pain. "Thank you, old friend, you will be remembered. For the recreation of Athreal, your soul is free." At that moment, Lade tore back his arm, and ripped Courier's heart from his veins, breaking through his ribs and skin-blood and gore spilling from his dead chest. Courier's body followed his swift movement- a dark shadow flooding from his body, screaming in pain- before he fell to the ground, one final tear falling from his socket.

Alex attempted to scream through his mask, but he was only allowed tears as it silenced him. He pulled against the chains, a shock of electricity buzzing through his veins as crimson blood stained the ground. Lade held the heart joyfully as a red soul was drawn out of the heart and reunited with the others. He smiled menacingly as he dropped the bloody heart beside Courier's decaying flesh. He cackled as he vanished into the darkness

Alex, left alone in the darkness, craving to be set free, mumbled through his mask of lies. He waited, until, suddenly, a loud crashing sound fell against the wooden door. Again, the sound emitted until the splintered door fell from its hinges. Zidal and Zorus stood in the doorway, motionless, afraid. Tears fell from Zorus's eyes as he rushed across the length of the room, staring at the horrible sight left in front. His loving arms wrapped around the lifeless body that once was his brother, soaking his own attire in his blood. Sorrowful, yet vengeful whispers drained from his mouth as his brother's body melted into his arms. "No…" he softly whispered through his tears. "No!"

As his body dissipated, Zorus clutched his only remains. His skin turning black and melting into the pool of blood beneath, Zorus wept. Soon, all that was left was a memory. An overbearing sense of ennui draped his mind in sorrow as his uniform was coated in fading memories.

He sat still for a moment, running his fingers across the fabric of his brother's cape. He took in a deep breath, tearing his cape from his uniform, a memory to hold him close. Lifting his sword from his brother's sheath, he tied the fabric around the handle. He unsheathed his own sword and replaced it with the memory of his brother. Zorus stood from his place- no longer able to bear looking at his brother's resting place- tears draining from his eyes, anger embedded in his soul. He slowly stood, in pain and agony, stepping forward and passing Alex along the sidelines.

"Zorus!" Zidal yelled as he neared her, a disordered expression plastered across his face. She stood in front of the doorway, blocking him from proceeding, but was caught off guard when he forcefully shoved her aside. Zorus stepped outside of the room and continued to walk down the hallway. Zidal, regaining her balance, rushed after him, leaving Alex helpless in the room. "Zorus, wait! We need you..." she cried.

Zorus halted, and strictly turned toward her. "Shut it! This was *all* your fault, Zidal! This mission has torn me away from the things I love! *We* could have been hiding." he spoke in a morose tone.

"Don't go... I thought that you loved me."

He lifted his finger and bit his lip, struggling to speak through a tear-filled voice. "I tried to love you, but I only lied to myself because I took pity on you. Those words you said were all lies; the feeling was never real. You pretended to care for me, and in the end, all that is left is hurt. It was all just a distraction; it was all fraudulent and you knew it. That wasn't love, in reality, you only distracted me from the important things. I still blame you for everything that has happened!"

"Fine, I know that you resent me, I know that you are mourning, and that I broke my promise, but we still need you, we need to defeat *him*. Believe me, I am grieving too."

"Haven't you heard? There *is* no way to defeat *him*... I should know, I tried… R and I tried. But he only came back, more powerful than before, more power hungry than before. I'm tired of all of this Zidal, nothing can change my mind!" he stuttered. "Just let me be."

Zorus turned around once again, and began to walk, but stopped once again as a hand rested on his shoulder. He listened but did not face her. "But Zorus," She exclaimed, wiping a tear from her scarred face, "We need you; we can't win this war without your skill." she paused. "*I* need you."

"No, I'm done Zidal! No more chasing around the villain, no more torture, no more heartbreak! I can't handle it any longer, I tried to appease you, I tried to follow your lead, but all this has led to is a dead end with no way back! I could care less if I ever saw you again! Take this as my resignation…" Zorus spoke with a passion of anger. He turned from her, and walked down the hall, disappearing before he reached the end. Zidal reached out her hand as tears drenched her uniform. She fell to her knees, covering her violet eyes.

S awoke to a bubbling sound emitting from the echoing hallways. A shadow loomed over him as the light from the hallway was covered. S glanced at his brother, who slowly opened his empty eyes, startled by the unknown noise. "Zorus… what is that?" he asked, fearful of his Master's doing. "It doesn't sound natural. It…" R ceased to speak as the sound of a clicking lock played from the large metal door.

"I don't know." S spoke almost silently, in fear as to what was to come. The tension rose, the handle of the door spun, and the door creaked open. A formless, dripping being of darkness stared into S's empty eyes as it slid across the cold stone flooring. R gasped as it neared him, his heart struck with fear, he ran into his brother's arms, holding himself closely. "Oh Death! What in the Abyss is that?!" the shapeless being tilted its darkened head, or what seemed to be its head, as it shut the large door behind him. The room was shadowed in a coat of distraught and fearful thoughts.

"I am Kellac, now blessed with life eternal, and the task to torture." a familiar voice emitted from the being's body, now more ominous and fuller. The being cackled as its body smeared across the floor. "You best prepare for an unbelievably wicked time. Master has commanded me." The oozing beast held its place as its skin continually reformed over its broken bones.

"What are you going to do to us, demon?" S asked, never removing his sight from the ghastly being.

"For the time being, nothing but an introduction, an answer to the questions held deeply inside your heart. I can sense your questions, go ahead, please ask them." it prodded, anxiously waiting for their voices.

S raised his voice, waiting for its answer. "What are you?"

"I am the first successful artificial Broken Soul, created with a power unknown to Darlids. With this power, I will live on."

“Broken Soul? That’s impossible, life is finite.” R started, backing away from the living corpse. “All of my studies have pointed the soul to the afterlife, a body can’t accept a soul when it’s unstable, decaying. How are you alive?”

“Pure will, young Darlid, pure will. With the right convincing thoughts, my soul is bound to my body, and here I stay, immortal, forever living, obeying the one who allows me to.” its voice bubbled vigorously. “Death will not force a soul into a place that it does not long to be, especially when that soul won’t follow him.”

“Why did you accept the Master's experiment? How did you know that you would survive?” S asked fearfully.

“I admit, I was afraid, clueless of the power that I would be granted with, but I was dying already, I wanted a second chance. He convinced me to live after my death.” The shapeless form bobbed as it spoke.

“How did you die? Was it of natural causes, or did *he* kill you?” R asked fearfully as the figure slid toward the large door.

“Once I was convinced, he took a knife from the counter, stabbed my heart, and drew it through my flesh until it reached my left thigh. I bled out, I screamed in pain, my body began to decay, but my soul lived on. Soon the pain left me, and I stood as what you see now, a decaying body filled with infinite power.” it cackled as it reached for the handle, opening the door toward himself. “I have elsewhere to go. Master will arrive soon.” It let itself out of the room, slamming the door behind him.

R let go of his brother and fell to the ground in relief. S too sat against the wall, waiting for the day that they could finally escape.

No Return

Wiping a tear from her eye, Zidal stood from the ground and turned toward the broken wooden door. She stepped toward the darkness, and after she entered, she sighed. "Zorus is gone Alex, he really left. I… I think it's my fault, I pushed him too far. If I only treated him better… if I just let him get what he wanted, Courier would've..." her somber voice played as she reached for the rusted key left unneatly on the counter behind Alex. She placed the key into the lock on the cuffs and twisted it to the left. The shackles immediately fell off of Alex's wrists. "What are we to do?" she asked in a quiet whisper.

Alex lifted his hands to his mouth and began to pry against the disgusting gag which was placed over his lips. It slowly began to rip off, and after a moment, his lips were free. "We… we have to find him, Zidal. I've got to talk to him, no matter what it takes." Alex spoke with urgency as he stepped toward Courier's remains. Nothing but a dark puddle of decay and tattered clothing sat where he once did. Alex bent down and grasped the strap of his blood-stained satchel from the ground before sliding it over his head.

Zidal waited, still, at the opposite side of the room, letting the key fall from her hands. It clattered as it hit the stone floor. "We'll never find him, he's too good at hiding. We may never see him again." Zidal stated, brushing her fingers over her scars. "It may be better to just move on and find the last remaining emblems." she remarked, though she was too upset at the thought, knowing that she would miss him more than any other soul.

Alex, while walking back to her, frowned. "We can't just let him be like this. Who knows what he would do to himself? Is there a portal nearby? I have an idea where he could be."

"I don't even know where we are Alex, let's get out of this twisted maze first." she spoke with a softness in her heart as she stepped through the doorway. Alex followed behind, the muddied walls of the corridor falling behind as they walked. They passed by many cells, the cries of strangers flowing through the air as they neared the exit.

The final doorway stood before them, reaching out toward them, begging them to leave. Zidal took the handle and pulled the door toward herself, an unexpected terrain resting behind. The air was warm, and the sun beat against them. The grass was soft, and the air smelled sweet. Zidal began to walk into the sunlight, warming her empty heart. "I know this place; I've been here before. But where did that dungeon come from?" she asked looking behind her. Nothing but an endless meadow grew beyond her sight. Shocked by what she saw, she retraced her steps. "And why has it disappeared?" Alex followed her for a moment, without responding, before she stopped, staring into the distant horizon.

"Where are we?" Alex asked as the pain of the mind wavering caressed his every thought.

"The Careless Meadows. Darlids come here in order to free themselves from their burdens. I came here after Kyron *died,* I wanted to free myself from my grief. But it only made the load heavier." Zidal sighed. "Here, I *do* know where a portal is. Follow me." Zidal claimed as she walked into the distance. "See that patch of flowers? That's where we are going." she pointed into the short distance. Alex nodded, taking in a deep breath. "So, where do you suppose he has gone?"

"Treesy. It's secluded and unknown to most of this world. If I know Zorus well enough, that's where he would be." Zidal wiped another tear from her eye as she stood in the patch of lilac flowers. She stretched out her fingers and slid them together, a portal appearing in the empty sky.

"Let's go." she said before stepping into the portal. Alex followed, stepping through the familiar dark substance. Drained of hope, he carried onward. After only moments inside the portal, he found himself stepping through another one, entering a familiar forest. Alex began to walk through the evergreen trees, following the secluded pathway toward the small village. Wooden buildings began to appear between the trees, a Darlid or two stepping by. Alex passed by two buildings before he stopped in front of the Mossery. "Well, are we going inside?"

"Zidal, I need to talk with him alone. Stay here, would you, I'll be back soon.`` Though skeptical, she nodded, stepping to the side, and leaning against the exterior wall. Alex took in a breath and pulled the glass door toward himself slowly. The small bell rang before he stepped inside, allowing the door to shut. Darlids sat at the dinner tables, talking, laughing, and enjoying themselves. It was busy, and cheerful, but he knew that sorrow resided too.

Alex searched the area and began to walk, before he was quickly stopped by the leaf headed Darlid, carrying a tray of drinks. "How may I help you, human?" he asked with a shy voice.

"Where's Zorus? I need to speak with him."

Cleave pointed at the back counter and sighed. "I've never seen him like this. He's been a sorrowful sight, haven't got a word out of him aside from his orders. Maybe you could talk some sense into him." he gave Alex a quick pat on the back before walking toward one of the round tables.

As Alex walked down the aisle, he stepped toward the back counter. Noticing his messy blonde hair, and his slumped over figure, he found his way to where he needed to be. When he reached the counter, he stood behind Zorus. He was wearing a shadow grey hoodie and a pair of black pants, spinning a blue bottle around his finger, labeled *spicy snart venom*. He didn't look up, but still, he spoke. "Thought that you might try to convince me to come back. I bet Zidal's not too far either, in front of the diner I suppose." he lifted his head for a moment as he took a swig of the liquid, immediately dropping his head back down. "So, what's the point of you coming all the way here? To get the same answer I gave Zidal? I resigned, kid."

"Zorus, I didn't come here to bring you back, I understand that this is a tough time for you." Alex assured him, as he sat on an open stool beside him.

"So then, what are you *actually* here for?" Zorus took another sip of his poison. "To mock my pain?"

"No. Zorus, we are all in pain because of what has happened. I wanted to make sure you were okay. I thought you might have wanted someone to talk to. I'm here to listen." Alex spoke calmly, as he shifted his position.

Zorus sighed, tapping his foot against the wooden floor. "No Alex, I'm not *okay*, I'll *never* be the same Darlid again. What happened broke me, what I witnessed will never be erased from my mind. I'm so lost Alex, all I can do is wait and watch while the world burns." he sighed. "What happened will never be forgotten, the blood has seeped into my mind and now it has stained, leaving me lost in a world that will never let me rest. Always… always the memories will come screaming back, the torture, the pain, the screams… I can still hear them, as if they're calling me back to my horrendous past, waking me up from a dream and pulling me back into the nightmare I thought was gone forever."

Zorus shuddered, taking a sip of his drink. "All the memories are flooding back, drowning me in sorrow. I can see it all so clearly, the blood, the cuts and burns, the knives and syringes laying across the counter, my bones weak and helpless. The shadows coming to life. *His* dastardly grin and his malicious gleaming eye watching, wanting us to suffer. I still feel the pain, I can still remember the wish to escape, the need for freedom, the desire for my brother's suffering to end… but it never did. The torture always returned, the pain always balanced on the tip of the knife, the scars on my skin there always there to remind me of the pain!"

Zorus leaned forward, pulling his hand through his golden hair gently. Tears bled from his empty eyes, staining the wooden counter with sorrow. Zorus took in a deep breath as he continued. "I remember how much I wept, I remember my fear and anxiety. I sometimes wish that I could return to the past and fight for myself, for my brother. I wish I had the ambition to make things right sooner before I became this... monster." he leaned back as he took another sip of the venom. "Listen, kid, the world is never in your favor, it always throws tasks at us to keep us busy. Some beings get the easier tasks, and few are given pain, suffering, and loss. Alex, those of us who take on those types of tasks, come back from them broken, unable to return to the life we once knew. It's not difficult to tell who has the *easy* tasks.

"Look, the world is full of suffering, we live to suffer, we breathe to suffer. Everything we do brings us closer to another terrible lie of a glorious life." Zorus wiped his cheeks, as he took in another shuddering breath. "But after all, Alex, if everything was bliss… well then, the world would be immensely boring." he sighed and glanced at Alex.

"I wish I could understand how difficult it must be to lose someone you were so close to, but it's only been a few hours, Zorus, it takes time to heal." Alex leaned toward him, the flaps of his coat dropping toward the floor.

"Hours? It's been weeks. Alex... you took a portal, didn't you?" Alex nodded. "Don't you listen? Taking portals *are* shortcuts, but time still passes. It could feel like only a moment walking through a portal, when in reality, you have been absent for weeks. That's what it feels like every moment that he's been gone. Weeks..." he spoke with a morose tone. "I'm so tired, Alex, my bones ache, my mind will never still, my eyes won't close. But there is no way back, there is no way to change my mistake, there is no way to return to the past to make sure *he* dies. None of this would have happened if *he* just died!" Zorus lifted his drink and took a sip. The liquid swished as he placed the bottle on the counter. "Oh Death, I wish *he* would just have died!"

"We still have a chance, Zorus, we still have a chance to defeat him, to get revenge. You still have the chance to rest your mind. Imagine how many more souls you could save." Alex remarked.

"Heh, there were only two Darlids that had enough power to defeat *him*, my brother and me. And even at that, he still came back. No Darlid could defeat *him.*"

"What about Death?"

"Death is no Darlid, he's a force- a god. He guides souls away from their bodies when they are too unstable. He seldom kills things at will unless it is necessary. It is difficult to persuade him to act against his own will. " he sighed. "Look, kid, I told you before, I resigned. I'm tired of fighting, I'm tired of losing, I'm tired of this idiotic war. And I know that there's no way to defeat him without… without… Death! I miss him!" Zorus's voice rang somberly as he slammed his bottle against the counter, venom spilling onto the surface. He sighed, his voice ringing quietly. "What… what were his last words? I know that you were there."

Silence rang through the shadowed room for a moment before Alex chose to speak. "He didn't want his death to get in the way of you fighting to the end. He loved you Zorus, he wanted you to know that he did everything for you." Alex remarked. "He wanted you to press on."

Alex grasped the strap of the bloody satchel and bowed his head as he removed it from his figure. He held it in front of Zorus, waiting for him to accept the item. Zorus glanced at Alex, noticing the satchel in his hand. He raised his eyebrow. "Where'd you get that?" he asked as he reached toward it and wrapped his fingers around the leather strap, taking it from him. He lifted it over his thin body, allowing it to rest against his side.

"It was sitting in the debris. I thought that you would want it." Alex noted.

"Thank you." Zorus replied as he opened the flap, reaching into its contents. He retrieved *The Book of Emblems* from the empty space and stared at it, drawing his finger across the textured cover. Flipping open to the middle of the book, phrases were obviously annotated, notes left behind from his brother. He scanned the pages slowly. "Courier... he was always good at studying." he stated as he turned the page. "The Broken Souls would surely have an advantage if you didn't retrieve this satchel." he flipped the page again, scanning the words. "This..." he stared at the page blankly. "Meet me at the mansion..." without any further explanation, Zorus disappeared, leaving no trace of his existence behind.

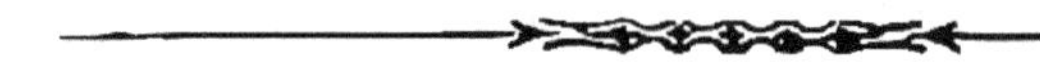

S awoke in the blackness of night, anxiety corroding his mind, the shackles tightened around his wrists. He glanced at his brother, who slept peacefully, no nightmares resting in his fragile thoughts. Moonlight drenched the stone room, creating shadows, monsters about the room. S sat; fear struck in his heart as the shadows crept through the room.

His own shadow rose against the wall across from him, a chill ran down his spine as he stared at it. The figure matched his exactly, yet for an unknown reason, a bright moonlight created its empty eyes and mouth. It grinned at S as it took form, ceasing to mimic his movement becoming a sentient being. "Wh... what are you?" S asked in fear as it stared into his soul.

"I am you, the darkness that resides in your soul. The fear and the demonic character which lies within your magic. Don't be afraid." it spoke in a low and shadowed voice, filling his heart with fear. "Ask your questions, I know you have them."

"What do you want from me?" he asked, staring into its sharded eyes.

"What do I want...? I want your soul, it belongs to me, there is no escape from my wrath." it spoke charmingly. "But of course, your soul is *yours*, it accepted me. You cannot control me without my consent, and I cannot control your soul without its consent."

"Why did my soul accept you?"

The shadow grinned as it began to step around the room. "Accept me? You are an unnatural being, a monster. With the potion's assistance, I corroded your soul, entered it without permission, and now it relies on me. Without the activator inside you, I would slowly consume your being, your soul is unnaturally powerful, delicious… More powerful than any other soul that exists." S swallowed in fear as the shadow halted over him. "I am a shadow demon… your friend." it rested its shadowed hand on S's shoulders, breathing quietly into his ear. S shuddered as its fingers peeled off of his shoulders, disappearing into the shadows. The being began to follow the light through the room, waiting for the soft sound of his prisoner's voice.

"Why are you here? Just to haunt me?" S asked, brushing his hand against the cold stone floor.

"Here?" he repeated. "I am here to free us. You are not the only one who is trapped. You see, I am powerless when you wear those shackles. I yearn to be set free, to destroy the very being that granted me your body. Only then will I be satisfied, and then I will leave you until you ask for my aid." the shadow leered. "You *are* going to help me, right?" S nodded, fearful of his appearance. "Good. Follow my instructions, and we will free ourselves from this dungeon. Then my shadow can be free, yet still bound to your being." S glanced at his brother and whimpered. "Ah, we shan't forget *my* brother."

"Your brother?"

"Indeed, my brother, Corbin, resides in his soul, craving the same thing that I do." the shadow remarked. "Though you cannot see him, for he is not your demon."

"Do *you* have a name?"

“I am he who they call Astaroth.” the shadow voiced cunningly. The light of the moon began to dissipate, and Astaroth smiled. “Until the morrow.” the shadow voiced before fading into darkness.

Repeated Misery

Alex stood from the wooden stool, confused, almost afraid. He stared at the entrance of the diner and stepped slowly through the maze of tables set in front of him. He passed by each of the tables, not a word dripping from his mouth as he reached toward the handle of the glass door. He pushed against the door and stepped into the woods as the bell gave a gentle ring. Glancing to the left, he watched as Zidal stretched out and stood. "How'd it go?" she asked somberly. Alex shook his head. "What now, then?"

"I don't know, he told me to meet him at the mansion." Alex took in a deep breath as he stepped through the forest. He could feel Zidal following behind him, her shallow footsteps keeping him allure. They passed by the wooden structures beyond them, distracted by the constant pain of their mistakes. The tall spruce wood trees shadowed over them as they exited the village, following the dirt path to the mansion. Birds sang as the sun gleamed overhead, light peeking between the needles in the trees.

A peaceful feeling loomed overhead as they traveled through the forest, though they trod on somberly. Through the midst of the trees stood the mansion, standing proudly. Alex and Zidal stepped toward the entrance, the large white doors standing before them, the skull carving greeting them. Alex slowly lifted his fist and gently knocked against the door. Footsteps rang through the hallway before the door opened, Zorus waiting for them. He wore his uniform once again, his sheath, holding his brother's sword, resting on his back. The satchel lay over his shoulder, resting against his left hip. Though he looked tired, a dark tint under his eyes, his hair done messily, and his emotion distraught, he gave a somber smile. "What's going on?" Alex asked.

"Follow me, I can explain." He gestured into his home as he walked through the hallway. Zidal and Alex followed him closely behind. The thin wooden walls of the hallway widened as they entered a gorgeous kitchen, counters crafted from the finest marble, blackwood bookshelves lacing the walls. There wasn't a section of the walls which wasn't decorated in books. The collection was enormous, only read through by one who no longer could. A table carved from the same material stood in the center of the room, matching chairs fitted with black velvet cushions surrounding it. A lavish chandelier draped overhead, hundreds of finely carved crystals hanging above.

Zorus pulled one of the chairs from under the table and tossed the satchel onto the surface before taking a seat. He then gestured the others to sit on the chairs beside him. Alex chose to sit by his right as Zidal seated herself on the chair by his left. Staring at his uniform, Zidal spoke. "Zorus, are you returning to your position in the Galaxy Knights?" Zidal asked. "It's not too late, I still haven't reported to the king."

Zorus let out a breath. "Nothing could bring me back to that Abyss of a profession! No, I am only going to return to the battle, until it is won, and we are freed from the torture. I will then be finished with my work, at peace, though still lost."

"But what has changed your mind?" Alex asked, staring at the satchel on the surface of the table.

"What is written in the pages of this book." Zorus lifted the flap on the satchel and retrieved the *Book of Emblems* from its contents. Finding the lace bookmark inside the pages, Zorus opened the book and placed his finger underneath a paragraph, which had markings beside it. "Here," he declared, "My brother knew well what was going to happen, it was far worse than we had initially imagined. Only, he didn't tell us, he wanted to protect us."

"What does it say?" Zidal asked, staring at the page, unsure of the misery which would be casted onto her people.

"There will come a day when a human shall find his way into the portal and, no matter the consequences, he will find the emblems, each of the eight, and they shall all be released one by one, whether by the Broken Ones or the living. Only fate shall know who will succeed in this dreadful battle." he paused for a moment, placing his finger under

another paragraph. "*The emblems, once each of the souls are released by the hands of the Broken Ones, and activated by the Drex potion will reincarnate Athreal, Son of the Dying Star, Bringer of Torment. Then they will be released once again, fused into one mass of power, and broken once again into twenty-three pieces. Each piece will find its way to a powerful soul, who yearns to live for eternity, and there it will rest until the body will accept it, recreating each of the living demons.*"

Zorus lifted his head and glanced at each of them, drawing his finger across the page. He pointed to another paragraph before continuing. *"Twenty-three days shall commence, and the world will be encased in darkness, disasters of a large variety will take place. Rec will fight against rec, and the death toll shall rise until there are none left but the Broken Ones. And the siege will not end until they can escape, and rule over all worlds."*

"This is much more disastrous than I expected." Alex remarked, rereading the words written across the pages of the book.

"I'm afraid that if they accomplish their goal, if they gain each of the emblems, there will only be suffering, there will be no way to *win.* We would fight against twenty-three demons, each one more powerful than the last. There will be no chance for mercy, there will only be torture until the Broken Souls are the only beings left alive. We need to find and destroy the remaining emblems before this horror comes to life." Zorus remarked.

"Every single living demon would rise again? I only imagined it to be a fable, it *was* only a fable. Their souls were shattered during Gehalla, they can't return." Zidal recalled in a voice of rage.

"Fable? It is written in prophecy, inside a book which the Darlids of the war wrote, having knowledge of the power which the demons held."

"There is no possible way for us to defeat every demon that ever lived, only the Shaens of Achnor had that ability. I'm afraid that if we don't destroy even one emblem, we will perish." Zidal remarked somberly. "How are we to accomplish this? The Olks are far greater in power than we, and there are so few emblems left. They are sure to reclaim all of the emblems before we have the chance to search for them."

"Here," Zorus flipped the page and found yet another marked passage, *"Before the potion is drunk, there is still a way to defeat the being that possesses the attributes of the emblems, the leader of the Broken Ones. Only the king of this world knows what can defeat it."*

Alex stared at Zorus. "Then we must meet with the king."

"Indeed, we must. Surely, he will have more information regarding the remaining emblems, and he may be willing to fight with us and aid us in finding and destroying the remaining pieces before it becomes too late." Zorus remarked.

"Are you sure? He could be reluctant in giving us such precious information. And he seldom wishes to use his skill in war." Zidal remarked.

"Yes, indeed. But we must take our chances, I believe that he should have been guiding us on our journey from the beginning. With him by our side, we would have been able to destroy each of the emblems, and the Broken Souls would be no trouble. It may take time to persuade him." Zorus claimed.

"Time? I'm running out of time; I may not be able to find the emblems for much longer." Alex acknowledged, noticing that the pain of the mind wavering was becoming less and less apparent in each of its episodes.

"The kid's right, we have to find those emblems before it's too late, destroy them no matter the cost. The Broken Souls are searching for the emblem of strength at this very moment, and we are just sitting here. Because it has been found once, there isn't much doubt that they can find it. I believe that we must find it, at all costs." Zorus agreed, as he closed the book. He took hold of the leather satchel and lifted the flap, sliding the book inside. He then tightened the lace and lifted the strap over his head, holding in his anxious thoughts.

"Shall we search for the emblem of strength then?" Zidal asked, desperate for the adventure to finish. "Where must we go and what must we accomplish?"

"We must, but it is much more important that we enlist the king himself to guide us for the remainder of this mission. Without him, I am certain that we will fail." Zorus declared. "The emblem of strength is the only remaining emblem that has a foretold location. Do you still have the map, Zidal? We should know where we will be going after we meet with the king." Zidal nodded as she reached into her pocket. Her hands caressed the edges of the paper as she lifted it from its contents, placing it atop the table. Zorus took the paper and unfolded it, laying it across the surface. He pressed his hands against the page, flattening out the map. He studied the page for a moment, placing his finger on Krysal city. "There, the emblem of strength is hidden within the depths of the city. Now we must certainly travel to Krysal."

"This is incredible news; we couldn't have more luck." Zidal stated.

"Then it is settled. We will travel to Krysal palace and speak to the king regarding the emblems and the destruction of the leader of the Broken Souls, then we will collect the emblem of strength, and finally, it is Alex's job to find the emblems of love and knowledge." Zorus finished.

Knowing something tender, so fragile, yet needed to complete the task, Alex spoke. "But the emblems of knowledge and love… they..."

"No, Alex, it is too important to put aside. I don't care where the emblems are, how difficult the tasks are, or how difficult it will be to destroy them, their souls need to decay so that the Broken Souls will not succeed. And even if we destroy one of the emblems, we still must destroy the Master of the Broken Souls."

Alex stared into Zorus's eyes, and took in a deep breath, knowing that his words would change everything. "Zorus, the emblem of love… it's…"

"It's none of our concern at the moment, we must begin our journey toward Krysal, we must retrieve the emblem of strength before it is too late." he took in a deep breath before standing from his seat. Zidal reached for the map and neatly folded it into her pocket. "Come, we cannot waste time." Zidal stood from her seat, followed by Alex, as they began to walk down the hallway. "Alex, you're going to need a weapon before we can continue." Alex reached toward his sheath, recalling the memories as his hand passed across the empty space.

Zorus stood in front of a dark oak door and wrapped his hand around the nob. He pulled the door toward himself and waited for the others to step inside. He followed them into the small, dimly lit room. There were more bookshelves lined against the side wall, cluttered with knowledge, two black couches standing parallel to them on the opposite wall. Above each couch, a sword was neatly placed as decor. Zorus stepped onto the soft cushion of the leftmost couch and reached for the sword. He gently lifted it from the hooks it was balanced on before stepping off of the couch.

Zorus stood before Alex and held the sword toward him. Alex took the sword from his hands and studied the blade. The grip was black as the night, yet it was easy to hold. The crossguard, lined with silver, bent upward at each end. The pommel was a silver sphere, a dark crystal fused in the center. The blade was sharp, used often, having seen many battles. "This sword is stunning." Alex remarked as he sheathed it. "Thank you."

"That sword was the first I owned." Zorus mentioned somberly, staring at the walls. He rested his hand against the wood and sighed.

"You're giving it to me, just like that?"

Zorus turned toward the door and stepped through, showing the others to the exit. "It suits you. Though the memories haunt me, the blade did a glorious work. Use it well." Alex nodded as he stepped through the front door. He followed Zidal through the forest, a feeling of peace and confidence looming overhead. The night had coated the sky with a blanket of stars, the light dimly lighting the mansion. The air was sweet, and Alex's mind was free, as he stepped through the growth. His joy lasted only for a moment before he turned back. He stopped and stared at Zorus. Zorus stood at the open door of his mansion, unmoving, but only a breath.

Alex walked back to the entrance of the mansion and stood by his side, staring into the hallway of memories. Zidal quickly noticed their absence and returned to the mansion. "Zorus? What are you doing?" she asked as she watched him lift the satchel over his head.

"Saying one last goodbye." he disclosed, staring into the open abyss. He held the satchel before him and smiled as he recalled the forbidden memories held inside. His grip tensed for a moment, before he let out one more anxious breath, delaying his decision. He tossed the satchel into the hallway.

"What...?" Alex voiced as Zorus reached into his pocket. He retrieved a small stone and bent beside the satchel. "Zorus, what are you doing?" he asked, reaching toward him. Taking in one last breath, Zorus applied pressure to the stone, a glorious lavender spark igniting as he dropped the stone onto the satchel, watching the flame consume the memories of his past.

S awoke in a cold sweat, screams filling the dense hallways, the sound of a knife cutting through skin playing closely behind. Yet another year had passed since the first Broken Soul had been created, yet the experiments never ceased. Glancing to the opposite side of the room, S's breaths calmed as his brother rested on the beaten down mattress. He stood from his place and walked to the mattress, the shackles tightened around his wrists, keeping his demon from destroying him. S placed his thin hand on his brother's shoulder, shook him gently and whispered. "Courier… wake up." R's eyes began to open slowly, confused, and afraid. He stared at his brother, realizing that screams played behind the thick walls.

"What's happening, Zorus?" R asked, rubbing his eyes. "Is *he* attempting to break another soul, endeavoring to make Darlids immortal?"

S nodded, sitting beside his brother. "He is trying to make them have form, a better body that won't melt too quickly… an immortal army." S shivered as he listened to the screams. Screams of pain and suffering and sorrow, screams that would embed into his mind forever, haunting his dreams. "He is experimenting on these Darlids, these innocent beings so that he can have an army… so that he can make us immortal with perfection."

"No… we can't have that happen, Zorus. We have to protect ourselves from these tortures, from his experiments. We need to escape before he even has the chance to begin the process. If we become broken, I fear that society will never accept us, I fear that we will be cast away, or even tortured more than we have been here." R embraced his brother as tears fell from his eyes. "The demons are corrupting us, we will never be the same, we will never be *normal* again." R looked past his brother, at his own shadow, which swayed across the wall. It mimicked him, though its voice ran deep inside him.

"Core, the demons, they are here to help us. Haven't you spoken to yours? Haven't you learned from it?"

"I have, but I don't trust demons. How can I know if the shadow won't harm me?"

"They crave freedom just as we do. They gifted us with power so that we can all be freed from this prison, so we may be able to destroy Master and live in peace." S glanced at the back wall and watched as his shadow grinned at him freakishly.

R waited in silence for a moment, listening to the screams play in the near distance. "I don't want the torture to continue, I want to be free, living amongst the peaceful ones. When can we be free and save the world, like in the stories?" he asked shyly.

"I'm afraid that the stories are only fantasies. We can try and we can fight for our freedom, but still, we may never be able to escape this prison, we may never escape the torture."

Course Through Winter's Gorge

The flame was an arduous memory left only as a lingering reflection in Zorus's dark, empty eyes. The wood of the mansion slowly burned to ash, crumbling to the ground as the fire cackled. The sparks of the fire flew through the dry air, sizzling before they dissipated into the darkness of night. The night sky was lined with a sullen lace of smoke and the glory of the luminous fire. Zorus licked his dry lips as he stared into the lavender embers, the pains of his past slowly burning away.

Zidal and Alex stared at the flame in awe, the embers burning brightly as the memories perished. Alex looked at Zorus and spoke calmly, yet Zorus never moved his sight from the flame. "Why did you ignite your home?" he asked, curious to his decision.

Zorus took in a deep breath, the smoke warming his body. "They mustn't have a trace of where I have been, or where I am going. With Courier gone… they'll be searching for me, *he* will want me dead at all costs." he spoke mournfully, and at the sound of his brother's name, he fell into sorrow. "It's all a memory that will be forgotten in time. All that matters now is that we destroy the remaining emblems, and *him*. Then I will finally be at rest."

The flame began to die into the night as Zorus looked into the distance. He nodded somberly at Zidal as he began to walk into the distance, leaving everything he once loved behind. His shadow followed him mindfully, replicating his somber movement precisely. The light of the nearly full moons bled through the branches of the evergreen trees and fell upon the shadow, creating a shallow smile upon its face for just a moment.

There was only silence as they stepped through the forest, trodden with needles. Soon, they found their way to a crevice of trees where the portal could be opened. Zorus glanced at the others and spoke with a morose tone. "The portal on the summit of Winter's Gorge is the nearest to Krysal city. We must begin our journey now, for the trek will be difficult."

Zorus stood himself straight and interlocked his fingers as he stared into the empty space. The view before him spun before it became a dark space, an abyss, where the portal stood. He stepped to the side and gestured his hand toward the portal, allowing the others to enter before him. Zidal gave a shy smile and wrapped her fingers around the stick of her scythe before entering the portal. She disappeared almost instantly. Alex followed behind, glancing at Zorus before walking into the Abyss. He too, dissolved into the darkness.

Zorus let out a deep sigh and looked into the portal. He glanced behind him at the dying flame, and stared into its brightness for a moment, letting go of his past before he stepped into the portal. It closed as he entered, leaving behind the life he desired most. Stepping through the darkness felt quick, and soon he appeared on the summit of Winter's Gorge, once again beside Alex and Zidal.

Zidal stood at the edge of the cliff, staring through the stars, witnessing the glorious palace and city from afar. Alex joined her side, and Zorus slowly stepped to their place. "We have a long way to walk, Krysal city lies at the foot of Winter's Gorge." Zidal remarked clearly as she smoothed her fingers over the scars on her shadowed cheeks. "It may take us a day to reach the castle."

"We don't have any provisions." Alex mentioned with urgency.

"We'll have to provide somehow. Hoswed are easy to find on this mountain if we get desperate, and the crystal trees grow a sweet fruit that should be in season." Zidal described as she turned toward the slope. "We best begin our trek now, or we'll never make it to Krysal. But Olkned was erected on Winter's Gorge. We must be careful." the others silently agreed to her thought as they began to walk through the frozen air.

The trek through the snow on the mountain was much more difficult than it had been the time before. The snow had deepened since they had last journeyed on top of Winter's Gorge, and they were higher up, as this time, they did not have a quick ride down the slope of the mountain. Their footprints left a mark of their arrival, and a track to where they had gone, leading any Broken Soul that found the prints to them. Though time was anxious, and they had little of it before they needed to find the emblem of strength, they continued at the same pace throughout the journey to save their energy.

Zorus stayed very wary as he trekked through the mountain, always searching for something, anything that could be lurking by him, searching for his presence. He knew that he would no longer be safe, that the Broken Souls were searching for his every movement, waiting to capture him, and to destroy his soul. His left hand always stayed near his sheath, and he was anxious to begin a battle, yet they never attacked, and the journey was silent.

Soon, they had found their way down the slope of the mountain, and nearing Olkned. Their minds began to fill with anxiety as they came closer to passing it. Zorus halted in a shadowed area, where it was impossible for the Olks to notice them and glanced at the others as they ceased their movement. He rested his back against the mountain wall and quickly glanced around the area, assuring to himself that there was not another being in the area to interrupt them. Zorus spoke with great urgency. "I must advance… without being seen. I fear that the Broken Souls will find me, but I must complete this journey."

"What do you mean Zorus, we'll be fine as long as we walk through the shadows." Zidal assured.

Zorus shook his head. "I know that they will find me, they are looking for me at this very moment. I cannot risk faring too close, Zidal. Do not fret, I promise that I will meet with you again, just a mile down the slope of the mountain." Zorus gave a weak smile.

"Are you sure about this? What if we get caught in a battle, and cannot win without your expertise?" Alex asked, unsure of his decision.

"The Olks are strong and steadfast in their skill, but it is not you who they desire at this time." Zorus said as he glanced into the city of Broken Souls, melted skin spread across the snow, pieces of the mountain broken and tortured. He watched as shadows passed across the ground. "I must go now… I'm sorry." he remarked before vanishing from their sight.

Zidal glanced at Alex with astonishment. A somber smile fell from her violet eyes as she stared into the distance. "Do you really believe that he was telling the truth? Do you think that he is waiting for us later down the slope, or did he decide that he won't complete this journey after all?" she asked as she began to step out of the hidden area.

Alex spoke as he followed her, careful of his steps. "I trust Zorus, he can be frightening at times, and show difficult emotions, but he would never abandon those that he cares for. He would never let us fall. He will come for us if we get into trouble." Alex declared as he stepped through the snowy terrain.

They waded through the snow silently, peering toward the village of Broken Souls, fearful of what could be waiting for them inside, what could be watching for the perfect moment to attack. Yet, all that could be seen through the passage were the stone buildings laid across the stone wall and the endless mounds of snow burying any sight of an Olk. An ominous feeling shadowed their bodies as they neared Olkned, and though they walked distantly from it, and hid themselves in the shadows casted from the mountain, they still felt the uneasiness of the Olks lurking nearby. The shadows of Broken Souls seemed to crawl across the stone of the mountain, finding a way to hide from their enemies.

Neither of them caused for a sound to be made, not even the whisper of their own voices, other than the slow, repeated fall of their shallow breaths. Anxiety rose through their minds as they carefully followed the pathway through the mountain, a constant pain eroding their chests as their hearts pounded heavily. Zidal's eyes were full of worry, a somber feeling drifting through her soul as she dragged her hand across the rough stone. Her limbs were tense, and her body ached not of physical pain, but emotional pain. The emotions that were drawn out in her mind were so intense, that the feeling could not be described.

Though it seemed as if they had spent hours passing by Olkned, the city of fear, they found their way around it quickly, and without any disturbances. The city seemed barren, as if all of the Olks had vanished, leaving to a greater work. Still, they trod in the shadows for a while longer, to keep away from anything still lurking near them. Alex let out a heavy breath, relieved to have crossed the path without any trouble causing a delay to their journey to Krysal city.

An ominous lavender flame emitted a light through the darkness of night. They held their place for a moment, skeptical of what could be lurking in the snow. Zidal soon began to walk toward the light of the flame, her fingers wrapped around the stick of her scythe, Alex following behind. The light glistened more brightly as they approached the flame, a fearful feeling drifting through the shadows. They stepped around a small corner, a being sitting in the cold snow.

Zidal's anxious breaths calmed as she noticed Zorus resting his back against the stone wall of the mountain. His knees were raised against his chest, and his head was buried within his arms. His body was lit with the glorious lavender light of the flame. "Something happened, something terrible, didn't it?" Alex asked in a fearful tone. Zorus lifted his head from his knees. Fearful tears streaming down his cheeks were now visible. He looked tired, shallow bags resting beneath his eyes, as if he hadn't slept for weeks.

"Zorus, you look awful." Zidal noted as she set herself down by the fire. Alex too settled down, listening to his fears, listening to the awful pains that had begun with the weight of the mission. "What's wrong?" she asked, staring into his empty soul.

Zorus spoke, his voice choked with tears. "My magic, it is becoming corrupt. Ever since Cour… oh, Death...! Ever since *he* has been gone, the void has been playing tricks on me." he took in a shuddering breath. "Can you not hear the voices? The whispers, the constant threats?" he asked fearfully.

"Voices? The only voices I can hear are our own." Alex assessed. "Zorus, what are you hearing?"

"I can hear voices whispering terrible things to me constantly, and they become louder in the void. The nightmares of my past have begun to return, nothing has been the same." he stared into the embers of the flame as he wiped a frozen tear from his cheek. "Along with the torturous sounds filling my mind constantly, my sight has defied me, my shadow won't imitate my movements."

Zidal glanced at his shadow, splayed across the mountain wall behind him, from the light of the ever-consuming flame. The same disturbed position was displayed, Zorus's ever so slight movements copied by his shadow. She returned her gaze to Zorus and spoke with a tone of concern. "I see nothing. Your shadow follows your every move."

“Oh, but it doesn’t. It has a mind of its own, awoken from a dying sleep. It has been haunting me, corroding my mind each day that has passed by. It craves revenge…” Zorus spoke fearfully.

“Zorus, are you sure that you want to continue on this journey?” Alex asked supportively. “Your magic may only continue to corrupt you, you may forget who you are, and what you stand for if you continue. You may find yourself yearning to harm yourself or others. I worry for you.”

Zorus took in a deep breath as the light of the flame reflected off of his skin. “I must continue. There is no turning back now.” he claimed, sitting against the stone wall. “My skills are needed. I cannot let the brokens souls take one more emblem. We must continue to trek to the castle on the morrow and speak to the king. He has answers that none of us could expect.”

Zidal stood from the snow and balanced her right hand on her scythe. “I’ll keep watch tonight. Zorus, you must get some rest.” Zidal commanded.

“No, I cannot sleep, the voices only return, keeping me awake. I fear greatly, the shadows desire me. I mustn’t rest when there is danger lurking near me.” Zorus stood and smiled gently at Zidal.

“Zorus, I’m afraid that what you are seeing is only in your mind. There is no threat near other than the Olks a mile back. You should try to distract yourself from these harmful thoughts, go, walk a while, find aliment for us. Don’t worry, Alex and I will guard the camp.” Zidal assured. “Be careful though, this mountain is infested with Broken Souls.”

Zorus gave a subtle nod before silently walking through the snow. Fearful of the Broken Souls that lurked further up the mountain, Zorus followed the narrow pathway down the slope of Winter’s Gorge. Only a moment of walking had passed, yet when he glanced behind him, there was no sight of the flame, or of his companions. An ominous fear played with his thoughts as he shivered in the bitter cold. His cape blew against the wind, following the powdered snow through the current, a chill falling through his body.

Zorus continued to trek through the snow in silent footsteps, yet the awful thoughts would not stray from his mind, they only grew stronger. He only became more fearful of his circumstance, yet he knew that he would never again be safe. His desire to receive the help and guidance of the king only amplified, knowing that he would be the only being who could help him lead his mind away from the task at hand. He struggled in breath as his anxieties grew more intense.

As he continued his journey through the snow, crystal trees began appearing on the side of his path, some flowering, others barren of leaves, and seldom had grown fruit ripe enough to eat. Under the light of the stars, and the two moons, the snowcapped mountain shimmered, the light reflecting off of the trees creating a glorious light that lit the path.

Zorus stood at the base of one tree and reached his frozen hand toward the shimmering fruit. "Greetings… old friend." a shadowy, yet familiar voice played behind him. Zorus dropped his hand to his side, and waited, silently. "Fear not, I am not here to harm you. Please, I desire to speak with you, but for a short moment." Zorus took in a deep breath before facing away from the crystal tree. He was startled as no being stood in front of him, only his shadow, waiting for him to respond. It smiled by the pale light of the moons.

"Astaroth...? It cannot be. You set yourself free from my soul years ago." Zorus remarked as he stepped closer to the rocky wall where his shadow lay.

"No, I did not set myself free, I set *us* free from the bond. Neither you nor I are bound to each other any longer, we never were. I still reside within your soul, I am still a part of you, I still grant you your magic. You still aid me." Astaroth spoke cunningly.

"Why then have you returned now, at this treacherous time?" Zorus questioned the shadow.

"The time has come to test your magic. Now is the time where it is needed most. It has grown strong, and you have been a reliable keeper of this power, but now you must prepare for the most treacherous battle of your life." the shadow frowned. "It will not be easy."

"What must I prepare for? Have I not done all that I can?"

Astaroth stared deeply into his soul and spoke quietly. "The torturer of your past, *he* you must battle against once again, this time, alone."

"But why? Why must I defeat him on my own?"

"Zorus, I am no longer bound to you. Your soul won't accept my help without a specific element, one you shall recall soon. I once asked for your aid, but now I must ask again." The shadow spoke with an ominous tone.

"What do you desire from me?" Zorus asked as his shadow created its own movements.

Astaroth smiled through his moon-lit eyes before speaking. "Destroy the very being who killed *our* brother." as the last word fell from his mouth, the shadow returned to its own state. Overwhelmed with power and confusion, Zorus fell into the snow, unconscious.

S felt uncomfortable as his hand was held inside his Master's viscous tentacle. He was still in pain, a large, forced scar healing a knife wound across his thigh. He stood in front of the small door made of keeler, held in chains crafted of the same material, awaiting his training. His Master reached for the handle of the door with his lower right tentacle and pulled the door toward himself. He led S inside, and as the door locked them inside the small space, he released him from his chains. The Tall Being gifted him with his sword before standing himself in the corner of the room, waiting patiently.

S glanced at his Master. "Are we not training? What have you brought me here for?" he asked curiously.

"There will be a battle, but not against me in training. I must witness how your magic has grown, and at the same moment, find weaknesses in my Broken Souls, find what I must fix in them. Your task is to defeat my first creation."

"I don't understand, Master. What if it destroys me first? What would be the point then?"

"I won't let it cause your destruction; I will cast it away if it comes too close. I need both of you to become strengthened." The Tall Being opened the door once again, allowing a familiar, dripping being to enter. He shut the door before S had the chance to escape. *"Show me your power!"* he commanded.

"Kellac?" S asked himself as he raised his sword. As the past few weeks had passed, he had become almost unrecognizable. He smiled grimly at S, waiting for him to strike. S swiftly thrusted his sword toward the being, impaling it with the tip of his sword. As it had no reaction, S drew back his blade and noticed that the skin he had ripped through had reformed, dripping over its own wound. Kellac stretched his claws forward, causing S's arm to bleed, as he was unable to counter the attack.

He remorsed in pain as he attempted to reach his magic, as he tried to dodge his opponent's next move. He took a step back as he struck the being oncc again, still attempting to escape. He glanced at his Master for a moment, a disappointed gleam in his eye, as if he knew that he could do more. His gaze then shifted to his own shadow, and suddenly, he was overcome with power, and he felt as if he was not controlling his own body.

Three more strikes of Kellac's claws came roaring back at him, but before a single claw could touch him, he escaped to *the void.* Quickly stepping through, he found himself able to fall from it and return to reality. He fell onto Kellac's back and impaled each of his shoulders. It roared in pain, reaching toward its tormentor. Again, S fled into *the void* before it could touch him. He returned quickly, drawing his blade across Kellac's stomach. Easily, he was able to fall beneath his counterattack and disappear before any harm came to him.

For a moment, he waited inside *the void,* regaining his breath. Again, he fell from his security, and thrusted his sword forward. It stuck into Kellac's heart, shattering his soul as he roared in immense pain, waiting for his misery to end. S stepped toward the back wall, watching in fear as Kellac's skin stained the floor. He knew not what he had done, he had killed, caused pain to something… alive. His sword clattered against the ground as it fell from his hands, his mind returning to him, his capability of controlling himself. With an unknown suddenness, he fell to the floor breathlessly, overwhelmed, his Master in awe.

Krysal City

Zorus was roused by the brightness of the rising sun. The snow was reflecting the sun's lilac light, creating a beautiful warmth throughout the mountain. Zorus lifted his head and studied the camp. The fire was nothing but blackened wood and ash, and everything was covered in another layer of freshly fallen snow. He stood from the freezing blanket of snow and glanced at Zidal. "What in Death's name happened?" he asked in concern as he searched the area. No other being could be seen beyond the bend of the pathway, shielded by a crooked stone wall.

"When you didn't return last night, Alex went looking for you. You had fainted beside one of the crystal trees." Zidal informed him as she let out her hand. Zorus took it skeptically and rose from the frozen ground.

He shook the layer of remaining snow off of his uniform and stared into the distance. "Where is the kid anyway?" he asked, scanning the area.

"He left to complete the task you failed to. Come, we should meet up with him." Zidal commanded as she began to step down the slope of snow. Zorus followed her closely behind, waiting for the worse to happen. He knew that something was not right, though he could not remember what had happened after he had left the camp the night before. All of his memories were blurred together into one thought, he was unable to differentiate them, unable to find a clue to what had happened to him. His footprints left a story in the snow of what had come to pass during these troubling times.

The trek was short, and soon after they stepped around the bend, his thoughts collapsed. Alex stood before a crystal tree, reaching to the ripest of the fruit which grew from its strong branches. He glanced to his right as he noticed their subtle movement. The fruit in hand, he turned them and smiled shyly. "Zorus, I'm glad that you're awake. Are you alright?"

he asked, handing each of his companions some fruit. He took a bite, filling his empty stomach.

"I cannot say that I am well, but nonetheless, I am alive." Zorus responded as they began to walk through the mountain pass. He took a bite of the sweet fruit, replenishing his energy.

"You must have been exhausted." Alex said.

"I was, but I fear that wasn't the reason I collapsed last night." Zorus shuddered through his words, attempting to reason with himself.

Silence rang for a moment.

"If it wasn't exhaustion, what caused you to faint last night?" asked Alex as he stared into the distant light of the radiant city.

"I can't remember it thoroughly. There were voices commanding me, a shadow following me, and then, suddenly, everything went dark. I felt overwhelmed with darkness and power. I don't know what's happening to me. Some things cannot be answered easily." he replied somberly.

"What can be done? This is making me really concerned." Alex inquired.

"We must meet with the king, only he knows what can be done. He knows the state of my mind, he knows how to defeat the ultimate evil, and he knows how to destroy the emblems rightly." Zorus remarked. "How much further are we from Krysal?"

"We shouldn't be much further from the palace. The slope of the mountain will reach its end soon, and then we shall have an easier journey ahead of us." Zidal spoke with a softness in her heart. "What do you suppose he will think of this?" she asked. "What if he chooses not to join us on this last stretch of our treacherous journey?"

Zorus glanced at her, following her slow steps, responding with uncertainty. "That can only be answered when we arrive."

Silence rang through the air as they stepped down the slope of the mountain, nothing but the sound of crunching snow followed their laborious footsteps as they ate. The bitter wind cooled their bodies as they trekked through the thick layer of snow. Their footsteps were filled with urgency, a strong desire to find their way to the king keeping them standing upright in their weariness.

Alex stepped with great difficulty, as the mind wavering grew strong once again. The pain in his mind was indescribable, and he was losing all hope of finding a way back home. At this moment, he knew that he would be unable to retrieve the life that he yearned for most, that he would be stuck in a world he knew so little about for the rest of his remaining days. Yet he endured, knowing that the trek would be worth it in the end.

Their legs ached as they continued to follow the steep slope down the mountain side, continuing their journey to Krysal city. It was becoming near, the light reflecting from the crystal buildings easier to notice. Glorious crystal trees passed by as they followed the path blanketed in snow. They became more numerous, and larger, each capped with glorious silver leaves and bearing ripe fruit. The slope became easier to step upon, and a calmness filled the air. They had entered the gorge, a beautiful space between the mountains they had climbed though, covered in snow and ice. A large river ran beneath a bridge constructed of fine marble, flowing rapidly through the icy terrain. The city of Krysal was built upon the rocky ledges of the mountains laid beside them, and above the river, built on marble bridges. Each building was crafted of the finest, and most vibrantly colored crystals.

At the end of the straight bridge, in which they were following, stood the Krysal palace. As tall as the mountains standing beside it, and shaped in the same manor, the castle erected of crystals stood proudly. Massive marble spears erupted from its edges, creating a glorious presentation. Light reflected from its glorious estate like the stars at twilight. All who witnessed the castle were struck with awe.

Zorus led the others across the bridge, peace running through his mind. He closed his eyes for a moment, only to find himself alone as he stepped through the city of Krysal. Becoming almost fearful, he glanced to his left, his brother stepping beside him. He smiled at him softly before fading away, returning Zorus to reality, Zidal and Alex walking by his side. Though his fantasy lasted only a second, he stepped across the marble bridge with somber elation, as they finally reached the entrance of the palace.

Two guards stood at the entrance of the palace, one standing beside each of the doors, wearing uniforms that reflected the light of the city, each holding a spear in the hand furthest from the doors. Noticing their arrival, the guards stepped forward, and in union pulled the heavy marble doors open graciously. Zidal nodded respectfully and entered beside her allies. With a slow, swift movement, the doors shut heavily behind them, leaving them inside the beauteous palace.

Two more guards stood beside the entrance doors in the same fashion. The throne room was nearly empty. An elegant chandelier fell above them laden with crystals emitting a glorious light. At the end of the room, there stood a pure white throne, crowned with ridged wings. Upon the throne, sat a figure hooded in a dark cloak. The hood which fell over his head shadowed his face, and they were unable to identify his features.

His cloak, lined with a crystal blue silk, fell to his elbows, and on each of its shoulders rested a marking of two triangles, each with a line falling through its center. At its center, it was pinned together by a rounded violet crystal. Under the cloak he was clad in a fine grey cloth which faded to white. Upon the fabric, crystal blue stems reached from each side and curled to a line in through the center. Between each stem a feather pattern lay on the centerline.

His pants were made of the same fabric, a darkness fading to light. Upon them, one large stem, alike the ones on his shirt, slanted down his thigh, and branched to his knee. In his right hand, he held a magnificent scythe as a staff. Its wood was strong, and the blade was glorious, marked with the same symbol, which was upon his cloak, yet again shining crystal blue. Upon his light-colored forearms, huge, jagged scars fell across, revealing blue crystals which resided beneath his skin.

They approached the king, and once they reached his throne, Zidal and Zorus bent on one knee. Alex, noticing their gesture, followed their movement, bowing his head low. "Rise." he commanded in a deep and shallow voice. They followed his request and rose from the ground. "So, you have returned, and you have brought the prophesied human. Even I was unsure if the legend would become a reality." he glanced at Alex. "Tell me, by what shall I call you?"

Alex choked in his words, unsure of how to speak to royalty, as he once was one who was spoken to as royalty. "Alex, your honor. What shall I know you by?"

"Very well, and by that, I shall call you. I am known by many names. Many call me by the name of *King Kardama*, and others remember me by the *Guider of Souls* and the *Bringer of Sorrow*. *The Ruler of this*

Gracious Land and the *Savior of Souls."* he spoke with power and prestige.

The figure stood from his seat gracefully, standing before them. He gently removed the hood from his head. His hair was pure white, shimmering in the light of the crystals, yet his face looked young, stern, and glorious, as if he would never age, though he would live forever. He lifted a crown upon his pearl white hair. It was crafted of gold, and had three spokes on the front, the two that stood on the right and left bending away from the glorious spoke in the center, which bore a bright crystal in its center.

Yet another large and rigid crystal scar was borne across the right side of his face, falling from the top of his head, cutting through his dim, violet eye, and ending at his chin. Underneath his left eye, which shined brightly, was drawn yet again the same symbol of two triangles. His ears were shaped as small horns made of the crystals which were found in the city, shing blue as bright as his scars. He was the most glorious of all creatures in Shawon, the most powerful, the most inspiring and compassionate.

The king spoke in a dark tone and leered. "I am he who they call *Death.* You may call me by those names.*"* Alex nodded, staring carefully into the king's sorrowful eyes. Kardama smiled softly and directed his attention to Zorus. "Zorus, I have noticed that your brother is not accompanying you, where has he gone?" the king asked solemnly.

Zorus shuddered, reminded of his pain. "He... was killed by the leader of the Broken Souls. Were you unaware? Did you not guide his soul?" he asked in sorrow. "Will I not see him again, even in the afterlife?"

"I was unaware of his death, his soul never called to me. I am afraid his soul has been shattered; the leader of the Broken Ones is much too powerful." Zorus bowed his head in sorrow. "I am saddened to hear that he has departed from life. Courier was one of the greatest Darlids to have lived. My deepest condolences." Kardama took in a breath and spoke again. "I believe that you have matters in which you desire to speak with me, and I must discuss your mission. Come, we will dine together, you all look famished, then I will answer your questions." the king turned away from them and began to walk toward a hallway. His cloak brushed against the air, the sound of his heavy boots and large scythe hitting the ground echoing through the palace.

They followed him closely, unwilling to stray from him. The journey was not long before they found themselves entering the dining room. It was well decorated, the table was crafted of marble and so too were the many chairs, lined with light blue cushions. Another chandelier fell from the ceiling above, creating a perfect light. The glasses were carved of fine glass, filled with pure juniper. The ceramic plates were decorated with pastel colors, creating flowers, four of which were plated with the finest of meals. The same design was carved into the silverware.

Kardama let out his hand and allowed for them to take a seat at the table. As they each took a seat beside each other, gently pulling the chairs from their place, the king found his way to the other side of the table and took a seat directly across from them. The king spoke as he lifted his fork carefully. "Please, eat, tell me of your triumphs and challenges which you have overcome in your journey, and soon we will discuss what you desire to."

R awoke to the sound of clashing chains. As he opened his empty eyes, the weight of the chains had been removed, only the shackles remained on his wrists. He stared at his Master in fear as he was lifted from his place and dragged against the rough stone ground as his Master forcefully led him out of the room, leaving his brother alone, sleeping. He knew that it was his turn to train his magic, his turn to experiment, but unlike his brother, because he was only seven years of age at this time, he would be unable to wield a weapon.

R picked up his feet and stepped quickly beside the Tall Being, finding their way to the small room lined with keeler. The Tall Being opened the door and shoved him inside, shutting the door behind himself. "*Tonight, we will study your power, you have the ability to read minds. Who needs to fight back when they can avoid every attack, knowing what is going to occur?*" the Tall Being depicted.

R stared at his tormentor's smile as he pulled the shackles off of his fragile wrists. Once the shackles were removed, R felt something he had never felt before, a power unknown, trapped by the previous pains he had encountered. He could feel his body morphing, his skin decaying, and his figure shrinking. His bones began to show, and he was protected from harm. Confused, he studied his boney hands in awe, curling his fingers and twisting his bones.

When his Master's sight laid on him, he too was struck with awe. *"Scelo... but the remainder of that rec were destroyed in Gehalla. It cannot be, they are the most cunning in battle, and built with a fine defense system. How could I not see it clearly before?"* he asked himself. *"No, this is good. I am making progress in this plan, if he is a scelo, so too is his brother, and this will mean that I will have the greater advantage when it comes to the final battle. I will have an army which will be undefeatable, living, yet dead."*

R looked into the Tall Being's eye and spoke softly. "What is happening to me? This is not something that should be happening to a mortal soul."

"R, fret not, this is natural for your kind. I had not realized it soon enough. Please, use this skill to your advantage, this will make you perfect for my envisionment. Now, I will begin to attack, and you must protect yourself."

R watched as four tentacles were drawn out of his Master's body, ready to attack. He waited for a moment, unsure of how to control his body in this state, unsure of what he had become. Glancing at his own shadow, he knew that he must trust his demon to save him from the one standing in front of him. He let it take control, he let it teach him how to control his magic. Cunningly, he was able to see his Master's every thought, every move.

Quickly, with great agility, he fell beneath his Master's swinging arms, saving himself from a worse fate. Following after, he bent his legs and took a leap of faith, flipping between the terror of tentacles. Knowing that an arm would cut down from above him, he dashed to the side before it could reach him. As he continued to dodge each attack, the adrenaline in his mind continued to rise, and his ability to see clearly became easy. Unless he calculated his own moves incorrectly, his Master would not have the chance to touch him.

Soon, he felt himself take control once again. His shadow trusted him with his new teachings, knowing that he would be able to remember how to possess his power correctly. He fought against his Master's will to harm him with ease, not even the tip of a tentacle caught on his rough bones as he continued his battle.

R, looking into his Master's thoughts, followed his own swiftly, copying the movements in his eyes exactly. His Master smiled, knowing that nothing he could do would harm his prisoner. He stopped suddenly, and his arms dissipated into his body. *"Very good R, you have done well. You have accomplished things that no other Darlid could dream to do at your age. You and your brother are very powerful beings, the last remaining of your kind, and with this unspeakable power, you will be unstoppable!"*

The Tall Being cackled as R stood in fear, the strength of his shadow holding near to him, giving him the power he yearned. As his flesh grew over his bones, he fainted, overwhelmed by his abilities.

Lore of the Past

As they had each finished their meals, filled with satisfaction for the first time in weeks, Kardama stared at them with dark curiosity. As each had told their story of their triumphs and challenges, the king had listened intently, creating an understanding for himself. Each word which was spoken was another piece to the puzzle, each misfortune, another clue to their victory. There was much sorrow as each of the three spoke, and fear was struck into their hearts as they recalled their trials.

Soon, all was spoken that could be, and the king sighed. “I see, your journey has been quite challenging, but nonetheless, it has gone better than expected. There is much we now know about our enemy and his allies, and with this, I have discovered that my intuition was accurate. Zidal, you and your company has been perfect for this mission. I thank you thus far, but we still have long to go.” he slid his empty plate to the side and rested his scarred arms on the table. “Knowing that the Broken Souls have acquired many of the emblems, we haven’t much time, but I understand that you have queries regarding your mission. I will spare the time we do have to answer your questions to my ability, knowing that with this information, your understanding of this world will immensely change. I am quite interested, what is it you are so curious to know?” he asked, touching the tips of his fingers together.

“There are many things we want to know, so many, that I’m not sure where to begin.” Zidal addressed.

“Then ask me all that you must, and I will answer them in the order which I see fit.” the king commanded.

Zidal thought for a moment, drawing her fingers across her scarred cheeks before speaking again. “It was said in the *Book of Emblems* that you have the knowledge of how to destroy the leader of the Broken Souls.

This may give us a greater advantage. How can one accomplish this?" she asked.

Zorus's voice followed. "What will happen if the Drex potion is drunk?"

"Why do the Broken Souls wish to return to Achnor, and why is it that only a human can break the seal?" asked Alex.

"If we fail and Athreal returns, how can we destroy him?" Zidal asked.

The king let out a deep breath before speaking with great mystery in his tone. "Ah, so you seek to learn of the war of Gehalla." His small audience stared at him with immense curiosity. "There is much explaining, and I must begin at the war of Gehalla. Many stories have been told of the fabled war, and I'm sure you are familiar with them, but much of it has been altered throughout the centuries to create the well-known battle between the humans and Darlids. In reality, this war was not fought in that manner, for the Darlids fought alongside the humans in effort to destroy the twenty-three living demons. I, myself, led in battle."

He continued with a soft, yet powerful voice. "Before the war had begun, humans and Darlids ruled together, I being the king of the Darlids and Technar being the king of the humans. There was peace and elation throughout the land, yet Athreal, gifted with extraordinary power, sought otherwise. He believed that because of our magic and abilities beyond the humans' imagination, Darlids should be the rightful rulers of Achnor. He had allied himself with several of his own rec, the killiosdt, and came to speak with me of his plans. His idea was despicable, and destructive... the blood of the humans would be forever stained in the dirt of Achnor.

"He knew well that the humans were well trained in battle, as we had also been, but he knew that they would be unprepared to face an ally which held unspeakable power. He wanted to betray the humans, he wanted war, destruction, and death until there were none to stand in his path. He wouldn't explain his plan until I agreed to his intentions. I knew it was well planned, none could have defeated him, and I was sure he could accomplish it easily. I opposed his proposal, and in response he exiled himself and his twenty-three followers in the farthest, most inescapable lands. He would never set foot near our kingdoms again… or so I thought.

"When he returned from those lands many years later, he came to me once again to convince me to take part in his plan to rule over Achnor. He revealed a vial which was filled with a potion he had created, the *Drex potion,* a concoction made from the forbidden fruit, called oru, which would intensify all power he already owned, making him nearly undefeatable. He offered for me to drink it, to have unlimited power, if only I would follow his plan and destroy humanity. I refused, and he remarked that if I would not side with him, I would be sided against him. Even with the pure knowledge that drinking the potion a second time could kill him, before my very eyes he swallowed the liquid. An immediate increase of power could be felt near him, and I had no ability to save him from his insanity. Little did I know, he had brewed twenty-three more Drex potions, allowing his army to become unstoppable. He and his followers were no longer killiosdts, they had become living demons.

"Testing his overpowered magic, and teaching me a lesson, he created a crystal spear and drew it across my face, leaving me with this scar and blindness in my right eye. I did not fight back, for I knew I would fail. He left me with the scar, and a warning: war would be set against the humans, and if I did not choose to side with him in a year's time, we too would be at war. He spoke of his army, one I feared too great to battle against. He had allied himself with the Broken Souls. There were thousands, all powered with new life. I feared that there would be too many to fight against, even with the humans and Darlids combined, it would not be enough.

"Though it pained me, I knew that I had to go to war against Athreal and his followers, I had to save my allies from that awful fate. At dawn, on the third day after the creation of the living demons, my army, allied with Technar's army, marched through the Hills of Gehalla, facing the sea of Broken Souls. Thousands of humans and Darlids, any that could fight, stood, waiting for their death. There, the horns of the demons blew, and the war had begun. We were no match against the Broken Souls, they were strong, and experienced, the only way to defeat them: striking them in their hearts and shattering their souls. The demons caused much destruction, many spears of stone grew from the ground and impaled hundreds of our warriors. At this time, hundreds of Darlids and humans had perished, blood seeping into the dirt, and not a single Broken Soul had fallen.

"We fought without break for eight days straight, and though we were growing weary, the Broken Souls never ended their rage. But this day brought relief, for the shaens, legendary humans who could wield magic, had returned from their war against the sorna, and had come to fight beside us. Many Broken Souls shattered, though the number of our dead was rising too. Many recs were brought to the brink of extinction, including the scelos. The battlefield was laden with bodies and the decay of Darlids. It seemed as if the war would never end.

"As the war continued, I realized that we could not endure this fight forever. A thought came to me suddenly, an awful thought at that, but one which would save humans from Athreal's genocide. A fabled spell which required the magic of a Shaen, would save Achnor from Athreal's wrath. It would require sacrifice, but it was a risk I was willing to take. Fighting my way through the battlefield, I found Technar, persisting in battle- though he was wounded- and I recalled my idea to him as we fended off the Broken Souls. With the combination of magic used by shaens and Darlids, a rift could be opened to create a world parallel to Achnor where all Darlids would be exiled. There our magic could increase. We would save the humans from their doom and have a fighting chance to destroy the demons. This grieved him deeply, but it was a risk he was willing to take for the benefit of all life.

"Technar, the elder of shaens, and I, against our desire, fled to a hidden place far from the battle. I bid Technar farewell and allowed for the portal to be opened. Darlid blood was necessary to open the portal in order for all to be cast into the parallel world. I offered my own, but it could not be spilt by my own hand. Technar drew his blade and slit my right arm, allowing my blood to stain the ground. The Shaen cast the spell, and before my eyes, a portal grew with a brightness that would cast away all darkness. The king of the humans and the Shaen sent me away with their blessings, and the portal began its work. As I stepped inside, each living Darlid, Broken Soul, and demon followed unwillingly. Everything was dark for a moment, and then I was in an entirely different world, surrounded by evil beings and all Darlid kind. The king of the humans spent his own blood to seal the portal, therefore, no being would have the ability to escape this new world… Shawon. Sealed by the blood of a human, it could only be opened in the same manner.

"Though the war had been won in Achnor, and peace reigned once again, Athreal's heart filled with rage unmatched, and he cursed me, and swore that he would destroy all of Darlid kind until only the Broken Ones remained. He gave me a week to prepare, for he too needed to plan his attack. Now knowing that our magic would be enhanced in this world, I met with the great wizard Sel, and asked him to create a poison which would destroy Athreal, meanwhile, I was preparing a spell which would destroy the remainder of the demons. My army prepared, they replenished their strength and honed their skills in battle, they learned how to best shatter the souls of the Broken Ones. The war would be lost, not by us, but by our enemy.

"One day before the battle would continue, Sel found me. He was drained of all his energy, for creating the poison took days and caused him to spend much of his magic. The poison would shatter the soul of Athreal forever, and peace would reside. But all spells come with a consequence. *Whomsoever laces their blade with this poison and pierces a demon's heart shall watch it perish, but he who kills the demon shall their heart rotteth and their skin crumble until death.* For the welfare of all Darlid kind, I took the poison and drenched the blade of the very scythe I carry this day and sheathed it.

"The morning after, we stood, awaiting the attack. The war began again, and there was much death on both sides. I thought that we had finally found a way to defeat them, we were finally going to spread peace across the land, but as soon as Athreal realized he was losing, he began to use keeler stone against the Darlids. He used keeler chains to cease our use of magic and, more fatally, he had crafted weapons from the forbidden stone, shattering the souls of his enemy immediately.

"At this, I knew it was time for me to take action. Having spent days creating the perfect spell, one which could only affect the demons, I used the majority of my energy to cast it. A shadow was cast across the battlefield and the war ceased, but for only a moment. I had given the shadows of the demons' sentience, and with this, they craved to devour the souls of their hosts. These, the shadow demons, are the only beings powerful enough to weaken a demon and are the only beings with the ability to destroy the Master of the Broken Souls. I watched Athreal and each of the twenty-three living demons fall, one after the other, weakest to the most tenacious. As their shadows ate through their souls, the bravest and most experienced of my army, the Knightmare and Shadlas, killed each one of the demons. But, as I had expected, Athreal's soul was too powerful to be corroded by his own shadow. He would need a more fatal sentence in order for his soul to shatter.

"Athreal raged as he watched his army fall, but he would not yield. He wanted revenge on me, and even with his shadow eating at his soul, he would not give in. As my legion continued fighting against the Broken Souls and the dying demons, I faced Athreal alone. He was powerful and would not back down from battle. His weapons were strong, he was quick and well trained. With a strike of his blade, I was left with yet another jagged scar draping through my left arm. I was in pain, and just as he, I would not yield. I continued to counter his attacks, and he too countered mine. Though it seemed impossible to strike him- each of us finding our match- with my determination, I felt my blade cut through his skin.

"Athreal screamed in agony, and immediately, as his body and soul began to decay, I felt my hands begin to harden and crack. I became immobile and knew that my deed would not be forgotten among the Darlids. I felt my mind fade, and my vision darken. I felt my bones break, and my skin cracking. I fell to the ground, letting my last words fall from my lips: *It has ended.* With my breath leaving my breaking body, the stone encasing me, my fragile body broke. I was born anew. My deed had not granted me with death, it granted me the power over death, and life everlasting. I became the most powerful being ever to exist and was given a new name: *Death.*

"Though Athreal's body decayed, *his* soul still lived. With the gift of my newfound ability, I took his soul and broke it into eight emblems, each with an attribute he once held. *Death:* the ability to destroy any being which stood in his path, *Destruction:* the capability to consume beauty, and replace it with ruin, *Magic:* the power over things imagined as impossible, *Life:* the true determination to be immortal, and overcome death, *Greed:* the intense desire to possess power over all life, *Strength:* the power that caused him to be unstoppable and cause fear, *Knowledge:* the gift to perceive the world in such a way that no other being could, and

Love: the tenacious lust he owned for death and destruction. With this, knowing that each emblem would be too powerful for any being to control, and would cause dismay if found again, I cast each away in hope that they would never be found again.

"Thus, the war ended… or I had expected it to. The Broken Souls retreated, their Master now destroyed, and none had been seen for centuries. Any which had been formed afterward were cast away, or their souls shattered. And now, they at full strength revealed themselves, with a knowledgeable Master and a Mastered plan. A devious idea to create Broken Souls at will, to torture innocent Darlids until they gave in. All this in order to reincarnate Athreal, and there would be certain doom. Many would suffer, and with the human's blood, they would escape and finish the battle once started centuries ago. It is imperative that the remaining emblems are found and destroyed by my hand." the king sighed, staring blankly at his reflection shining through the marble table. All that could be said, was said with diligence. Every word was heeded, each syllable was noted.

There was silence for a moment, a peaceful time of deep thought. A new understanding was set, and all which was said was remembered. A new knowledge resided in each of their minds. "Is this all that you desired to learn of?"

Zorus opened his mouth and spoke. "Sire, we do wish for one more thing." he declared respectfully.

"What is it that you so desire?"

"We need you in order to complete our task. Without your power, without your ability, we would surely lose the battle… Athreal would be recreated." Zorus admitted. "We ask that you join us for the succession of this task, so the Darlids of Shawon never suffer again. We ask you to help finish a battle once begun so long ago. Only you know the spell which can destroy the emblems forever."

The king nodded solemnly. "Though I have responsibilities of my own, I see the urgency in this task. Indeed, let us find the remaining emblems, let us end this suffering."

S sat beside his brother, both in chains, both in pain, but not physically as their Master had ceased to cut into their skin. Instead, after forfeiting that method, he began to torture their minds, placing thoughts into their hearts which could never be forgotten. They too felt pain in their bodies from being forced constantly to change their physical state, though it wasn't nearly as noticeable as the devious thoughts. Each day was filled with an unforgettable pain, a hope depleted in the darkness of their minds. This method was more malicious and caused more lasting harm than before. There wasn't a night that wasn't filled with fear.

Their Master had plastered images into their minds, torture of other Darlids, breakings of their souls, torment to the weary and young. He had spent much time with them, speaking, telling lies, telling things that caused their nightmares to come to life. Psychotic words, which only one who cared so deeply to employ torture could enjoy. Words that only one who wanted to inflict pain on others, who wanted to stay in power could love.

The demons haunted them, the forced thoughts causing their presence to linger. Their shadows betrayed them, leaving them alone in utter darkness as their minds continued to deteriorate. Nothing was as it seemed, there were only shadows. They felt weakened, as they were kept in chains, the ability to use their magic, to keep themselves hidden only accessible when they too were free. The voices became more present, whispering the same demented words into their ears, words which had no meaning to them other than to torture. "Bring us home, let us aid you. Send us away, or later betray you."

But all of this was necessary in order to make them more powerful. The longer the thoughts lingered, the more the demons chipped away at their fragile souls, the only thing to satisfy them, their fear. And soon, they would be bound to each other, one demented soul broken with another, when only the element was adopted into the body of the host: *one drop of their enemy's blood.*

The Soul's Desire

Kardama stood from the marble table, his scythe held in his firm grip. He gently slid the wooden handle of the scythe into the ropes resting on his back and beckoned the others to stand. The others graciously followed, stretching out their worn bodies as they began to walk behind his prestigious steps. "Your majesty, do you know the whereabouts of the emblem of strength?" asked Zidal as she drew her fingers across her fragile face.

"I am afraid I haven't the slightest clue. Indeed, I did cast each emblem away, but to places I knew not. Only those who were brave enough to search were able to locate most of them." the king let out a deep breath as he stepped into the palace corridor. "Still, I am curious as to why the emblems of love and knowledge haven't been located." Alex bit his lip, knowing that soon, even against his own anxious and tortured mind, he would have to reveal the emblem's location. He wasn't brave enough yet, he knew that recalling the true hiding places of each would cause much pain, and he wasn't ready, knowing that pain was already lingering. Soon he would have to break through his painful thoughts and reveal that which would change everything. Alex knew the pain, the torture this thought was gifting him was obvious, he couldn't hide his anxiety.

"Alex, are you okay?" Zorus asked, placing his arm around his shoulder, as if he were his brother. He held him further back from the others for a moment, being careful to follow behind Kardama. "Is something wrong? Is there something you want to tell me?" Alex followed the pattern of his breath cautiously, waiting for the mind wavering to cease its tricks so he could concentrate on the task at hand.

"I'm just trying to process everything that has happened." he lied as he felt tears forming in his eyes. His anxious thoughts encased his mind, reminding him of things he didn't want to remember. "Zorus, I don't think I'll ever get to go home. The mind wavering has almost completed its course, the immeasurable pain has become finite, and it appears less often. My mind is beginning to work in a way I can't understand. I won't be *human* for much longer." Alex looked into Zorus's empty sockets, his pained emotion bleeding into his every thought. He felt sick knowing what had happened, knowing something that would change the motive of the mission, something that would increase the anger ever resting. He didn't *want* Zorus to know.

"I'm sorry, kid. There's no escape from pain, I should know. All we can do is endure." Zorus sighed. "I'll look out for you, and with all of my power, I will be sure that you make it home before it's too late. That's a promise, and as long as I live, I will not break it." he spoke in an intense and serious tone, one which a promise could not be forgotten.

"Thank you, Zorus. I don't know how I'll ever repay you."

"You won't have to…" Zorus smiled softly, yet in such a way that sorrow bled from his emotion. He gently shoved Alex aside as they followed the king through the palace entrance.

Kardama nodded at the guard standing on the right side of the door, lifting his crown from his head. The guard took the crown gently from his hands, swiftly stepping into the castle to return it to its resting place. Silence filled the frigid air for a moment as the large doors were shut behind them, leading them into the last stretch of their long-endured journey. Warm breaths filled the air with a cool fog. Kardama turned toward the others, determination spread across his expression. "Alex, please lead us to the emblem of strength. Search for it in your mind, find its hiding place, bring us to its destruction."

Taking in a deep breath, calming his anxious thoughts, Alex began his search for the emblem of strength. He thought of the feeling of strength, the ability to overcome anything in his way, whether it be physical or emotional. The force of the emblem entered his mind, drawing him nearer to its resting place, but only for a moment as his thoughts began to corrupt. Tears streaming down his cheeks, he fell to his knees in weakness. There were too many people he missed, too many tragedies had happened, his home seemed too far out of reach, all his thoughts overwhelming with weakness, each torturing him as to keep him from locating the emblem. His thoughts erased the determination to complete the mission, his mind had destroyed the hope that remained and caused him to cry out in pain.

A gentle hand suddenly rested on his shoulder, and a force unknown overwhelmed his thoughts, calming his pain, stretching his hope forward. Staring through teary eyes, Alex looked upon the king's glorious face, peace drenching his body. He took in a shuddering breath before standing from the snow-laced ground, The king releasing his soft grip. "North." he pointed slightly to the left of the palace, a beautiful cascade of frozen juniperfalls displayed behind.

"North? But that means…" Zidal shuddered. "The emblem is beyond the Krysal Falls. Kardama, we'll die if we proceed!" she exclaimed, fear shown through her trembling eyes.

"But we will perish knowing that the Broken Souls will never succeed in their mission to return Athreal to Shawon." the king proclaimed.

"What's beyond the Krysal Falls?" Alex asked weakly.

Zorus spoke, staring into the abyss of icy falls. "The Krysal Falls have often been called *The Labyrinth of Ice,* a place where one can easily get lost inside, but can never find their way out without great difficulty. None who have entered have found their way out, and seldom choose to seal their fate inside." a gentle breeze filled the air, bringing a blanket of clouds with.

"Not only is the labyrinth impossible to find your way through, but this territory is known to be crowded with Broken Souls, a home where they can hide away from harm. They are the only beings who know how to escape, living beyond any Darlid's imagination." Zidal added, brushing her shadowed hair from her face. "Kardama, there is little chance for us to succeed in finding the emblem if we are surrounded by the enemy, lost where none can be found."

"Indeed. Winning this fight will take courage, we mustn't lose hope. We will destroy the emblem, we will succeed." Kardama smiled solemnly, a feeling of confidence raining upon them. "Let us win this long-fought war, even if it costs us every drop of blood we own..."

Kardama stepped forward, the others following his footsteps anxiously. The air was bitter, and their fearful thoughts rained upon them like a summer storm. Zorus's mind raged, a thought of insecurity falling upon him. The last words the king had spoken ate at his thoughts, corroded his imagination. Holding back from the others, he stared at his hands, breathing heavily. "Blood…" he whispered underneath his breath. "One drop of the enemy's blood." anxiety unconsciously filled his mind as he continued to relay the thought. He watched as his hands began to shake uncontrollably. *He knew what he had to do.* It would cost his own sacrifice, but he had already lost too much to care.

The voices of his allies played in the distance, slowly fading away as his own breaths became more rapid and unclear. His hands trembled as he reached for his sword, wrapping his fingers around the soft fabric of his brother's cape. He gripped the handle of the sword tightly and unsheathed it, drawing it closer to his being. Carefully, he placed the blade onto his right wrist, his skin attempting to hide itself, keep it from its own harm. But he would not allow it, he continued to force his skin to blanket his bones, ready to spill his own blood. *He was his own worst enemy…* and his soul desired to become powerful once more.

Taking in a deep breath, Zorus applied pressure to his wrist, and with one swift movement, he slit his wrist deeply. His body began to weaken, he would no longer be able to change form as long as the wound remained. Immediately, he felt an increase of power, a binding to another soul. "Zorus?!" Zidal screamed, rushing toward him. His hands still and ever trembling, his mind overwhelmed, he fell to his knees, dropping his sword into the fresh snow. His blood seeped into the ground, staining the snow crimson. What he had done to himself was the only thing he wished to exact his revenge on, the one thing that tortured him for years on end. He drew his own blood. He was becoming the very being he wanted to destroy.

Though his vision began to go blurry, in shock of his own gesture, he noticed Zidal fall beside him, Kardama and Alex rushing to his place. "Zorus, what have you done to yourself?" she asked through a shaky voice. Her hands shaking in fear, Zidal reached toward his bleeding wrist. "You once saved me, so let me save you now. I won't let you…" Zorus pulled his wrist away from her gentle hands, shoving her away from his figure. She fell into the snow, shocked and afraid.

Listening to Zidal's fearful tears Zorus spoke. "I know what I must do." Reaching out, Zorus gripped the handle of the sword. As his vision began to clear, he stood from the snow, sheathing his sword. "I must destroy *him.*"

"You can't fight him alone, you'll get killed." Zidal remarked, repositioning her figure.

"Then I will die exacting revenge on the very being who killed my brother! The being who caused so much ruin in my life!" he screamed. Calming his voice, controlling his anxious breaths, he spoke again. "Please, Zidal… I can't lose any more souls. I must do this alone."

"No…" Alex whispered. "Zorus, please…"

"Kid, this isn't your fight, this is mine, and mine alone. I can't keep living in a world where *he* still exists!"

"And a day will come where he does not, but today is not that day. We have a better chance of destroying the last remaining emblems than destroying that being." Kardama spoke with a powerful voice, one which could conquer the mighty, and persuade the unconvinced.

"No, you don't understand. This *must* be the time." Zorus raged, turning away from the others. As he began to walk toward the unknown, the others followed.

Kardama stared at Zorus with powerful eyes, sensing his intentions, reading his soul. "You have been playing with a force that is uncontrollable, Zorus. Yes, the shadow demons are powerful, and they are the only beings that can destroy the leader of the Broken Souls, but they can be misleading. They are the most devious of liars. Your soul will be fully consumed before you have the chance to find *him.*"

Zorus stopped coldly, knowing that the king knew much more than he could imagine. "And it is a risk I am willing to take. Even if it kills me." The breeze began to grow stronger, the fabric of his cape riding against it. "It's best if you just forget about me. Save the world, destroy the last remaining emblems before Athreal can be recreated, but forget about *me!* I can take care of myself, my strength is unknowingly powerful, my magic is well trained, my swordsmanship is unparalleled, and my determination is unmatched."

"Your soul is stronger than any other I've known, even my own. You *and* your brother's, and it was that alone that made me fear you. And now, I also fear for you, for you are tempting a demon when you yourself are mortal." The king stood tall, patiently waiting for his student to listen.

"You are not only putting yourself in danger, but you too are putting every living being in danger. You have great power, and as an ally, you would be unstoppable. If we lose you to the Broken Souls, there will be no victory."

Zorus shuddered. "I would never side with those that destroyed me!"

"But the devil has his ways, and even the most pure of heart can sin." Kardama spoke with great authority.

"I know you want to persuade me to finish what was once started centuries ago, and I will, but I must finish what *I* started first. I will return, and I will help cause the succession of this war, but not now." Zorus remarked.

"Are my words all for naught?!"

"*You* don't understand...!" Alex began, courage running through his veins, before Zorus forcefully stopped and turned toward him.

"What don't I understand, kid?!" Silence rang for a moment as the tension rose. Alex opened his mouth, finding himself unable to speak. His tongue felt as if it were knotted. He couldn't tell him. He was cut off before he could make a sound. "Heh, you can't even make up a good lie to keep me from my fate." Zorus stared into the glistening sunset, drawing his fingers through his knotted hair. Taking one last glance behind him, he spoke. "There is no word that could change my mind. Goodbye." with the last trace of his word, he disappeared from their sight, bringing himself to a long-awaited fight.

"No." Zidal spoke softly, a somberness trailing behind her note.

Alex spoke with a fear unparalleled, a sorrow unmatched, the king and Zidal staring at him with unbelief. "There is only one emblem left to destroy…"

The sounds were horrific. The spilling of blood, the cutting of bone, the melting of decayed flesh, the screams of a suffering Darlid. Even with his eyes shut tightly, even as he covered R's empty sockets, S knew that the memories would stain. He knew that the thoughts would haunt them for the rest of their lives.

Sitting uncomfortably against the cold stone wall, his ankles chained with keeler, he unwillingly listened to the Tall Being's description, blindly imagining what was happening before them. "*Immortality is only gained through sacrifice. Don't be afraid, all will be well when you are broken. You will be more powerful than any being you know.*" their Master's voice rang through the laboratory. *"Never underestimate the power of the mind, your mind will heal your pain. Trust me…"* a gut-wrenching slice of the knife played as it ran through moist skin. Droplets of blood slowly clattered against the metal of a rusted bucket which lay beneath the table. The smell became immediately pungent, the scent of warm blood filling the air.

"*The time has come to test my methods once more. I have failed time and time again, each attempt to artificially cause one to become broken ultimately ending in their doom. But you have sacrificed yourself to a worthy cause, and even if this too fails, I will be one step closer to achieving the impossible.*"

The knife crashed against the floor, drops of blood landing on S's face. The Tall Being wrapped his viscous tentacle around the patient's arm. It was a grotesque sound, challenging the horrific shrieks he had heard only days before.

The sound of his wriggling, dripping skin distorted the sound of his voice. "*There. Now, with my perfected formula, there should be no problem saving you from your presumed death.*" the whimper of the Darlid's voice followed the Tall Beings' smooth, devious sound. Deep, echoing footsteps played for a moment, followed by the clash of metal tools before he returned to his place.

S listened as the point of the syringe was plunged into the Darlid's heart, the liquid draining into his veins. The air became silent for a moment, and S slowly opened his left eye. His heart sank as he watched the dead being rise from the table. Allowing himself to lift his eyelids completely, S's sight was restored. He stared at the being in fear. It was no longer recognizable, it was a completely different being, powerful and now fearless. Dark, decaying skin flung off of the broken creature's body, splattering against the wall as he roared. The being shook its head violently, the stems of its antlers swinging about the area.

"Perfect, you are absolutely perfect! Finally, my formula has been perfected, and immortality has been reached. Yes, you still decay, but the magic within you is more powerful than you could have once imagined!" the Tall Being cackled, admiring his success.

Where

"Where are you going, Zorus?" the whispering abyss of voices echoed inside his ears as he stepped through the cold, endless vat of nothingness. *Where was he going?* He had no answer to the figureless echo of sound, he wouldn't answer it. He knew his exact intentions: *to kill the very being who started it all,* but there was not a thought in his mind, not one clue that would lead him to the one he wanted to destroy. He had to trust his heart in order to find where he needed to go. He wandered aimlessly through the Abyss searching for a feeling, one which would anger the hearts of the pure.

Zorus glanced at the slit in his right wrist, blood staining the skin around it. His skin shivered as he drew his thin finger over the forming scar. He wasn't afraid to see his own blood, he was used to crimson stains coating his skin. What he did to himself though could never be forgiven. He gave himself pain *intentionally,* just as his tormentor had. A reminder to a past so horrific, his thoughts would never still. He knew that because he drew his own blood, he had lost a great advantage in his skill until it healed completely. But he knew the power and guidance of the shadow demon would be worth the mistake.

His footsteps echoed through the empty terrain as he stepped forward, never seeming to change position. He wrapped his fragile fingers around his shoulders, warming his thin coat of skin from the chilly air surrounding him inside the void. He turned his head in both directions frantically, wondering if there would ever be an end to his search. He felt that he would die before he reached the hiding place of this demon. A harmony of shadows rose above him once again, breaking the silence. "Zorus… you want my help, don't you? I know where *he* is." the shadow confessed cunningly.

Zorus stopped walking for a moment, swallowing his fear. A blanket of shadows cloaked his freezing body. "You do?" he asked in a deep, nervous voice.

"Ask me, Zorus… ask me *where*." the shadow begged.

"Where is *he,* Astaroth*?* Where must I go to destroy *him*?" he asked in a chilled voice, awaiting his answer. "I must know. My mind will not rest until *he* is dead."

"Ah, he is somewhere very hidden, a place none would imagine. Follow your thoughts, I will lead you to his hiding spot. We *will* destroy *him.*" the symphony of droning voices sang. The voices of the shadow demon had grown stronger through time, each word which was spoken was believed by the mind of their host. The demon fed off of his fear, his anger, and most of all, his wish for revenge. This fueled them, bringing many voices into one.

Zorus took in a deep breath before beginning to follow the directions implanted in his fragile heart. It had been broken many times, ripped into pieces. He had suffered much pain, witnessed much sorrow, experienced things that felt like *death.* He was no longer a *Darlid.* He knew he had become a monster, something unnatural with powers that should not have been wielded by a mere child. His vision was clouded, and he knew that nothing was as it seemed. His life was a nightmare, and he was never waking up.

Though he knew that he must follow his intentions, each moment, it became more difficult to trust himself. The whisper of voices guided him cunningly, directing him to the one he desired to kill. His energy was becoming insufficient, and he knew that he would not be able to continue using his magic for long. He could almost feel himself falling from the void, slipping back into reality where nothing had changed except for his disappearance. If he could hide in the void forever, he would. Then there would be no more pain, no more sorrow, no more torture… but his body and mind were becoming weak.

What he had left behind would be forgotten, the words *they* said would be nothing but a memory. They didn't really care for him… he could tell. Everything spoken was a lie to keep him from accomplishing his only desire. They wanted his advantage in a mythic battle, one which he knew would never begin if *he* was dead. He had his agency; he had the ability to choose his own fate. No one could care for him so much as his brother did, and nothing could bring him back. He could care less if he died, leaving the world to one much better. He would be doing it for a great cause, taking vengeance on the most evil being that he could possibly imagine. Not one could be more evil than that being, not even Athreal, in his eyes.

The anger raging in his soul, his energy dying, his newfound power overbearing, it became more difficult to keep himself from slipping out of the void. His breath became heavy, and his head ached more than could be imagined. His vision began to blur, and the freezing air of the void amplified, a constant wind blowing flakes of snow in his direction. Though he attempted to keep himself from returning, reality continued to split through the void. "Do not fall now, Zorus, we have much to trek. Use your magic, stay in the void." the shadow pleaded. He stopped for a moment, kneeling to the ground, reviving his lost energy. The void surrounding him faded, and he was left in a freezing terrain, snow blanketing his body.

"I… can't." he admitted with heavy breaths. "It's taking all of my energy. Soon I will have none left to destroy *him.*" His body began to shiver, strong gusts of wind blowing through him.

"You will have the energy, *I promise.* You must return to the void, there are far more dangerous beings awaiting you in Winter's Gorge. Cooperate, Zorus." Zorus did not answer the shadow's song. His body stilled as if he was frozen, awaiting an end to his misery. The air chilled his body, the loss of heat causing him to lose energy, and all of his hope. The air around him became ominous, and he quickly understood where he was: *Olkned.* Blackness surrounded him, and the eerie cries of Broken Souls raged with the wind. He whimpered, knowing that he would lose the battle before it even began. He would not be able to fight against anything that came his way in this condition.

"My energy is insufficient." Zorus acknowledged.

"Fine. I'll do it myself." the shadow raged. "Zorus… why don't you look at me?" it asked.

With all of his remaining strength, Zorus turned his head to the right, gazing at his shadow. A feeling filled Zorus's heart, one which he had not felt in years. He was overcome with power, and suddenly, he felt as if he was not controlling his own body. The pain was overwhelming, a furious pressure holding onto him. He attempted to cry out, yet no one could hear him scream. His voice was left only to his thoughts. He was stuck in his own body without any control. He couldn't speak, he couldn't move, all he could do was think.

His once frozen figure stood effortlessly from the snow, breathing in the fresh, crisp air. His mouth opened, yet the words he wished to speak did not flow from his own voice. What he heard played tricks on his mind. "Ah, I haven't felt like this for years. To control the vessel once again, I feel my power returning, his depleting as I consume it. Your soul is strong, but not enough. It cannot deter my magic."

Zorus heard himself cackle, laughing in such a way he could never imagine. His chest pounded with an unusual feeling of joy, though nothing gave him the sense of elation the shadow portrayed. His mind became frantic as he realized that he could no longer control his own body, yet he could still think, still see, still feel, still know that he was no longer himself. As he couldn't overwhelm the power of the shadow demon, his magic, his abilities, his hopes all washed away as the demon took over his body. "Do not fret, I am here to help. I am here to destroy the being who tortured *us* for all of those years, to destroy *he* who killed *our* brother." The demon had persuaded him too well.

Zorus felt his body erupt in pain as the shadow demon attempted to use his magic. The world around him flashed between the void and reality, neither one taking control. He wanted to scream, the pain unbearable, yet his mouth would not open. The void faded once again, and his body hit the floor. "Ah, I see, you used your abilities to their extent. Fortunately, your energy is sufficient, and your body still has the ability to fight. *I need practice anyway.*"

Astaroth scanned the area through new sight, locating each of the cunning Olks hiding themselves away before they attacked. It wasn't difficult to spot them, as fresh coats of a dark, inky substance dripped from certain areas of the mountainside. Zorus felt his dominant hand reaching for his sword, his fingers wrapping around the soft fabric of his brother's cape. The sword was unsheathed silently as the soft sound of crunching snow played in the near distance. "I know you're out there. Please, come out and show yourself." his voice rang clearly.

A figure stepped out of the shadows, a familiar being, its height reaching only to his knee. With one enormous green cat eye balancing on its neck, and having only two limbs, it wasn't hard to recognize who was standing before him. "Nidaret." The shadow cocked Zorus's head. "How could you possibly defeat me with your size?" he chuckled. "I only want to make the fight *fair."*

The nidaret nodded as its body began to expand. Its body morphed until it stood a foot taller than Zorus, its tangled antlers stretching and retracting as it stood. "So, you're here to fight me. You think you can defeat me this time. I promise, that won't happen. *He* would be proud when I show that I have captured you." the nidaret cackled. "You can try your luck against me, but you will only fail."

"I won't let you get in the way of *Master's* demise. You best be prepared; my magic is stronger than it has ever been before."

"*Master?* Since when have you called *him* that? Even when I first received unlimited power, you despised referencing him as such." the nidaret snickered.

A grim smile spread across Zorus's face. "You'd be surprised." He lifted the sword into the air, settling into his battle stance. "Let's get this over with you pathetic demon."

"I forfeited your demise once; I will not allow it to happen again." The nidaret smiled a toothy grin. "I see you aren't taking advantage of your *protection.*

"As I said before, I prefer to keep things fair. I won't *disappear* either."

The nidaret grinned. "I know you too well for your lies to go unnoticed."

"You'll just have to trust me." Zorus felt his body move, watched as he unwillingly lunged toward the nidaret, sliding under the cascade of antlers raining down on him. His sword brushed against its slick skin, the inky substance draining from its body. The nidaret threw his horns toward him, strangling his arm with its grip. Though it was painful, the shadow demon continued to thrust his sword toward the Olk. His thin hand slipped through the tangle of antlers as he stepped beside the decaying being.

Confused by his gesture, the nidaret stumbled backward, catching himself on the rocky sidewall. "Is that the best you've got?" he asked, swerving to the right. Astaroth forced Zorus to duck beneath the attack, throwing his blade against its antlers. "You will lose this battle easily if you choose to continue fighting that way. I could match your power tenfold."

Even in the freezing air, Zorus could feel sweat slipping from his brow. His body continued to follow the movement of the shadow's wish, paining the feeling in his mind. Each strike of his sword, every dodge of an attack, his body matched perfectly to the desire of the shadow demon. Even with the unmatched skill he had developed over years of forced training, and his own desire to become wondrous while wielding a sword, he could never fight the way the shadow controlled him. The shadow never missed an attack, always found an opening to strike. Each one of his movements perfected by the knowledge of the shadow. He was now confident in *his* demise.

The nidaret began to falter in his steps, waterfalls of blood and melting skin dripping from many open wounds. Realizing that the being he fought against held power greater than he recalled, he knew that he would not have a will strong enough to survive. The whips of his antlers, and strangling of his horns began to weaken, the shock of Zorus's skill distracting him. Each time he attacked, the scelo slipped from his grip, each attempt to slaughter him missed. The nidaret was taken off guard by the sudden thrust of Zorus's blade toward his stomach. Stumbling backward, he fell to the ground with a great clatter, Zorus standing above him.

The wounds in his broken body too great, the nidaret was unable to move, unable to strike back. He began to breathe deeply as the blade was set against his throat. The shadow spoke through Zorus's voice. "Even without the use of my magic, you still failed to destroy me. You performed substantially worse than I knew you could have, and now your demise is set." As the nidaret's antlers stretched weakly toward his body- attempting to wrap against his skin, attempting to save himself from his fate- the shadow lifted his sword, slicing the antlers clean off. The horns sunk into the snow, staining the pure powder ebony. "You're nothing but a useless worm, I never understood why *he* claimed you were one of the best. Your creation was absolutely disgusting. You were a pathetic, dying creature in hope of everlasting life." the shadow chuckled. "I'll tell *him* you died with good intent."

The nidaret whimpered as Zorus raised the blade above him. With the swift movement of the sword, the blade slid cleanly through the nidaret's neck, cleaving its head from its body. Instantly, the nidaret's soul shattered, never to have sentience again. The shadow stared into the nidaret's green eyes as they darkened, its decay melting into the snow.

S opened his eyes, a fearful feeling filling the room. The moonlight pouring through the gaps in the wall, S stared at his shadow, waiting for something to happen. "What do you want?" he asked, whispering in attempt to let his brother sleep. Rest was something they scarcely had now that their magic was becoming more powerful, and even when they could, fear forced them to keep their eyes open. S knew it would be unfortunate if his brother woke from what little sleep he had.

The shadow stretched across the wall and followed the light around the room, moonlit eyes appearing on its figure. "I want my freedom." it demanded. "You and your reluctant brother have failed to destroy *him* countless times. You have had many opportunities, and yet you still choose to live in fear, shackles wrapped around your wrists forbidding you from using your gifts." Astaroth raged.

"We will free ourselves from this prison. You must remember that Courier and I have been planning this out for years. We just have to wait until the time is right, I'd say no more than two years from now. You'll have to trust us." S remarked, his voice deep and tired. He was more mature and learned, though he trusted his brother's plan, for he was more intelligent than any other being he had met. "R still has more to plan. If we act too soon, something could go wrong, and we could find ourselves dead at *his* feet.

"Fine, be *his* marionettes for now, continue to falter in your steps, continue to lead yourselves closer to a life serving him, but know that every day that passes while you do, I will be there to remind you of the task you must complete. Your soul looks delicious S, don't let it go to waste." With those words, the moonlight faded into darkness, and S found himself alone, his brother still sleeping peacefully across the room. What Astaroth had said was right, the longer they stayed in this place, the closer they came to becoming *his* servants. S would destroy the Tall Being if it was the last thing that he ever did.

Labyrinth of Ice

"One emblem remaining? What about the emblems of love and knowledge? No one knows where they are, or if they even exist." Zidal spoke, confused and afraid.

Alex cowered into the snow; his tongue frozen in place. He opened his mouth, struggling to find the right words. A tear slipped across his cheek as he spoke. "It's my fault. I tried to warn him, but he wouldn't listen… and now he's gone… *really* gone. If Zorus had known sooner… but it's too late. *I killed him, I let him die, I let the Broken Souls take it."*

"Alex, explain yourself. I'm afraid we do not understand. I have not felt Zorus's soul yet leave this world, there is still hope that he lives. He is well trained, almost undefeatable." Kardama spoke with warmth, the frigid air blowing against his cloak.

Alex let out a breath, a cold mist forming before him. "Zorus thought he was bringing himself to destroy the leader of the Broken Souls, but he will only die knowing the unfortunate truth. *He* has his ways, and even with Zorus's skill, he is destined to fall by the hands of the enemy." Alex swallowed his tears. "He *is* the emblem of love."

"But that's impossible. How could this be?" Zidal asked, fear tainting her emotion.

"The reason Courier's soul was unable to be guided wasn't because it was shattered… It was because his soul *was* the emblem of knowledge. Lade released his soul, sending it to recreate Athreal. I witnessed it, I could feel it, the sense of knowledge around him was extraordinary." Alex spoke with a somber tone. "It was only then that I realized Zorus's soul contained the emblem of love. When I met with him again, my mind confirmed it to me. I couldn't bring myself to tell him… to warn him, and now he will die returning the emblem to the Broken Souls." Alex stood from the snow; his hands placed over his eyes. "I'm sorry."

"We have to go after him, please Kardama, we must save him from this awful fate!" Zidal spoke through a teary voice. "We've already lost Courier; I refuse to lose him too!"

Kardama sighed, his face shadowed by the hood of his cloak. "I am afraid there isn't enough time, by the time we reach his destination, he will have been silenced for many days. All we can do is carry on, hope that we can destroy the emblem of strength before it is too late." Zidal fell into the soft blanket of powdered snow beside Alex, tears falling into her cupped hands. "I'm sorry. There is nothing we can do. He has sealed his fate." Kardama stared into the distant labyrinth of cascading juniperfalls, a somberness filling the air. "You beings have such tender emotion, you care so deeply for others, those we cannot control. A type of emotion I haven't felt for centuries. Indeed, it is sorrowful that one more soul is lost forever, but we must press forward, working toward the greater good." the king placed his hand on Zidal's freezing shoulder. "Come, our destiny awaits us all."

Zidal placed her hand on the stem of her scythe, gently wrapping her fingers around the pole. "I could end it all right now, take away my life, choose to leave this world." she spoke softly as her grip tensed. "I could end my misery…" as the scythe began to slide from her ropes, Kardama gently placed his hand on hers. "I could erase my existence, destroy what could have been. Because life without those I love is not one worth living. Because the world could be better without me." Zidal loosened her grip, fixing her posture. "But part of me is afraid of what will happen if I do, part of me wonders if I'm strong enough to escape the grasp of a second chance." tears streaming across her cheeks, Zidal weakly stood. "But with a purpose, a destiny to defeat the Broken Souls, I know that I must continue living. We must find the emblem of strength."

Kardama nodded softly. "Zidal, you are incredibly brave, sacrificing a desire for the greater good. Alex, you have immense strength, fighting for a world you know so little about." Kardama took Zidal's hand and helped her stand from the snow-laden ground. "Though our hearts are filled with sorrow, we must begin our trek at once. Alex, you are the only one who can lead us through this labyrinth. Do you have the strength?"

Alex lowered his hands, revealing his tear-stained face, and weakly nodded his head.

Alex stared into the entrance of the labyrinth, his mind laced with strength, mirrored by a melancholy emotion. His body ached and his mind swelled with the familiar motion of the mind wavering. Taking in a deep breath, Alex stepped toward the darkened space, leaving behind nothing but his footprints and frozen tears. The king and Zidal followed closely behind, a feeling of confidence and sorrow balancing between them. Silence rang through the air as strong gusts of wind sent dark clouds above them.

The air around them grew darker the further they stepped into the labyrinth. An inky-black substance caked the walls, dripping onto the frozen ground. Silence rang through the tunnels, the icy walls echoing back any sound that entered the empty halls. Soft sounds of crunching snow played in the distance, Broken Souls lurking in the shadows. Each step which was taken was filled with anxiety as they knew that at any moment, they could be attacked. Even with the sorrowness that filled their fragile souls, they never lost their guard.

Alex stepped with caution, following the emotions that coated his mind. The corridor seemed to go on forever, not a single break in the ice had yet been seen. The walls began to cave out, widening the area surrounding them. Sections on either wall were carved out, hiding areas erected for the Broken Souls to sleep without fear, for even the most powerful of beings have something to fear. They continued to trek through the seemingly endless icy terrain, a deep, anxious knowledge following their every step.

Glancing behind him, Alex slowed his step to a halt, his expression in awe. The others followed his gaze, understanding what he had found incredible. Though they had stepped for what had seemed like miles through an empty walkway, openings in the walls of the maze were now visible from every direction. Even more to their disbelief, a blockade stood only a mile from where they stood, the entrance they took now being an impossibility. Returning their gaze to what stood before them, another frozen fall stood before them, the endless corridor now ending with a right turn. "It's no wonder no one had ever found their way through the Krysal Falls. The labyrinth is constantly modifying itself, as if to ensure no one knows how to explore this area." Alex observed. "Even with the advantage of knowing where the emblem is, we'll never be able to find a pathway directly to it."

Alex took the right turn, the others following him behind. Looking behind him, the ice which was blocking the left had dissipated. Confused, he began to follow the straight pathway. "It is true, no one has found their way through, but how would we know about the dangers of this maze if no stories were told?" Zidal asked as she followed Alex through a right turn. "The only beings known to reside in this labyrinth are Broken Souls. They know the ins and outs of this maze."

Alex took another right before turning around and following another straight pathway. "What you speak of is true, Zidal. But why would such a thing matter in our travels?" Kardama asked gracefully.

"If we could find a Broken Soul that could lead us through the labyrinth, we could retrieve the emblem of strength with ease." she acknowledged, her soft voice carrying through the soft breeze.

"But trusting a Broken Soul can lead to a plenitude of risks. With hundreds living within the Krysal Falls, they are bound to release the soul of the emblem." the king declared, following Alex through a small tunnel.

"We've been walking for miles and not one Broken Soul has appeared. How do we even know if they still reside here?" Alex questioned as he took two lefts.

Kardama spoke. "Oh, they'll show themselves..." Alex stopped in his tracks, glancing behind him. The realization came to him, and a sudden fear corrupted his mind. Who stood before him was neither Kardama, nor Zidal, but a pair of hideous creatures, their skin bleeding into the ground. Their figures resembled that of a horse. Their muzzles long and aligned, a sharp horn balanced on the tip of their noses. Two snake eyes glowing emerald-green appeared on each side of their faces. Thick, scaly spines crept down their necks like a mane of hair, leading to their slick, black bodies. Lengthening from their backs, a leathery tail, covered with spines, grew, developing into a tattered hand. From the center of each of their chests, a fifth leg grew, each of their broad legs ending with a long paw, thick blade-like claws extending from each toe.

The differences were subtle, but each had their own unique properties. The being who stood on the left grinned cunningly, the bottom jaw split unevenly through the center. Its tongue draped uncomfortably outside its mouth, tightening around its broken jaw. The other, which stood proudly on the right, had been slit through the stomach, decaying intestines slipping out of its open wound. From the center of its chest, its rapidly beating heart hung from only the veins it was attached to.

Before he could move, two stale hands wrapped around his forearms. Alex's breath became heavy, his heartbeat rising anxiously. "This is when you ask your questions." the one on the right spoke, his voice smoothly shifting from Kardama's to one much deeper and more sinister. "Go on, we know you have them. We will declare our bargain when you are finished."

Alex took in a breath. "Where are Kardama and Zidal?"

The Broken Soul on the left began to answer, her voice trembling as it became less sorrowful. The sound was still clearly feminine. "Taken." she said simply, her tongue caressing her lips.

"Where? And by who?" Alex queried.

The male began to speak again. "They are now prisoners to the Broken Souls, captured by others who reside here." the Broken Soul brayed.

"Will they be killed?"

"Enough with them. They should no longer matter to you. What happens to them is none of your concern." the female spoke, shifting her weight. "What else do you desire to know?"

"How were you able to follow me without being noticed?"

"Easy, you were distracted with the transitions of the maze. We have been trained with such silence that your notice of the other's disappearance was non-existent. The sounds of your allies' voices led your mind astray as you expected to be safe." the one on the right answered.

"Who are you?" Alex questioned.

"I have been given the name of Atlas, accompanied by my sister Ambush. Given second life, we are the most powerful of the pfesen rec, steeds with the most impeccable imitations of voices." Atlas reared, his three front legs swinging chaotically. "We were sent by the Master of all

Broken Souls to find and release the soul of the emblem of strength, and we will not end our quest until it has been completed."

"You have the ability to lead us to the emblem. We ask you to bring us to the emblem, and in return, we will free your comrades." Ambush promised.

"What if I choose not to lead you to the emblem?"

Atlas raised his hoarse voice. "Then you and your allies will bc sentenced to death. Once you have fallen, there would be none to stop us from massacring the entirety of Darlid kind, and without Death, Broken Souls will be the only creatures residing. There would be no *heroes* left to stop the Master from accomplishing the ever-important quest."

Alex swallowed fearfully, glancing over his shoulder. He bit his lip, his mind corrupted with anxious thoughts, feeling alone, and afraid. "What will it be, boy? The location of the emblem or the death of everyone you care for?" Ambush asked sneeringly.

After a moment of deep thought, Alex sighed and spoke with agony. "I will lead you to the emblem of strength." The broad hands loosened their grip on his arms and took his hands. With a firm shake from both pfesens, Alex committed to a deal he could never break.

R awoke in the silence of the night, the fear lingering from the nightmare which corrupted his mind. His breaths were heavy, and his fingers were trembling. He was unable to discern the shadows in the room from monsters which existed in his dreams, the darkness corroding his perception. R glanced at his wrists, the shackles binding his arms tightly, though he could move freely through the room. The pain of his magic being blocked from his own use was unbearable, like a hare trapped in a small cage, unable to use its speed to escape the predator.

His brother was nowhere in sight. It would be unusual if he woke in the middle of the night when S was asleep. The Master called for his training more often, his torture, his pain now that he was older. R wondered if they would see each other again, if three nights ago was the last he would know of his brother's existence. With only two years until their plan would take action, he needed the presence of his brother in order to plan their attack.

With a shift in the light, R watched his shadow creep across the wall, smiling grimly at him. He knew that the shadow held sentience, that its presence was evil. S attempted to persuade him of the goodness the shadows brought, of the power they could give him, but R knew that his mind had been corrupted by the teachings of the demon. Corbin would never corrupt him; he would not let the shadow take over his innocence.

"Have you made up your mind yet?" the shadow asked. "It has been three nights, and still, you have failed to comply with my offer." Its voice taunted him.

"You don't understand, Corbin." R began, his voice becoming more mature. "Decisions take time and thought. I must find the most logical answer, or I may regret it in the future."

"Think? You have had hours upon hours to think… time is of the essence; you are losing it very quickly. I fear soon you will no longer be yourself, but a slave of the Master. Your brother even sooner, his mind will become corrupt if you do nothing to save him."

"Zorus has a strong heart, he will never fall into the deeds of the Master, neither will I. There is no logical reason for me to take part in his battle, only fear, and death. It is our destiny to destroy this being, and we will not die until he has breathed his last breath." R felt a tear slip from his empty eye. "I will not give in, I will never give up in the hope that I can find my way out of this tiny world of mine, into one which I know is infinite."

"You want to take my offer then?" Corbin asked cunningly, using R's plea to his advantage.

R swallowed his tears and nodded softly. "As much as I don't trust you, as much as I know you will betray me in the end, I know that I will need your power in order to defeat the Master. I know that Zorus will need the help of his shadow too. If either of us decides to disregard your wish to destroy the Master and escape, we too will fail in our efforts to succeed."

The Shadow veered its head to the left, pondering R's words. He spoke through his crooked voice. "Very good, I will consult with my brother. Let us hope that yours follows through." Corbin cackled before he disappeared into the darkness of the night.

R closed his eyes, anxiously rocking back and forth on the surface of his tattered bed, attempting to sleep, attempting to find reason to his existence, to his hopeless life.

Zorus stood from the ground, his hands quivering, his mind shaking with an immeasurable amount of anxious thoughts as he regained control over his body. The amount of adrenaline in his veins was unreal, the power he held was unlike any other force he had felt. He had done the impossible, no mortal before him could have defeated a being such as that. His confidence rose with the confirmation that Astaroth could complete the impossible.

"What have you done?" he asked, relieved that words flowed smoothly through his lips again.

"I only demonstrated the power you wield Zorus. Your magic is incredibly strong, you have the capability to accomplish all which I have done, you need only to expand your mind, reach for things you thought were once impossible. No, not yet have I added the strength of my own power, nor have I explored the opportunities available through your magic. Exterminating *him* will be easy." the shadow spoke deviously. "Control your thoughts, Zorus… you can overpower me."

"Where do I find him? I need to finish this… now." his body held in a constant tremble, Zorus stood from the ink-stained snow, staring into the distance. He swiftly sheathed his sword, waiting for the deep echoing voice to answer him.

A dark, shadowed feeling draped over his mind, corrupting his imagination as Astaroth spoke again. "Continue on the path I have set for you. Have patience, soon we will receive the gratification of his death." the shadow chuckled. "Soon all the pieces will be in place for the greater goal to be accomplished."

Closing his soulless eyes, Zorus focused on the task at hand, finding the path that was set for him. Breathing in the crisp night air, he restored his sight, admiring the glistening reflection of the stars on the pure-white snow. He began to step through the snow shakily, though filled with power and energy, leaving nothing but deep footprints behind. There was nothing that could get in his way now, he would destroy the very being who corrupted his life, the one who destroyed all his hopes, the one who killed the only person he loved. He could feel it in his heart, though not everything would be right, he would have his satisfaction.

The light of the twin crescent moons flooded his figure, sending him a glorious light to aid him on the final stretch of his journey. Never before had he felt so passionate about one feeling, one to destroy another soul. The breath of the wind brushed coolly across his bare skin, chilling his bones, and sending a tremble of anxiety through his veins. He wrapped his arms around his chest, warming his body from the freezing air as he stepped through the continuous lane of snow and rock, smothered in the decay of living corpses. Those that still resided in Olkned now feared him, knowing what he had done. He was not afraid of any other being, knowing not one could exceed his power, none but himself.

The air was silent, and the constant crunch of the crisp snow sounded beneath him. Something seemed to counter the balance of peace in the night. He could feel it inside him, there was a being lurking in the shadows with one desire: to destroy him, soul, and body. Zorus halted in his movement, reaching for the stem of his brother's sword. He drew his hand across the smooth pommel, wrapping his fingers around the tattered cloth of the valiant cape. His fingers latched tightly around the handle, his soul ready to unsheathe his weapon and rip the blade through the demon's heart.

He waited patiently for the being to show himself, to appear out of the shadows, but only a familiar, crooked voice filled the night air. "Ah, so you have arrived at the very place where it all began." the echoing voice cackled with a glorious intent. "What an unwise decision, S. I thought you would have known better, coming here has only corroborated your destruction. You attempted this very feat before, only to fail. It is only certain you will fail again, but this time, your loss will be worth your life, and the lives of many others."

With heavy breaths Zorus searched the snowy canvas in awe, unable to find the source of the voice. To no avail, the terrain was empty, and the echoed sound played from every direction. With an unexpected suddenness, Zorus released the grip of his sword and fell to the ground in agony. That awesome power he held instantly dissipated; the familiarity of magic vanished. A familiar, weak feeling entered his soul, a weight on his ankle calling to his past. *Keeler stone,* a weapon against the powerful that would cause them to become weak, force them to accommodate and fight with strength they still owned until there was none left. "Death!"

A shadow loomed over his sunken body, though it did not reach for him. Swaying limbs furled above him, deviously waiting for his suffering to begin. "One could say the powerful use their power unwisely." his tattered voice filled his mind with dread. "Though, keeler stone is too a powerful thing, it can block even the most powerful of forces."

"*You...*" Zorus spat.

"Ah, S, you thought you could play against the rules, find a hole in the balance. No, I knew your intentions, I knew you would find me, I wouldn't allow for my own downfall... at least with such an unfair advantage." Zorus reached for his sword, lightly gripping the handle.

Zorus glanced at his shadow, begging it to strengthen his skill, yet the guidance and skill of the shadow felt unreachable now. "Why would you ever trust a demon? You thought that a being as powerful as a shadow would be your only chance of defeating me, and I must admit, you were right. You are playing with an uncontrollable force, foolish of you to think it would protect you..." a chorus of laughter filled the silent air. "The shadow demons only help themselves; they tell lies only to gain their own strength. True they are the only beings who could possibly destroy me, but when they do, it will be they who have all the power." Zorus felt his lungs fill with heavy breath as his confidence drained. Lade chuckled. "What is it you want?"

"I want answers, you corrupt analyst!" Zorus demanded as he rose from the icy ground. Though he knew he hadn't the power to defeat his greatest foe, his strength and knowledge of his own skill increased with his unmatched determination. Drawing his icy blade, he faced the demon, his disgusting, deformed face haunting him. The same jagged scar stretched through his empty right eye. He couldn't bear to lay his eyes on him for more than a second. He held his blade before him, listening to *his* daunting words.

"That's not all you want, is it? I know you desire to destroy me, and I won't let myself stop you from attempting. You see, war is in my blood, and I desire to take everything you live for away from you. I desire to cause you misery."

"What is your point, demon?" Zorus asked in a sorrowful rage. "You've already succeeded in that."

"Ah, but the hopes you still hold can be destroyed too. There is more I want from you, something you cannot fathom as even being a possibility. I will bring you to your breaking point, such that you will willingly give me that which I desire.`` The smirk smeared across his face drew out, creating a freakish grin. Each of his tentacles raised into the frigid air, awaiting the battle to begin. *"Ask your questions..."* the words slipping from his deformed lips, Lade lunged toward Zorus. With his quickened reflexes, he bent toward the ground, lifting his sword above him. Lade's thick skin caught on the tip, ripping across the blade.

Zorus attacked with more force than he had ever before, using his skill in swordsmanship in a way he never thought he could. Though, his skill was easily matched by *he* who trained him. Throwing back an attack which was easily countered, Zorus spoke. "What hopes are there left to destroy? You took everything from me!"

"Ah, so you desire for me to show you how I can break you, soul and body. Where should I begin?" Lade questioned himself as he threw his tentacle around Zorus's thin waist. "No, I have not taken everything from you... not yet. Your claim only strengthens my theory, for you see, you believe that your brother is the only being that cared for you. You believed that he was the only being you could have the capacity to care for. Your love for him is immense." Zorus forcefully lifted his arm through his vice-like grip, tearing through his viscous skin. The decaying tentacle uncoiled, reforming the torn flesh.

"His death was unnecessary, cruel and torturesome. You will die for his fall!" Zorus raged as he struck forth his blade.

"You truly don't understand, I have reason for everything I choose to take part in. His death was necessary for my plan to come to completion." Lade announced as he lifted himself from the ground, avoiding the swipe of his enemy's blade.

"You aren't making sense!" balls of sweat began to form on his forehead, drenching his blonde hair.

"Ah, so you are not aware that there are only two emblems remaining?"

"Have the others failed to successfully find the emblem of strength? Have your followers released the emblem?"

"I fear that they still have much of a journey to complete." he spoke cunningly. Reaching to his left, Lade wrapped his arm around the circumference of an icicle, as broad as a sword, ripping it from the rocky overhang. Whipping his arm toward his fleshy chest, Zorus raised his blade anxiously, blocking the attack.

"Then how is that possible?" he questioned, swinging his sword, the icicle clashing against it. "That could only mean that you have found either the emblem of love or knowledge, and that is impossible!"

"So, the human never told you... I thought you would have known by now, but you never were a good listener either." Lade chuckled, drawing the icicle toward him. Zorus stumbled in his steps, catching his balance as he anxiously, fearfully listened. "That only allows me the satisfaction of your reaction. *Your brother was the emblem of knowledge."* Zorus lowered his blade, a dark realization shadowing his mind. His body shook and became weak. He fell to his knees, the sword dropping into the snow, his thoughts shattered and his soul empty. Lade's grin expanded. "So, I can break you more than you expected… how queer."

Zorus sat in the snow, his breaths heavy, unable to think straight. "Put the pieces together, S. Why would I kill your brother in such a demonic fashion?" his demonic voice rang through his mind. Zorus's breaths became heavy, his mind filled with anxieties never felt before. Everything became more clear, disturbing his soul with great immensity. He couldn't forgive himself for his stupidity, he knew he would die by *his* hands, but was so blind to see that he would be putting the entire world in danger by doing so. He was speechless, not one word could fall from his lips as his anxiety drenched his soul. His throat was sealed, his body was frozen with disbelief, and all he could do was listen.

"It never occurred to me when you were children that your purpose and benefit to me would be to recreate Athreal, but now, it is all so clear." time began to feel slow, each word dripping from his tormentor's mouth lingering longer than he would have wished as his thoughts bounced quickly across his mind. "Your brother always learned quickly; he knew more than any other Darlid could imagine. His mind was never filled to its capacity, he always knew more, always wanted to know more. He wanted to understand the workings of this pathetic world. The realization came to me quickly, only the emblem could hold such a power; therefore, he must be the living embodiment of knowledge." Lade chuckled as he continued to step about Zorus's bitterly frozen figure.

"You were much more difficult for me to confirm my theory on. I couldn't possibly kill you first without affirming that your brother was the emblem of knowledge. After I released the emblem from your brother's heart, confident with my assumption, the confirmation came that a living being could indeed hold the emblem of love too. I first looked to you, for if your brother held the emblem of knowledge, it could only mean that you held the emblem of love, but you always seemed so cold-hearted." the grin across his face widened. "But as I observed you, it became quite obvious. The immense love you showed for your brother's pathetic soul, the way your mind could trick you into loving someone you so clearly despised before, the difficulty you have had letting go of those you have cared for. That feeling, the strength of the emblem, you wield it… and I crave it."

As the immense feelings of ennui and sorrow cloaked his restless mind, each word Lade spoke began to fade, each syllable became more difficult to derive from the last. "You belong… to me…" the last words he understood fell from the lips of that monstrous creature wickedly before all he knew fell from his grasp, all his being dissipated. He fell to the ground and remembered no more.

S awoke to a strange sound, like two walls ramming into each other in a constant beat. His vision was blurry, and his head ached immensely, but he had the strength to stand. S stepped toward the large metal door, noticing light flooding through the opening. Placing his fingers against the door, using all of his strength, he applied pressure against it. Slowly, the door swung open, leading into the empty hallway. S glanced at his brother, sleeping under the influence of the Master's drugs, and after assuring himself that there was no other soul lurking in the hallway, he stepped out.

S turned toward the left length of the hall, staring at the all familiar door which stood mockingly at the end. He had seen it plenty of times, always aware that it would lead to the outside world, that it would lead to his freedom.

As curiosity over-swept his mind, he took in a longing breath and followed the corridor to the door, dragging his hand across the smooth stone walls.

The beat continued to play, growing in immensity as he stepped closer to the door. S could feel his heart rate rising as he neared the door, his arm reaching toward the smooth metal of the handle. His footsteps soon echoed the pulsing beat, challenging him to race for his freedom, until his hand finally smoothed the handle. Everything became silent, not even the dripping of dew drops echoed in the corridor. He felt his heart suddenly stop, his breath rising as he pressed on the handle of the door, pulling it in toward himself.

The sensation was overpowering. Sweet air filled the corridor, unlike anything he had tasted before. A light brighter than could ever be described flooded into the darkness of the hallway. The vision of the outside world blinded him, beaconed him to leave before he lost his chance, but he knew he couldn't. The taste was enough to satisfy him for the time being, he would not break his promise, he would not leave his brother in this wretched place just so he could taste freedom.

He could taste a life beyond this prison.

Letting out a deep breath, S slowly closed the door, letting his fingers slip from the radiant handle. His freedom would come, but not today, not for months, he would fight his way through his last days remaining in his prison, fighting for his brother's life until they both could feel the warmth of the sun across their skin.

S smiled, this being the only time he would while he still remained in the Master's care. Losing a breath, S turned away from the door, his

Master standing above him. The devious, murderous grin of his Master bled into his heart, staining his mind with irreversible nightmares. He knew that he would be heavily punished because of what he did, he knew that his exploration would cause him exceeding pain, he knew that he could have put his brother at risk too, but stil, he fell to his knees in surrender, asking the Master to remove him from the sight of his freedom.

Path for the Weak

The freezing breeze rushed across Alex's cheeks as he steadied himself on the pfesen's slick back, matching the chaotic beat of his five legs as it galloped. He took in a heavy breath, holding onto the spines of the pfesen's main with all of his strength as it galloped through the snowy labyrinth. The air was pungent, the scent a mixture of decaying flesh and fresh blood. The tips of Alex's boots coiled underneath Atlas's hanging intestines, the constant tapping of feet hitting the ground followed by snorts of chilly air moving forward. Ambush followed swiftly beside her brother, anxious for their task to be completed. "Left there!" Alex called, pointing south as the walls of the labyrinth narrowed. He tightened his grip with his thighs as the pfesen's whipped to the left, knowing that if he failed to, he would be left behind in the middle of an endless maze. Even with the claws extending from its tail wrapped tightly around his waist, the force of the turn pushed him toward the side.

Galloping down the icy pathway, an intersection appeared. Despite the fact that a wall stood at the end of the road, the only possible directions leading right or left, Alex did not stutter. "Continue straight!" he called. The pfesens did not falter in their step as they phased through the cracked wall. The labyrinth was much easier to navigate now that he had the help and knowledge of the Broken Souls by his side, the illusions now easy to see past. Many of the walls seen before were merely reflections to trick the common eye, each time any being changed direction, the reflections appearing in different positions. With the illusions now more obvious, Alex could trust his mind in which direction to follow with certainty. Still, he was caught wondering how he would be able to outsmart the pfesens and take the emblem of strength for himself.

Hours had passed since he had first encountered the pfesens, hours since he last knew the whereabouts of his allies. The labyrinth was enormous, and even with the knowledge of the illusions, it was easy to get turned around. Still, they would not rest until the emblem of strength was found. Alex's throat was becoming dry after the numerous times he had to shout directions to turn. His hands constantly slipped from the slick spines of the pfesen's mane. His head was becoming dizzy, and his eyesight began to blur as the thick breeze stretched against him as they galloped. His back, tightened by Atlas's claws, began to feel sore and his thighs were weakening as he continued to cling to his body. His breaths were heavy, and his soul began to feel depleted of energy as he had ridden far longer than he ever had before.

Along with the physical pain he was experiencing, the mind wavering was causing his very soul to ache. As it was nearing the end of its course, completing his full transformation into Darlid kind, the pain was becoming far more difficult to manage. Still, he continued to press on as the time of Athreals' recreation was nearing. He could not give up, he would not give up, not after all he had been through, not after how far he had come. He knew that he may not ever return to the life he once had before, but he finally had a purpose in life, a reason to fight for something.

Upon their enduring gallop, a wall of stone appeared in the near distance. "Straight ahead!" the pfesens listened to his direction, cantering toward the cliff. Near feet before the stone, the pfesens reared, turning away from the wall. Alex held tightly to Atlas's mane, sliding across his slick back as they reached higher. As they landed, their movement faltered, and they faced the wall.

"We cannot pass through this wall, for it is stone erected by the elements." Atlas brayed. "We can go no further, where is the emblem?!" he demanded, his intestines swaying in the crisp wind.

"Have you led us astray in attempt to postpone its destruction?" Ambush questioned.

"No. As much as I do not want the emblem to be destroyed, I have followed its force perfectly. It is very close…" Alex silenced himself for a moment as he looked to the cloudy sky in realization. His heart was pulled toward the peak of the rock before him, begging him to reach it.

He spoke with a demolition of hope. "The emblem is located at the peak of this cliff."

"At the peak of the Mirror cliffs?" Atlas asked.

"You seek us to climb the most tenacious mountain to ever have risen?" Ambush questioned. "You will *pay* if the emblem cannot be found atop this peak."

Alex swallowed his fear as he gazed into the foggy sky, speaking with little confidence. "I promise, with all of the being that remains inside me, the emblem is atop this frozen cascade. We must ascend in order to collect it."

"Very well, young human. We will ascend. I would hold on tightly if I were you." Atlas commanded.

"You're not going to let me dismount?" Alex asked, cupping his fingers around the claws of Atlas's tail.

"Do you think us fools? If we let you free, you would leave us behind. And, besides, you are far too weak to climb this cliff, the mind wavering is almost complete, is it not?" Ambush questioned cunningly.

"All the more reason to begin climbing now. Once it is completed, I will no longer be of aid to you." the pfesens snorted, extending their claws toward the rocky cliff. Each of their front claws wrapped around a protruding stone, they heaved their bodies up, gripping the rocks below them with their two back claws. Attempting to balance himself upward, Alex gripped the slick spines of Atlas's mane and elevated himself. Wrapping his arms tightly around his neck, held himself up. Though he was holding himself onto his back as well as he could, if it were not for Atlas's claws holding to his waist, he would surely have fallen.

Glancing below him, they had climbed well above the snowy ground of the labyrinth, a drop from this height fatal. His vision extended across the ledges of labyrinth walls; the paths now easy to distinct. The movement was steady, each second that passed, two steps skyward were taken. The pfesens were careful of fragile shards, immediately grasping a different stone when pebbles began to slip off of the cliff. Climbing was in their nature, as if they were born on the edge of a cliff. They never took rests, a determination to reach the emblem driving them to reach the top.

Alex held tightly to the slick skin of the pfesen, attempting to keep himself from meeting a great demise. Their steps never slowed as they continued to scale the Mirror cliffs. Though the trek became more perilous as they climbed, as the shards of frozen juniper, creating the appearance of crystals, began reflecting the light before them. Though the pfesens did not slow their step, they began to stutter and lose grip on the thin ledges they had chosen. The reflections caused their eyes to deceive them as crystal shards began to appear where they were not on thc facc of thc prccipicc.

The peak of the mountain never seemed to be nearer than the step before. The only acknowledgement of their rising movement, the fall to the icy ground. The tension began to rise as anxieties echoed through the crisp air. Their steady breaths began to lengthen as the air began to thin upon their climb. The pfesens brayed quietly, though no word was spoken. Alex's grip began to loosen as the freezing air bit at his fingers, but he held tightly to the spines of Atlas's neck, determined to live beyond these cliffs.

Finally, their breaths heavily filling their lungs, their strength beginning to falter, and each step becoming more difficult to devise, they began to slow their movements. Lifting their heads, a ledge appeared in the distance. Though the rocky ledge still stood a long distance from the peak of the Mirror cliffs, the pfesens drew their last length of energy and swiftly pulled themselves atop its surface. Upon the cliff, the pfesens collapsed, and allowed Alex to sit upon the ledge, their claws still wrapped around his waist.

Their breaths were heavy, and their muscles were sore, yet the determination still flowed freely through their bodies, and their desire did not cease. Ambush slowly rose onto her feet, her four eyes searching the area before her. The ledge, though the path was thin, led beyond a corner, slowly rising to the peak of the cliff. "Come brother, we haven't much further to trek. The climb should be easier with a surface to walk upon."

Atlas placed his feet beneath his swollen body and lifted himself from his fallen position. His heart swung freely beneath him as he stood upright. "Human, where is this emblem? Must we trek one thousand steps more?"

Alex, speaking through heavy, broken breaths, stood from the icy ground. "No, it seems only a short walk further." Atlas shook his head, allowing Alex to mount and take hold of his spines. The pfesens stepped slowly through the icy terrain, weak in soul and body. A great cloud of fog surrounded them as they had reached a height unreachable by most. The cold, crisp air froze their broken bodies, a warmth ever wished for. Their bones ached every step they took, their joints cracking as they broke through the thin layer of ice forming around their melting skin.

Taking in a deep, sullen breath, the pfesens took the corner, leading themselves into a cavern. As they stepped into the cavern, a light and warmth unknown entered their hearts. It was a small cave, a circular room with only one opening. It was a peculiar room, a strange violet light encompassed the area, bringing warmth into the cave. The ground was soft, covered in leaves of grass and a vibrant array of flowers. In the center of the cavern grew a glorious flower, its thin stem blossoming large petals of ice. It gave a bright and glorious glow and filled all who witnessed it with a strength unknown.

Alex and the pfesens basked in its glory as they had finally found the very item they had been searching for. As they had finally reached their goal and found their once lost strength. Atlas stood in awe near the entrance of the cavern, wonderstruck, Alex held tightly to his back. Glancing at Ambush, he nodded, allowing her to stand before the glorious flower. Her tail flowing swiftly, she reached out her hand and gently pressed her claws against the stem, plucking it from its resting place.

Ambush stared in awe at the crystal petals surrounding the stigma, letting out a frigid breath. Her body filled with a strength unmatched, and her soul ignited with hope. "What a shame this glorious flower must be destroyed. After such a treacherous climb to find it, only to let it shatter between my fingers."

"I beg you, please do not destroy it!" Alex yelled, struggling through the pfesen's grip. "You do not understand the pain it will bring to this world if Athreal is recreated!"

"That's the point," Atlas began, "We are doing this to return him to his rightful place, ruler of all. Let the ritual be completed, dear sister." Despite his struggles, the being's grip only became tighter. There was no escape from his grasp, there was no chance to save the emblem from its fate. He had failed, he knew nothing could be done, the world was doomed.

Ambush raised her crooked voice as she lowered the petals into the palm of her hand. "For the reincarnation of Athreal, your soul is free!" in an instant, she cupped her claws around the glass petals and crushed them between her fingers. A violet soul escaped from the shards of broken glass, returning to its rightful place. All of the warmth, light, and strength disappeared, leaving them in a darkened, joyless cavern. Ambush flicked her tongue across her broken jaw as a grin appeared on her dragon-like mussel.

Tears pouring down his face, knowing he had failed, that there was nothing he could do to prevent Athreal's reincarnation, Alex spoke. "You got what you wanted from me, now take me to my friends. You promised."

"Indeed, we did." Atlas recalled.

"Oh, we'll take you to them..." Ambush's words echoed with a nasty cackle.

"Ah, S, you think that you are smart. You think that you can try and escape from me, from this, your home?" the Master's voice of delusions echoed through the stone room. S struggled through the grip of the chains bound around his wrists and ankles, though his strength would not comply. He was bound to the table once again, unable to escape the tortures his Master would cause him. "You knew that there would be consequences to your actions, and yet you still disobeyed me." The Tall Being lifted a knife from the countertop and began to strike it against a stone.

"It seems that torturing your mind is no longer enough, you must be punished physically in order to remember your place." The Master lifted the knife from the stone and neared the table. S shook with fear, knowing the pain would be all too real. "Now, I understand that the shift in your power is only temporary. Once your wounds heal, you will once again have the ability to change form." the Tall Being grinned with evil intent. "Oh, how I've missed slicing through your skin. This is pure bliss to me."

S laid silently; his lips unable to part. He was speechless, afraid beyond explanation. His eyes shut tightly as he was unwilling to watch his own skin break. He squirmed as a sharp pain pierced his side, and though he wished to call out, he knew no one would hear his cries. He felt his cold blood running down his brittle skin as the knife was drawn out of his body. S slightly opened his eyes when the Master unexpectedly stabbed his left side. S groaned in pain, coughing, and gagging through the piercings in his body. Slowly the knife was drawn yet again from his body, laced in his own dripping blood.

His body ached with a pain unimaginable. This wasn't the first time the Master had cut into him without consent. It had been happening more frequently than he last recalled. He barely had time to heal from his wounds before the master cut into him again. It all hurt.

Tossing the knife to the side, the Tall Being carefully lifted his shirt, revealing the wounds he had created. His skin was dyed crimson as his own blood streamed across his chest. "You must continue your training; S. I only need those wounds to heal more quickly. Then you can prepare yourself to serve me in the final days." the Tall Being cackled as he returned to the table of objects.

He lowered his reach and opened a small drawer beneath the top of the table. He rummaged for a moment before retrieving a needle and thread. The needle was thick, and the point was sharp. S whimpered as his Master returned to his side, threading the string through the eye of the needle. A shock of pain ran through S's body as the needle pierced through his broken skin, stretching, and pulling it to reach the end of the cut. Swiftly the needle ran through his skin, dragging the thick string through his insides. After many strokes, the Master tied the end of the string in a tight knot, keeping his skin in place, and forcefully ripped the end of the string.

The Tall Being then stood on his opposite side, preparing another string to tie together his body. The needle again pierced his skin, running through his body to fix the very slice his Master had created. S waited patiently for his wound to be sealed, pain the only thing he could feel. Tears ran across his dry cheeks, the only way to comfort himself. The string ran through his body a multitude of times before the Master finally tied the end of the string and once again ripped the remainder of the string off of the end.

The Tall Being sighed, removing the chains from S's wrists and ankles. "Ah, the most joyous moments in life never seem to last, do they? Each moment of pain, each second of misery is what lasts. There is no escape from the tortures of life, they always return." the Master tightly held S's hand as he lifted him from the medical table. "Now, return to your room and never again think that you can escape again."

Loved and Lost

Taking in a deep, crip breath of the murky air, Zorus awoke from his long-lasting slumber. Blood dripped down his face, amongst many other wounds which stretched across his body, pooling on the stone floor. A once silent mind was instantly constrained with thoughts as he became aware of his existence once again. Every demonic thought echoed through his mind, each of his failures, all of the pain which he had endured through his life. All hope was lost. His mind had gone insane from the horrors he had lived through. There was nothing left for him, nothing but the constant pain and sorrow which never seemed to end.

The rush of fear and anxiety intensified as he realized where he was, the sight of the small, dull room all too familiar. His only instinct to react failed as a familiar, binding sensation rushed through his body, a weight on his wrists reminding him of a life filled with misery. He was incredibly low on energy, and his magic was unreachable, bound inside of him, unable to escape. As he shifted his weight, the steady clatter of chains echoed through the small space. His mind and body were equally weak, he had not the energy to attempt to escape.

His breaths were slow and steady, and his empty eyes followed the shift of light as his shadow creeped across the wall. "Why did you leave me? We failed. *He* still lives. You knew I could not destroy *him* on my own. You knew that you were the only being that could possibly defeat *him.*" Zorus demanded with a weak voice. Silence rang for a moment as he waited for an answer, "You cannot fool me, I know you are present, Astaroth."

The shadow stirred, and a gentle, blue light formed his enchanting eyes. The shadow smirked. "It was you, Zorus. Your fear and anger was so intense that your mind would not allow me to control it. I tried to warn you, but now we are both doomed. I am afraid that it is too late now, there is no escape from his wrath. Soon we shall join our brothers… Goodbye, old friend." the shadow spoke softly as his figure faded into the darkness.

Zorus sat in silence for a moment, regret plaguing his mind. Thoughts began to fade, a desperate plea repeating as he finally lost his will to be. The shadow was right, death seemed more appealing than an attempt to escape. His soul was filled to its capacity with emptiness, the constant agony demolishing all hope, harrowing all memories. No physical pain could satisfy him, his aches in body pained him far less than those in his mind. The world no longer seemed of purpose; he was no longer needed in one as such. He had failed himself, and everyone he had ever cared for. Though, now, no one pleased him, no one cared about him, he was alone and obsolete. Zorus let his eyelids fall, awaiting his freedom by death.

The loneliness consumed him.

Loneliness… a feeling so immense that a mind as impaired as his could not contain. All he could do was wait, wallowing in his tears, drinking them in as sorrow became his only comfort- allowing himself to be consumed by the thoughts, the fears… the pain.

One without such monsters inside their minds could not fathom the immeasurable grief felt, caused by nothing other than his own corrupted mind. Not one soul would dare care for a monster such as he. Not one would care to commune. Such was the life of one like him. One who could not linger in the pain but allowed himself so anyway because the feeling of pain was at least a *feeling.* Because the pain and sorrow *wanted* to be there when so many others did not.

The pain within his mind could only be compared to that of a true wound. A knife dug deep into his fragile heart, repeatedly stabbed back into the same wound, ignoring the incessant bleeding draining from his core. But despite the pain, the horror, the knife continued to draw itself out, only to pierce through again, unknowing of the constant pain it infused.

And still he endured- somehow through the pain- when his whole being craved nothing more than to crush itself from the inside out and become oblivious to the world. Oblivious to those that *pretended* they cared. That feeling continued to follow him throughout his life, proving to him his greatest fears again and again. The people who care never know how to, never care to *try* in fear of hurting him more- leaving him to his own worst enemy: himself.

The mind is the creator of all sorrows. It is the soul, the *spirit*, that invents the fear, the pain, the hopelessness inside the mind. And yet, to be in control of that power was unobtainable. The mind and the soul aren't always on the same page. The feeling of loneliness was always there, always lingering, and the one who could cure it all, had also administered a blow. All he could do was wait, wallowing in his tears, drinking them in as sorrow became his only comfort…

And as he began to drift away into an oblivion, Zorus was startled awake- the handle of the metal door rattling before it opened, creaking eerily. A silhouette stood in the doorway as light entered the room. Zorus lifted his arm above his empty eyes, attempting to make out the figure's features. "So, you have finally awoken." a crisp, devilish voice broke through the silence. "I was beginning to think you *never would.*" the being chuckled, the door slowly shutting behind him. Dark, tattered wings stretched out from his figure as he stepped closer, his features now more visible in the darkness. "Master says that this experience will be the most rewarding of his existence. If only *he* could savor your defeat."

"So, the emblem of strength has been released then? I *am* the last piece of the puzzle; I *am* his victory."

"Indeed." the figure chuckled.

"Why have you come to me? To mock me, to pain me? Nothing can hinder me any longer, my mind is cold, and my emotions are as one." Zorus spoke with a weak, quiet voice.

"I've come to keep you company as you wait, one can lose patience when death is near." The figure leaned his back against the wall, an inky substance caking the wall as his wings draped across it. Zorus could see his malicious smile from the corner of his eye, joy lacing his mind for such an act.

"*He* broke me, there is no return to the Darlid I was before. There is nothing left for *him,* Kyron." Zorus sat, unmoving, his weakened body stilled by the overwhelming thoughts in his mind. Taking in a deep, sullen breath, he only allowed his lips to move. "Why? Why am I still alive? Why had he not taken the victory when I finally faltered? The world is doomed because of *one* selfish act, and yet he won't claim his triumph… I *crave* the taste of death."

"And yet, *he* claims that you can be broken more. He delights in the witness of your suffering. He craves to cause you to suffer, mind and body, until there is nothing left. Then will he be satisfied; then will he allow you to fall into Death's hands." Kyron chuckled devilishly. "He merely wanted to stretch out your suffering before your demise."

Zorus raised his hand to his cheek, smudging the blood across his skin. "My entire life was pain. When will he let me rest?" he asked with a mournful voice.

Kyron pulled his fingers through his slick hair. "The time is nigh. If that is your deepest desire, I will deliver you to him."

"I don't desire to live any longer. I cannot watch the world suffer anymore. There *is* nothing more for me."

"Very well." Kyron lifted the silver key from his keyring and bent beside Zorus. He unlocked the chains from the wall, and allowed them to clatter across the floor, though the cuffs still laced his wrists. Letting out his hand, Zorus took it, coating Kyron's hand in his blood as he weakly stood. Kyron let go roughly and glanced at the blood staining his skin with pleasure. After attaching the keyring to his belt, he smiled grimly at Zorus's weak figure, and he reached for the metal handle of the door. A dim light entered the area as he slowly led Zorus out of the room.

Zorus placed his fingers on the rough, damp wall, smoothing them across as he followed his guide to his final resting place. His glance followed his own steadied footsteps, his leather boots drenched in blood and heavily torn. Nothing could wake his mind from his deliria, it was set in thought that there would be nothing better than an end to all he knew. It was more calming to him knowing that his spirit would not live on after his body gave in, that he would be set free, taken from this Hell he called life. His breaths calmed and his mind was blank. Depression filling his soul, no thought had the strength to focus.

As the sound of Kyron's footsteps faltered, Zorus came to stillness and looked upon a splintered door, hiding what he wished to find. Kyron took the handle and pulled the door toward himself. He bowed courteously and gestured into the Abyss. Zorus hesitated for a moment before sealing his fate, entering the room. The door shut silently behind him, leaving him in darkness. He felt no different, for his mind was already encased in innate darkness.

A voice echoed through the space as his vision began to clear. "You are truly a broken being. Never have I seen a Darlid so hurt, soul and mind." the Master spoke. "I was right. You would be the most powerful Broken Soul in existence. It's unfortunate that you cannot become one." A malicious chuckle followed as the figure stepped out of the shadows. His figure was as awful as he remembered, he couldn't bear to look at him, conscious of his dubious defeat. His smile stretched across his skull, chilling all who witnessed it. As Lade neared him, his left arm extended, gently wrapping around Zorus's shoulders.

Zorus willingly followed as his tormentor led him toward a wooden post standing crookedly at the end of the room. One he knew all too well, for he *died* here, witnessing what awful fate had occurred. The ground was stained with his brother's precious blood, his soul and body. The chains were tattered, stained with an appalling tale.

"I see, you haven't even the strength to speak." As they ended their trek, Zorus weakly fell to his knees, letting his arms out in defeat as *he* attached the chains to the heavy cuffs held to his wrists.

Each chain connected, his arms fell to his sides effortlessly, his figure bending over as he stared at the stone. There was nothing he could do to save his soul from this atrocious fate, nothing that would change his mind to fight for his life. He had already lost, his fate was sealed, all that needed to be completed was his sacrifice.

Lade stepped out of his view for a moment. A generous clatter sounded as he searched through his desk before returning with a sheath in his arms. A third tentacle extended from his right side, wrapping around the handle of the sword. Revealing the sword, he tossed the sheath aside, drawing his tentacle across the blade, studying the sword in detail. It was all too recognizable. The smooth blade agleam, a long bone, scarred and worn, lying across the blade as a guard, the pommel a grinning skull, and *his* tattered cape wrapped tightly around the handle and edges of the guard.

"This was your brother's, was it not?" Zorus's lips did not part, the words slipping past his ears, nothing mattering. He could not bear to remember him, not when he knew that soon, all of his memories would be obsolete. Though, the being understood exactly what his mind intended. "Ah, well then, you shall die in his honor."

Silence rang for a moment, nothing happening, both unmoving before Zorus's voice weakly played. "Just *end* me now. Free me from my prison." Zorus begged. Lade smiled with evil intent, knowing that he must be patient for the moment to arrive. His torture wasn't complete. Allowing him to suffer longer was more pleasurable than committing the act. There was still something missing, he would not destroy him until all hope was lost, just to find a single glimmer.

Light fled into the room for a moment, fading soon after. A familiar, sorrowful voice played as footsteps echoed. "Why must you take me here? Have I not suffered enough? Let me go!" chains rattled violently as tears flowed through her voice. She fell to the ground in protest, crying as she stared into the empty ground. Kyron tugged against her chains, forcing her to sit straight, to witness what sight had been before her. Her violet eyes quivered as she realized what was happening in front of her. "Zorus…"

Zorus did not shudder, his body and mind unmoving, yet her voice, her sweet reminder, allowed a gentle tear to fall across his cheek. "Ah, now we may commence." lifting the sword into the air, Lade stepped gently about Zorus's unmoving body.

"You… you are still alive. I thought you were killed, I thought we had lost." as Zidal spoke, Zorus let out a heavy breath.

"Have you any last wishes, any final regards?" Lade asked condescendingly, interrupting her thought.

"No… No." Zidal spoke inaudibly with anxious tears. "You cannot die, you cannot give up. Don't leave me now, I can't lose you too!" her voice rose with tears, though he did not stir.

"Nothing…" his weak word fell from his dry lips. "Nothing can stir me."

"No… please, fight back! Take back your life!" lunging forward, Zidal pulled against the chains, yet Kyron's strength held her back, his grin lingering above her, keeping her from saving he who would not save himself. In pain, she halted. Tears strained across her scarred face as she spoke with a deep desire. "You may have naught to live for, but… I… I love you. I cannot… watch you suffer." she spoke weakly through a choked voice, tears pooling beneath her. "I don't want to watch you die; I don't want to watch you give up your soul to this cause."

The words, though he heard them, did not cause him to quiver, to open his mind and see a light in life. "End me." his final words fell from his lips distraughtly.

Lade stood behind him, holding the sword lightly above him. "For the reincarnation of Athreal…"

"No!" Zidal screamed, knowing she had not the power to stop the ritual from commencing.

"Your soul is free!" When his words ended, the blade fell, ripping through his skin. The sword glided smoothly through his body, shattering bones, and rupturing his heart before the point of the blade touched the stone ground. A shadow arose from his body, screaming in agony as it dissipated. Blood leaked across the blade, pooling beneath his slumped body as a bright blue soul arose from his remains, returning to that which would become Athreal.

It wasn't a murder. This was his own self-annihilation. This was of his own doing, and he had craved it.

S awoke in pain, his sides aching beyond imaginable pain. It was a sharp and uncomfortable pain in his chest, covered by the stitches the Master had placed. He winced, his hands cupping around his sewn wounds. His brother gently opened his eyes to the sound of his misery. R slowly rose from the broken mattress and sleepily walked toward S. Sitting beside his brother, R spoke. "What did the Master do to you? I thought he ended his experiments through physical torture."

"Don't worry about it, Core, I'm fine. I just have a little stomachache." S declared, attempting to comfort his innocent brother. "The pain will subside eventually."

"Don't lie to me Zorus, I know the Master's work. I know that type of pain. He cut into you, didn't he?" R asked, staring into his brother's empty eyes. S sealed his lips, unwilling to speak of his tortures. But he knew that his brother could see past his lies. He knew what he had been through.

His mind was broken, and his hopes were diminished. All he had done to get to where he was, was all for nothing. He knew he could get close to escaping, but alas, the chance to truly be free would never come. His once chance to escape was taken from him, atoned for by his painful sacrifice. But he knew that he could not leave his brother behind. He loved him too much.

"Please, tell me what happened." R begged.

Reluctantly, S lifted his shirt revealing the stitches on each side of his chest. His brother gently ran his fingers over the bumps on his chest, wondering what he had done to deserve this pain.

S winced, the pain all too real. His suffering would never end, the suffering of his brother would never end. He knew that his suffering caused his brother pain too, to see that the only Darlid he trusted was losing himself. "Everything we do has a consequence," S began, "Everything we think that will bring us joy, only takes us to another miserable reality."

"What did you do? I don't understand, why did he have to punish you?" R asked, anxious for his brother's response.

S thought for a moment, but he knew that it would be foolish to tell his brother what he had done. He was a terrible example.

"It's better I keep it a secret, Core. The truth will only bring misery. I cannot relive that moment again; else the pain will only return tenfold." S slumped his figure against the wall, allowing the rough fabric of his tattered shirt to fall against his skin. He stretched out his fingers and ran them through his dry hair. "I don't want you to worry about me. No one should have to. I'm the one that should be worrying Courier, I should be the one that has to look out for you."

"No, we have to look out for each other. We both have to be there for one another. We both have to protect each other. The pain will never subside if we don't." a tear fell from R's socket, dripping onto the cold stone floor. S gently wiped his cheek before his brother embraced him. Startled by his sudden gesture, S wrapped his arms around him, allowing his tears to stain his clothing.

As time continued to pass, R's cries began to fade as he fell asleep in his brother's arms.

S stroked his caramel hair, staring at the shadows strewn across the wall. A smile grew across the shadow's face, a reminder to the deal they had created. They were powerful beings, S knew that. A small glimmer of hope entered his heart as he remembered the plan they had begun. The Master would die, he would perish for all of the evil he had spread through the world. He would finally pay for all he had done to them. He would fall by the hands of those he tortured.

Prisoners

Alex awoke to the sound of gentle tears, a quivering of chains rattling through the empty area. His crystal blue eyes slowly opened, bringing him out of the darkness he once resided in. The room was dim, the only light entering through a small window far higher than he could reach. The area was crafted of stone, damp and covered in a thin layer of moss. A murky scent filled the air, it was pungent. A large metal door stood across from him, locking him inside of the room like a prisoner. Chains fell from the back wall, leading to him where tight shackles wrapped around his wrists.

Glancing to his right, he noticed Zidal waiting beside him, softly weeping into her hands, her soft, shadowed hair tangled across her back. The pfesens kept their promise, they indeed brought him to his allies, though still a lie was hidden beneath their words. They were now trapped, once the heroes of the story, they were now Lade's pawns. Alex sighed, allowing his anxieties to coat his mind, allowing all hope to fade. Zidal lifted her head and looked at Alex, surprised to see him awake. She wiped a tear off of her shattered cheek before she spoke. "Alex, you're awake." she spoke through a shuddering breath.

"Where are we? How long have I been here? The last thing I remember was the destruction of the emblem of strength." Alex questioned with great confusion.

"I've lost count. I have been held captive for weeks." Zidal whimpered in a hopeless voice. "You arrived only three days ago, unconscious from the bitter air of the Mirror cliffs."

Alex shifted his position, leaning his thin body against the wall. "I sense we have failed. I cannot feel the presence of the emblems any longer. Has Zorus… Oh, Death, has he perished?" Alex asked in a disturbed fear.

"Do not remind me of the pain, for I witnessed his demise!" Zidal spoke, her voice raging in pain. "The reincarnation of Athreal will surely commence, and the world is doomed." tears began to stream across Zidal's face once again. "Zorus was right, it was all my fault. I should have listened; I should not have brought *them* into this mission." she whispered beneath her breath. "I take all blame."

Alex placed his hand on her shoulder, stroking his fingers across her back. He spoke through a teary voice. "How could it be your fault when the final decision came to his alone? How could a single soul be the cause of the world's torment?"

Zidal had no response to his words, silencing herself in grief and agony. She exhaled, a deep, cold breath exiting her lungs before she spoke again. "I don't know Alex; I'm so lost in this world. Everything I do seems to lead to a tragedy. Everyone I choose to love is destroyed." she spoke lightly through her tears. "My life is not one worth living anymore; not when pain and suffering is all that is left, not when evil has prevailed and all is lost, not when we are trapped here with no escape." Zidal's head fell into her hands, her warm tears and soft cries falling into them.

"I'm sorry, there's nothing we can do now, there is no escape from this torture. The world will surely perish, but it will, knowing that we tried." Alex took in an exhausted breath, slumping his figure against the stone wall, dampening his coat. All was silent beyond the sound of Zidal's tears, a moment to reflect on all that had commenced. His mind was worn, and his body ached beyond explanation. He was so tired of all that he had endured. Tired of the fighting, the adventures, the losses. The echoes of the mind wavering beat inside his mind one final time, all that he was before ripped from his being, all that he once was torn from his heart.

The anxieties that once flowed through his mind ceased as his hope depleted. All that he once knew was destroyed in one instant, never to be brought back to life again. He could feel it in his soul, he was something much different than he could once have imagined. His soul was now connected to the world in a way that could not be described, as if he belonged in one as such. His heartbeat marched beside each of the living souls that belonged to the world, a sudden realization coating his mind, a final thought to bring back hope to all.

Alex sat straight, speaking with urgency. "Zidal, it's not over yet." Zidal raised her head, watching Alex's movement with tear-filled eyes. "Athreal cannot arise without the creation of a Drex potion. One such creation which requires an almost impossible ingredient to find: an oru."

"Of course, how could I forget such a thing?" Zidal queried, fixing her posture. "Even with every emblem released, they cannot prevail. Oh, how this brings hope to the world." Zidal cried in shallow joy.

Alex placed his hands beneath him and stood from the broken ground as he began to pace about the room. The chains clattered against the floor, scraping against the rock as he stepped through the dimly lit area. "We need to find the oru." he directed, knowing that doing so could cost everything. Stepping toward the large metal door, Alex slowed his pace. He leaned his figure against the door, his arms folded across his broad chest. His tattered robe draped across his back, gently moving through the breeze.

"Have you lost your mind? The oru is hidden in the tower of Sel, the location is unknown to Darlid kind. Searching for it could kill us, or even worse, if we found it, the Broken Souls could take it from us." Zidal anxiously pondered. "We're trapped in here, anyway. We wouldn't be able to search for it even if we knew where it was." Zidal sighed, once hopeful, now derived from peace.

A sudden question filled Alex's heart. "Where is Kardama?" Alex asked with urgency. "He will know its whereabouts. He is our best chance at succeeding."

"I… I don't know. I was separated from him once we arrived. I can only imagine how tremendous his torture is, for he is Lade's true foe." Zidal spoke with fear in her tone.

"We need to get out of this place. We need to escape, it's our only chance. We need to find Kardama before it is too late." Alex watched Zidal's slumped figure, curiosity draping his soul. "We need to devise a plan, Zidal. I can, but not on my own." Alex lifted his figure, turning toward the locked entrance. He wrapped his fingers around the bars held inside the window of the metal door and peered into the hallway.

What he saw disgusted him; the sounds of sludging ink echoed through the hallways, dozens of Broken Souls marching through the broken corridors, lurking, protecting.

"It's no hope Alex, even if we escape from this room, it would be impossible to get past the Broken Souls. Even if we pass the Broken Souls, it would be impossible to find Kardama. And, even if we find him, it may already be too late." Zidal raged, burying her head in her lap. Her muffled voice echoed through the cell. "And if you haven't already noticed, they have hidden our weapons."

Alex ignored her demeaning thought, scanning the area before him. "It doesn't make sense though. How can there be so many Broken Souls here? It's like the number of broken beings has tripled. What happened?"

Zidal sighed, a solemn breath echoing through the empty space. "I can't have answers for everything this world gives, Alex. Only then I would feel a useful piece of this world." she dropped her head, a gentle tear slipping across her fragile cheek. "Even if the most skilled of commanders devised a plan to escape this prison, we would eventually perish by the hands of the Broken Souls." Alex listened as soft whimpers began to shudder through her voice, muffled by the silky touch of her uniform. It had been stained by the blood of her enemies, tampered by those she despised, and colored by her tears.

"Fine, if you so believe that escape is impossible, allow me to demonstrate the power of logical thinking. I believe that there is an answer to everything, a solution to every problem. Sometimes it just takes a little time to figure out." Alex let out a confident breath as he led himself to the back wall. He rested his weakened body against the roughness of the stone wall and slid onto the floor beside Zidal. "I will get us out of here, I promise." Zidal refrained her voice from echoing his words. She knew that she could not dissuade him from his insanity.

Zidal awoke to the creaking of the metal door. She was used to this strange happening. Lade was insanely cruel, but even with his desire to punish those he saw insignificant, he would not allow hunger to be the cause of their suffering. Her sullen eyes gently opened, the broken being entering the room, two plates balanced on either hand. Glancing to her side, she noticed that Alex was missing, though his chains were strewn across the floor, leading behind the open door. A shadow of his figure was visible, peaking slowly around the open door, waiting patiently. The figure, blood and decay leaking from his standing body, bent before Zidal and placed the two plates before her. The aliment was not unlike what it had been before, dry, brittle, and tasteless. The being stood, the keys on his belt gently shaking, a toneless ringing echoing the prison cell. He slowly searched the area, knowing something was missing. "Where could that human be?" he asked in a voice coated in a thick slime.

Attempting not to look toward her friend, Zidal smiled shyly and shrugged, lifting a piece of the brittle food toward her mouth. The broken being began to retrace his steps, urging his way toward the halls. He needed to warn the Master. Suddenly, before the broken being had time to react, Alex leapt out of the shadows, wrapping his left arm around the creature's throat, and placed his right hand over its leaking mouth before it could make a sound. "Thank you…" Alex said as he yanked his chain across the creature's neck, forcefully tightening it against his throat. The being silently choked before falling lifeless to the ground; a once powerful soul diminished from reality. His broken body melted across the stone ground, barely a trace of his existence left behind.

Alex bent to the ground, retrieving the keys from the sticky mess, along with a worn dagger that lay hidden in a sheath beside the keyring. Alex tied the light sheath to his belt, ensuring its safety. Quickly, he unlocked the chains held to his wrists, allowing them to clatter across the floor as they fell to the ground. Zidal watched silently in awe, wondering things she couldn't find words to ask. Alex rushed to her side and lifted her arms, one by the other, releasing her from the thick chains. Sticking the keys in his coat pocket, he let out his hand and helped Zidal stand from the cold floor. "How...?" she managed to ask.

Alex pulled her to her feet. "I'm not entirely sure myself, I didn't know that I could do something like that." Alex let go of her soft hand, glancing toward the doorway. "Quickly, we have to find Kardama." Zidal nodded, though still unsure if she could believe what had happened. Hope had never seemed so strong in her being. Alex stepped toward the open door, his hands resting against the doorway. Glancing to his right, he noticed dozens of Broken Souls walking the length of the hallway, turning the corner. Some were shivering, some twitching, all demented, broken beings. To the left, one thin Broken Soul lagged behind. He slowly unsheathed the dagger, watching the Broken Souls pass by. Zidal stood by his side, awaiting his plan to commence. She was still unsure of his plan, worried that something could go wrong.

Curious as to why the door remained open, a short, stubby hound-like creature peaked into the cell. Unsuspectingly, the hound fell to the ground in a painful whimper, Alex's dagger being drawn from its now dissipating body. Glancing to the left, no Broken Soul in sight, Alex silently gestured for Zidal to follow him into the corridor. As silently as they could, they slowly walked through the hallway, passing many cells which held Darlids of all kinds slowly, and painfully suffering. They were *his* experiments; they would become Broken Souls all too quickly. Halting his movement, Alex waited at a crossway, deciding which way he was best to go. "We'll never find Kardama, his prison is a maze." Zidal hopelessly whispered. "Which way should we go?"

"For the sake of our lives, we should probably go down the paths with the least Broken Souls. It may be counterproductive, but we don't really have the weapons to fight off dozens of powerful beings." Alex remarked as he stared down the empty right hallway. Zidal, though skeptical, agreed with his thought as he began to step through the hallway toward their right. Their steps were slow, almost silent, though they were sure that the Broken Souls could notice them regardless of their actions. The hallways were dark, coarse, and damp, layered in coats of decaying skin. The scent was awful, it was a pungent rotting smell that could only reveal something unpleasant.

Alex was uneased by the fact that they had not encountered another Broken Soul as they traveled down this hallway. Something told him that there was something wrong, that maybe he was just bringing them to an inescapable trap. Despite his fear, Alex continued to trek the hallway, Zidal walking closely behind him. Nearing them was yet another intersection. Alex quickly chose to go down the left path, though both ways had no trace of another soul lurking inside. Zidal didn't question his motives and continued to follow him despite the feeling that they would ultimately get lost. She didn't dare make a sound, knowing that one voiced cry would catch attention.

Alex continued to step through the hallway, his hand dragging against the damp wall as a guide through the pitch-black maze. As he continued to get nearer to yet another crossway, a shallow blue light bled across the empty halls. It was quite luminous, bright enough that the darkest of creatures could not behold its glory. Alex removed his hand from the damp wall, reaching toward the light, one which was too glorious to turn away from. They had found Kardama.

Freakish cackles echoed through the near-empty room, lit with dim light. S opened his eyes, glancing at his brother, knowing that there would be no protection from what was to come. *Night locks.* Bitter formless creatures that would consume anything that they deemed delicious. S knew that they would live, that the night locks would not consume them, they would only eat that which was rotting, decaying, yet still living. The Master had created them to punish those that would not obey his rule, both living and those that had become broken.

He named them a present to them, yet he knew that the night locks would gnaw on them just enough to feel uncomfortable and in pain, but not enough to cease their powers from working when needed.

It was a painful process. The creatures were ceaseless in their work. Their hunger would never sill. The only way they would stop there feeding would be by the Master's call. They would only obey him.

S watched as a small dark blob squeezed through the small opening underneath the metal door, followed by many others, making their way toward him and his brother.

S closed his eyes tightly, anxious to feel their teeth chew on his skin. There was no escape from their hunger, they would not let go until they were satisfied, not without fire. S was no Master of pyro though and creating a flame would take great energy. He felt it then, the night locks coating his feet and arms, devouring all that they wanted. Causing him pain despite his infinite pleads for them to let him go.

He could feel his skin decaying away, though it would not be enough to kill him. The torture continued.

S could hear his brother's shy whimpers playing from across the room. He knew that he too was in pain, he knew that he could do nothing to save him and that caused him more dread than the feel of the night locks devouring.

Hope Returns

Alex stepped toward the brightness of the light, unaware of his thoughts, unknowing of his actions. Zidal slowly followed him, anxious for what was to come. Alex reached out his hand, urging himself toward the light bleeding through the cell door. His hands wrapped gently around the bars as he peered into the cell door. "Kardama." he whispered, awed that they had found him as quickly as they did. Alex shook himself out of his trance, clumsily reaching for the bars on the window of the door. The sight before him left him in horrendous awe. The king was held strewn across the stone wall, each of his limbs spread equally apart by the force of the chains. His head hung down, his chin resting across his chest. The scars, each cut across his eye and arms, shined with a glorious crystal blue light, signifying his pain and sorrow.

Alex dropped himself from the sight and reached for the keys inside his pocket. "We have to get you out of here." he whispered, glancing in both directions. He quickly placed the key inside the lock, turning it sideways before removing it. Placing the key inside his pocket again, Alex wrapped his fingers around the thick handle, pulling the door toward himself. The metal was thick, and heavy, unlike any substance he had ever touched. "Zidal, help me pull this open." he begged, pulling at the unmoving entrance. Following his command, Zidal gripped the handle and tugged against the heavy door. Slowly, the door unlatched and creaked open.

Anxious to save Kardama, Alex let go of the handle and squeezed through the thin opening they had created. Zidal quickly followed, hopeful to save her king. Kardama was breathing heavily. He was in pain, his mind equally as hurt as his body. His regal head fell forward, unable to sustain the weight any longer. His breaths were heavy and slow, his lips peeled open to retrieve each breath. His cloak was heavily torn, and his hair was tangled. Thin cuts had opened his skin all about his arms and legs. Turquoise blood dripped from his figure, a puddle forming beneath his hanging body.

Alex let out an anxious breath, kneeling on the cold stone floor before him. Noticing his maneuver, Zidal copied his respectful gesture. Weak and tired, Kardama slowly lifted his head, knowing of their arrival. His pure white hair draped over his eyes. "Rise," he weakly commanded, and at the sound of his voice, they stood. "This is no place for respect." Kardama remarked as Alex retrieved the key, unlocking the cuff on his right wrist. The chain fell against the wall as Kardama's weakened arm fell to his side. His left leg was released next, followed by his right. Finally, as he fell to the stone ground, Alex removed the shackle from his left wrist. Weak, and tortured, Kardama fell onto his knees, his hands catching him from his sore fall. He coughed heavily into the stone; his strength replaced. The bright, blue light faded from his scars, darkening the cell as the final chain hit the ground.

Alex bent down and let out his hand. Kardama took his hand gently and rose from the frigid floor. "What happened?" Alex asked, confused and afraid.

The king took in a deep breath, as if he was constrained from the sweet taste of air for days, dusting his attire. "Lade has provided me with the highest degree of torture. I am both mentally and physically weak, and the pain in my bones has caused me to suffer." he remarked, glancing at the chains behind him. "Keeler stone, though very rare, it is insanely powerful." Kardama's voice rang clearly. "The stone is greedy and consumes all power that it is given. Weeks have passed, and each moment that I have wasted chained in these insipid shackles, yet another soul perishes, unable to be led away from their body." he sighed, staring at the door. "Thousands of souls have unwillingly become broken because I was kept in those chains, and each time a single soul perished, my heart pained me. It is too late to save those souls now."

"It's true, we have seen them. The number of Broken Souls has tripled since we arrived in *this place.*" Zidal remarked.

Kardama lifted his head, painful feelings coating his mind. "But what pains me more than the fallen souls is this dark disturbance in the air. I fear that yet another soul has perished with the inability to escape. Tell me, where is Zorus?"

Alex dropped his head, shaking it slowly and grimly. "I'm afraid that he, as his brother, has been taken by the hand of Lade. There are no emblems left for him to take, his succession is nigh."

"This cannot be. How could such a powerful, heroic soul give up his life for the demon's work?" Kardama sighed. "He became too greedy. He forgot who he was and why he was fighting. It is as I feared, the fate of the world is no longer safe. War is upon us, the second war of Gehalla is at hand."

Zidal sighed, a sullen breath warming the cold area. "Kardama, his plan is all too devious, he knew how to get what he wanted almost effortlessly." Zidal cried. "And now, he will find the oru, and the potion will be created. There is no chance for us to end his recreation." she admitted, fearfully.

"The oru, that is a name I haven't heard for centuries. The forbidden fruit, hidden in the tower of Sel." Kardama inquired. "Indeed, if we destroy the last remaining oru, his rule will never commence. We must do all we can to rid this world of his evil." Kardama attempted to lift himself from the ground, swiftly falling back onto his knees in pain. "I am weak, though now that I have been released, my magic is returning. Hundreds of souls are begging me to bring them home. The weight of one thousand souls is too much for one to bear. You must leave without me; you must locate the oru and destroy it at all costs."

"We cannot do this without you." Zidal remarked in a teary voice.

Kardama glanced at Alex, staring into his crystal blue eyes. "The legend is true, you are truly the savior of this world, Alex." the king smiled solemnly, staring into his soul. "I sense a great power in you, Alex. The legend tells of something I couldn't deem true until this moment." he smiled regaly, weakly standing from the stone. Kardama stood before Alex, gently placing his right hand on his forehead. "The mind wavering has completed, and as a result, you are no longer human, nor are you of Darlid kind."

"Who am I?" Alex asked, awed.

Kardama removed his gentle touch. "A deity. A legendary being who holds ultimate power. Power you may not yet know of, but I can see it already. Your skill has improved tenfold, both in strength and in reason. You have the ability to surpass *his* power." Kardama smiled with pride. "You must find the oru, you know where it is. Enter the tower of Sel you only need these words: Death will forever conquer." Kardama stated as he dropped his hand, falling to the ground once again.

Alex's eyes glimmered a bright light for just a moment as his mind was enlightened. He knew what they must do in order to accomplish this task. "What about you? We can't leave you here, it's too dangerous." Alex pleaded.

"Do not worry about me. I have much to do, many souls to save before it is too late. Please, forget about me, I will find you again." Kardama groaned in pain, holding his arm across his stomach. "The weight of these begging souls aches me. I must do this alone. Please, leave before *he* realizes what has happened."

"No, Kardama, we won't leave you here!" Zidal assured, letting out her hand. "We cannot lose another, *I* cannot lose another!" the king's violet eyes locked on hers, a proud smile stretching across his face. He took in a deep breath, gesturing toward the exit. "Please! We cannot lose someone of such importance."

"Zidal, many of great importance have perished, and many I could not save. Your allies, your *friends* have died for causes that will lead to something much worse for those who remain. You must go, you must save this world from impending doom before it takes place. *You* are of much importance." Kardama dropped his head. "Go, before the chance is taken from you. You must escape this wretched place. You will see me again, I promise."

Hesitant to leave the king's side, Alex stepped toward the loosely opened door and slid himself through the thin opening. Zidal followed behind him, her gaze never leaving Kardama's royal figure. Her touch slowly falling from the rough metal, the door instantly slammed shut with power unknown, the king locking himself inside, attempting to rescue those souls who still had a chance. "No…" Zidal whispered in agony. She sighed, unsure of her emotions.

Alex gently placed his hand on her shoulder, glancing into the dark hallway. "Don't worry about him, Kardama has magic unlike any other being, he can save himself." Zidal looked at Alex. "Come on, we should get out of here while we still have a chance." though fear coaxed her mind, Zidal took Alex's hand and followed him through the hallway, now dark and barren of light. Neither allowed their lips to move, both knowing that the thinnest of sounds could summon a Broken Soul. The single dagger they had collected would not be sufficient enough to fight against many Broken Souls, especially those greater in size and power.

Stepping through the cold, barren hallways, it soon became clear that no Broken Souls had crossed the path they were taking. The slick decay of those beings were no longer coating the floor, the bubbling, eerie sounds the Broken Souls created falling far into the distance. Where had they gone? The area around them was immensely dark, not even the light of a torch could light their way. Alex dragged his hand across the wall beside him. The texture of the rough stone never halted, there was never another opening in the wall to change direction.

Soon it became clear that the hallway was reaching an end. Reaching his hand forward, Alex felt a wall before him. Dragging his dry hand across the wall, his palm hit a handle. This was it; they had found their way out of this horrid place. Carefully, Alex let go of Zidal's hand, assuring her that they had found their escape from this treacherous maze.

Alex grasped the round, metal handle, pulling the door toward himself. Light bled into the dark hallway, highlighting shadows, ridding the feeling of fear from their eyes. The outside seemed quite desirable to those who had been locked in that place. Alex stepped beyond the door without hesitation, entering a new, glorious terrain. The air was sweet, and the warmth of the beating lavender sun filled his heart with peace unmatched.

Glancing behind him, he noticed Zidal's sullen expression as she waited behind the door. Her figure was covered by shadow, the darkness of the area behind her unpenetrated by the sun's light. He gave her a weak smile as he gestured for her to follow.

Zidal sighed, looking back toward the hallway behind her, drawing her hand across the open doorway. "We will get you out of here." she promised, leaving the darkness behind as she entered the Careless Meadows, the building she was once held in disappearing behind her.

S opened his eyes, weak, yet sleepless. Each day that passed felt slower and slower, the torture, the pain, the sorrow, and guilt never ceasing. They seemed to merge together, each week seeming like the one before. Each moment never actually passed. It was always he and his brother suffering, enduring, the days never seeming to get nearer to the day of their escape. Only one more year, then they could take action on their plan. Then they could finally rid the world of *his* impending treachery. Never had hope seemed so dim, yet so present in their lives. Their power, their training, the promise of the shadows. They would succeed.

S let out a deep and sullen breath, glancing at his brother. It wasn't a pretty sight. His dark hair was matted, his skin was thin and brittle, showing the outline of his frail bones. He was unbearably tired, and though the nightmares continued to fill his mind, when he wasn't training with the Master, he was sleeping.

S didn't feel too dissimilar. His blonde hair was tangled, covered in dirt, blood, and the decay of those he was forced to fight. Dirt was smudged across his face, and small specks drifted into his empty eyes, irritating them. He was basically starving and could feel the structure of his skeleton through his skin. His mind was coaxed with anxieties and fear, knowing that each day could be worse than the one he was already experiencing.

His lungs ached, filled with dust and smoke. He couldn't help coughing often. Sometimes blood would flood his mouth, spray across his ragged clothing as he choked. It wasn't a pleasant flavor, and the texture was far too thick. He feared that he would die before the day his Master would be killed, and that frightened him sorely. His brother had hope though, he knew that they would escape soon. He always thought that they would succeed.

The weight of the chains on his wrists pained him, a power inside yearning to escape, consumed by the strength of the metal. He wanted to break free, he wanted to release all of his emotions, he wanted to destroy the endless loop of time that forced him to remain in the same place. His brother didn't deserve this suffering, *he* didn't deserve this suffering. The darkness inside of him could easily shine. Once he was released, once he and his brother were released, everything they wanted could be theirs. They had the power; they had the ability. They were *deities.* No other could defeat them… no, they must use their abilities for good. What would be the point to escape the torture only to inflict others with the same feeling?

The waiting was unbearable. He wished that the day would just arrive, that he could finally end the suffering that he and his brother had to endure. He wished that he could just free himself from the pain, from the horrors which haunted his every thought.

S glanced at his shadow, the image of a smile drawing across his face. The shadows played tricks on his mind, he knew that they had sentience, that their deeds, promises, and wishes were incomprehensible to the minds of mere children. They were incredibly persuasive, and children were much easier to manipulate than a more experienced being would be, especially children like he and his brother who had only known a life such as this. He knew that the shadow could have been lying, he knew that he could have made the promise for his own benefit rather than for theirs.

It was too late now; he had sold his soul to a being with much greater power than he could ever perceive. His life, his fate was no longer in his control. His thoughts were bound to a monster's. Knowing that another being knew all of his thoughts, that another soul could feel all of his pain and regrets only strengthened the feeling. He shared his power with this terrible foe, and he accepted it.

He was the shadow, and the shadow was him. He knew it, there was no changing his mind. The shadow was his deepest, darkest regrets, his pain and suffering, the urge for revenge. The shadow was the part of him that he couldn't control, the pieces of his soul that craved pain. There was no difference between he and his shadow other than the feeling of consciousness.

Soon all of their suffering would end. He only had to wait another year, then all of this pain would finally be released from his body. Then he would never have to feel this hurt again. Then he would finally feel joy. There was that feeling in the back of his mind though, the one that knew there was a chance that they could fail at their task, even after all they had worked toward. It wasn't an easy thought, but S knew that he would have to give up if the Master wasn't destroyed. He couldn't risk himself being the successor of Athreal. If it came to the option of death or serving his Master for all of eternity, he would gladly take the blade. Even with the whimpers of his brother, he would rather end his own life than watch the world suffer because of himself. That was his choice, the rest was up to R.

Tower of Insanity

The air in the meadow was sweet and the fragrance of the flowers flowed through the sky. The grass was soft, gently swaying in the breeze, its light sego color bleeding through the various hues of blossoming flowers. For miles, all that could be seen were the endless planes of flowers. The breeze felt calm, as if it could carry away the cares of each and every soul. Nothing could surpass the feeling of the Careless Meadows, all that was terrible in the world could not exist in this place.

Alex let out a deep breath, gazing into the violet sunrise. Zidal stood by his side, sorrowfully staring into the distance, wondering, hoping that all would turn right in the end. Hoping that they could soon be freed from this terror and the world could be savored. He spoke, interrupting the silence. "The beauty of this meadow is indescribable; I feel like I could stand here forever."

Zidal redirected her gaze toward Alex's longing complexion and spoke. "Such a place can take away all the feelings in your body. Some that come to this place never return, addicted to the relief of pain." she looked at the ground, speaking with a morose tone. "We shouldn't stay here. We need to find the tower of Sel."

Alex searched the area, as if he was looking for somewhere to go, somewhere to finally defeat this evil. "I can't explain it, but I know where the tower is. I know where to go. It's a different feeling, one unlike the beacon of the emblems. After Kardama touched me, it was like I had been to the tower once before." as he spoke, Alex began to walk into the distance, Zidal following closely by his side, listening. "It's here, hidden in the meadows."

"How is that possible?" Zidal asked, intrigued by his proposal. "There's nothing for miles."

Alex glanced behind him. “We escaped the prison only moments ago, though now it seems to have disappeared. Zidal, it hasn’t disappeared, it’s invisible, blending into its surroundings. It only makes sense, this place has the ability to hide things in plain sight, the tower of Sel is here.” he paused. “That prison, that laboratory was built here in effort to find the tower, but the tower would be impossible to find unless you already knew where it was.”

Zidal nodded thoughtfully. “Let’s just hope that we’re not being followed.” Alex nodded in agreement, drawing his fingers over the pommel of his dagger. It was rusted and coarse, having been used for many slaughters. The blade, still coated in the inky decay, was strong and reliable. Though one small weapon would not be enough to hold off more than one Broken Soul at a time, especially Olks.

Alex sighed, thoughts cascading through his mind like a waterfall, one idea never standing still. His mind was free. Free from the pain of the mind wavering, though still coaxed in the feeling of sorrow and loss. The feeling of hope resided, though he knew that failure could follow. He knew that there was always something following them, there was always something that could go wrong, there was always another problem to face while they fought through the final stages of this battle.

The sound of their pounding footsteps and singing birds filled the near-silent air as the flowery meadows passed beneath their feet. The breeze was soft, and the world was colorful. The feeling of fear and destruction could not be felt in such a place, there was only hope. The wind carried away all of the sorrows and pain that played through their minds. The wind took away all of the pain and replaced it with the feeling of hope. Never was there a time more hopeful for them than while they wandered these meadows.

Stretching forth his hand, Alex halted forth his movement. “It should be here.” he declared, waving his hand through the air as if he was searching for something.

Zidal stepped forward, walking straight through the area Alex had been searching. “There’s nothing here Alex. If the tower of Sel was transparent, I wouldn’t be able to step through it.`` She spoke with a manner of intelligence.

"It's not transparent, Zidal. It's like that prison, it's hidden unless you know how to enter it." Alex stated, moving his hand down as if he was drawing it across a wall. "Found it." he declared, cupping his hands around the knob of the door. It was smooth and round, crafted of a fine metal. Alex waved Zidal over and opened the door toward himself as she returned to his side. As the door was opened, the tower appeared to them, standing as gracefully as a palace. Alex and Zidal stared at the tower in awe. Its pinnacles were crafted of fine marble, stretching toward the endless sky. The structures bent and whirred in the air, creating massive spikes which stood from the top of the tower. The door was made of glass and the knob was formed of gold. Vines and flowers climbed the tower walls, reaching toward the heavens.

Alex glanced at Zidal and nodded, gesturing for her to enter the palace. Alex followed her inside shortly after and shut the door behind him as he entered, the tower once again hidden from the outside world. The inner workings of the palace were as wondrous as the craftsmanship of the outer shell. The marble staircase stretched cylindrically around the room, the gold bannisters following the trail. Glass doors opened to a variety of rooms while countless bookshelves laced the hallways with knowledge. Bottles of unknown potions stood within the bookshelves, along with blooming flowers and worn books. Wooden desks and decor stood proudly throughout the tower, papers and books scattered about.

"Where do we begin to search?" Zidal asked, awed by the magnificence of the tower.

"I don't know, but the oru is bound to be within this tower. It's best we split up, then we can cover more ground. I'll search the upper room while you look here." Alex declared, looking toward the peak of the tower.

Zidal nodded as she stepped toward an open bookcase, dragging her hand across its length. "Good luck."

"You too. And be careful. Watch for Broken Souls."

"I will." Zidal smiled, gesturing toward the staircase. "We should begin our search before it's too late."

Alex agreed to her remark, placing his hand on the smooth banister. With hope, Alex began to ascend the spiraling staircase. The climb would be long, for the pinnacle of the tower was taller than any built before it. Alex stepped each stair carefully, a royal aura filling his soul, dignity and pride filling his heart. The marble was smooth and clear, lavender light reflecting from its surface. The climb was simple and calming, a peaceful air falling through the center of the spiral. Alex looked to the wall on his right as he climbed the tower, drawing his hand against the smoothness of the marble. Glancing through the crystal windows as he passed by, he witnessed the glory of the Careless Meadows which stood proudly beyond the glass, calling his name, whispering things to him which could only be described as miraculous.

Soon his ascension neared to an end, and he found himself standing before a glorious glass door, calling for him to enter the room beyond. Clutching the gold handle, Alex opened the glass door and entered the study. As the entrance area below, this room too was filled with books, shelves of items lacing the walls, papers strewn across the floor, and piles of clutter strewn across the wooden desk. Greenery grew recklessly throughout the area, covering the walls in vines and filling the room with a fluorescent scent. It was a small room; the search wouldn't take long and when he had fully searched the room, he could return to the base of the tower to help Zidal. He wasn't sure what he was looking for, but he would know when he found it.

Beginning his search, Alex made his way toward the cluttered desk in the center of the room. Three books laid wide open alongside a pile of papers, a feather pen, and an inkwell which had been tipped over staining the fine wood in ink. A well-used candle sat on the right corner of the desk, still ignited. It was a peculiar thing, but Alex paid no heed to it. Alex bent down, pulling a drawer toward himself. The contents of the drawer were fairly bland. Just a couple more books and a glass sphere rolling around the near-empty space.

Closing the drawer, Alex headed toward a nearby bookshelf. It was carved of pine wood, and not a single scratch or dent could be found. Books filled the shelves with knowledge, along with a few ceramic pots which grew a variety of plants, numerous unused candles and even a few glass bottles stood on the shelves. What was the most curious of all was the fact that everything was clear of dust. Alex ran his finger across the wood studying his clean finger. It was a mysterious thing.

Alex lifted one of the ceramic pots from its place, studying the flower which grew from its soft, white soil. Its petals were warm and lustrous, and it gave off a fervent scent. Though, this plant did not bear fruit, and therefore was not the oru. The next three pots contained the same sort of shrub. All gave off a mossy scent and grew bristly leaves from their branches. Small red berries grew from the ends of each branch, surrounded by night-blue flowers, but these were also not the forbidden fruit. The final two pots contained the growth of two dying weeds, shriveled and dried. None of these could be the oru, rather something used by Sel to create potions and medicines.

Alex drew his fingers across the books on the shelves. They all shared titles of a similar caliber, each one informing the reader on how they could create different potions and spells. They were all immensely complex and only the highest skilled wizards even stood a chance at creating the potions without fault. Those who failed risked death. Other books related to the botany of certain plants, many of which were growing inside the tower of Sel itself. Some even described the care of certain animals.

Before continuing his search, Alex glanced at the glass bottles with curiosity. The first was filled with a bright teal liquid, engraved with one word: *Demothar.* A paper label was tied to the rim of the bottle with twine. The second held a translucent indigo substance with the label: *Abstroce.* The third, similar to the others, was filled to the brim with a cloudy white liquid and was labeled: *Milk.* Alex lifted the milk bottle from the shelf and unscrewed the lid. He brought the rim of the bottle beneath his nose, smelling the liquid. It was still fresh, the sweet, creamy scent filling his nostrils. Putting the rim of the bottle to his lips, Alex drank the sweet liquid. It was fresh and tasted finer than any dairy product he had consumed, though this tower had been abandoned for centuries. It was mysterious how some things never seemed to change in this tower. It was as if everything inside this tower was locked in time, unable to decay. Screwing the lid back onto the bottle, Alex returned it to its place.

Alex began to turn away from the shelf to search for the oru elsewhere, but before he moved on, his crystal eyes were drawn back to the first bottle. Curious, Alex took the bottle labeled *Demothar* from the shelf and examined the label. It read:

Whomsoever laces their blade with this poison
and pierces a demon's heart
shall watch it perish
but he who kills the demon
shall their heart rotteth
and their skin crumble until death.

Alex's eyes lit up, he had heard those words once before. This was the antidote, if they failed in finding the oru, this poison would aid in the destruction of Athreal. Alex turned his head, ensuring that no other soul was in the room with him. He knew what he needed to do, but he couldn't sacrifice himself at the knowledge of others. Alex unsheathed his dagger, placing it on the ground. Prying the cork from the bottle, Alex bent to the ground and slowly poured the glowing liquid onto his blade, thoroughly lacing his blade with the poison. His dagger shimmered in the light of the sun, reflecting the pain that would inflict his heart if he destroyed the demon. Alex reached for his blade, but startled by the sudden sound of bashing wood, Alex dropped the bottle onto the ground. The glass shattered, and effectively vanished just as quickly. The evidence was gone, his fate was sealed. Anxiety began to coax his mind; Alex quickly sheathed his dagger.

Alex lifted himself from the ground, the pounding sound only becoming louder. Ignoring the sound, Alex returned to the shelves, searching through the piles of clutter. The thump played again. Alex quickly rummaged through the various items piled on the wood. *Again.* Finding a singular book on the shelf, which was tattered unlike the others, Alex took it from the shelf. *Again.* Opening the book, a small hatch opened. *Again.* There it was, a round fruit as white as snow. It gave off a powerful feeling. The oru had been located. *Again.* Alex took the forbidden fruit from the inside of the book, hiding it in his pocket. *Again.*

Silencing himself, Alex listened for the sound to play again. A thunderous sound echoed through his ears once again, this time sounding just behind him. Dropping the book onto the floor, Alex turned his head toward the glass door. He knew he wasn't alone.

A feeling caressed his thoughts, S knew that he was no longer in the cell. *Where was his brother? Was he safe?* His own fate was much less significant than that of his brother's. R was much stronger than he could ever be, he knew that he would be able to defeat all of his foes and save himself from a life such as this. If only he could escape, then all of S's nightmares would cease to exist.

That wasn't the problem though. S needed to know where he was, what was happening, and how he could save himself from the pain that was sure to follow. First, he needed to gain control of his body, pull himself from the darkness that he created for himself. He needed to feel the rise and fall of his chest as he breathed, and the constant pounding of his heart against his ribcage. Carefully, he wiggled his fingers, smoothing them across the textured fabric beneath him. He could feel his toes, barren, bandages wrapped around them. The heel of his foot brushing against a rough surface. He could feel himself on a slight incline, laying on a table.

S opened his eyes, his breaths slow and laborious. Everything around him was a blur, but that emerald eye was unmistakable. He knew where he was, he could feel the bounds around his chest, stomach and legs, and the heft of the chains around his wrists and ankles binding him to the table. Three tentacles hovered above him, each accomplishing a different task. One held a syringe, filled with a pungent silver liquid. The second on his right held a bloody knife. It was unmistakable, he knew that it was his blood, the familiar pain in his knee confirmed that. The final arm flowing from the Master's left shoulder held a damp cloth, drenched in blood, mucus, and alcohol.

Why was he here? It wasn't uncommon for him to find himself on this table, screaming and crying, pain inflicting his every thought, but not like this. His Master was *correcting* him, he knew it. He was trying to fix his imperfections. His perfect imperfections that he had dealt with since the moment of his consciousness. His spine was slightly crooked and the bones in his left arm did not have a sufficient amount of marrow. His flesh was thin and weak, although it was meant to be. He knew that he had imperfections. He knew that the Master would do anything to make him a perfect being, one which would become a deity. *What was he going to do to him?*

The Master leaned closer, bringing the tools nearer to his helpless body. S wanted to scream, he wanted to take control of his body and escape this experiment, but he knew that wouldn't happen. This procedure had been his life, his every day, his every thought. The pain lingered. There was never enough time for him to heal, it was always another experiment. He was never free, he was never left to his own thoughts, he was never happy. This was his reality; this was why he existed… to be tortured.

The Tall Being took the cloth in his arm and draped it across S's mouth. The scent was strong and unpleasant. He knew that he wouldn't be conscious for much longer. That would only mean that pain would be more unbearable when he woke. Next, the needle of the syringe was set into his left eye-socket, gently caressing his dried skin. Slowly, painfully the needle was inserted into his brain. He could feel the liquid drain into his mind, causing natural movements to cease. His limbs were limp, and his heart slowed its beating to an irregular pace. He would wake when all had been done.

Now he could dream. Sweetly, softly dream. Dream into the darkness of night. Dream into the terrors. Dream until there is nothing else.

The Beginning

Alex stared anxiously at the glass door, the pearl-white marble becoming black from the stains of decaying flesh. A woman grinned at him from behind the glass, her beauty destroyed by her decaying skin. Her icy dress draped lusciously down her body. Her hair, as black as night, fell across her shoulders, dripping onto her apparel. And her eyes, two beautiful glowing emeralds, locked into his. They filled his soul with dread, and as hard as he tried, he couldn't look away.

The woman was accompanied by four broken creatures which took the form of foxes. There they waited patiently, never a movement in their figures. Not a word was spoken and not a step was taken. Alex quivered. He couldn't proceed forward, else he would be captured once again, taken captive by the Broken Souls. He was trapped at the top of the tower, caged in like a bird, with no exit out.

Her cold, dead eyes stared into his, an enchantment slowly encasing his mind with dread. Letting out a sullen, fearful breath, Alex began to back away, never losing eye contact. The fones barred their teeth, growling ferociously as slobber dripped down their muzzles. Alex's heart rate rose, and it wasn't long before his back hit something. Something *alive.* Alex swallowed his fear as his breaths became heavier. Silence, not a sound falling from his mouth, Alex waited. "Hello, boy." a thick, raspy voice played behind him, though it was clearly feminine.

Before he could react, he felt his arms stretch behind him as a pair of heavy cuffs cased his wrists. "Let me go!" Alex screamed, knowing all too well what would happen if the oru fell into their hands. Alex pulled against the strength of the Olk behind him, attempting to unsheathe his dagger, but to no avail, he was held back. "Please, no!"

The being behind him crackled ferociously, placing her two remaining hands on Alex's shoulders. Alex turned his head back, gazing up at the charmer's crooked beak. "We wouldn't want to fail our precious Master, now would we? You are a crucial part of his plan, and we would surely perish if we set you free." Merchel leered, her serpent slithering across her chest.

"How'd you get in here?" Alex questioned, eyeing both of the Broken Souls.

The woman in the doorway turned the golden knob and pulled the door toward herself, allowing herself and the pack of fones to enter the room. She placed her soft hand beneath his chin, lifting his head upward, examining his figure. Soon after, she quickly removed her hand, Alex's head falling from her hold. "Too fragile, too insignificant. Do you think one such as I would allow such a devious plan to be retold?" her voice was silky, and though it was intimidating, it was sweet and convincing. "Master would cast me aside if I explained his marvelous works to the enemy. But you did your part. You lead us to the tower." she smiled, her lip cleft by the decay. "Now, we must proceed. If I am not mistaken, the forbidden fruit has been found."

Alex stared at her with uncertainty knowing that his worst fear had become reality. He had led them to the one place he couldn't. He had the one thing that would cause them to succeed, for Athreal to exist once again, and it was all his fault. Anxieties flowing dangerously through his mind, Alex collapsed onto his knees. "What have I done?" he asked himself, wishing he had never set one foot outside. "What have I done?!" he cried more audibly; the regretful expression strewn across his face.

Merchel coughed, tugging on the chains. Forced to stand, Alex struggled against her powerful grip. Her talons only held tighter as he continued to pull forward. "Come now, *they* are waiting for us." Merchel commanded as she began to walk toward the staircase. Alex struggled against her grip, attempting to pull himself back as they continued to near the stairwell. The woman and her pack of fones followed at a near distance, ensuring that he couldn't go back. Against his own will, Alex was forced to follow the broken beings to the base of the tower. The journey down the stairs was quick, though he struggled to escape his fate the entire way.

The entire tower was stained ink black; books and torn papers were strewn across the floor. Shelves were knocked over and wooden desks were splinted across the floor. If he was being captured now, Zidal had already been taken. She had fought for her freedom, and ultimately failed in the task. Alex felt at fault, he couldn't imagine the pain she had been through. He had caused the suffering of this world. He was the reason this journey began in the first place. He could never forgive himself for what he had done, for what he had abandoned. He could only move forward in the hope that all would turn right in the end.

The Broken Souls led him out of the tower with great difficulty. As the woman stepped into the Careless Meadows, she shut the door behind her, the entirety of the tower vanishing from sight. Merchel shoved Alex onto his knees, forcing him to look at the sight before him. The view before him was shocking. Hundreds of Broken Souls surrounded the hidden tower, waiting silently to complete their long-awaited task. Decay ran along the grass of the fields, sorrow and fear engulfing the aura of the meadow's skies. Along with Merchel and the woman, A third Olk was present. Kyron forcefully held Zidal to the ground. She was slumped over, tears were streaming across her cracked cheeks, her dark skin reflecting the light to the lavender sun. "Zidal…" Alex said anxiously, though barely audibly. Her breaths were heavy and the thoughts inside her mind weighed heavily in her mind. She knew that there was little hope left.

Kyron's wings draped across his back, dripping into the soft grass. "I assume the oru has been located?" he asked patiently through the sound of Zidal's tears.

"Don't fret, the human has it. I'm sure of it." Willow's voice echoed through the meadows. Alex grimaced, knowing that she was right.

Alex's mind began to stir. Everything they needed to have Athreal arise again was in place. There was nothing he could do. They were *his* prisoners and there was no escape from the torture and pain. Everything would succumb to his power as he erased the world's history. As he caused all to become his puppets. As he finally achieved his greatest desire. The fight would be nearly impossible, and even if there was a way to get close enough to him, the chance Alex had to kill him with one final blow was small.

Alex glanced anxiously at his captors. "Well, should we *proceed*?" Merchel asked.

Kyron nodded. “Indeed, there is no time to waste.” he said, unlocking the chains held to Zidal’s wrists. Slowly, she brought her hands before her, looking at them fearfully. Those were her hands, they had done so much in her lifetime. They had held others, they had caught her tears, they had shed blood. Her mind was filled with grief, the feeling of failure overwhelming her mind, depressing her with a feeling that could only be described as yielding her soul. She was filled with an immense and torturous feeling of ennui. There was nothing she could do to fix what had been broken. She was a lost soul, yet to be freed from her mortal prison.

Zidal swallowed her tears, weakly speaking. “I have failed.” she admitted fearfully. “I do not crave to live in a world such as this.” she revealed somberly. “There is no soul that could save me.”

Kyron bent by her side, resting his soft hand on her shoulder. She shivered, the memories flooding back, his touch calming her dead soul. “Zidal, I still love you. Every day I have lived on, knowing that I could never be with you again, and it all became pain. I’ve missed your gentle touch, your soft-spoken words. The only Darlid to ever steal my heart was you, and you still have it.” Zidal trembled at his words, knowing that she couldn’t bear to be reminded. It hurt too much. Her thoughts shattered; thinking was no longer an option.

Kyron leered, knowing that she had finally *broke*. This was the chance he had been waiting for. He gently stood, taking one of his twin scythes from his back. He stared at his reflection shining off of the silver blade, smiling with evil intent. His silky voice played as he set the scythe by her side. “The choice is yours. Continue to fight, to *save* this pathetic world and fail, or set your soul free. If a decision cannot be made, your fate will be set...” Zidal’s hand caressed the coarse stick of the scythe, recalling her thoughts. Her fingers gently wrapped around the stick, feeling the splinters of wood.

Alex watched her carefully, knowing all too well how convincing Kyron could be. His body began to shake, he knew this feeling. It was becoming clear that one more soul could be lost. “Zidal, please.” Alex begged; his eyes filled with fear. Zidal retracted her grip, listening to his voice, her soul void of hope. “Consider your life. Save what can still be saved, you don't need to give up your soul. There is still hope." Alex pleaded, tears glazing his eyes.

"Thank you," she whispered through tears, "but I've already made up my mind. I made up my mind a long time ago, I don't know why I am still fighting Alex. I've lost so many souls, I've watched them die, I've watched agony overwhelm them and consume their souls. The same has become of me. I am of no worth to this world, and I cannot live knowing that I couldn't save them." The tears began to burn, the feeling of sorrow corrupting her mind. "*I lost all those that I loved.* I have been betrayed. I have caused pain. I have failed the world. I cannot forgive myself." her voice was somber.

Silence rang for a moment, the Olks watching patiently. "I know it's painful. I've been here with you. I've watched two of my closest friends die for the causes of evil. I've seen the pain, I know the grief, but we have to move forward." Alex let out a painful breath as tears streamed down his face. "I cannot lose another. I've already lost so much." Alex recalled, stuttering through his voice. His chest was heavy, and his soul ached. "Don't give up your soul. Fight for your life. I couldn't bear to watch you suffer." his throat closed, unable to speak another word.

"I can't take it anymore. The pain is too real, nothing can overwhelm the feeling I have inside. I feel so insignificant, so alone, so… *unloved.*" Zidal admitted.

"You're not thinking straight. Zidal, can't you see, the Olks are trying to manipulate you!" Alex revealed, aware of their devious plan. "Please, don't give up your life for something so surreal. We will get through this, I promise. It may not be today, but we will put an end to this suffering." Alex spoke with hope in his voice, yet fear followed.

"I…" Zidal bit her lip, glancing at the figure looming above her. A longing feeling entered her soul, reaching toward something indiscernible. She couldn't shake the feeling; she couldn't break the promise she made to herself. *She knew what had to be done, and if she failed, the world would suffer the consequences of her actions.* "Nothing can change my state of mind. The decision was easy. To finally be freed from this life… it was an offer I gave myself that I couldn't refuse." She choked on her words. "I'm sorry." she voiced, her fingers wrapping around the stick of the scythe once again.

Alex pulled against his restraints, forced back by Merchel's powerful grip. "No!" he screamed. "Please, no!" As the words left his lips, he felt the serpent slither onto his body, wrapping around his face, its vice-like grip stopping him from calling out again. His fears became more apparent as the thought of what would become came closer to reality. He didn't want it to. He didn't want to suffer the pain of losing another friend. He didn't want her choices to put the world in danger. He knew what would happen if she let her blood stain the grass.

Zidal lifted the scythe from the grass, holding it upside down, the tip of the blade resting against her stomach. She gripped the stick tightly with both of her hands, one held shakily above the other. Breathing in deeply, she took in all of her last thoughts. Every horrific memory coated her mind. Every sorrow she had felt came back to haunt her. The faces of those who had died before her were scarred into her brain. Soon she would be like them...

Her violet eyes opened into a void of nothingness, her thoughts corrupted, her soul empty, yearning to find freedom. "I'm sorry." she repeated as she thrusted the blade into her body. The blade impaled her stomach, teal blood draining from her wound as it curved upward and slid out of her back. She let out a few shuddering breaths in pain as her body began to lose function. She could feel herself fading, she could feel herself *changing.* The pain began to dissipate as her heart failed to pump, her thoughts fading into another world.

Alex wanted to scream again in pain, in horror at what he had witnessed, yet was unable to because of the serpent's terrible grip. Tears poured from his eyes, his mind and heart aching with a feeling of dread.

After a few moments painfully watching her suffer, tears staining his face as sorrow and regret drenched his mind, her body slumped forward, and her dark skin began to melt away. There stood her lifeless body. Her corpse left there, waiting, vengeance completed by her own self-righteous suicide. The pain reflected in her dead glassy eyes was unbearable, her tormented life taken by her own hands. The image stained, and though her reasons were unjustified, her suicide was completed.

Kyron smiled darkly, knowing what was to come. Stepping before her decaying body, he latched his hand onto the stick of his scythe, ripping the blade from her stomach, holding it upright. He stared at Zidal's inanimate body- lifeless and obscured- grimly, as if he was waiting for something to happen. Alex watched with disgust and fear, pain embedded in his mind, waiting for something, anything to happen.

Slowly, Zidal's precious, dead, violet eyes began to glow, the color fading before an emerald hue took over. A smirk slowly bled across her face as she slowly lifted her head. Her tangled, shadow-colored hair draped over her uniform, stained with her own blood, decay drenching her body. She stretched out her fingers, the newfound power encasing her soul. Zidal cackled freakishly, laying her dead eyes on Alex.

This was the beginning of the final days.

S awoke from his nightmares, cold sweat running down his forehead. His breaths heavily fell from his mouth, breaking through the silent air. The pain immediately returned, every inch of his body screamed out in misery, pleading for an escape. A terrible feeling of pain jolted down his spine. He could feel where he had been cut into, he could feel what the Master had tried to correct. The pain was unbearable, and he refused to move from the position he was placed in. He had been given medication to ease the pain, though it instead increased the awful feeling he had in his spine. His eye sockets also ached, and it was hard to see out of the place the Master had injected the needle. His chest ached more than it ever could have before, as if tens of rocks had been thrown against his chest. It was almost impossible to breathe, and each of his breaths were incredibly heavy.

His clothing was drenched with his own blood and puss. All he could smell was the drying blood. He wanted to throw up, yet he was too starved to even attempt to. The chains were wrapped tightly around his wrists. Even at a time where he was in pain, the Master would not allow him to move freely. There wasn't a way for him to use his magic with this amount of pain anyway. He was suffering at the extent of his own will; his fate was only determined by that of the Master's wish. He couldn't move, he couldn't see, he couldn't think straight.

Everything was a blur. It was hard to keep his eyes open, yet he was unable to fall asleep. He was exhausted and thirsty. His whole life seemed to be nothing other than frequent pain. He was a marionette for his Master's ploy, and he would obey. After all of the pain he endured, he would obey. After all he had witnessed, he would obey. And even when he obeyed, the torture would never end. For all his remaining days, the torture would somehow return, he knew that for a fact. The chances they had to destroy the Master was low, even with the plan they had devised over all of these years.

He wished that he could just end it all. If he could never escape this prison, then there was no point in life. There was no point to live if all he ever felt was pain, but there was nothing he could do but wait. Eventually he would heal, and soon after that, he would destroy the Master and end his evil doings. But, what else could he do while he waited. He needed something to ease the pain, something to distract himself from his Master's doing. It was no use. No amount of thoughts could distract him from the pain in his bones. It felt as if his back had been broken, only to reposition it in a straighter form. *When would the Tall Being ever end the torture?*

S glanced to his right weakly. R wasn't there, and he could only imagine what he was going through. The thought made him sick, causing him to cough heavily. The coughing became so strong that his own blood spewed out, staining the already disgusting floor. The pain was too much. S began choking on his blood, regurgitating whatever was left in his body. It stung. Tears flowed out of his eyes like great rivers, he didn't feel nearly like himself. This was the most physical pain he had been through. For the first time in what he could remember, his cries became vocal. He could hear himself weep as his body slumped onto the stone ground. He wrapped his arms around his knees, desperately seeking some form of comfort. With little effort, he gagged, choking up another puddle of blood.

He could feel his soul echoing the pain. The shadow… his shadow screaming inside him, begging for the torture to end just as much as he did. His cries were overwhelmed by the pleads of the shadow, for as he felt pain, the shadow felt it increased tenfold. He wished the pain would just end. He wished he could fall asleep and wash it all away, but it would only return when he woke again. His greatest fear: knowing that the pain would only return.

"Please… let the pain end." he whispered through a painful, teary voice. There was no answer to his call though, he was left to drench himself in blood, to wait in pain.

Broken and Betrayed

Zidal was broken. It was a thought that never occurred to Alex, that she had the power to live again. He knew it was possible, and he knew the Olks were convincing, rather, he never expected her to fall into the hands of the demons and help them with their cause. She had her second chance, this time her guilt allowing her to cause pain to others, to be more powerful than she could have imagined while *living.* Kyron smiled with great elation, letting out his hand. Zidal gently took it, rising from the soft ground as her insides dripped from her decaying body. Blissfully, Zidal embraced Kyron. What was missing in her soul finally felt full. Her soul *was* full, filled with power and greed, the thoughts in her mind now focused on a greater cause: *recreating Athreal.*

"Oh, how I've missed you." Kyron's voice echoed, his thick tongue sliding across his lips. His hand caressed the back of her head. Her soft hair flowed between his devious fingers as he pulled her closer, his tattered wings blanketing her body. Their lips touched, a long-awaited kiss finally ending the torture- his thick tongue caressing her own. Once so far from each other, both living in two different realities, now finally together again. Something so desired, yet so far from reach finally returned. The warmth of their love embraced their surroundings as they fell deeper into their greatest desire.

Kyron let his tongue slip from her mouth, sliding it across her neck. Zidal fell from him, staring into his eyes, like black holes.

Zidal buried her head into the warmth of his chest as he stroked her back. "I knew you would eventually come to your senses, Zidal. To finally have unlimited abilities, to live without the fear of death, to be with those you love. These are the benefits to being *broken.*" Kyron stated, kissing her cheek. As he gently let her go, Zidal fell from his embrace, her heart filled with joy unmatched.

Alex stared at her, awed, afraid, and betrayed. The feeling sunk into his soul deeper than a blade. The truth seeped into his mind, his thoughts coaxed in anger and confusion. This was it; he was finally on his own. He had no one but himself to rely on now. He had no one but himself to keep him alive. It was up to him to end the suffering and the torture. It was up to him to keep Athreal from reincarnating. It was up to him to save a world he knew so little about.

Zidal approached him, a smirk neatly drawn across her shattered face. He gagged, the scent of newly spilt blood and decay, which could only come from a recent death, filling the area. He looked up at her, his eyes swollen with tears. "Zidal, how could you?" he asked with a cracked voice, tears streaming down his soft cheeks.

Zidal chuckled. Finally, she wasn't the one to suffer, someone else could let their tears fall instead. "I was so blind." she admitted. "I now see so clearly," elation filled her voice, "the power is immense. By *him* I am now undefeatable. By *him* I am immortalized. By *him* I can have a second chance. And what better cause to live than to bring back *he* who created this life?" she let out a sorrowful breath. "Alex, I now see who the true villain is… and that's you. If you succeed in the task, I once tried so hard to accomplish, true horrors will corrupt this world. Peace and elation would never return to this world."

Alex let out a shuddering breath. "Open your eyes. *This* isn't life. *This* isn't joy. You became the very thing you swore to destroy." he quivered, beginning to feel nauseous.

Zidal snickered, amused by his idiocy. "Believe what you want, but my mind has been opened and I know the truth. The Broken Souls *will* be victorious." she claimed, her voice raising in glory.

"You're not the Darlid I knew. *She* would do anything to prevent this. *She* would do everything in her power to fight against the cunning of the Broken Souls. *She* would fight no matter how difficult it became. *She* was a warrior, a savior, and now *she's* gone, fighting for the very thing she once tried to destroy." Alex spoke, his throat clogged with tears.

Zidal smiled somberly, the memories were so faded. Darkness corrupted her mind; she was no longer that Darlid, and she never wanted to go back. “You try so hard to resist the truth. Master won’t allow such foolishness. Now that you have served your purpose, only *he* knows your fate.” she straightened herself. “Your life is hanging on the edge of a cliff, one wrong move, and it will fall…” she turned away from him, staring into the mass of silent souls, awaiting her destiny.

Zidal's figure blended into the sea of Broken Souls as she left Alex behind. Kyron stood before him, his dead gaze landing on Alex's fearful, diamond eyes. He smirked, bending to his level. "I believe you have something we require." Alex looked down, avoiding his luminous stare. Kyron chuckled. “Give us the oru, and we’ll spare you… for now. Otherwise, the Master has *plans* for you.”

Alex turned his head away, refusing to make eye contact. “Never! I will not give in! I will not allow this world to be cursed by the hand of a demon!” he bantered, his eyes swelling with rage.

“Very well,” Kyron’s voice rang quietly, “Master has his ways. He who cannot be convinced *will* be forced. You will be tired.” Straightening his figure, Kyron looked into the obedient crowd and called out. “Take him away.” he snickered as he began walking into the distance, once beautiful now covered in blackening decay. Many of the Broken Souls began to follow his regal step, leaving Alex behind. Zidal quickly found her way to his side, taking his hand in hers.

Alex watched helplessly as the mass of broken Darlids trekked through the Careless Meadows. His attention shifted as he felt a familiar pain in his side. Four huge, sharp claws dug into his abdomen, lifting him into the air. It was only a moment before he was set onto the back of the pfesen, though, this time he was unable to hold onto his mane as his hands remained cuffed. He could feel Atlas’s thick, moist intestines tangle against his legs, the constant beating of his heart thumping against the tip of his boot. His grip tightening around his waist, the pfesen followed the sea of broken beings closely, his sister trotting by his side. His step was unsteady, his five feet marching in an uneven beat.

Tears caressed Alex’s cheeks. His vision was a blur, though there wasn’t much to see. He felt nauseous knowing that his time was coming close to an end. He could have given them the oru and waited for an opportunity to defeat them. He could have escaped unscathed and devised a plan to put an end to the suffering before it began. But he didn’t. His fate was now in their hands. He knew that torture was ahead of him. He knew that they would stop at nothing until he gave in and gave up the forbidden fruit. No matter how hard he tried, they would take the oru and recreate Athreal.

Alex was taken out of his thoughts as the pfesen brayed. "The oru will fall into *his* hands." he heard his own voice play back to him, though it was not he who said it. The voice clearly flowed from the pfesen's broken lips, taunting him. It was a strange phenomenon, that another creature could replicate any voice without failure. "Athreal will be recreated." his voice played again, echoing back the very words he feared most. Alex tried not to believe the words he spoke, but he knew the pfesen was devious. He took what he feared most and reflected those feelings back at him with his own voice. *It was his voice. These were his thoughts. He knew it to be true.*

The journey continued in silence. The beauty of the meadows began to fade as the sun settled and night blanketed the sky. Only the heavy breaths of the pfesens complemented the flow of the wind. Alex's tears were silent, but the sorrow was real, and all hope was lost. His breaths were steady and his heartbeat with the same, rhythmic tempo. Everything he had worked for was lost. Every Darlid he had met had either died or been separated from him. Every attempt to keep the Broken Souls from their victory was stopped. Despite his best efforts, he knew what Zidal had said was true. *The Broken Souls would succeed.*

With great suddenness, the conglomeration of Broken Souls halted. Atlas froze, waiting behind the group of decaying beings as the prison appeared where there once was nothing. One by one, the Broken Souls entered the building, disappearing from his sight. It wasn't long before they reached the entrance door, the same repeated routine happening once again. The broken pfesens navigated the dark hallways easily, bringing him into an empty prison cell. As the painful grip fell from his side, Alex slid onto the cold, stone floor. The pfesen cackled before the metal door slammed shut, the sound of clicking locks playing after.

Alex leaned against the damp wall and sighed. His cuffed hands sat uncomfortably by his sides. His dagger rested against his right thigh, though it was of no use in his circumstance. It would likely be confiscated too. Attempting to beg for his release wouldn't change his fate either.

Saving his energy was the best thing he could do for himself. He looked about the room, but nothing of interest caught his eyes. The room was frigid, moss growing from the moist walls. From a crack in the left wall, drops of juniper constantly fell into an ever-deepening puddle. To his right, a small bed stood bound to the wall, though its mattress was just as uncomfortable as the stone he waited on. Other than those few things, there was nothing to explore in this small cell.

Darkness surrounded him. He felt helpless and alone. Once again, he waited patiently in prison. Arrested for crimes that didn't exist. Imprisoned to keep him from spreading *lies* about what he had been through. Punished in an attempt to do good. It seemed to be something of a usual sort. The good were always the ones to be silenced. Soon the world would be corrupted with Athreal's rule, and all would fall for his false glory as no one would be there to oppose him.

Sudden realizations caressed his thoughts, causing him to grieve at his own stupidity. *He would never return home*. He had so foolishly left, hoping for something more in life than the same repeated schedule, the same responsibilities, the same melodious rhythm repeating each and every day. And to a point, he had achieved the very thing he wanted, but it cost him much and he would never be able to return. He had been through more pain than he would have imagined before he decided his fate. He had starved, fought for things he was clueless about, he was bruised and scarred, he had watched his friends die and betray him. It was all there. It had all stained. These thoughts, *these memories,* would never subside. They would always be there to torture him. They would always be there to remind him that he was of no worth… and it was all true to him.

Alex closed his eyes, deranged of hope and energy. His back slumped against the wall, his arms and legs spread out weakly. Gently, tears slipped from his wetted eyes. His fate was now sealed in the hands of the Broken Souls, and he knew that he would soon die. He would be martyred for crimes he didn't commit. His name would be deteriorated, and he would be known as a curator evil, an opposer of the *truth*. There was nothing he could do now. There was no one else to save him but himself, but he didn't see the reason to try. Soon the Master of the Broken Souls would complete the task he had tried so hard to prevent. Athreal would rise again. All his efforts would be obscured, and no matter what he did, he would die. He wanted to rescue this fallen world, but it seemed like an impossibility after all that had happened. It seemed as if there was no hope… the world was destined to fall.

S reluctantly followed his Master as he pulled him through the darkened hallway, reaching for his brother. R clumsily followed the Tall Being's step; though his legs were shorter than the others, therefore causing him to be left behind. He quickened his step, attempting to keep up before the Master suddenly stopped in front of the small keeler door. The Tall Being sent them inside after he opened the door, following them behind to keep them from escaping. His eerie voice echoed through the empty space as the door slammed behind them, locking them inside the small room. *"Today you will both explore the depths of your magic together. Your magic is strong, but together, it could be much more."*

The Tall Being grinned as an arm emerged from his shoulder, taking the key from his pocket. Slowly, he removed the shackles off of each of their wrists, allowing their magic to take hold of their beings. Immediately, S sent himself into the void, escaping his Master's clutch. He had explored the void many times before, the barriers always stopping him from escaping the training room. Though this space was small, it was a paradise for him, an escape from the tortures he endured. He realized that he couldn't remain in the void forever though, as his energy rapidly depleted as long as he stayed. Each time he chose to exit the void, he was mentally and emotionally tired, and though he had to finish his training for the day, he begged his Master to let him rest.

After having visited the void a multitude of times, S had found strange glitches in the void. He had found a crack in the wall that he could fit himself through, though he could never exit the void while he waited there. It was a secret room of a sort, one which he enjoyed spending his time in, though no other soul could see it. There was a strange form in the area that resembled a bed, and beside it stood a nightstand. The most unusual part of that room though was the fact that if he placed anything inside, it would disappear until he wanted it again. It intrigued him nonetheless, and he tested it often.

Strangest of all things that occurred in this realm was that for as long as he resided, time would cease to pass, and though he could spend hours within its chambers, he would always return to reality the very moment he left. And, if he wasn't careful, he would arrive in a different area and position than the moment he left. *Teleportation.* At least, that was how it seemed to anyone who had not visited the depths of the void.

As S wandered the void, a thought crossed his mind. He wondered if he could bring others into the void with him if that was even a possibility. Then he remembered his brother. If any other soul would ever be allowed in such a place, he would only take him. S sighed, knowing that he would have to return to reality for a moment only to attempt this feat.

S lowered his eyes, finding himself back in the very place he had begun. He glanced at R, knowing that his Master was curious as to what he was up to. S thought for a moment, and then an idea came to mind. "R, take my hand." The Tall Being watched with earnest curiosity as his brother took his hand. S closed his eyes, traveling into the void once again. As he opened his eyes observing the void, his brother stood beside him, studying the area in awe. S smiled, giving out a shy chuckle knowing that he had discovered something amazing. "Courier, I'm going to let go now," he said. R nodded understandingly as S cautiously let go of his grip. Immediately, he found himself alone in the void again.

Panicked, S returned to the room beside his brother and took his hand once again. The Tall Being cocked his head before S returned to the void again.

The void was a place where color could not exist. Where it was both light and dark. Joyous and sorrowful.

"What's going on, S? This place is so strange."

"I'm not sure. I don't really understand the rules of the void. At least, that's what I've come to call it." his grip tightened around his brother's hand. "Here, I want to show you something." S tugged R's hand as he searched for the crack in the wall. Turning sideways, he fit himself through the glitch, pulling his brother through with him. "This area is strange. Here, let me try again. Maybe in a room such as this, you can remain in the void." S wondered aloud as he gently let go of his brother's hand. To his awe, R did not vanish, but rather stood worryingly in the center of the room.

R gave a weak smile, attempting to understand this strange place. "I don't understand. This place is quite curious. Never in my life would I expect such a phenomenon to occur." R stated as he studied the area about him. "How could such a place exist?" he pondered. S shrugged, seating himself on the bed-shaped form in the center of the room. "We could spend hours here, escaping the Master's tortures. We could train and prepare ourselves for the final battle. The possibilities are endless!"

S frowned. "As much as I'd like that, I can't spend very long here. My energy drains fairly quickly while I wait here, and after my energy has completely drained, the void collapses around me and I am forced back into reality. Trust me, I've spent hours here determining my limits." S shook his head, his weak bones shaking in the frigid air. "There isn't a simple explanation to any of this. I really wish there was."

The room around them shook, items shaking and breaking apart. "What's happening?" R asked, fear in his expression.

S studied the area. "My energy is low. The void won't last much longer with the state I'm in. Take my hand R, we best return to the Master's training session." S gave a weak smile as he let out his hand. R took it and followed him as he squeezed through the crack in the wall.

"What happens if the void collapses while you're in that room?" R asked, looking back.

"I don't know, I've never tested it. I fear that I would be obscured from reality if I let myself decay within the void." as his words fell from his mouth S let go of his brother's hand, returning to reality.

The Master showed a toothy grin. *"Brilliant."*

The Fallen

Alex awoke to the sound of rattling metal. A clear feminine voice ran through the bars of the prison door, he knew who it was. “Lade is ready for your trial.” the voice said as the handle of the door shook. The door opened, light seeping into the darkness as she spoke again. “You’ll have your chance. Agree to his terms and he may spare you. Revolt and death may be on your path.” The figure smiled, her dark, bleeding skin blending into the shadows. Her freakish smile brought fear into the room. “I know you too well though, you would never give up something so important for the sake of your own life. You’ve sacrificed yourself time and time again.”

Alex grimaced. “He can’t break me. I have a plan.” he admitted.

A plan. Indeed, he had a pan. It was one which would likely kill him in the end. It was a plan that would cause him to suffer all pain and perish. It was a plan which required his freedom, or better yet, escape in order to succeed in it. He had a plan, and that plan was the greatest risk he could take.

“And what would that plan be?” Zidal asked. “No plan would suffice. He will always be successful in his attempts.”

“It's a risk, one I am willing to take, but I refuse to relay my thoughts to someone who betrayed all of Darlid kind!” he spat. Zidal scoffed as he stood from the rough ground. His hands were held neatly behind his back, chained together. Zidal beaconed him to follow her, gesturing him toward the opening. Though slightly reluctant, Alex made his way toward the dimly lit hallway, hoping that he would not make a mistake in his plan. Alex followed her through the musty hallway, his head hanging low. He pondered his thoughts, trying to make sense of every part of his plan. Everything had to happen one way. One mistake and the plan would fail.

One mistake and he wouldn't be able to stop the inevitable from happening. He would have to sacrifice his own life, but he knew one thing for certain: *Athreal had to rise again.*

This wasn't going to be simple. Of course, he had to be reluctant. Of course, he had to refuse to give the Broken Souls the oru- they would get it anyway he was powerless. His plan was complicated and frightening, but it was the only chance he had to save this world from its awful fate.

It wasn't long before they reached a large and crooked door. Zidal opened it toward herself and showed Alex in before she followed him inside. Alex studied the room in remorseful awe. It was much larger than he had expected, and it was cylindrical in shape. Rows upon rows of steps rose toward each of the walls and dozens of Broken Souls sat upon the steps to observe. They jeered as he entered the room, their bright emerald eyes piercing the darkness. An ominous light fell from the center of the ceiling appearing from an unseen source. At the front of the room stood a podium and a seat on either side. On one chair sat Kyron, the Master's most trusted advisor. The second seat remained empty, showing its splintered wood.

Hanging from the deepening ceiling held above the wooden podium was an ominous chrysalis. Its thick hide was composed of a sticky, translucent skin, reflecting all color so it appeared white. Though, within its dense walls bubbles of pulsing colors emitted. It was immediately clear what those colorful lights were, the power they emitted was too great to be unnoticed. They were the souls of the emblems. Alex winced, knowing that two of those souls once belonged to two noble living beings.

Alex was struck with awe, so much so that he didn't notice the indication to move forward. Zidal gently, though carelessly, shoved Alex's back, forcing him to step toward the center circle. Alex stepped toward the center of the room with careful steps, unsure of how far he was permitted to go. Suddenly, once he had reached the center of the room, Zidal gave him another shove, this time powerful enough that he fell to his knees. His body hit the white dirt painfully. Sighing, Alex lifted his gaze toward the center podium and waited. Zidal smirked as she stepped toward the front of the room, taking her place on the empty seat as decay fell from her bones.

Kyron rose from his seat and stepped behind the podium, his wings gently falling behind him. Immediately, the room fell silent, and the Broken Souls watched with great respect. Kyron spoke. "Today we witness a great end to our suffering," he announced, "Finally, we are brought to the end of our perilous wait. The Master will converse with the human. The oru will be brought into our possession. And finally, the fate of the human will be set." Alex remorsed at the sound of his words. He knew his risk would be the cause of his demise. It had a great possibility of failing.

The demeanor glanced to his left before he spoke again. "I now present to you our faithful leader." At the end of his words he bowed and returned to his seat beside the podium.

A roar of gleeful cheering entered the area as a figure emerged from the leftmost side of the room. His figure was stern and powerful, a daunting aura emitting from his bones. His luminous green eye gleamed against the darkness as three of his tentacles emerged from his melting body. He stood gloriously at the podium, his terrible glare watching Alex with deep intent. His distorted voice pierced the silence of the room. "We have waited an eternity to finally set our Master free," he began, gaining the attention of the congregation, "but now all the pieces are in place to set his soul free. He will be reincarnated." He gave his followers a proud look. "One final item must be taken, the oru. And after we have it in our possession, the Drex potion will be created." The stadium of Broken Souls cheered, knowing well what was to come.

Alex cringed, ducking his head away from the crowd in shame. Now was his only chance to set things on the right path. All his other chances had been taken. He had failed all those times before. He wasn't going to fail this time. "Rise Alex, son of man." The Master's voice rang clearly through the room. "Speak."

At the sound of his command, Alex took in a shallow breath lifting himself from the ground. He stared at the Master of the Broken Souls uncomfortably as his hands shook within the chains. His voice trembled as he attempted to speak. "What do you ask of me?" he questioned, quivering through his words.

"The oru. Release it from your possession and return it to its rightful place and you shall live." the skeletal mass of viscous skin declared.

This was the beginning, he had to decline. "No. I decline your offer. I would greatly prefer death over the reincarnation of a being who would only bring destruction." He could hardly believe what he was saying. Not too long ago he would have found himself saving his life over something so small, but he knew the impact it would make if he gave up something such as this. They would get it anyway, but he needed to declare his standing, his beliefs. He had nothing to lose now, he had already lost it all. All that was left now was his impending doom. He waited for the Broken Soul to speak, to close his anxious mind with one phrase. One phrase which would declare his death. Fear lingered, the room was silent for only a moment, but each second felt longer than it should have.

Suddenly, the Master began to chuckle. Soon, the chuckle became a cackle, a maniacal laugh which ailed all others. The room filled with laughter as each and every broken being joined in this hysterical idea. Alex studied the room with great confusion. *What had he said? What was going to happen to him? Was death something to laugh about?* The laughter soon died out as each voice became silent once again. "Death?!" the Master enraged. "You think that I would kill you before I fulfilled my calling?" His freakish smile widened. "Oh, but you have sealed your fate. I know you have the oru in possession. We will still take it from you, but only now you have chosen to suffer by the hands of the demon rather than side with him. Oh, how unfortunate." the Master coughed.

"But you said…" his voice was abruptly silenced.

"Oh, but I didn't. I said: *Release it from your possession and return it to its rightful place and you shall live.* I never said you would be killed if you didn't. You could have played it more carefully. You could have declined without setting your fate. But how precious this is to see a single soul sacrifice himself to Athreal, Son of the Dying Star. When he returns, he will be pleased. *To kill a human again.*"

Alex recoiled in his words, stepping back as his eyes became dark. He felt nauseous and dizzy. It wasn't too long until his body hit the stone. The laughter about the room emerged again, this time much more fervent and paralyzing. He should have waited. Athreal was supposed to rise again, it was the only way he could destroy him, but now his fate was set. He chose death rather than service. He chose to die rather than to betray the Master of all emblems. "I take back my words!" Alex called out, attempting to save himself from his ignorant plea.

"Your words cannot be recalled. Everything said in this room is true. Once a deal is set, it can never be broken." the Master said. His words caused shivers to fall down Alex's spine. He couldn't find a loop in his phrase. He couldn't find a way to escape his sentence. "You should have asked the rules before you led yourself into an inescapable doom."

Alex shivered, unable to find the words to say.

The Master raised his leftmost tentacle and silenced the room. The area became hushed before he spoke again, this time his words sounding deeper and more disturbing. "Zidal, search his person. He's sure to have it on him."

Zidal stood from the seat she was waiting on, her sullen voice quietly echoing through the room. "My pleasure." she said freakishly. Alex dropped his face into his cuffed hands as tears began to coax his eyes. He could feel Zidal's dripping figure hovering above him, ready to steal the most important item from him. He should have listened, not just to the Master of the Broken Souls, but to his tutors and mentors. He should have held his tongue before he put himself into dangerous situations such as this. He should have destroyed the oru, crushed it into a million pieces instead of taking it for his own. He should have cast it away, never to be found again. But he was too ignorant. He didn't know he would be caught so suddenly.

He felt Zidal's soft, yet decaying hands run across his frail body. He did not recoil at her touch; he didn't care anymore. There was nothing he could do to stop the inevitable from beginning. It was the beginning and the end. *He was the Fallen.*

Zidal searched his entire figure, her fingers deepening into his pockets and forcing their way into his cupped hands. Finally, she reached into the leftmost pocket on his robe and took hold of the forbidden fruit. There was nothing he could do, nothing but wait for the inevitable to happen. *He was the cause of this world's impending doom.*

"Here Master, the oru has been located." Zidal's voice rang. The crowd of Broken Souls lit up in excitement, cheering as Zidal handed the small orb to the Master before taking her seat once again.

Lade lifted his boneless limb into the air, showing the oru to all. "Here the oru has been gained. We are one step closer to *his* joyous return. We will bask in his glory. We will worship him. We will serve him with all of our might." The Broken Souls cheered, excited for the return of a Master that was only fabled to them. They were going to be the most powerful beings to ever live.

Alex felt hot streams of tears bleeding from his eyes. He had done what he had to do, but now he had to find a way to destroy Athreal before the whole world became broken. Before he was murdered because of his ambitious stupidity.

The cheering ended again as the Master of the Broken Souls began to speak again. "The time has come to create the fabled Drex potion. Athreal will have risen again within a fortnight, and then our service will be given to him." A freakish smile formed through his translucent skin. Such joy should never have occurred for such a devious plan. "Son of man, you have the exciting privilege to watch me create this potion and to witness the reincarnation of Athreal firsthand." The Broken Souls cheered again. Alex did not join in their gleeful action. The tears only streamed down his face more quickly. This was the first time in his life that he had ever felt true fear and sadness.

Alex felt a forceful grip holding to his arm. The being forcefully pulled him up from his seat and dragged him toward the now open door. Broken Souls followed after him, filing through the door to get back to their posts. There was nothing he could do now. Nothing but watch. Athreal would rise again. *This was the end, and it was his fault.*

The Master's smile didn't fade. He was pleased with their sudden finding. *"Brilliant."* he repeated, unable to express his admiration through mere words. *"Extraordinary."* the Master brought his tentacle to his chin as S let go of his brother's hand. He studied their appearance, now waiting on the opposite side of the room. To them it had felt like they had spent the entirety of their day within the void. To the Master, only mere seconds had passed by. *"This idea changes everything. Everything about my studies. Everything about my theories. My*

experiments. My training." S swallowed his fear, staying in one place as he worried what would happen if he moved.

The Master paced across the keeler stone floor, pondering all of the possibilities. *"I already thought it extraordinary before: the ability you had to transport yourself anywhere almost instantly. But now, my understanding has widened. You can teleport not only yourself and any object you hold to, but you also have the ability to bring others with you-so long as they hold your hand."* The Master's bright emerald eye landed on their frightened figures. R quivered, clinging to his brother.

"And what of you R," the Tall Being continued, *"Is there something else hiding within your abilities that we have yet to discover? Please, don't hold back. This time is to learn, not to be timid."* R shrank, knowing that the burden upon him was more than he ever wanted to bear. *"Don't be shy... what's on your mind now?"*

R took in a laborious breath, collecting his thoughts. "I can feel your thoughts. I can feel everyone's thoughts" R began. "I know things I shouldn't know. I learn by the knowledge of others. I understand because others understand. I always know what's coming next." R shied away as the Master began stepping toward him. He began to shiver as his luminous smile enlarged.

"Please, do demonstrate. R, elaborate on my feelings. What am I thinking of at this moment?" the Tall Being asked, hoping to have R reveal something more to his abilities.

R stared into the Master's emerald eye. That freakish, lifeless, overwhelming stare that encapsulated the soul. He could feel his every thought. Every movement of images. All the knowledge he could access. *He could find his weak point. He just needed to stall long enough.* R began to speak, retelling the thoughts about his Master's mind, while at the same time searching for an advantage. "You're excited, Master. You feel that everything is coming together… finally." he stalled for a moment. "You feel the recreation of Athreal is closer to happening than ever before." He recoiled at the sound of that name falling from his lips.

"Intriguing. Your abilities are stronger than I had initially anticipated. Knowing how to counteract every move your opponent throws at you isn't the only power that will leave you as the victor." The Master smiled. *"Continue."*

R continued to speak as he searched his mind further. "You know that we are powerful. You know that your experiments were a success. Each hour you come closer to a perfect version of a Broken Soul. Soon you will have it all. Soon you will be the successor of Athreal." There. He found it. It was all too obvious. How could he have missed it before? He would have to relay the information to his brother eventually. Not now though, they still had to train.

"Very good." the Master said. *"And your brother?"*

"Somehow, I know that S's mind is easier to access, as if our blood relation connects me to his mind more clearly." R looked up to his brother, his empty eyes longingly staring into his soul. "You're empty, S." he claimed shallowly.

"Empty?" S questioned, leaning against the back wall. "What do you mean?" The Master watched curiously, wondering what would come of this conversation. It was quite curious to watch S feel uncomfortable at his own brother's words.

"Your thoughts are constant, S. There is no flow, just the same pattern. I've noticed it before. You're always repeating the same things in mind. Things that I won't dare say aloud. S, your thoughts scare me. Please don't..." R said cut off by his own tears.

"I'm sorry R, I shouldn't be thinking that way. I..." he stopped for a moment. "I'm sorry I frightened you. Things will work out, just you wait." He attempted to stay careful of his words, knowing that one wrong phrase could reveal their entire plan.

"Very well. Your training today is complete." The Master returned to them, cuffing their arms. An immediate loss of power surged through their veins. *"Return to your cell. We will continue tomorrow."*

They obeyed.

Elixir

Alex awoke from his painful slumber as the door of his cell creaked open. He was incredibly tired. Dark circles had formed beneath his eyes. After so many days of waiting in a prison cell with so little nutrients to fill him and nothing to do, he felt completely fatigued. His muscles had grown weak, and his legs were useless. His poison-laced dagger had been confiscated from him the day he had arrived. There was nothing he could do.

The figure entered the room, and under the scarce flickering light, Alex could barely make out his features. He knew who it was though, it wasn't difficult to discern the Master of the Broken Souls from any other. His melting skin shined a glorious white hue unlike the dark, void-like decay of his followers. The shadows were just strong enough to make out the feverish grin on his face. Alex grimaced.

"Ah, so the son of man still lives." the Master chuckled to himself as he neared him. "To honor you and your willing sacrifice, you will witness the creation of the Drex potion. You will be the only being- other than myself- that will witness the reincarnation of Athreal." Lade stepped closer to him, revealing the key which he held. He began to unlock the chains from the wall, though he did not release him. "Ah, so you choose silence. Would you rather not reveal the elation this brings?"

"This is no joyous creation." Alex spat weakly. It hurt to talk. His throat stung with a dry raspiness which had lingered for days. "All will be doomed when he returns."

"Isn't that the whole point of this recreation? To destroy all which had come before." Alex struggled to find a direct answer. The Master smiled and pocketed the key. His tentacle merged into his body as he turned away. He expected Alex to follow him, and though he despised the fact, he would not disobey. "So, you won't disagree?"

Alex weakly stood from the ground, attempting to walk without falter. His muscles ached increasingly, but he forced himself to endure the pain. There had to be something he could do to stop the recreation from happening. Lade stepped through the open door before him. He reluctantly followed him into the hallway. "True, I do not disagree with the statement. I understand why he is to be recreated."

"But you do not agree that it should occur. Why is that, son of man? This world is not your own. Why care to put a stop to its destruction?"

"I…" Alex struggled to find the words. Everything seemed so unclear now. His mind was broken and mournful. He knew that the destruction of so many lives would be terrible. He knew that whatever he said, the Master of the Broken Souls would find a way to twist his words. The whole world depended on him to save it, but he couldn't find a straight answer as to why. "I can't find the words," he admitted. "Why would one want to destroy a world such as this?"

"If I elaborate on my thoughts, will you elaborate on yours, son of man?" Alex nodded reluctantly. "The answer is quite simple… revenge. This world and every Darlid among it must be erased to atone for the sins of their ancestors. The entirety of Broken Souls were destroyed that day, save but one."

"You...?" The Master smiled, knowing well of the past.

"I have lived as long as Kardama himself, yearning for vengeance for the very day all my allies were destroyed." The Master almost seemed sorrowful. "After Athreal had been destroyed and all Broken Souls were exiled, their souls all eventually shattered. I was left to my own sorrow, and eventually my own research. After centuries of research, thousands of experiments, and dozens of deaths, I created an elixir that would shame all others. One which could bind the souls of Darlids to their bodies." he spoke with great pride in his voice.

"With the power to create Broken Souls at will, why are you still determined to reincarnate Athreal?" Alex asked, with genuine curiosity.

"Power. Ultimate power." The Master smiled. "You seem to have so little understanding. With the reincarnation of Athreal, so comes the reincarnation of all of the demons." His words contained a powerful feel. "But, until he is recreated, I'm afraid you cannot fathom the importance. With his return, the rule of Broken Souls will be inevitable. The destruction of all Darlids- *the impure-* will commence. Only the broken will remain. Kardama will be sacrificed for revenge of the past."

They entered the room. It was fairly empty aside from a cauldron sitting upon a wooden fire and the colorful chrysalis hanging above. The feeling was incredibly powerful, but Alex felt sick knowing that with that power came souls. On the left side of the room, a splintered wooden chair sat beside a stone countertop which was covered in various ingredients and tools. The Master shut the large metal door behind him and gestured for Alex to take a seat on the lonesome wooden chair. He followed the command, his eyes never leaving his terrible figure.

"Ever since that day, I have dedicated all of my time to the recreation of Athreal and the creation of his army. I not only studied the whereabouts of the emblems, or the creation of the Broken Souls themselves, but I also attempted to mutate living Darlids to have abilities unlike any other soul. I created elixirs, and I was successful. But only once." the Master spoke in such a way that made Alex's mind turn. It was as if he was *trying* to reveal something. He chuckled as he made his way to the counter.

He was successful before. But only once. Alex needed to think. That statement was a clue, and he knew who *they* were. Alex thought for a moment, realizations jumping through his mind. It only made sense, the way they spoke in secrecy, the strange and awesome powers they held that couldn't be comprehended by the mere fact they were Darlids. It had to be: "Zorus and Courier..." Alex whispered, barely audibly. "They were your experiments?"

The Master smiled knowingly. He seemed to be enjoying his queries. "For a time, they were. From the moment they were brought into this world until their successful resistance sixteen years later. Indeed, they were the last remaining scelos- they had slowly died out over the centuries after the war- but I gave them their magic. And I trusted them with it, all but too much. They were to be the successors of Athreal. They were to be the most powerful beings in existence after they had become Broken Souls."

"But the emblems of love and knowledge themselves were embedded in their souls. Why didn't you just take them then?"

"Ah, if only I had known. Even with my constant search for the emblems, I was unaware of the locations of the emblems of love and knowledge. The whole time they stood right beneath my feet, and still, I was too ignorant to see. The revelation only came to me recently, and even though I had let them get away before, I knew that they would eventually return."

Lade took a large glass bottle- which was filled to the brim with juniper- and began pouring the contents into the cauldron as he spoke. "Though I wish that all had gone right, and they could be rulers by Athreal's side, it is not so. Their destiny was elsewhere. Their destiny was to bring him back. In a way, they did fill their duty. They were his successors." he said, glancing at the chrysalis above. The Master returned to the counter and retrieved another, smaller bottle, filled with a glowing liquid of a blue hue. It was as if he had drained the light of the stars themselves.

"And what if you fail? What if Athreal rises again, only to be destroyed before the task can be accomplished?" Alex asked as the Master began to drain the starlit liquid into the cauldron. He continued the elixir's creation with time and care. He poured with such precision that only one who had created a potion as such before could accomplish. Once the correct amount of the liquid had touched the boiling juniper, the Master tossed the bottle aside. The vile shattered and the starlit liquid adhered to the floor.

"I don't have any doubts, son of man, he *will* be successful. The Broken Souls *will* take their rightful place as rulers of Shawon. And with your aid, Achnor too." Alex cringed at those words. *He couldn't let Achnor fall into the hands of the Broken Souls.* It was his calling to end the torment of the Broken Souls entirely. But if he wasn't able to save this world, at the very least, he must save his own.

Alex continued to watch the Master work. He delicately lifted a large metal ladle off of the counter and began to mix the starlight into the boiling juniper. Silver steam began to fill the shallow room. "Now, as promised, explain to me why you wish to save this pathetic world. Don't be deceived. Nothing can change my mind; it is set on one belief. But please, I yearn for an answer." The Master returned to the counter once again, this time retrieving a pile of dry leaves. His second arm holding the ladle, he took a handful of a dull yellow powder in his third.

Lade returned to the dark cauldron staring menacingly over the liquid. As he crumpled the dried leaves into the cauldron, he released the powder too. He immediately began to stir the liquid. The steam became an evergreen hue, and the scent was pungent.

"I suppose, logically, I believe that every soul deserves a life. There shouldn't have to be vengeance. One should not have to rule over the others." The fire began to die, only a faint lilac light glowing from below-giving off a warm feel.

"And yet you believe that Kardama should rule overall, and that the Broken Souls should be destroyed. As I suspected, all logic is flawed, Alex. You contradict yourself in your own beliefs. So, I ask again: why are you fighting for this world?" Lade took the ladle and dipped it into the liquid, filling the bowl of the spoon with the potion.

Alex thought for a moment, unable to find the words to say. He was never good with words. He was never good with speaking. The Master did have a point. All views could be flawed in one way or another. He didn't have a reason. He didn't know why he was here. He didn't know why he was fighting anymore. "I don't know," he admitted. "All I can describe it as is a feeling. It feels right. Like I'm supposed to keep this world at peace. That I'm supposed to let good prevail." he choked on his words, knowing that what he said would be turned against him again. Lade would always find a way to twist his words. He had centuries to learn and ponder the same questions.

"There you go again. Flaws. Good… Evil. It all depends on your perspective. In my perspective, *you* are the villain." The Master took a small vile from the counter with his free arm and lifted it to his eye level. He took the ladle in hand and carefully and precisely poured the pungent liquid into the opening. "You claim to have a reason to fight for this world, yet your logic implies that you are only 'saving' it because you have been told that you will." He carefully set the vile on the counter beside various ingredients. He then set the ladle down carefully beneath the counter. "Prophecy. Legends all have their flaws. One cannot simply believe what they have been told when there is no proof of it. I deem your reasoning flawed once again. You must have another reason. Why do you fight?"

Alex stumbled in his words. "I suppose I do not have a reason to fight."

"If you do not have a reason to fight, why do you still? You could easily give up on everything." To this, he did not answer. He had no answer. Even though it pained him, he would not answer. He would let the Master win with words, but he would not allow him to win the battle.

The Master ceased to speak. He knew he had won.

Lade returned to the boiling cauldron and let the fire die. He then returned to the counter and opened a drawer beneath the counter. He carefully dug through its contents and then revealed the oru. He gently set the white fruit onto the counter.

The Master retrieved a stone mallet which blanched against the leg of the table, and with one swift movement he smashed the berry into a lethal dust. The odor filled the room with a powerful scent, one which could not possibly come from such a small object. Lade gathered the white dust and allowed it to trickle into the vile. The color began to fade, transitioning into a beautiful blood-red shade. Instantly the overpowering scents canceled each other out, fading into a sickeningly dry, sweet metallic aroma.

The Master plunged a cork into the bottle's opening and violently shook the liquid. The crimson hue became more prominent as the liquid finally stilled. The Master grinned, staring into the crimson potion with pride. "Perfection."

The Drex potion had been created.

R watched his brother questioningly as he continued to pace about the room. "Core, we're running out of time." S said as he changed direction once again. He pulled his fingers crusted through his tangled dirty-blonde hair. It was crusty and uncared for. The strands felt dry and dead. The shackles around his wrists slid against his skin. It had been so long that he barely noticed their presence. It always felt unnatural when the Master took them off.

“We’re not running out of time, Zorus, we could set this plan into action as soon as we want. We are running out of time to reach our set deadline.” In his ninth year, R had become quite logical in his thinking.

“You will be of age in two weeks. Then soon after, the Master will begin training you with the sword. That was the plan. As soon as he allows you to wield a sword, we will strike him down and escape once and for all.” S spoke with a maturing voice. “The shadows promise to aid us in our battle, and we will be successful.” His words had a concerned tone to them.

“You sound unprepared. We have been working toward this for years. Why must you now struggle to comprehend our escape?”

“I suddenly don’t feel prepared. What if this works? I don’t know where we are going to go after we escape. I don’t know how *normal* Darlids function. I don’t know how we are to survive on our own.” S found a dry spot on the wall and leaned against it, slowly collapsing to the floor. He let out an anxious sigh. “We’ve lived by the rule of the Master all of our lives, even if it has been terrible. I don’t know how we are supposed to thrive on our own. I’m not sure I’m ready to do this.”

“And what if it doesn’t work?” R asked, genuinely intrigued with his own thoughts. “Then what? We would surely be immensely punished for our attempt to escape. Then we would live life exactly as we have before. Unhappy. Tortured. Forced to fight. Forced to train. And eventually, forced to side with the Broken Souls and use our unparalleled magic to aid in the succession of Athreal.”

“You’re right. We can’t keep living in a life such as this. We cannot give our souls to the Master and let Athreal prevail. We have to succeed. We have to destroy him.”

R smiled. It was soft, and barely noticeable, but he smiled. “I’m sure we will find a way to survive on our own. There will be Darlids in the outside world who can help us figure out how to live. And when we learn how, for the first time, we will be able to *live*.” S glanced at him with a look of confusion. “This isn't *life,* this is a nightmare. When we are free, we will have *awoken* from this dream we call reality.”

R stood from the uncomfortable cushion and made his way to his brother. He sat beside him, giving him a comforting hug. “Things will all work out S, you just have to trust me.” *S.* He hadn’t heard his brother call him by his experimental letter for years. It almost felt comforting to him, though he knew it to be a curse among words. He felt weakened by his brother's words. All of these years he had told himself that he was to protect his brother, that he was to comfort him. But here he was, the opposite occurring.

"Do you think that the Master suspects anything?" S asked, glancing at his brother. He began gently stroking his back. He could feel the ridges of his spine poking his fingers. To anyone else, this would signify malnutrition, but knowing of their origins, this was completely normal for him. Even favored among the scelos. "When you were searching through his mind, did you see anything?"

"No, I was too busy searching for something else." R refrained from acknowledging what he had found. *There would be another time.*

"If he does suspect anything, he's doing a very good job of hiding it. Our resistance is deceiving him now, but I fear that even attacking him without his knowledge will be a mistake. He could be more powerful and resistant than we expected."

"Don't worry. We *will* succeed."

Remembrance

Alex grunted feeling the cold stone floor beneath him. His moist breaths flowed evenly throughout his body, the pain enveloping his soul. Eerie sounds flowed through the silence, and he could feel the shadows misting over his body. He could feel his fragile heart beating, screaming at him as his consciousness overtook his mind. *He was alive.* He didn't want to be. Anguished, he forced his eyes shut, hoping that if he never opened them, reality would never be what he knew it now was. He had failed. Everything had gone wrong; everything had become what he hoped it never would become.

The Drex potion had been created. There was no turning back, there was no stopping the recreation of Athreal. *How long had it been? Three days?* Athreal could already have returned for all he knew. The entire world could be facing its doom and Alex was just waiting, hoping there was a way he could stop the inevitable from happening. He was too weak, too demented. *There was nothing he could do, and he knew that as fact.*

Alex hadn't seen anyone else since the creation of the potion. Only the couple of servants that would supply him with his daily supplement. He knew that he could refuse to eat. He knew that he could starve himself. He knew that he could allow himself to fall to his own self-destruction and end the misery of knowing that everything he worked for- everything he tried to save- was going to be destroyed, and yet he still ate. Something in his mind screamed at him, telling him he could still do something. He knew that they were all lies, but he still decided that he could believe in them. He needed to believe that he could do something, to gain vengeance for his friends, and for the rest of the world.

What could he do though?

He was an insignificant human attempting to save a dead world.

Alex forced himself to open his eyes. The same dead area appeared before him. There wasn't much light to expose the area, but there wasn't much to look at anyway. It was an empty space, damp and grotesque. Walls lined with moss and a pungent scent filtered through the air.

Shadows roamed the room. The shadows were deceiving. They drifted across the walls, following the shifting light like animated beings. The shadows almost seemed sentient. They were beings created from fear, formed of the most demonic thoughts which lingered within the mind.

This was no place for the innocent.

As a prince- his past, innocent self- he never imagined himself locked away. It would be blasphemy for someone to even consider jailing the prince. But here he was, locked away. Helpless. Unable to fight for his life and the lives of all others. The world was doomed.

What was his life like before he arrived in this doomed world? Though a blur, he could still remember it faintly. As the prince of such a broken kingdom, his life was lived in solitude, the same schedule playing through each day, the same tutors teaching him, the same princely duties needing to be completed each hour. Life had become rather boring, and he wished for nothing more than a little adventure in his life. And that adventure had come. That adventure had broken him. That adventure had killed the people he loved.

Death, he didn't know what was happening on the surface. What had happened to his parents? How long had they gone mourning their son's disappearance? How long had they searched for him, only to find the remains of a once unbroken man? Had they cared? Had they worried for him?

And now what? He was here. Dying. Never to be seen again.

Alex shivered away the tears, the worries, the pain. The pain of his loved ones not knowing of his existence killed him. It was more painful than the demonizing pain of the mind wavering.

The weight of the chains about his wrists consumed his mind. They felt heavier than they did before. His body had grown weak. They weren't ordinary chains either. They were formed of a metal he thought that he would never hear the name of again, let alone be chained in. *Keeler stone.* The stone itself wasn't rare within his kingdom, but it had been forbidden after the rebuilding of the kingdom. It was said to have the ability to cease the use of power any soul bore and force one's mind to tire. He could feel himself tiring. He could feel himself drifting away.

The pain soaked him. The horrors made him bleed out. Every vein in his body felt tight, his heartbeat slowing, unable to keep his blood flowing evenly. His breaths were low and sullen, his lungs rejecting new air to open his mind.

If he was not killed by the leader of the Broken Souls, Athreal himself, or some other Broken Soul, his mind would destroy him. The thoughts, the feelings, the pain. All of this- already overwhelming his mind- would soon capture it and send him into his own self-destruction. *Only a little longer. He could survive. He needed to. He needed to destroy Athreal.* Alex gently closed his eyes again.

With everything that had happened during his residence in this corrupt dimension- with every wound he acquired, every sorrow he felt, every failure he had allowed- he couldn't bring himself to try anymore. He could be dragged around by the villains- pushed, tortured, corrupted- but trying was no longer an option. He had been killed. He was no longer the person he thought he was. He could no longer care. He *should* no longer care. There was nothing he could do, and so he should do nothing.

His death would come to him soon enough. He didn't have the energy to care any longer. Why eat when the last meal he had could be his last? The pain in his stomach was a constant reminder of his demise. Soon. Why drink when the dryness of thirst could comfort him? Why move when all his body wanted to do was rest? Why think when his mind wanted to die?

Everything was a blur. Even through closed, blackened eyes, his thoughts, his mind was broken.

All he could see was the blood. The pain. The torture. The memories. Each friend that he lost. Every creature that he killed. Every tortured soul reincarnated for a cause that could not be reprimanded. A will that could not be corrupted. An idea that would only swell until it became a reality. A dream. *No.* A nightmare.

He never thought that his mind could feel so corrupted. There was always hope. There was always one last thought to pick him up and keep him determined. Now there was nothing.

There was always someone else there to stretch out their hand and lift him up. There was always someone. Now it was him, and him only.

There was always a place to go to where he could confess all of his sins and feel free. Now he was left a sinner. And the torture would follow.

Alex could feel the torture already. His mind swelled with an immense convulsion. This was torture. This was pain. This was what nightmares were made of. Living things. Living thoughts. Demons crawling through a space which seemed convoluted.

His mind was a labyrinth of lies where the demons played. The demons crawled through his thoughts, whispering to him, breaking through his already fragmented core. His mind was the Abyss, a living, breathing Hell.

He could feel his breaths becoming more rapid as his heartbeat ceaselessly against his chest. His mind quaked and his soul ached, the beasts within corrupting his mind. *Why couldn't he just end it all?* The whispering abyss of voices overwhelmed his mind. The silence was diverted as the voices continued to whisper to him in an unintelligible harmony. The words were too quick, yet too slow. The voices played tricks within his mind; he couldn't understand. All of his mind was pain.

He cried out, terrible screams leaving his body. With all his might, with all his strength, with all his heart and mind, he begged to be set free.

The voices faded.

The pain didn't leave him. The pain only began to corrode his mind, weakening his soul. He could feel himself drifting away. He squirmed, tossing, and turning against his being. There was no comfortable position. All his thoughts were pain. All of his feelings were pain. Wherever he laid, his entire body ached. All he wanted to do was rest. But he couldn't.

The pain wasn't just physical. All his thoughts were pain. *He shouldn't have left. He should have lived in captivity.* Everyone he had cared for was *dead.* They were obscured. Everything he had done had failed. The world was doomed, and it was all his fault. If he had never arrived in the first place, the search for the emblems would never have occurred.

The truth. He knew the truth. The human's arrival was the beginning of a legend. That legend was true in every aspect except its end. He would fail. Just like he had at every other thing. Just as he knew he would. *He had already.* Athreal would return. He would be forced to open the barrier and curse his own dimension as well. He would die a pitiful, wicked death. He wouldn't be remembered for his attempt to save a world so fragile, but rather as the one who doomed two.

He would die a martyr.

Alex could feel the dry dirt on his face cracking as tears melded into his skin. He didn't know that he still had tears in him. He felt as if he had bled every last one of them. The pain was too immense. The memories tortured him beyond reason. He was broken. If he were of Darlid kind, he knew that he would already be *one of them.* He would already have joined the very beings he had been trying to destroy.

What was a villain anyway? The Broken Souls were as much evil as the *heroes* were. They were fighting for a cause that they thought was right. Maybe their cause was the right one after all. Maybe the legend wasn't wrong. Maybe it just had the wrong perspective.

No. He knew it wrong. He knew that he had to do all he could to try and protect this world. He had to do all that he could to save all beings from mass destruction. Even if it killed him. Even if he couldn't achieve it. Even if every action caused him pain. At least he would be dying fighting for what he knew was right.

The pain returned.

The feeling was unbearable. The fear, the torment, the worries. His soul wanted to cry out. He wanted to scream until the pain was no more. He felt as if his body and mind would fall into an oblivion, twisting inward into his own destruction. It was overwhelming. No words could describe the pains he was enduring with perfect accuracy. There was too much. Every pain, every emotion rinsed his mind clean.

All he could see was pain. All he could hear was pain. All he could taste was pain. All he could smell was pain. *All he could feel was pain.*

Alex fell onto his knees, enveloping the pain within his body- both physical and mental. With all the strength that still remained within him, he cried out. Though only a simple phrase, a whisper that none but himself could hear, he prayed. "Death, save me."

A voice played within his mind. One he knew too well. Sweet and loving. "Son of man, you possess a glorious burden. You mustn't let evil reclaim the world." A calming sensation gently touched his mind. A simple breeze entering his soul, casting away the demons inside. His troubles began to fade, the pain relinquished, strength entering his soul. Only for a moment. But that single moment was pure bliss. Relief. Truth. A sign.

"How am I to save this world? I am locked away and helpless."

"I will come for you, son of man."

The voice faded.

He knew this to be true. He knew this to be his purpose. Yes. Even if he failed, he had to fight against Athreal. He had to banish evil from this world.

Alex lifted his hand to his face, the chains ringing through the silent room. He wiped his tears across his skin, washing away the dirt. Washing away the stains, the imperfections. He was clean again.

R was pacing the floor again. A constant flow back and forth within the small stone room. *Their prison.* He had been doing that a lot lately, like something was turning within his mind he was pondering something beyond S's comprehension, and for the sake of his brother's concentration, he hadn't cared to ask. He was becoming impatient though. What had R come up with that had got his mind stirring?

S shook his head as R turned around and crossed the floor again. He was wasting their precious time. Time was running out; they didn't have much longer until their plan had to come into action. Much longer and the Master would catch on. If that happened, he would do everything in his power to stop them. They would go through more pain, more torture, more brainwashing.

S studied his brother's pacing. It was so different. So worrying to him.

R started mumbling to himself out loud. S couldn't make out many of the words, so he chose to mostly tune his brother out. He closed his eyes, listening to R's innocent, ponderous voice. "Master… he must… defeat… no, that's not… wait, maybe…" his voice trailed on in a rambunctious flow of thoughts.

S, for once, felt particularly relaxed. In pain, still tortured and weak, but relaxed. The train had been less harsh recently, and he found the more they pretended to obey, the less the Master would punish them for their mistakes. His swordsmanship had become Mastered, and training only increased his awesome ability.

The Master had chosen to start the training with R a couple of months before his tenth birthday and found that his skill was already accurate. He was pleased with R's ability to learn so quickly, and luckily, he was still unaware of the secret training S had shared with his brother. They both needed to be ready to defeat the Master, and S wasn't taking any chances.

"More… no, less… we can't do it like.... No, no… why can't I think...?" R stuttered, circling the room once again. "Think Core, think…"

S took in a deep breath, allowing his mind to flow a little more freely. They would be free of his horrific place soon enough, he just had to be patient. *Patience.* It was more difficult a task to follow through than one could imagine. He just wanted the pain to end. The demons had promised that their pain would end. *And he trusted them.*

S hadn't conversed with Astaroth in weeks. His shadow appeared less often, and when it did, it seemed to shy away… like it was hiding something.

Secrets. So many secrets. The shadows refused to tell them everything that would occur when they were free. There was no speak of reward, or payment. They had explained that their reward would come in their own due time, and S chose to believe them. If he didn't believe them, if he didn't choose to do what they said and allow them to take control, then their chances of escaping immensely depleted.

R never really trusted the demons. It was like he knew that there was something deeper, something darker hidden behind the promise. What was a promise anyway? *A lie.* A promise fulfilled was still a lie, and yet Darlids still accepted them as truth. As a security. And S had fallen into that trap too.

They would escape.

"Please… no, I can't… Master... *weakness.*"

S perked up, his empty sockets staring at his brother in awe. "What was that you said?"

R stopped in his tracks, turning toward his brother, his fingers lightly drawing against his lips. "Huh?"

"What you just said… about a weakness?" S stood, his mind agape, hoping what his brother had said was true. "You found the Master's weakness?"

R sighed, his legs shaking. All that pacing must have worn him out. R went up to his brother, sitting beside him. "I'm sorry, Zorus, I should have told you earlier. I just couldn't find a way to incorporate this into the plan."

S nodded slowly. "When did you learn of this?"

"When Master was exercising my abilities- four weeks ago, I think- I also took the time to find his weakness. It was exhausting to do both at once, but it might be worth it if we can use it right."

"Core, what is his weakness?" S asked earnestly, placing his fragile hands on his brother's shoulders.

"Fire."

The Return

Alex awoke to the sudden sound of flesh hitting metal. His eyes burst open alight, his heartbeat quickening. Shivers trailed down his spine and his chains chimed as his body shook.

Sounds like this were usual within a dungeon. Darlids would fight against their captors, Broken Souls would brawl over territory, and some would even make noise just to inform others that they were there. Alex still wasn't used to the sounds. He found himself startled by them more often than not but could still tune them out if he found something else to concentrate on.

Alex closed his eyes, drawing in a deep breath as his heartbeat began to slow. He was in no real danger. The Master wanted him alive. Though he was still in pain, at least he would live another day. At least he knew that there was still a chance to follow through and defeat Athreal before the world became too much of a mess.

If only he could get his hands on his dagger…

Bang! The fluttering sound echoed through the corridors once again. Alex gently rubbed his swollen eyes and lifted his head, attempting to peer through the window of his cell door. *Bang!* He couldn't see much. Just a few shadows passing by. It seemed like a couple of the Broken Souls were brawling over a disagreement.

The shadows moved quickly and silently over the window of the door, creating a thrilling scene. *Bang!* Though, Alex had to imagine most of what was happening beyond the door since his view was limited.

Bang! This time the sound was much clearer. One of the figures slammed the other against his cell door, dank sludge spewing through the crevices of the door. Alex squeezed his eyes shut as the viscous liquid splattered against his attire.

Upon opening his eyes, the sounds had stopped. A single shadow, tall and brooding, stood above the door. It was hard to see, but Alex thought he could make out the outline of a smile across its face. It was simple, and almost calming. A smile so unique and genuine. One which could save the souls of any yearning being.

He could hear the clatter of the lock as the key turned within. The lock clicked and the handle began to shake. Gently, the door began to open, revealing a figure which immediately elated his soul.

Kardama.

The magnificent being stood shadowed in the doorframe, posture standing tall and firm. His glorious scythe was held uprightly in his right hand, black ooze dripping fervently from the tip of his shimmering blade. His royal attire was stained with black decay, ripped, torn and maimed. Teal blood ran across his cheeks gently, scars and wounds awarding him the assurance that he was alive. Though he presented tired eyes and a weak body, his smile comforted him.

The horrors were over. He was free.

"Kardama, is that really you? Or has my time come to leave this torturous life?" Alex asked, voice weak.

"I have come for you, son of man. Your pain will be relieved. You have a second chance at life, this I grant you." His voice was rasped and broken, as if he had spent all but a sliver of his strength. Kardama stepped forward, his scythe acting as a walking staff, and smiled faintly at Alex. The large metal door closed behind him, masking their conversation. The tiredness in his eyes became easier to notice as he stepped closer.

"I never thought I'd see you again." Tears welled into Alex's eyes. "I never thought that I would see anyone again. This is a relief."

Death smiled, though he could tell that there was sorrow held within. "But the war is far from over, and the forces of the Broken Souls are becoming overwhelming. I am afraid that relief is still yet to come."

"And the souls? Have you saved them?"

"It is done, son of man. I spent weeks kept in the cell unnoticed bringing dying souls into the spirit world, saving all I could before their minds fell to the darkness. Not a moment did I waste to rest, not a moment to eat, and my energy is spent. I have saved all the souls I can. All but one." The king stared longingly into the darkness.

Alex cocked his head as Death bent to his side, revealing a key held gently between his calloused fingers. His shimmering pearl white hair fell over his sullen violet eyes. "You have done all that you can. Every soul saved is another kept from joining the enemy. Every soul saved gives us a better chance." He spoke with frail determination. "One soul lost is nothing to fear."

"I have lived centuries, losing more souls than could be counted." As the chains fell from his wrists, a great weight was removed. Alex could feel his soul returning, the power he didn't know he held before. "Alex, this last soul is the most important one I can save." The king let out his hand, helping Alex stand on his shaky legs. It had been weeks. He thought that he wouldn't ever be able to stand again and would be left to die lame. "That soul is you."

"What?" Alex asked, attempting to take a step. His entire body was thrown off balance for a moment before Kardama caught him, holding him upright again. He looked into his burning, desirous, eyes.

"I'm afraid you won't be completing your mission." Alex looked at him, his awe, overwhelmed with questions. The king frowned. "Alex, this world is doomed. Every Darlid that remains within this realm will die. Athreal will return and curse this world until his revenge is met. You, though, can escape. I am going to lead you to the portal so you can return home."

"No. I was brought here to save this world. Sending me back will do nothing." Alex said remorsefully.

"Legends have their flaws, Alex. You can stay here no longer. If you remain in this dimension, you risk cursing both worlds. If you attempt to destroy the demon, he will get ahold of your soul and break the barrier." Kardama spoke with firm assurance, lightly placing his hand on Alex's shoulder. "I can watch my world burn into ashes, but I can't share the burden of cursing both worlds."

"I refuse to leave this world as it dies, knowing that I can save it. Please, I was sent to this world to save it. Brought here because fate knew that I could do something. Commanded to do everything in my power to save it from its own self-destruction." Alex wobbled on frail, boney legs. He was so malnourished, *so hungry.*

“I cannot allow it. I cannot cause more suffering than I have already. I should have died that day. I should have let Athreal rule this world to prevent the suffering it will cause now.” Kardama leered into the distance, the darkness- the shadows- talking to him. “I created this world in order to keep yours from being cursed. I can’t allow this dimension to fail its purpose.”

“You did all you could to save them. Now let me. I have a plan.” Alex tried to smile with tired muscles. The king let out a deep breath. He seemed to be considering, though his mind seemed to stray.

“Alex, the choice cannot be yours. I am going to return you to Achnor whatever it takes, even if it kills me, so your world does not suffer my mistake. You cannot persuade me otherwise.”

Alex gently shoved himself away, his temperament raging through his veins. He stood on weak legs, attempting to stand tall, to uphold his argument. “No. I refuse to leave this world knowing that I did nothing to fight for its survival. That I left allowing its destruction to commence.

“I was forced into this world with one purpose- to save it from its demise- and if I cannot save it, then I *will* die with it. If you won’t allow me to fight against the demon and save this world, then I will sit here and rot away in this cell until you change your mind. If I am dragged all the way to the portal and forced to return home, then I will do everything in my power to come back and have my vengeance for the ones who died. For my friends. For all the Darlids who still remain living.” Tears began to boil against his dry skin, a passion only true emotion could express.

“I cannot leave this world knowing that I did nothing. That I escaped while the entire race of Darlids is cast into extinction. It’s genocide.”

The king sighed somberly, knowing that what he would say could change fate as it was. “Son of man, is your arrogance so adamant that you would risk everything? Is your mind so closed that you would forget the pain that this could cause? Are you really willing to sell your life to the demon in order to save this doomed world?”

Alex let out an exhausted breath. “Yes.” The king stared aweingly into his eyes. “I would do anything in my power to save this world from its destruction.”

“It seems that I have met my match. Alex, son of man, I grant you my blessing to go to war against Athreal and reclaim this world. May luck be on your side.”

“Thank you. But I can’t do this on my own. I can’t defeat every Broken Soul that crosses my path. How willing is Shawon to fight for its life?”

The king thought for a moment, his heart pumping against all others, feeling the hopes and dreams of every Darlid. “Very willing. This is their home. They would do anything to cast out the demons and allow for this world to be saved. To live without fear, in peace.”

Alex smiled, regaining his balance once again. “Then go, reach the people. Call out to them to fight for their home. Ask them to form an army beyond the ranks Athreal could have dreamed. Teach them to destroy those who want to claim their home for themselves.”

“And what will you do? Where will you go? You cannot face him yourself.”

“I can, and I will. This is my choice. I will be waiting for your army to accompany me in battle. We will fight to the end.” Alex took in an endearing breath, courage filling his soul, and unknown strength finding itself within him.

“If I cannot persuade you otherwise, please, take my scythe. It is good and strong and will aid you in the final stretch of battle.” The king stretched forth his hand, offering his blade to Alex.

Alex shook his head. “You will need your scythe, to protect those who inhabit this world.”

“And what of you? How will you fight with no weapon?”

“I have one, my dagger. It was taken from me when I was sent here. I am going to find it, and when I have, I am going to pierce that dirty demon’s heart and watch him suffer as his eyes burn out.”

He expected an objection, but the king just nodded silently. “Very well. As you wish, son of man. I intend to see you again. Good luck, son of man. My warriors will gladly fight beside you in battle.” He touched Alex lightly on the shoulder and smiled somberly.

The king sighed, as if he were making a difficult decision. "Alex," he began, "You are no Darlid, but knowing what has occurred, because of your bravery, I want to grant you the title of Knightmare for the rest of your days."

"Me, Knightmare? But…"

"Son of man, no soul deserves this title more than you." Alex nodded and argued no further. "You are the hope the people need."

The king let go, reaching into his coat pocket. When he removed his hand, he stretched it forth. Within the palm of his hand was a small round fruit, bright red and speckled with dark splotches.

"Before I leave you to your fate, take this, it will return your strength and deplete your hunger."

Alex took the small berry and inspected it. "What is this?"

"It is a Newblood fruit, the only known to Darlid kind to have the ability to regenerate one's strength. This is the only one known left in existence, and I have held onto it for centuries knowing that one day, I might consume it when all hope is seemingly lost. I was not wrong to think that. It is needed more than ever to restore one's strength. You need it far more than I do." The king glanced toward the door. "Please, eat it, I cannot stay here much longer."

Alex looked at the speckled fruit once again, before quickly popping it into his mouth. It was sweet and soft. A sugary syrup ran down his throat as he swallowed. He closed his eyes, taking in a deep breath as the substance filled his stomach. His body began to feel whole once again. His aches and pains, bruises, and cuts, began to feel as if they did not exist. His legs ceased to shake, and he could stand fully without trouble. His weakness, drowsiness and sorrows began to fade as his body once again regained its health.

"You will have to remain here until your body has regained its strength entirely." Kardama said.

"Thank you, Kardama. All hope would be lost without you."

"No, all hope would be lost without *you.* You are truly the hope of this fallen world." He said no other word as he turned away, leaving Alex alone in the dungeon, a new hope residing.

S sat against the wall of the room, eyeing his brother thoughtfully. *Fire. His weakness was fire. How were they to use fire?* R was right to wonder how to incorporate fire into their plan. They were both Masters of the sword, and there was no way to ignite a fire within the room they initially planned to deal the dead- the training room.

Their time was running out. They couldn't reinvent a plan that had taken years to devise in a mere two weeks. That just wasn't a possibility. They still had to follow through the plan that they had originally thought of, but now, they had to find a way to make fire an addition.

Their shadows were of no help in this situation. Astaroth had merely told them that their minds were not as learned in the mortal world as theirs. So they were on their own, attempting to find a way to destroy the beast once and for all before their fate was sealed inside this Abyss of a prison.

They would *not* become the Master's pawns.

"Have you come up with anything yet, Core?" S asked through a tired voice. "This weakness of his has thrown in a huge complication to our plan."

"Do you think I haven't been trying? I spent weeks thinking over this on my own and haven't a clue how we could work fire into the plan, let alone ignite one." S sighed, slowing his pace- which he would begin each time he was in a ponderous state- and stared at the large metal door before him. "I don't think that Master has any Striker Stones around. At least, I've never seen them. But if we could find one somewhere, starting a fire wouldn't be a problem.

"This is what I've been thinking about the majority of the past four weeks. If I knew where a Striker Stone was, then I already have a brilliant plan in mind that would surely succeed. I am already aware that the Master has a stash of lighting fluid in his laboratory that I could get my hands on next time he takes me in. I could easily hide that away and douse both our swords in it without his knowledge. But this isn't possible without the stone." R began to draw his fingers over the cut in his lip- a sign that he was thinking deeply.

“Striker Stone? What’s that?” S asked, genuinely curious.

“It's a small stone that when pressure is applied, it creates a spark. They are really fast at creating fires, so one must be careful when using one. I read about it in a geology book Master left around. Quite wondrous, don’t you think?” R said, leaning his back against the mossy stone wall.

“That is amazing. What does it look like? How is one to know that stone from any other rock?”

“The scent. It smells strongly of sulfur.” R pulled his thin fingers through his matted hair, brushing it out of his empty eyes. “And it's usually no bigger than the tip of your pinky finger.” R set his hand in front of him and wiggled his fingers. “They’re pretty hard to spot even if you did know what they were.”

S rolled his head, looking about the bland room as he thought. The Master had to have some of those stones. He used all sorts of things to create potions and elixir, medicines, and drugs. The stones must be lying around somewhere. S had seen him ignite fires for potions before, why hadn’t he paid attention as to how? There had to be a way that he could search that room, there had to be.

“Core, I know what I have to do, but it may be risky.”

“What? Will this infiltrate our plan? Or worse, will this risk your demise?” R’s voice was filled with sudden concern.

“I’m going to have to sneak out of the room again.”

“What?! You can’t do that. Remember what happened last time when you almost escaped? Master tortured you endlessly.”

“I know, but our entire plan depends on it. I’m older now, I know my boundaries. This will all be worth it in the end. If it means finding a stone and killing the Master, by Death’s name I’ll do it.”

Blood of the Lost

Sorrow filled the air as Kardama quietly shut the metal door behind him. He didn't want to leave the human by himself again, but he had a feeling that he could manage. He had made it this far, hadn't he? Alex would be able to find his way through this twisted maze and retrieve his weapon, ending the suffering of all Darlid kind.

Still, he feared for his life. He himself had fought against the demon and had only defeated him at the cost of his own life. A poison which would never be created again. Sel had lived his life fully and had thanked Kardama with the utmost gratitude as he set his soul free. He had left the world with a smile, saying that his work would always be with him, trapped in time. But it wasn't enough, the demon was still here.

Kardama couldn't waste time. He had a task, himself. He had to unite an army. One which could be put against the Broken Souls.

The hallway before him was silent, caked with viscous decay- black and pungent. While searching for Alex, he himself had shattered the souls of many Broken Ones. It was gruesome. And seeing their blankless faces, emerald eyes, and questioning spirits of a lost soul had broken his heart. They didn't deserve to let their spirits fall into oblivion. When they had chosen a second life, they didn't know that they would forever be in Athreal's debt. But they were his followers now. A few more souls destroyed was better than more living in bodies too unstable to control, serving someone with a plan that they couldn't understand.

The hallways were quiet now. Kardama was sure that he would find more Broken Souls through his escape route, but the corridors were strangely empty. *Where had they all gone?*

On his trek through the labyrinth which was this prison, he had slaughtered beings time and time again who would have otherwise reported his escape. They were just guards, doing their job. Protecting their prize, but he had killed them. He had met each of these fallen souls once before. It caused his heart to ache knowing that he had destroyed the souls of those who chose the wrong path. Every soul deserved salvation, but they themselves chose a life of pain instead. Their blood and decay stained the walls, a reminder as to what he had done.

Now as he walked these crusted halls, they were strangely empty-quiet like a forgotten grave. Not a single Broken Soul walked the corridors of the facility, and yet hundreds still lived. They had to be hiding somewhere, lurking in the shadows. They were creating a ploy to recapture Death himself to end his salvation of souls. His focus became more intense, as he couldn't risk being locked away once again.

Where had they gone?

He couldn't risk pondering on that question for long though, there were far more important things to be focused on. Still, he kept his hand on the stick of his scythe.

Tired. He was so tired. Scars, bruises, cuts and wounds caressed his body with a longing pain. His warm teal blood drenched his attire, sliding gently down his skin. His cloak was tattered and ripped to the point that it barely functioned as it was designed to anymore, covered in decay and blood.

His mind ached with an unfathomable ailment. He had spent so long saving those dying souls in secret, leading them to a safe place. A home. He hadn't had much of a break between when Alex had freed him, and he had found him in return. There was a constant flow of yearning souls. It had taken all of the energy that still remained in his being, and even as he walked through these halls, he could still feel them calling to him. He still had a responsibility to save them before Athreal could take them from him.

His physical mind remained aware as he attempted to find an exit, but his soul continued to enter and exit his body as each spirit called to him. He needed to reach them all. He needed to save them all. They were always grateful when he came when he sent them to the life beyond. But he couldn't spend as much time with each soul as he desired as the flow of constant death continued.

Death.

They called him *Death. Guider of Souls* and the *Bringer of Sorrow. The Ruler of this Gracious Land* and the *Savior of Souls.* Some feared him. Others worshiped him. But all he wanted to do was to save those who would listen.

Three. Only three souls had refused his offer within the last week, claiming that they knew the right path was that with the Broken Souls. This saddened him deeply. But he was a righteous deity, he couldn't force his people to do that which they did not desire. They had their agency.

Though, then again, some did not. For the past decade Kardama had met souls which he could not touch. One section of their soul was tied to their body unnaturally, and no matter how hard they pulled toward him, they always continued to be drawn into their melting body. Experiments by the Master of the Broken Souls to benefit his own cause.

Kardama himself had been granted a second chance at life. Though with his second life he was given immortality, and the power over death, he was not broken and became a god himself. A gift, the makers called it. Granted to him for his bravery… for his choice to fight the demon until his very last breath. His desire to kill the betrayer of Darlid kind for the safety of the world.

Yes, this immortality had been a gift. He had the power to save all of those souls who would otherwise fall into the hands of the demon. He could save each being from a second, more painful death, or from the awful pains of living in their decaying bodies.

But there were still those who would choose the wrong path, no matter how much Kardama pleaded with them to live in a better eternity.

Watching his people side with the demons caused his soul to ache. He had seen it done to too many valiant souls. The ones he had held so closely to him in their mortal life.

Zidal had been one of them. The second of his Knightmares who had chosen that path. Hers was much more terrible than Kyron's though. Done by her own hand rather than that of the enemy. That pained him too much. He could remember it so clearly, more vividly than any other guidance he had taken part of.

There was always a moment where a Darlid's body stilled- body slumped and beginning to decay, yet the heart still beating- before the soul decided to leave into a better eternity or return to their body and serve the demon.

When Kardama's guiding soul had reached her, he was shocked, his mind unable to discern the situation. He wasn't expecting to see her again so soon, let alone like this. She had just come to beg him to escape with them a mere day before, and now her soul was departing mortal life.

He had always sensed an aura of sorrow from her being. A never-ending pool of grief and sadness. The never-ending fighting, the tasks, the responsibilities… it was all too much for her fragile heart to handle. There wasn't enough love given back to her for her accomplishments. Her thoughts always reverted back to the failures that she had encountered.

It was all too much. But he never thought… he never *knew* that her altered mind would curse her soul with enough fear to cause her own self-annihilation.

She was surrounded by broken souls, yet none touched her. Alex was held back by a serpent, silently screaming for her to live and fight against them. But the Knightmare. Her melting hands cupped gently around the handle of Kyron's scythe- a blade which he had gifted him for his bravery- borrowed by the hands of a dying soul. Her teal blood caressed the blade, which ran through her stomach until it pierced through her back. Tears washed her sinful face clean, yet she knew that she had to be the one to let herself *die.*

Her spirit stood keenly in front of her body- bright and glorious- staring curiously at its dying movement. Everything she saw was moving much more slowly than reality would assure, allowing her a few extra moments to decide. She didn't look at Death, though she spoke knowing he was there. "This is what it feels like to have no pain." she said, the memory of her voice clear. "This is what it feels like to die. It's just another moment, isn't it?"

Death spoke through sorrowful chords. He thought he could feel his physical being crying. He could feel the tears streaming down his cheeks. "Indeed, it is yet another moment in an endless eternity. But you can leave it now, you can join the others in endless joy now. There is no more need for sorrow, for pain…"

Zidal looked at Kyron longingly, seeming to want something Death knew was too out of reach. She licked her lips. "I can't leave this. I made my decision already, before the blade even touched my skin. Kardama, I have sinned, and I can't face a place of joy- a place which you rule- knowing that."

"But with death, you have been forgiven. The Kingdom is waiting for your return, knowing of nothing you did in your mortal life."

"There is someone on the other side whom I promised to share my life with, and that was cut short. I need to return to him. I need to keep that promise."

"You can't keep that promise, Zidal. Even if you return, that would be no life. Only pain. Only sorrow, serving the one you know will destroy all remaining bliss in this world."

"It's a risk I'm willing to take. When I step back into my body, and forget this occurrence, as new information- truth as I might see it as- enters my mind, there will be no turning back." She looked back at him and smiled somberly. "When I return, I hope you kill me. Run your scythe through my broken heart. I don't want to be the villain, but there are also reasons you couldn't begin to understand that gives me reason to return as a broken soul."

"Please Zidal, take my hand. I promise you things will become right. I can't watch another one of you *die.*" Kardama let out his ethereal hand, but Zidal shook her head.

She looked back at her body. "Even when my mind is altered, I want you to know that my true soul, my *true* mind, wants Athreal to be defeated and for joy to be returned to this world." She sighed. "Promise you'll kill me."

And before Kardama could answer, she stepped into her decaying vessel, and Kardama's spirit was transferred to another dying soul.

He had lost too many of his closest allies, the people he believed to be his closest friends. He felt it in his soul when Courier and his brother both were killed. He knew they left. He knew they were taken from him by the hand of the demon, broken to a point he could not save them. He wanted to save them, and now he would never see their spirits again.

That was a pain he never thought he would have to cope with. Knowing that a soul couldn't choose salvation or a second life, it was disturbing. No power could shatter a soul before its second life… none except that of the demon's.

All this time, and he still couldn't admit it, even to himself. He never *killed* Athreal. He just delayed his return, his destruction of this world.

After centuries of freedom and peace in a world that he had created, why would the demon choose to show his face now? How had he plotted for so long to find a way back to fight for the world he once lost? Where had he been hiding for this eternity?

The Broken Souls had been prowling about the surface of the world ever since the New Beginning. With no master to serve though, they were mindless and voiceless. Just another Darl walking the ground. When had everything changed? When had the knowledge of the Master's return come to the knowledge of the Broken Ones? There had to be some sort of connection within the minds of the Broken Ones and their Master. But how?

And Alex. He wanted him to live, to go home, because he knew that if he died, he would never see him again either, and he would be at fault again. If he just went home, he could live knowing that he had saved the one who could change the fate of the world. If not, Alex risked the fate of two worlds. He couldn't be at fault again. So he was going to protect him, whatever it took. He was going to summon an army and destroy that Death forsaken demon. He was going to shatter his soul and have his vengeance. For the ones he lost.

Kardama brought his mind back into reality, noticing that he had found his exit. He could feel tears streaming down his face. Everything was out of his control. Everything was so overwhelming. How could he- *The God of Death-* be filled with so much sorrow over the fallen?

He was coated in the blood of the lost, and no amount of pure water could cleanse him of his sins.

R awoke on the doctor's table. *In the laboratory.* He had been taken in, and the familiar sense of pain enveloping his body. He could feel the shackles wrapped around his wrists and ankles, keeping him tied down to the table. His blood trickled cleanly across his stomach, and he could feel sutures sewn across his abdomen.

The Master had left him inside the room on his own, trusting him too much for his own good. He often left R alone after a procedure, allowing him to heal in solitude as he attended other errands. He forgot how smart R was for his age though. Many would have to spend decades of their lives studying to achieve the amount of knowledge he held within his still ever developing mind. The knowledge was never enough. He always wanted more. His thirst for knowledge was insatiable.

The Master had left a pile of books on the side table for him to read while passing the time, knowing that his intelligence could benefit if his plan came to completion. Once his experiments were proved to perfection, there wouldn't be much hope for R and his brother. They would be broken and forced to side with the Master.

He and his brother were not going to let that happen though. Siding with the Broken Souls was the last thing they would ever accept.

He could faintly read the titles from the sides of the books. The titles intrigued him. *The Second Soul, Following Fate, Darls and Mortals,* and one other which had faded too much sat atop each other. He was tempted to pick one up. He could probably finish two of them and start the third before the Master returned...

He couldn't waste his time reading today though. He had a plan, he had to collect the lighting fluid before the Master returned. R sat up, his stomach scrunching up. He winced in pain, gently clutching the left side of his abdomen. The pain was unbearable- almost too much to remember what his plan was. Almost too much to follow through. He would not give in though.

Taking in a few uncontrollable, hyperventilated breaths, R sat completely up and slid off of the doctor's table. His feet hit the ground with a sharp thump. He could see the keys to his chains resting on the counter just three feet ahead. It was much too far for R to reach while in chains, but Master was far too trusting.

Master had forgotten that he had left another chain on the desk beside his books. With enough force, R could knock the key off of the counter and send it flying to his feet.

R stretched forth his arm, his hand brushing gently over the cover of the stacked books. He could feel his fingers caressing the rusted metal chains, but only at the tip. He attempted to stretch himself further, his abdomen continuing to scream as he pulled at his wound. The chains taunted him as he reached for their security, the only chance he had at helping he and his brother escape this wretched place.

Finally, his boney fingers connected with the metal loops and wrapped around them finely, pulling them into his grip. R took hold of the chains and held them close to his aching chest. The chains collapsed to the floor with a mighty clang. R glanced at the door fearfully, making sure that no one would come to check on him. After waiting a moment, no one having come, R redirected his attention to the task at hand.

The line of links was long enough to act as a whip, allowing R more than one chance at throwing the links at the key. R looked at the key and lifted his hand, aiming for it. He sent a powerful blow. *Strike.* It had missed the key, leaving a small dent in the counter. *Strike.* The chain nearly hit a glass bottle. *Strike.* He missed by a few inches, hitting the floor instead. *Strike.* The chain hit the key, sending it a jolt forward.

R gleaned at the door again, anxious that someone could walk through at any moment. He couldn't stop now though; he was too far. *Strike.* The key was finally caught off balance and came crashing to the floor. *Strike.* R hit the key again, sending it forward. It was still too far though. *Strike*. The key pulsed forward again.

R set down the chain and bent forward, reaching out toward the key. He could feel the corroded metal between his fingertips as his stomach bleed out of his sutures. The pain could be ignored. *It had to be.*

R retried the key and fit it into the shackle on his wrist. He unlocked the cuff and let it fall to the ground. It felt good to be free again. He followed suit with the other three shackles bound to his body and set the key on the doctor's table. He would worry about putting it back later.

Now he had to find the bottle of lighting fluid. R stepped up to the counter. He knew that this shouldn't be too hard, as there was only one compartment to store equipment inside the laboratory. That was the cupboard beneath the counter.

R found himself bending down again as he opened the cabinet. That sent a jolting pain up his chest. Everything hurt. Inside the cabinet, there sat many forms of equipment. There were a variety of dry ingredients waiting in small wooden containers. Many different surgical instruments were placed inside too. R smiled as he was able to recognize what each was. A few scalpels, a set of clamps, and some forceps, needles and syringes, sharp knives, and blades. He had to ignore those too.

The last form of substance came in liquid form, all held in glass bottles with labels stuck to them. R rummaged through the shelf of liquid ingredients, reading the names on each label. *Trepfia.* No, that was for sealing cuts. *Hyginnia.* That was used to cure drowsiness. *Glycelation.* A medicine for the common cold. The master never used any of these on R and his brother. It was no wonder each bottle was near full. *Butannicoliy.* The more technical name for the lighting fluid. Yes, that was what he was searching for.

R lifted up the bottle. It was small enough to fit in his worn-down pocket. It seemed that the amount of liquid would be far too little to ignite, but from what he had read, only a small dousing would do the trick. R pocketed the bottle and shut the cupboard.

Now he had to put himself back, lest the master became suspicious. R walked back to the doctor's table and collected the key. He sat himself up and retrieved the length of chains he had used to hit the key off of the counter. He placed those chains neatly beside the books, where he had found them, and began to chain himself up again.

After all, four shackles were attached to him once again, R looked at the key. *What was he supposed to do now?* His best idea was to throw the key and hope it landed roughly where it needed to be. He only had one shot. R looked back at the counter, set his eyes on his target, and with hope, sent the key flying. It ricocheted off the edge of the countertop and landed on the floor beside the cupboard.

R grimaced and hoped that it would be convincing enough that the Master wouldn't question it.

Letting out a deep breath, R reached over to his left and took a book off of the pile and began reading.

Two Edged

The warm, damp scent of moss flowed evenly through the air- entering Alex's nose. How long had it been since Kardama had left? The last thing he could remember was relaxing himself against the wall as the Newblood fruit reinvented his strength. He could feel his mind and body reconnecting to the world, begging him to stand and begin his journey to save Shawon from its impending doom.

He was the Knightmare now… Somehow, he felt like he had so much more weight on his shoulders, so many more people looking up to him. He was their prophesied savior.

Pain still lingered within his mind. There were some things that he could not forget. Things that had happened that had scarred him. Things that he had seen that he could never forget. Blood had stained his mind in a pain that could never be reversed. But it made him stronger… more determined. He would do this for the ones he loved.

Alex stood from the damp stone ground, and carefully peered out the barred window on his door. He listened, waiting for any sign that a Broken Soul may be lurking within the silent hallways. Looking for a fresh trail of ink. To his amazement, the corridors remained quiet- too quiet. He almost didn't trust himself as he placed his hand on the handle of the door, slowly applying pressure as the door began to creak open.

He knew that there must have been someone waiting beyond the door, ready to strike when he attempted his escape. But when the door had fully opened, all that was left before him was an empty hallway- violet candlelight flickering beyond. The stone walls were caked in dried decay, seemingly having been left there to rot for weeks. Moss and chilled dew ran across the walls. Small puddles of juniper congregated beneath dripping cracks- the beginnings of stalagmites forming.

Alex carefully shut the door behind him, glancing in both directions. Every sound he emitted screamed through the echoing corridors with a terrifying sound. His footsteps alone could alarm any nearby Broken Soul.

Alex knew that his poison-drenched dagger was hidden within the Master's laboratory. That's where he had seen it last, while the Master created that awful potion with the ability to bring Athreal back into existence. He could see it so clearly, resting on the countertop beside the other ingredients. But it had been weeks since that had occurred. There was a possibility that the dagger had been moved, destroyed even. And after all those weeks of pain, Alex could not remember the pathway to that laboratory.

So Alex decided to turn right, and lurk toward the dim, violet light flickering in the distance. It was incredibly silent in the hallways. Even the cells surrounding Alex's were void of sound. Alex didn't dare look inside, but he could have sworn that every single cell was vacant. The thought made him shiver. Had he been completely abandoned? If it were not for Kardama's appearance, would he have starved to death?

Alex didn't ponder the thought for long. When he reached the warmth of the candle's fire, he found another crossway. The pathway continued straight, but also curved toward the left, and turned toward the right. This place was a maze in itself, one which only the Master could have memorized.

Alex peered into the twisting hallway to the left, the pathway fading into the distance as darkness consumed it. He couldn't remain in the same place for too long, knowing that he could be found and recaptured. So he took the hallway to the left and clung to the slick wall as he continued through the corridor.

The silence continued to flow through the chambers as if he were the only living being remaining in the prison. He could hear juniper splashing against the stone, the sound of fires crackling, of insects crawling across the walls. The shallow sound of his breaths rang within his ears. Even the most silent of sounds were audible.

This caused great concern within his mind. The silence was not a comforting sound. It was taunting. A silent creature waiting in the darkness. Watching. Lurking. He was weaponless, helpless, afraid. Once he encountered another soul, his life would be taken from him in an instant. He had no efficient way to defend himself. Only his bare hands.

Doors began to reappear within the walls- entrances to places he could not know. They were all locked, unused. He knew that they were not what he was looking for.

In the distance, he could faintly see a hallway leading to the right. And even in the silence, he swore he could begin to hear the sounds of chatter forming from that direction. For all he knew, it could just be his mind playing tricks on him. Of all the places to be, the mind was the most frightening. It could create the most realities, the most fears, the most sorrows.

Despite his fear, when he had reached the hallway, Alex entered it. The sounds of laughter, of talking, of a congregation began to rise in a disturbing crescendo, becoming more clear as he stepped further into the hallway. *Had he been here before? It seemed so familiar.* Flickers of light began to bleed from the cracks beneath the doors, a light draft blowing through. The sounds began to increase in volume, and Alex could feel his heartbeat quickening. *This would be his end.*

The door to his left was cracked open. Alex stopped for the moment, despite his danger and peered inside. The room was nearly empty. Only a table and a chair stood inside, and it seemed that a bottle had been tipped over on top of the table. Alex shook his head, continuing through the hallway.

The next door Alex passed was a crack open, the one across the room locked and dark within. The following two were left half open, lavender lights bleeding into the hallway. The next in succession was left a crack open full flames lighting the room, and as he continued forward, the sounds seemed much more clear. Alex gently placed his hand on the door, his other against the frame, and pushed the door open. It creaked and moaned, yet the broken souls were not alerted, so much more interested in *something else.*

The flame illuminated the room with a warm lilac light, and something stood boiling within a cauldron. Then he saw it, as glorious as he could remember, his dagger sat waiting for him. He reached out, starting for the dagger. And then he heard the voice. It was quiet and muffled, but he could still make out the words. "It is this day that we reincarnate Athreal. We will give him new life, as we too receive life beyond all others." Alex knew that voice.

Alex stalled, biting his lip as he glanced at the dagger again. The blade was important but so was the distant dialogue. He was drawn to the sound of the voice. He had to witness what was happening. What he had caused. Alex turned away from the dagger, stepping toward the source of the sound, toward the light.

The door was left a crack open, and he immediately recognized the room to be the same as he was tried in. He stood at the corner of the door and peeked in, amazed at the amount of Broken Souls that waited within the room. Thousands upon thousands were seated in the balconies, as if every single Broken Soul that existed was seated in the room, excited for the return of their master.

He could see the disgusting, pulsing mass of colors hanging from the roof like a chandelier, locked within a translucent chrysalis. The souls of the emblems, awaiting to be recombined into one being. The Master of the Broken Souls stood at the podium, holding the Drex potion in his tentacle for all to see. His grin was disturbing, an abyss of hopes and dreams waiting to be destroyed.

The Master spoke again, drawing the attention of the crowd as the room became nearly silent. "After centuries of work, after decades of searching, years of planning, months of fighting, and weeks of finding the emblems, finally all have been found and destroyed for our cause." The Broken Souls let out a foreboding cheer as the Master continued. "After so long, our enemies have been slaughtered, many souls have converted into our religion- the soul truth of this world- and above all, the son of man has been captured and locked away, granting all souls and Athreal to cross the portal into all worlds."

Alex cringed, though he knew that he had a chance to escape- to fight back and end it all. Even if it caused his demise.

The Master continued his speech. "On this day at the twenty-third hour, by the power of the Drex potion, Athreal will be recreated. The twenty-three living demons will rise again- in you, his followers- the ones chosen before to be the strongest of them all. The Olks."

Lade extended his tentacle to the right, directing the Broken Souls' attention to the Olks. Alex stared at them, considering the fate of the world. He counted, the number of Olks reaching exactly twenty-three. They came in a variety of recs. From enormous beasts to a royalty. Among them were a few he recognized. Kyron the damenor, Merchel the charmer, Willow the queen of the ugly trees and her hounds, and Zidal... *But what about Lade? Was he not the strongest of all the Broken Souls? The creator?*

As the Master spoke again, their attention was brought back to his disturbing figure. His enormous, terrible smile plastered across his face. "Let us not waste another moment. Athreal *will* rise again." The Broken Souls cheered again, filling the room with an ominous sound.

Lade, the Master of the Broken Souls, drew his tentacle across his body, begging for silence. The congregation of Broken Souls obeyed.

Alex watched in a panic, knowing there was nothing he could do to end the reincarnation. He had heard the legends, studied the stories- all but for a moment- but he knew that this would curse the world. All he could do was watch.

Lade lifted the bottle for all to see, ripping the cork from the lip and brought the potion to his face. "For the reincarnation of Athreal," He paused, placing the bottle to his translucent lips, "your souls are freed." The Master tipped the bottle, consuming the potion, draining it into his mouth. An ear-splitting shriek erupted from the chrysalis as its malleable skin began to tear itself apart, the colorful souls wailing as they reunited with *their* body.

The souls danced in the air until they reached the heart of their body, recombining to create the demon. "The transformation has begun." the master said with a cackle.

Lade was Athreal. He always had been. His broken body, his tangible soul waiting, hiding, searching until his power could be returned. And it did. He had never been defeated, only delayed. And his chance to return had finally come to him. He wasn't the prophet of a demonic religion; he was its *god.*

The colorful souls melded into his heart and compacted together, skin beginning to form over his tortured bones. A true form accumulating over his melting corpse. A true second life made possible. The bright light of the combining souls swelled, brightening the room before it dissolved as skin grew over his chest.

The room grew dark, and silent for a moment. Alex could only hear the sound of his own breath.

The silence was broken as a sound was emitted, a grotesque, pulsing sound echoing from the depths of Athreal's heart. As the sound flowed in an even crescendo, a bright green light culminated from his chest, shooting toward the Olks- gifting them with power unknown.

As the power struck the souls of the Olks, they fell to their knees, the newfound power choking them from the inside. Given power once through their conversion, they now realized that they were weak. Their newly gifted power was overwhelming, a power that should never be held. A power that could curse worlds. A rebirth.

As the Olks began to rise, the last bit of decay ceased to drip- their viscous skin returning to its original state just as the demon before them. They were reborn as the world's doom.

The Broken Souls remained silent. Respectful to their master. Alex could feel the power shadowing over the room. It was a depression unlike any other, a feeling he could not escape. *He was all powerful. He would succeed.* Breathing became a laborious task. He couldn't move. His thoughts screamed within his mind, begging him to run, to retrieve the dagger and hide until he was forced to face the demon, but his limbs ceased to function.

Finally, with a bout of energy streaming through his veins, Alex sprinted away from the room, the terrible looming feeling following him. He had to break through the cursed feeling, pretend that it did not exist, hope that it did not catch him. His only chance to escape was held by a sickening feeling, one that his hope could not evade.

Reaching the doorway, Alex stepped inside. He let out an anxious breath as he grabbed the rusted dagger- coated in the poison- tying it to his waist with a small rope. He had to destroy that *thing*. Even with the corruption of the power playing with his mind, he knew he had to destroy it. He could not let Athreal destroy all worlds.

Alex turned to escape but was greeted by a terrible face. "Hello, son of man."

S awoke cold in the night. It was dark, and his brother lay asleep. Just one day before his brother had managed to steal the fuel from the doctor's room after his weekly torture session.

R had said that their next task was to coat their swords in the fuel he had collected during their next training session, then light it the time after- the day they had set to kill him for the last half decade. S would have to sneak about the prison and find the stone before that date or risk failing the task altogether.

But this would be much more dangerous. That task would be even more dangerous than even his brother's. The last time he had snuck around without permission, he almost never came back. He almost ended it all because of it. There was too much pain. But he had to risk it. He had to find the stone.

S glanced at the shadowed wall, his perfectly projected figure falling in place. The shadow shook, fingers twitching, hair swaying. But these movements were not his own. "Astaroth?" The shadow blinked, his eyes forming of blue light. "You told us that we were on our own."

The familiar, demeaning voice of the shadow echoed in his ears. "Indeed. We have been studying you from a distance and have realized that we underestimated your abilities. You and your brother have created a plan that was beyond our own. Yes, it is less complicated, but it was set in plain sight, right before our eyes, and we missed it. This plan has more of a chance of succeeding than we ever imagined."

"But why have you returned? We can complete this mission on our own. You abandoned us. Why would we accept your aid now?"

"We are only here to guarantee the plan succeeds. Please, by all means, complete the task in the way you have devised, but let us guide you, protect you, and watch for the Master's warnings." The shadow smiled through his eyes. "We still have a deal, Zorus. You are to help us escape in exchange for your magic."

"But how can we trust you? How can we know for certain that you won't turn on us? Maybe Courier was right, how can we trust you?"

"You have nothing but my word, and a promise from a shadow demon is not one to be broken." he said. "But, ah well, if you would rather we stay out of this, we can leave. We can take back the magic we had granted you and leave you on your own. Who knows if you can defeat the Master with dueling skills alone." his cunning voice echoed through the barren room.

The shadow followed the light, crossing the room as the moonlight drifted across the walls. S sighed, considering. There was little chance that they would succeed without the aid of their magic. Their magic had kept them from failure so many times before. And what would it be like waking up the next morning with his power removed? He could not risk betrayal this close to the final battle.

"I'll consider." S remarked. "As well as you could be lying to me, I know for certain that we cannot risk failure. We cannot allow ourselves to falter because we gave up our magic so easily. Whatever you're planning, we will find a way to save ourselves from your torture in the end."

"Very well, the choice is made. Until we meet again, dear friend." Astaroth placed a hand before him, bowing deeply before the darkness swallowed him. S sighed, laying his head against the wall as he closed his eyes. Their time would come. Soon they would be set free.

Recruitment

Chaos. Everything was chaos. Through his good eye, Kardama witnessed *chaos*.

Everything was a blur before him.

The surge was unlike that he had ever seen, never before had the recs of Darlids fought against each other like they were before him. Krysal city was a disaster. Pain and worry now spread through the gentle clouds and peaceful sky. Crystal buildings were cracked, some even shattered. Lavender flames engulfed the entire city. Trees had fallen, bridges were broken, and the beauty of the city was taken from it in an instant.

The people who were too weak to fight for their own survival were barricaded inside their homes as the civil war went on outside. Others dueled outside their homes, across the marble bridges attempting to slaughter their opponent. Darlids who were once friends had now turned against one another, seeking the same triumph all others were. Only one kind should remain.

Kardama began to silently weep. He could feel cold tears slipping down his cheek, his sullen breaths visible by the bite of the chill air. His people- the people he had cared for so lovingly- had organized themselves into troops of their own recs, ambushing others that were unlike themselves so that they would be the only remaining rec. *That's why the death toll had been so constantly increasing recently, they had been killing each other...*

He could constantly feel the omnipresence of his soul leave his body constantly to save the spirits of those who had fallen in the confusion- collecting memories of their deaths as he continued his trek. Each farwell was different, many of the souls chose to accept his mercy, realizing that their minds had been altered, allowing themselves to be trapped in a fit of rage until death. Others- though realizing their alteration by the soul of all evil- decided that it was the path they wanted to take, returning to their dying body, and joining the cause.

The king wanted to save them all. He wanted them to all live peacefully together, but he couldn't force his people to do his will.

He wouldn't remember every encounter. By his own name he wanted each soul to be remembered in some way. But he knew that it was an impossibility. He knew he would forget in time.

His place was that of pain. Forever and always.

It wasn't a difficult mystery to solve- knowing their minds had been altered without reason. *Athreal had been reincarnated. His presence had caused chaos.*

At the moment- though he wanted to do all that he could to end this disaster- he had to return to the palace and begin the recruitment with his own forces. Only fate knew if they were still loyal- if they hadn't... changed. What was it that was implanted inside the minds of the Darlids that made them fight each other as such? That made rec turn against rec in the final days? There had to be more than the reincarnation of Athreal that caused this rage.

Kardama sighed, taking in the fear as he always did, allowing a calm and caring presence to be felt from his aura. He walked through the center of the city on a blistering marble bridge, passing the buildings, the fighting, and the anger with his hands held behind his back, walking proudly, regally, and calmly. Battles stopped as he passed them, Darlids dared to stop and stare at their king- unable to understand how one could be so calm in a situation as such.

The fighting, the fear, and the chaos all stopped in that moment, as if time itself had waited for Kardama to pass by. The people looked at him, knowing that only a soul such as his could bring hope to a fallen people. And he would not fail them.

Death nodded toward his subjects before entering his crystal palace, knowing that the commotion would begin again as the doors closed behind him.

As soon as he was no longer visible, not needing to uphold his appearance, Kardama sped his step as he frantically made his way to the Shadla quarters. Muffled voices sounded from behind the pristine white door. He anxiously pulled the door open, slamming it into the crystal wall beside him.

Despite the ruckus he had made, the Shadla's continued to argue against each other. Their voices rang in a temperament only created by the powerful force Athreal had sent across the world. His power was so great, so infinite, that every being felt the aftereffects of his reincarnation. He feared that the strength of Athreal's power would cancel out even that of his own. The demon's soul cast a shadow over Kardama's great kingdom.

The seven Shadlas sat together in a council, each placed at an equal distance around a table. Papers were strewn across the marble table, stained with ink. Glasses had been toppled, spilling drinks. Everything seemed to be in disaster just as everything else had been.

"Enough!" Kardama yelled, begging them to calm their anger. He could not bear to watch his subjects fight against one another as if they were each other's enemies. His heart ached with a soreness unbearable at the sight. Their argument ended at the startling sound. As they noticed him, the seven Shadla's desisted their bickering and stared at him, stilling their voices.

"My lord, you have returned." The Shadla closest to him said. He was a horned beast, cloaked in lizard-like scales.

"What is the cause of your agitation?" Kardama asked. "What has gone awry while I was away?" he asked, his voice calm, though his mind raging in fear for his people.

"Nothing, my lord," the eldest of the council began, "But that of our own minds. Something has opened in the minds of every Darlid, telling us things that we cannot disagree with. Each rec is of their own, only one should remain."

"Yes, it is true." another stated. "Most of the citizens have chosen to riot and kill each other in a frenzy. We, at least, have been more civilized. But our discussions have been ending in disagreements recently, none of us can agree on what to do, your majesty."

"We have sat ourselves here in this council attempting to agree on the best way to end this purge." one of the female Shadlas said. "But each of our ideas has countered the other, and we cannot find a way to bring peace to even ourselves."

"My lord, please, we need your guidance." the lizard beast declared. "Only you can still our minds."

Kardama sighed, considering their words. They looked at him with pleading eyes, knowing that no soul other than their king could advise a plan that would succeed. They knew- somehow through their mask of fear and confusion- that something was awry and that they had to end the pain. They *knew* that Kardama, *the god of death,* would be the only path that would end without tragedy.

Kardama knew that he could not lay these words easily on his allies. "This is the work of Athreal." he declared, acknowledging their rage against each other. He could see the shock on their faces. As if not one had considered the god of all contemptuous thoughts and discord had risen once again. Fear immediately struck their hearts, just as he had intended.

Kardama took in a powerful breath reorienting his thoughts before he spoke again. "Despite our attempts to destroy the emblems, Athreal has returned." The Shadlas cringed at their king's remark.

"We are in a state of emergency!" Kardama yelled, walking the room up and down. A power unknown entered his voice, as if he was speaking without thought, as if the words themselves were what was uniting the Shadlas. "Athreal has been released, the Broken Soul army has increased tenfold within the past eight years, and each rec has begun to kill off all others. Chaos is reigning. The end of the world is at hand.

"The time has come to make use of your skills, to recruit an army even larger- even more determined- than that of the Broken Souls. We must take back our lands and free ourselves from the enemy. Only then can we have peace for the eternity to come!" He paused for a moment, taking a breath. He could feel a stirring within the minds of the Shadlas. His commanders- his best warriors- looked up at him with a careful regard, taking in his words with care. His aura had touched their minds, had called them back to reality. "I cannot fathom doing this on my own. I can recruit as many as I can, but I need your aid to expand our army."

The eldest of the Shadla's stood, a motion expressing his agreement. He had a stiff expression, and a warming welcome. He bowed before he spoke. "We are loyal to you, and to you alone, your majesty. Tell us, what is it we should do, and we will make sure your wish is granted."

"Recruit, my friend. We must still the hearts of our people and bring them together again to fight against evil for the greater cause." The Shadla gave a faint smile. "I need one of you to rally up my troops- all of them- to be ready for battle. I need the rest of you to visit the six major cities and recruit the people with the same message. Any who are willing to fight, to die even, for the safety of the future.

"And what would that message be, my lord?" another asked, still sitting. The others nodded, a questioning tone in their mumbles.

Kardama thought for a moment, trusting his mind to declare the message. "Listen well to my words, the same message *must* be repeated accurately, else the world remains in chaos." he declared. The Shadlas stared at him, concentrating on his words. Many of them quickly bent over to dip their feather pens into ink, throwing papers out of the way until they found a blank page to rewrite his words on.

Kardama cleared his throat before speaking. "The world as we know it is in danger. Our lives, our homes, our families will be taken from us. Evil has entered the heart of all men, and every soul wishes for the same outcome- that of the death of all others but their own kind.

"Let us change our hearts, let us realize our mistakes, let us recognize that our minds have been tainted. Open your hearts and see the truth. Recognize the lies that have been planted inside your minds as the curator of pain has returned... Athreal has risen again, and he yearns for this chaos. He *wants* you to fight against one another. He *wants* you to hate each other. He *wants* this war and turmoil to distract from his greater purpose.

"He has caused your minds to fail and to think that only one rec should survive. He has caused you to forget that you are killing your friends, destroying the lives of your loved ones, and causing his plan to succeed. He only wants to expand his own army, to kill off those that oppose him and bring as many to his cause as he can. His lies feel like the truth, but the world will be his before killing each other off does any good.

"Let us now stand together for a greater cause, to stand against this evil and reclaim our home- to regain our lives. Peace will reign again, but only if we put our hearts together and fight for the same cause. The same hopes and dreams. We must destroy the monster who oppresses us before the time becomes too late.

"Please, any that are willing, take up your weapons and follow me to the Careless Meadows- to the place where the final battle will commence. To the place where we will have our victory. A place where we will rid the world of any evil that remains. A place where we will declare peace once again!"

The Shadlas stared at the king, struck with awe. None dared to disturb the silence he had left, but he knew that his message had been clear. He knew that they had found their truth.

"I will remain here, declaring my message and uniting the people of Krysal to fight for the greater cause. To cease their arrogance and stop fighting each other. To fight and defeat the greater villain before it's too late." Two more Shadla's stood, agreeing to the same cause.

"And then, after we have gained the greater part of our armies, where should we go, my lord?" another Shadla asked.

"Take the people through the portals laid about the cities and bring them to the Careless Meadows as soon as possible to meet against the enemy army and fight for the greater cause."

"It will be done, my lord." he said standing, followed by the three others.

"Very good. I must be off to begin this recruitment." Kardama nodded, trusting his Shadlas to do the right thing. Then he left them, rushing again to the front of the palace, hurrying to bring the people of this kingdom together… to save it.

The Master tugged on S's arm as they made their way toward the training room. R whimpered- though to seem more weak and in pain than he was. Their plan was coming to a conclusion, it was only mere days before the assassination would take place. Today was only a step in the path to their succession.

The Master halted at the door crafted of keeler metal and retrieved his key with one of his two remaining tentacles. As the door unlocked, he shoved his captors in and locked the door shut before they could react.

S was used to this kind of treatment. It was terrible and he would do anything to end it, but he wouldn't oppose his Master just yet.

He and his brother stood from the hard stone ground, grunting to show their weakness. The Tall Being liked weakness. It meant that he was still in control, that S and his brother would do as he commanded. But their weakness was just a ploy. They had taken weeks to recover, many of their training sessions waiting inside the abyss to heal themselves before finally submitting to the Master's tests and completing the tasks effortlessly.

Today would be different. Today was the next step.

R nodded at him with a gentle smile as the Master unlocked the chains and released them from their wrists. S could feel the power flowing through him. The magic, the abilities, the strength. He felt so powerless with the chains absorbing his magic, though he knew that was not the case. His skills with the sword had improved greatly. He could defeat a hundred men on his own.

S drew his favorite sword from the weapon rack as his brother's shackles clattered to the ground. The blade was strong and well-crafted. It was sharp and the handle fit in his hands as if the sword itself were made for him. He felt a different kind of power when wielding his weapon.

Once R took his sword of choice from the rack, he gently grabbed S's empty hand as planned and they immediately entered the abyss.

Time stopped. They would return to the master when their task was completed. Their stay in the abyss would include more than just their own rehabilitation.

R clutched his brother's hand, knowing that if he let go, he would return to reality. He couldn't face the Master on his own. S wandered through the small space- only as large as the room they were in as the keeler lining on the walls confined his magic. After a moment, he found the crack in the void and squeezed himself through. His brother followed and as he entered, he let go.

This was the only space within the void that he knew of that did not act the way it should. A rip within reality. He and his brother had spent many hours within the space, making it into another home within their prison. Things wouldn't disappear if S let go when he took them here, so it was here they held their stash.

R bent down, removing a bottle labeled *Butannicoliy* from his pocket and removing the cork. S set his sword onto the floor of the void beside his brother's and watched as he dumped the liquid onto the blades of the swords. He thoroughly laced the metals, allowing the blades to absorb the fluid.

"Are you sure that the lighting fluid will last until we need it?" S asked his brother.

"Yes. It won't expire, plus the swords will remain here. You know how the void works differently with time." S nodded, though a little skeptically.

When the remainder of the liquid dripped out of the bottle, R stood, leaving the bottle in place. "We should get going."

"You don't want to stay in the void today?"

"There's too much on my mind. The task at hand has been completed. Let's just get our training done." R nodded at his remark, setting the swords aside and replacing them with the ones they had stolen and claimed to lose weeks before.

"Let's just hope the Master doesn't realize we've switched weapons." S nodded in agreement, taking his brother's hand, and exiting the safe space. Letting go of his hand, they both returned to the room to complete their training.

The Song of Hope

"Hello, son of man." The voice rang clearly behind him, no longer disturbed by a viscous gurgle of chords. A once hideous voice returning to that of its origin. There was still a clear indication of who the voice belonged to. There was still a raspiness- a desire to cause destruction- hidden in his words.

The aura of the being behind him was binding. A feeling of hopelessness and dread filled his soul as the creature stepped closer, laying an incomplete boney hand on his shoulder. Alex shuddered a feeling of fear and of anxiousness filling his heart. He felt sick, yet unable to move, to think… to feel.

He could see the hand on his shoulder morphing as it gripped him tightly. Light colored skin slowly grew over the tangible bones, no longer decaying and dripping from his body.

The creature spun him around, allowing him to take in the full picture of the king of the Broken Souls. He grinned ceaselessly, lips growing slowly over his cracked skull- now healing from centuries of decay. His dark hair regrew, covering the top of his skull in luscious locks of obsidian. His left socket remained empty, though his right eye glowed a bright green hue like a celestial body. Horns pierced through his skull, short and fragile now, though slowly extending just above his broken ears.

From his shoulders grew four arms, one protruding from the front, and the other extending out from his back on either side- penetrating the broken skin on his shoulder blades. The bone structures of fragile hands grew from the stubs of his arms- the tentacles strengthened by new bones, bloodred muscles grown on top.

He was clad in black, cloths colored gold and crimson draping across his shoulders as a cloak. In his front right hand, he held a staff carved from a large metal spire, crooked and deceiving. He held a regality in his stature and a firmness in his voice.

And from his back grew two leathery wings, flapping in the draft as they molded into their true structure. Though weak and frail now, the wings of the demon would extend infinitely, holding a powerful strength to carry the regal beast into the skies. To hold him above his subjects and to declare to all others that he was almighty.

His appearance was that of a true nightmare.

Alex quivered, gasping, and choking for air, unable to withstand the presence of Athreal. He could feel his insides twisting inside of himself, a sickness caused by the company of the demon. He watched as his skin pulsed restlessly, convulging as blood spurted from open wounds. His smile widened as another one of his developing hands clutched his throat. He gasped for air, gripping his fists tightly.

This is the end. He thought. *After all I have been through, after everything I've done, this is where I die.* He could feel the grotesque skeletal hand holding his neck with an unimaginable strength. He felt himself stop breathing, his lungs begging to be filled, yet unable to take in the sweet air. *I was foolish. I never could have done this alone. I was the savior of this world, and yet, I am going to let the world fall to the hands of the demon. I have failed.*

Alex closed his eyes, taking in his last thoughts as he accepted his fate. His mind exploded with regrets before he felt his body slam against the cold, stone wall. Suddenly, his lungs filled with air again and he breathed heavily, gasping for the sweet relief. He brought his hand to his throat and opened his crystal eyes looking up at the beast from below.

"Did you seriously think I would kill you? When I still have use for you, son of man?" Alex didn't answer. His body ached. He was bleeding where he had collided with the wall, and his left arm felt sprained. "You thought to escape. You thought to defy me. You thought that you could find your rusted blade and kill me." He chuckled. He stepped forward, tapping his staff against the ground. "But you still forget that *I* am in control. *This is my world now."*

Alex shuddered, unable to speak, unable to emit a sound. All he could do was watch as Athreal stepped closer to him, extending his back left hand. He gripped his hand- damp with blood- around Alex's wrist and forced him to his feet with a mighty tug. Alex knew what was happening before he felt the coldness of the shackles tightening against his wrists.

"And that means you are *mine."* his voice sang quietly into his ears as he shoved him forward. His face met the wall with a powerful impact. His nose shattered against the stone. The shock of pain held his tongue. He found himself unable to scream, unable to move as he hit the ground again. Blood spurted from his face, leaking down his face along with his tears.

The demon laughed maniacally. "I've experimented countless years in the realms of torture. I know what can break someone's soul and body without killing them. I know how to inflict pain without death... and sometimes, that's the most enjoyable part- knowing that you will not die."

Alex felt a forceful kick to his gut, forcing blood to spill from his mouth. He coughed, attempting to ignore the pain. *It... cannot... end... now.*

"And what's even better...? An adult can take more torture than a child." Athreal lifted up his broken body, staring at him with his empty eye. "You *will* open the portal back to Achnor whether you want to or not. There are endless ways I can cause you pain. Endless ways I can torture you before you give in. Don't think you have a chance against me. *I will not die again!"*

Alex stared; his vision blurry. He could feel his cold blood and tears running down his clothes, staining his attire with failure. He wouldn't be able to stay conscious much longer. He could feel his mind falling to his pain, attempting to kill his consciousness to save him from the pain. But he would not give in. He could not fail now...

He couldn't fail...

Alex felt a cool liquid running down his throat, the taste was bitter and gamey, but he could feel it healing his mind. "This will allow the pain to ease... for now. I still need you to stay awake."

"Why...?" Alex asked through a shallow, dying voice. "Why don't you just kill me now? You can have this world to yourself, but I will never give in. I won't let you have Achnor."

Athreal smiled. "You will. Everyone breaks eventually."

The king of demons stepped forward, lifting his staff before him. Alex watched it plunge forward, colliding with the stone wall. The stone cracked, pebbles falling onto Alex as he struck again. A hole appeared in the wall as the demon struck again, chipping out the stone. He beat upon it again, exposing the outside terrain. Again. The wall collapsed upon itself, revealing the meadows along with the Broken Soul army.

Athreal grasped Alex by the back of his neck, lifting him up and showing him his accomplishment. "Look at my army," he said, "Look at all that I have accomplished in my years hiding away. No one will stop me from my desire. Not even Kardama can destroy my army. And even if he could, no one can kill me again.

"There is no weakness this time. There is no one to *create* that weakness this time. I am this world's future. Even if I have to kill every last living Darlid, this world will be mine."

Alex struggled in the grip, unable to escape knowing that the words the demon spoke were true. He looked upon the mass of Broken Souls- an ocean of dark terror standing before him. The mass was great, legions upon legions of souls stood before them with a lust for blood and an unmatched hope to have their victory.

There stood the twenty-three demons standing proudly before their army. Commanders and unstoppable warriors waiting for their leader's command to strike. Thousands upon thousands stood in the midst of the meadow, too many to comprehend. The world- both worlds- were doomed to Athreal's victory unless Kardama could construct a larger army with more experienced warriors.

He knew that it could not be accomplished. He knew that they would still be outnumbered. The world was doomed… *it always had been.*

Athreal forcefully threw Alex onto the grassy ground, the feeling of his grimy, slowly forming hand letting go of his neck followed by his plunge into the soft grass. Alex coughed, sitting up onto his knees- his hands held by the chains behind his back. "Ambush! Carry him for me, will you? We have work to do."

Alex heard the corrupted brays of the pfesens as the broken demons stepped forward. They were two of the twenty-three, their skin and bone reforging. Dark crimson scales were beginning to grow from their skin, coating each of their five legs and bodies. Spilled intestines and gore merged back into their bodies, regrowing the chipped off pieces of their skulls. He could feel a power almost as strong as the demon himself as they stepped closer.

The first of the two- it's broken jaw reforming- lifted Alex from the ground with the claws of its tail. She gently set Alex on her back, now rougher and shinier with glimmering red scales growing in their places. Her brother Atlas grinned at him with his four eyes, glimmering a distasteful green hue.

It chuckled, forming a taunting voice in its chords. "You have failed. You could never be the savior of this world." The voice was familiar, a clear respectful tone flowing clearly through. It was that of Kardama's, a ploy to break his hopes further. It wouldn't work though. His hopes were already low. His faith to accomplish his task was dry, and the words only left a scar where he was already cut.

Alex looked forward, watching as the king of the demons stepped forward, his wings fluttering behind him as a regal cape. He stood before his army and spoke. "Now is the time to become the heirs of this world, to take it for ourselves and bring vengeance to our ancestors!" His voice was loud and clear. The entire army cheered at the sound of his words, even the ones the furthest from the front. "Now we head to the capital- to Krysal city and open the portal to claim two worlds!" Again, another cheer bellowed through the empty space.

Athreal gave a nod toward the pfesens and at his command, they reared, sending a mighty call through the meadow. A demonic braying that commanded all who stood with them to follow. Alex struggled to stay balanced on Ambush's back, but the strength of her grip on his chest held him up firmly. He cringed as its front three feet made impact with the ground, beginning to march forward.

The entire army beyond him began to follow in a steady pace, following the twenty-three demons with pride. Athreal walked back toward his subjects, his facial structure now built better. He stopped beside Alex, mounting Atlas, and steadying himself on his back.

"My reign will commence." Athreal declared in a voice only loud enough for Alex to hear.

Something didn't feel right though. The very aura of his being felt diminished as a new presence filled his heart. A powerful hope, a determination that lessened even the pain of his broken body. He could feel a thumping in his heart, a constant tempo calling to him. A sound claiming that there was still a way. A knowledge that even when all hope seemed lost, there was still more than one outcome to this battle. *He could still win.*

Alex turned his head, looking toward the source of the thrumming-beyond the army of broken beings. "No, you're wrong," he declared in a firm voice, "There *is* still hope."

Athreal turned his head, searching for the source of the sound. Both stared in awe as the entire army halted, knowing that their reign would not be won- not yet.

In the distance marched a second army, its size matching that of the Broken Souls- continually increasing as more Darlids entered the meadows through the portals. The people, armed and ready to fight for their world, faced the army. Their voices rang loud and clear. Every soul sang the same tune, hoping for the same outcome. Every soul wished for the same cause, fought for the same dream. The people of Shawon had come together to destroy the Broken Souls once and for all.

At its head stood Kardama himself, holding his scythe regally before him. He led his army forward, a peaceful, calming feeling reigning from his being. A feeling that overwhelmed the demonic aura of the demon.

Alex felt himself smiling. "He really did it." he whispered to himself.

"No… By Death's cursed name- this cannot be!" Athreal yelled in a rageful agony. He looked toward his commanders. "Charge toward the people. Kill until there are none left. We must not jeopardize our reign." the commanders nodded before turning toward the army, sending it toward the people.

Alex was thrusted forward on the back of the pfesen, charging toward the army. There was hope. The song rang clearly in his head. He too began to sing for the same cause, knowing that he still had the *weakness.* He still held the blade that could destroy the demon.

S woke in the night knowing that the task he had to complete this night would be dangerous. If he failed, he might never see the light of day.

S glanced at his brother, watching him sleep- though still uncomfortably. He could not wake him. He did not want him to lose sleep as he anxiously waited for his brother's return.

S sighed, standing from his place. His wrists remained cuffed, though the chains on the wall did not keep him captive. He was left to find the Striker Stone and bring it back before he was found.

S reached for the handle of the door and pulled. The door- though heavy- was luckily open. He used what strength he had to open the door and squeeze through the crack he had created. This was one of the rare times he was grateful for how skinny and frail he was. If he was any bigger, he would not be able to fit through the crack of the door. He glanced back one last time, ensuring to himself that his brother remained asleep.

S took in a deep breath, looking down the dark hallway. It remained empty. He knew that the Master would be elsewhere, torturing some other innocent soul. He would still have to be cautious though, he couldn't risk being caught again. S crept down the hallway, finding the door to the potion room. It was only three doors away from that of his own chamber, and he had visited it often in his years.

The door to the chamber was left open by his master, knowing that no soul would enter without permission… or so he thought. S touched the cold metal of the door and traced his hand across its width as he entered the room. It was fairly dark, only the firelight of three lavender candles illuminating the area.

Items were scattered about the room. There were tools lying on the floor and across counters. Empty vials and ingredients sat patiently on the countertops. The cauldron in the center of the room remained stagnant, though a fermenting liquid bubbled inside. S quivered, wondering what despicable potion the Master had created this time. But that was not the task at hand. He needed to find the Striker stone.

S stepped toward the littered counter, searching its contents for the item he desired. But the clutter gave no indication of the stone. There were piles of crushed, dried leaves. Berries and chipped gemstones laid dormant. Vials of venoms and other liquids waited for their use. These were only the ingredients.

S moved to the bottom shelf, opening the cupboard door beneath the counter. This held equipment to create *his* potions. There were spoons and tongs, stirring sticks and vials. And in the midst of them all stood a pile of small berry-like stones.

S took one of the stones lifting it up to his nose. Remembering R's description, he took notice of the scent. It was fiery, like brimstone, a sulfuric scent coming from its pours. It was very small and could fit on the tip of his smallest finger. He knew that the stone was the one he was looking for.

Placing the stone in his pocket, S turned toward the exit of the room and began his way back to his room. The way back was more daunting than the way there, for if he got caught now, the consequences could be much greater. Still, he had a feeling in his heart that the Master would not find him.

Eventually, S reached his room, and squished himself between the door and the wall. Closing the door behind him, he locked himself back inside and rested himself against the wall. Now he could sleep knowing that the task was completed, that they were one step closer to destroying the Master once and for all.

Stone Soul

The armies clashed with a merciless rage.

Kardama lifted his scythe with a determination unmatched, hewing the head from a Broken Soul's neck. He had to fight, he had to protect his people. He brought the people into this fight only to watch them die. Thousands upon thousands had heeded his words, joining him for this very cause. And as his army advanced, clashing with that of the demon's soldiers continued to file out of the portals behind.

He was proud, though his heart still ached. He would lose many for the sake of the world's survival.

Kardama could hear the sounds of death around him as he swept his blade through three rampaging Broken Ones- blood spilling, people screaming, and weapons clashing. He could feel his soul constantly transferring from spirit to spirit as his people died, returning to the life beyond. But he knew that as Darlids died, so did the broken souls. He had to concentrate on the fight, he couldn't even take a second to remember the ones who died. And his soul ached because of it.

Decay was caking the ground in massive puddles. A dark, viscous liquid forming of the dead- both Darlid and Broken Soul- stained the ground. He could feel tears streaming down his cheeks as he attacked another and struck down another broken being. His blade ran through the chest of the deformed being as another attacked from behind. He felt a claw run through his back as he turned to destroy the being.

The Broken Soul died easily. He could feel the blood trickling down his spine along with the decay and blood of his enemies. He let the pain rage through his body. He could feel the pain, the rage, the sorrow, but he was still immortal. The pain, fatigue, and ailment would not kill a god.

He cut through another body, letting the being fall to the ground as it decayed into the grass. Surrounded by death, he knew he couldn't save them all. But he needed to save at least one. *Alex.* He needed to find Alex. Though the fabled savior of this world, he could not accomplish such a task on his own.

Kardama halted his fighting for a moment, searching with corroded vision through the legions of Broken Souls. In the midst of dark decay, he could see colors fly, Alex's blue robe fluttering in the wind. It was far and only a small speck within the armies, but he knew that to be him. He was kept captive, uncontrollably riding a reincarnated pfesen, its dark red scales glimmering beneath the lilac sun. He had to free him from his captors.

Kardama filed his way through the legions of Broken Souls, killing those who got in his way. His dark cloak was smothered in dark decay, the blood of the ones he killed drenching his kingly attire.

The beasts granted second life were strong- even stronger with the gift of Athreal's power granted as he rose again- barring sharp teeth and great ambition. But their strength could not save him from Kardama's blade. He sheared through ranks of decaying beings, amputating limbs, and severing heads as he rushed to give Alex aid.

Kardama grunted, throwing his scythe behind him as a viscous claw caught his hood. His swing drifted above the Broken Soul's head as it ducked below. The Broken One leaped and bared its teeth, snagging its sharp fangs on the hood of his cloak. Kardama raised his weapon, smashing the butt of his scythe into the beast's skull. The bone crunched and the being dropped to the grass ripping the hood free from the cloak.

Kardama spun around, cleaving the head off of a broken beast before plunging the blade of his scythe into the beast's heart. The beast fell, staining the grass obsidian.

Taking in great breaths, Kardama frantically searched the meadows again. Spotting Alex with his good eye, he began to run again. He pushed through the ocean of broken souls, losing strength and stamina as he followed the fleeing pfesen. Death slammed his scythe into the heart of a Broken Soul, impaling another behind it. Jumping over the decaying corpse, he threw his scythe through three more of Athreals followers, advancing toward the galloping pfesen.

The pfesen looked toward him, acknowledging his presence with four golden eyes, as if to challenge his authority. Kardama knew that he was one of the demons, for no Broken Soul retained the color in their skin or the strength of their bones. The pfesen- Alex held within the claws of its tail- charged through the army of Broken Ones, galloping toward his opponent.

They clashed. The beast was strong and tall, determined to kill the very being who granted death. Kardama swung his scythe forward, lacerating the scaly skin of the beast. The pfesen did not cringe as its blood- as red as if it were still *alive*- spilled across its chest.

"Alex!" Kardama yelled as jumped aside from the pfesen's buck. "What has happened to you?" he asked, considering the blood streaming down his face. His nose was shattered, and his arm was limp. His hands were chained behind his back and the claw of the pfesen gripped his waist tightly.

"It's nothing to worry about." He cringed as he spoke. "I need to get to Athreal. I have my dagger." he said, glancing at his side where a sheath lay.

"What is the importance of the dagger? Would you not consider taking my scythe?" Kardama asked, throwing his blade against the leg of the pfesen. Blood streamed through the cut he had created, but the bone was too strong to be hewn from its body.

"Demothar, Kardama. It's laced with Demothar!" Kardama ducked as the pfesen reared, avoiding its three enormous claws.

"But that's impossible. There was only one potion and Sel died over a millennium ago." Kardama raised his scythe blocking a swipe of the pfesen's claw. He threw his blade behind him- ducking as another claw came upon him- shattering the soul of another Broken One.

"I found it in the tower of Sel. It was preserved by a time spell. It was as if he knew this day would come." Kardama smiled proudly as he ran to the backside of the pfesen. He threw the blade of his scythe onto its thick tail. The pfesen hissed, enraged by the pain. Blood seeped from its hind, though the tail was not served yet.

"You know the consequences of this, son of man?" Alex nodded. Kardama sighed. "If you pierce the heart of the demon, you may never leave back to your world. You may never *wake up* again. Alex, I cannot allow you this destiny. Please, let me take the dagger and slay the demon myself. It is my duty." Kardama swung his blade again. The pfesen screamed as its tail came loose, dropping to the ground as it decayed.

Death let out his hand, helping Alex from the back of the beast before it galloped into the distance to warn its master. "I cannot let you. I am supposed to be the savior of this world. I *must* face Athreal."

Though it pained him, Kardama knew that he had to trust the boy. *He had his agency. He was the fabled hero.* "Very well." Kardama lifted his scythe, breaking the bond of the chains with the impact of his blow.

Alex faced him again, smiling faintly. "Please, Kardama, fight with me."

"You bring hope to this world, Alex. I will fight with you, though not by your side. With the Demothar laced on your blade, I must bring a weakness to the demons. I must cast the spell I had created long ago for this very purpose… even if it kills me."

"Kardama…"

"Alex, this duty is of my own, just as yours is your own burden. Go. Save us."

Alex nodded graciously toward him before he turned into the sea of Broken Souls- lost to his sight.

Alex charged into the black sea of Broken Souls, drawing his dagger from his sheath. He couldn't thank Kardama enough for freeing him, and he regretted having to leave him to fight on his own. He knew that the king had his own demons to face. He had to protect the people. He had to defeat the twenty-three living demons before things got too tragic.

Anxious thoughts raced through his mind as he cut his way through the army, toppling Broken Ones, and shattering their fragile souls. He could see his target faintly- hovering in the air with enormous wings; like those of a dragon's. The king of the demons waited patiently, causing destruction and death as he flew through the meadow.

Enormous stone spikes, like sharp stalagmites, emerged from the ground, cutting through the ranks of Darlids fighting for the safety of their world. Alex cringed, knowing that he couldn't save them all, knowing that Death couldn't save them all. He had to ignore the death, the killing, the horror, focusing on his own task- to kill the king of the demons and save this dying world. *It was his duty.*

Alex pushed his way through the ocean of decaying bodies, holding his sprained arm gently. His whole body ached, yet he felt strong, determined to end this battle once and for all.

Alex slammed his dagger into the heart of a broken beast, shattering its soul as he fell beneath another attack. Pulling his dagger from the lifeless corpse, he threw his blade into the heart of another. It fell to the grass, staining it with viscous decay. Alex took in a deep breath, thrusting his dagger into the neck of a third, shattering its soul as it dropped into the soft grass.

He could feel tears forming in his eyes. He couldn't handle the killing, all of the death and pain. His face erupted in pain, his shattered nose bleeding and swollen. His limp arm ached, useless to his battle ahead. His legs begged him to slow his step, to rest and heal.

He remembered his allies, the people he had come to love and trust while in this world. *They had all died. He had lost so many.*

He could see them in his mind, imagining the pain they were going through before they died. The ones he witnessed were so clear, the blood and decay stained within his mind. He was disturbed, he was pained, but their deaths still pushed him forward.

Still, he pressed forward, knowing that his actions would determine the world's fate. He would win this battle… for them.

Alex plunged his dagger into the heart of a Broken Soul. He watched it fall. *He watched it die.* Again, he threw his blade, shattering the soul of a broken beast.

Alex looked up as he killed. He could see Athreal flying above the ranks of Darlids and Broken Souls, sending spikes through the earth to destroy his enemies, to attempt to bring them to his cause.

Alex was right there. Just beneath him.

He had to find a way to defeat him.

Kardama watched Alex charge as he swung his scythe again- killing a rampaging Broken One. It died easily. He needed to find a safe, secure spot where he could cast his spell. He was immortal, but that didn't mean that he couldn't feel pain.

He needed time though. It had been centuries since he had first casted the spell. He could remember the words, he could remember the motion, but every spell had its own consequence. Doing it again would take all of his remaining strength- mind and body. He would have to rely on the others to finish off the demons once he animated their shadows.

Kardama swung the stick of his scythe, allowing the blade to cut off the heads of three Broken Souls fighting before them. They fell lifeless to the grass, decaying more quickly than they had before.

Kardama studied the warring armies, thankful that his own ranks still outnumbered that of the Broken Souls. But he knew that the Broken Ones were stronger, and even an army double the size could fall. Between him only stood decaying corpses and dead land for a fair distance. The Broken Ones had determined that Death himself was too tenacious. They realized that he couldn't die and had begun to focus on the Darlids; many of which were weak and had little training with a weapon.

There was so much death around him. He was losing so many souls. But he couldn't focus on them now. He had to focus on his spell. This was his greatest opportunity.

Kardama lifted his scythe into the air and spoke. "Convert." As he spoke those words, a black trail of smoke began to stream from the tip of his blade. Remembering the motions, he had to create to activate the spell, he drew his blade through the air, drawing the symbol of shadows. It was a spherical shape, holding two parallel lines within it. It was fluid and smooth. Death drew the symbol carefully, recalling the slow, swift movements he had once created.

The black smoke danced in the air, curling around itself; constantly flowing in a perfect pattern. The sphere held its shape in a perfect uniform pattern, expanding in size until it was as tall as Kardama himself.

The first symbol completed, Kardama stepped to the side- the smoke still trailing- and began to draw a second. This time, it was the symbol of demons. The shape was much more rigid. It had seventeen corners with sharp points at each end. Within the center of the unique shape, the symbol of death remained stagnant.

Kardama cut his scythe through the air, perfecting the shape. For if he created the wrong symbol, the spell would go awry- cursing him instead.

Completing the glyph, Kardama stepped back, studying his work. It was perfect. Precise. Lifting his scythe high above his head- smoke still trailing from the tip- he spoke the words. "You who bear the heart of a demon, let your shadows gain sentience, turn against you, and eat at your souls until death." At the end of his words, Kardama plunged the pointed butt of his scythe toward the black-stained grass.

With a sudden impact, his scythe was ripped from his hands. It clattered into the grassy ground; the spell unable to activate. A dark, luminous figure stepped through the symbols of smoke, destroying the glyphs. The smoke faded as the figure appeared.

Even though broken and maimed, Kardama could recognize the figure well. *Zidal.* Holding her scythe before her, she smiled cunningly, asking Kardama for a battle. A battle to see whose faith was more determined. A battle to find which fate would overtake the world.

With sullen eyes, Kardama retrieved his scythe and attacked.

Alex looked into the sky, the demonic figure flying above and causing great destruction. Athreal's body was almost made whole. As he flew, his wings continued to extend. His horns were fully grown like enormous spikes, the flesh had covered the majority of his body, though some muscles still showed through.

Alex looked over his shoulder again, trying to look toward Kardama as he thrusted his dagger into the heart of a Broken Soul. He wouldn't be able to kill the demon until the spell had been casted, but he still had to fight. Every Darlid among them still had to fight. There would still be death until the king of the demons was dead.

Alex looked to the complex of rocky spires, noticing that the Broken Ones kept their distance. After having killed dozens of them, there was a fairly enormous gap between him and the army of broken souls. This was his chance. He only had to focus on one.

Alex ran between the spikes hiding beneath them for protection. The ground and rocks were caked in decay. The enormous rock formations had killed thousands, crushing the helpless and obliterating those who could not run. He could feel the viscous substance beneath his boots as he walked.

Alex glanced upward; he knew that he had to climb the rocks if he wanted to fight the demon himself. The formations had many openings, and ridged edges to hold to. Alex stepped toward one of the rocks. It would be more difficult to climb knowing that he only had one useful arm. He could use his left arm, but the pain would be more prevalent when he applied more pressure to the sprain.

Alex began to sheath his dagger. "Escaped, have we? Attempting to fight the king of the demons yourself? Now, that would be tragic." Alex turned toward the voice. Through the midst of the spikes, a figure emerged. Kyron, rebuilt by the curse of demons, his features were more prevalent, and his structure was well built. His strong features made him look more handsome. His wings were large and strong, and his build was impressive.

"Your guess is correct, demon" Alex responded, drawing his dagger.

"I suppose I can't let you get what you desire. Oh, son of man, did you really think that you could defeat a demon with such weaknesses?" Kyron smiled through emerald eyes, holding his scythe upright. "How about two?"

Alex shivered. Even killing one would be immensely difficult before the spell was cast. And he couldn't waste the Demothar on one of the twenty-three. He would have to improvise, to stall until the spell was cast. He could dodge attacks, he could talk, but he couldn't use his blade.

"I can kill two demons. I *will* kill them. This world is depending on me, and I will not let it die." A rush of anxiety pulsed through his bones, begging him to flee. *But he wouldn't.*

"And how would one such as you plan on defeating a god? You have no magic. You have no potent blade." Alex ducked beneath the swing of Kyron's scythe as he charged toward him. "You won't even attack me back.

"You're right. A dagger would be of no use against a scythe." Alex stepped to the side, feeling a breeze as the scythe swept by him. "But what if that wasn't my plan in the first place? What if I'm just waiting for the opportune moment to strike?"

"Why would I ever believe that an insignificant human could pull off a ruse such as that? Athreal will succeed." Kyron shoved Alex against one of the rock formations.

"How do you know that?"

"I'll show you." Kyron reached for Alex, and unable to react quickly enough, he took him by the neck with a powerful grip. "Because he is stronger." Kyron lifted his scythe and threw an attack with great force. The impact hewed his left arm from its socket, letting it fall to the ground in a puddle of crimson blood. He tossed Alex to the ground, beside his severed limb- which would not decay like that of a Darlid's.

Alex screamed in pain, holding his hand to his shoulder. "Though I cannot kill you before your purpose is complete, I can still show you who's more powerful."

Alex cringed, his vision blurring as tears filled his eyes. The pain was so immense that he could not feel anything else. The blood loss. He had to contain the blood loss. Alex sheathed his dagger, removing his cloak. He wrapped the stained cloth around his shoulder, tightening it as best as he could with his one remaining arm. The stream of blood began to lessen as the cloak soaked up what was there.

Alex spoke through a shivering, pained voice. "You think that can end my determination? I can still win. There is still hope."

A sudden wave of darkness exploded across the meadows when he finished his words. The power washed over him, and he could feel a comfort within him. He heard Kyron scream. He watched him fall as his shadow corrupted him.

The spell had been casted.

The scythes clashed with a great clanging sound. Kardama could feel the rage swelling within Zidal's heat. She had finally chosen to oppose the very god of this world, choosing to side with the king of the demons.

Great sorrow filled his heart as he avoided a well-planned attack. He never wished to fight against his allies if they turned. Especially those he had once considered friends. *It pained him.*

But he knew that he had to do what he must to save the peace of the world, even if he had to kill her. He remembered her own words. The things she had told him before she decided to return to her decaying body. *"Promise you'll kill me."* was the last thing she had said to him before she departed to a demonic life.

Kardama swung his scythe again, allowing it to be caught by her own. He wasn't ready to kill her. He could see it in her emerald eyes. Though demonic and powerful, the sullen glimmer still remained. She was still herself somewhere. She still wanted to save this world, even if she fought on the wrong side. But her soul was corrupt. He couldn't let her live that way- alive yet unable to control herself.

He would keep his promise.

"Zidal, search deeply within yourself. You know who you are." he said, slamming his scythe against the stick of hers. They held the stance, pushing against each other's weapons with determination.

"I knew who I was. I was wrong all those years." Her scythe slipped from the hold, cutting through the air. "Athreal will save us. Athreal will grant us power. Can't you see? I'm more powerful than I ever was before. I'm more powerful than you."

"But what makes you think you can kill a god?" Zidal swung her scythe. Kardama lifted his scythe, but with slower reflexes, he found that he could not block the attack. The blade cut through his abdomen, spilling teal blood. He cringed in pain. He could feel his eyes going blurry, but he knew that he could not give up.

"I know I can't kill a god. But you still have a mortal presence. I can still incapacitate you." Kardama held a hand to his stomach, raising his scythe before it struck him again. The blades clashed.

"I will not give in. The demon will fail. The demon will die. Alex will complete the duty he was sent for."

"The human cannot defeat a god either. He will open the gateway to Achnor. Athreal might choose to torture him until he cannot fight anymore, but he won't kill him until his purpose is completed." Zidal said as she threw another attack. Kardama lifted his scythe, hitting hers with a forceful impact. He could not fight, but he had to defend himself. He couldn't faint when he still had a duty.

"I have faith in Alex, just as you once had faith in me." Kardama expressed stepping aside from a swing of the scythe. "I will keep my promise."

"What promise?" She asked, throwing another attack.

"The one you asked of me before you *died.*"

Kardama's determination swelled, the pain in his body decreasing as hope filled his heart. He would complete his task. He threw an attack toward Zidal's heart. His scythe hit against solid metal; her reflexes enhanced by her now demonic soul. She *was* one of the twenty-three. He swung again, blocking a swing toward his thighs before ducking beneath another attack. She was quicker than any living being could be. More determined. More powerful.

Death knew that he could not shatter her soul merely by attacking. They could be evenly matched, fighting each other for eternity if he did nothing. He had to cast the spell and kill her at her weakest point. It would be difficult, but he knew it was possible.

But he couldn't cast the spell while she was still standing. Kardama threw his scythe toward the left, watching as Zidal's weapon followed. He hit the stick of her scythe, shattering the wood.

Her weapon rendered useless, he swung again, swerving his attack, and cringed as his blade met her leg. With his powerful impact, bones cracked, and blood and decay spilled. Zidal screamed out in pain, falling to the ground. Her scythe fell into the grass, and she stared at Death with broken eyes.

Now lame, she was unable to fight back, and Kardama had another chance to create the spell. He stepped back, speaking quietly. "Convert." Once again, a dark trail of smoke bled from the tip of the blade.

Kardama drew his scythe through the air, carefully recreating the symbol of shadows followed by the symbol of demons. He watched Zidal before him, caressing her useless legs as dark tears streamed through her eyes. He looked Zidal in the eyes as he spoke "You who bear the heart of a demon, let your shadows gain sentience, turn against you, and eat at your souls until death."

He sighed as he thrusted his scythe into the ground. The spell stole his energy to curse those he wished. The air around him exploded with light, and the symbols of shadows and demons erupted, crossing the entirety of the world to curse the demons. Kardama fell to the ground in weakness, his mind and body drained.

As the spell hit Zidal, she screamed in pain again. Her shadow gained sentience, devouring her soul and mind as she sat helplessly on the ground. Weakly, Kardama stood from the ground, and walked back toward Zidal; scythe in hand. "What are you doing?" she asked in a pained voice.

"Fulfilling a promise." His heart ached, but he knew that it was for her good as well as the world's. He watched the fear in her eyes as he plunged the blade of his scythe into her heart, shattering her broken soul.

The light in her eyes faded, and her body decayed into the grass along with all the others who had died this day.

He fell to the ground, weakened, but glad knowing that the spell had been dispersed. Alex had the best chance he could give him.

Alex watched as the demon cowered in pain, sprawling himself against the ground. Though weakly, he stood and stepped toward the corrupted soul. Taking hold of his discarded weapon, Alex lifted the scythe with his remaining arm. He looked down at Kyron, staring into his soul as he cried out in pain; both mental and physical. "There is still hope." Alex plunged the scythe into the demon's heart. He watched as his eyes became lifeless. As his body decayed in the grass. Soon, only the stick of a scythe showed where the body died.

Alex looked up, shivering. He was dying. He could feel the blood dripping from his wound. The sight of the severed arm still made his mind turn. The pain was unbearable, but he knew he must endure. He still had to kill the king of the demons.

The spell had been casted. It had affected each of the twenty-three with the same caliber. Soon each would be killed by another Darlid as their shadows ate away at their souls. But Athreal would not be greatly affected by this ailment. He would be weakened, but the shadow could not control him as such. He was too powerful.

Alex sighed. He left the body where it was and searched for a sloped spike. Luckily, there was one that was shaped on a low enough slope that he could climb, not needing to use his hands much. Grabbing hold of a ridge, Alex lifted himself onto the rock formation and began to climb toward the sky. He could see Athreal waiting for him above.

"Athreal!" he yelled with a weak voice. The demon looked toward him, standing uprightly at the highest point of the rock. He looked shocked. "I have come to challenge your power. I have come to kill you and save this world from its destruction." He took a breath. "Your demos are dying one by one. You are the last foe in my way for salvation."

"Son of man, I accept your challenge." At that moment, he watched as Athreal flew toward him speedily, knocking him off the rock. He hit the ground with an intense impact, but the softness of the grass, soil and decay broke his fall. Athreal loomed above him.

Alex stood from the grass and drew his dagger. Alex charged toward the demon; dagger extended. He only had to strike him once, then it would all be over.

He watched closely at the grinning demon. An enormous spike of stone grew from each hand. Four weapons created by dark magic. The battle had begun.

Alex breathed in deeply as Athreal charged toward him and threw his four arms toward him. Alex ducked beneath the spikes, throwing his dagger above his head. The blade clashed against the rock, blocking the attack. He pulled his dagger back and swung it toward the demon's leg. Athreal dropped an arm toward the blade, catching it before it hit him.

Athreal bent his body and threw three of his attacks toward Alex's damaged body. Alex closed his eyes, lifting his dagger- small and fragile- in the air to block the pressure. He heard the materials ring, and opened his eyes again, applying force against the massive rocks. He ducked beneath the forcefully thrusted rocks as his dagger slipped.

"You really think you can kill the king of demons with a mere dagger?" Athreal asked, mocking him.

Alex didn't respond, swinging his dagger toward him. Athreal struck back, knowing how to block an attack such as his with perfection. Athreal swung another one of his spikes as his other was occupied. Alex ducked, the stone club an inch above his head.

Alex backed away from the attack and reoriented himself. He threw his dagger forward, catching it against another rock. "I know who I am." He said with a determination unmatched. He stumbled back and glanced at Athreal in agony. The pain rang through him, but he would not fail now.

Athreal studied Alex, swinging his spikes toward his legs. Alex felt the sharp stone scrape against his thigh, and blood began to leak ceaselessly. Grunting in pain, Alex threw his sword forward, catching another stone and pushing it back. Alex ducked as he released the pressure, allowing Athreal's weapon to soar above him. Leaping from his crouched stance, Alex threw his dagger toward his enemy's face, yet it was blocked again by two spikes, as if he knew what was coming.

Alex dropped beneath another attack, raising his weapon. Their weapons struck against each other again. Alex couldn't bear the pressure. With all of his might, his strength in his one arm was not enough. The pressure of the attack pushed him to the ground. He felt his back hit the grass and looked up as Athreal stepped toward him.

Aware of his mistake, Alex knew that this could be the end of his triumph. Athreal bent down, dropping two of his stone daggers. He held onto Alex's shoulders, holding him to the ground. "Did you ever really think that you could defeat me, son of man? You couldn't even land one blow..."

With weak words and a sore mind, Alex spoke. "Demothar."

"What?" the demon asked "That elixir died out after Sel himself died. There *is* none remaining."

Caught off guard by his words, Athreal lessened his grip. He seemed almost afraid, as if he had already lost. Alex weakly lifted his arm and pushed his way through Athreal's forceful grip. He thrusted his blade upward, and the demon did not react to the blow. "Then let me show you!"

The dagger sunk deeply into his heart. He could feel it sinking into his flesh, taking hold of his powerful soul. He could hear Athreal screaming in pain, decaying beneath his blade. It was an eerie tune, but he knew that it meant it was all over.

The demon's blood dripped over his weakened body. He listened to his screams but didn't move. The body was destroyed, never to be the host of the creature again. He had done what he must.

The Demothar took over his body, and before it cursed him to his own death, it showed him the soul of Athreal. It begged him to take control of it, to choose its fate. Alex reached out and touched the soul, shattering it into infinite pieces, never to be found again. He called them *Hatred.* And if any being felt this upon them, it would be only for a little time, for every soul showed anger at one time or another. His soul would be the presence of a feeling, still there, but the pieces would never be found again.

Alex could feel his body breaking. The spell began at his legs, rendering them useless as they were cast into stone. He held still, turning his head to the side to watch the world around him, knowing that he had done something great. Every remaining broken soul perished. He could see their bodies decaying, soiling the grass with their deaths. The entire mass of Broken Souls was screaming in pain as they died.

Darlids cheered. From what he could tell, one third of the army still remained.

He had saved the world. The fable was true. He felt a bitter-sweet feeling as he watched everything fade away. He had accomplished the impossible and saved an entire race of people. And now he had to leave it behind. *dead.*

Alex felt his insides harden. His limbs became immobile. His senses were taken from him.

He let out his final breath.

S awoke with fear in his heart. That fear was accompanied by anxiety and excitement. Today was the day. The day that their fate would be set. The day that they would either defeat their Master and find a new life, or the day that their master condemned them to eternal service. *S would make a fine demon...*

The silence was interrupted by the metal knob of the door shaking vigorously. S glanced at his brother with empty eyes, who sat up at the noise, eager for the day to finally be over. The door opened, revealing the Master, with one gleaming emerald eye, he smiled. Though he did not know the fate that would become of him this day. The day they had been planning for years as they were trapped in the prison.

"Come, you're training today will be very important. With the lessons you will learn today, you will be my greatest warriors."

S stood from the ground, following the master through the metal door. He glanced over his shoulder, watching as his brother followed him. He gave his brother a gentle, excited smile as he turned the corner, going down the all-familiar path toward the training room. S tapped his pocket, feeling the familiar roughness of the Striker Stone in his pocket.

The Master opened the door before him, watching his prisoners eagerly as they stepped into the room. As S and R entered the room, the Master followed behind, locking the door behind him.

"Today, you will be testing your skills. You will both battle against me, your Master and trainer, until I declare that you have one. I will not go easy on you. There will be pain." The Master stepped toward S, looming above him as his right tentacle emerged from his shoulder, holding a key in his grip. He unlocked the chains, allowing them to fall to the floor, doing likewise to R. *"Please, choose your weapon."* he begged, drawing a sword of his own.

S glanced at his brother, choosing one of the swords knowing that it was not the one he was going to use in the end. His brother chose another one- slightly rusted and dented and nodded. S took his brother's hand and stopped time as they fled into the void.

Despite the fear, S did not hesitate. He and R found their way to the hidden rift in the void easily and let go. "Are you ready? This is it." S asked.

"It's now or never, dear brother." R replied. "Only tomorrow knows if we will succeed." R smiled.

S held out his hand, taking the sword from his brother's grip and laid them on the ground. Reaching into his mind he found the blades they had hidden in the void and retrieved them. Their grips were black as the night, yet they were easy to hold. Their crossguards, lined with silver, bent upward at each end. The pommels were a silver sphere, a dark crystal fused in each center. The blade was sharp, used often, having seen many battles. They were made for them.

He handed one to his brother, pulling the stone out of his pocket. Taking in a deep breath, S applied pressure beside his blade, hoping that the sword would ignite. A spark flew from the stone, igniting the blade in an ominous lilac blaze. It felt warm in his hands- powerful.

Lowered his blade, touching his to R's. Both blades alight, S nodded and followed his brother through the rift in the void. Upon their exit, they returned to the training room, holding their Master's weakness.

The Master studied them, stunned, though not entirely intimidated. S knew that the Master wouldn't die without a fight, and with this, he was ready. "It's time. I made a promise, and we both agreed to the terms." With his words, he felt his consciousness transfer. It was an uncomfortable feeling being able to think within his own mind, yet only watch his body move, unable to control the movements. *Astaroth's consciousness was controlling him.*

Similarly, as his head moved out of his control, he noticed that his brother's movements were also unnatural, controlled by that of his shadow demon. Even with empty sockets, he seemed more soulless, more powerful than before. He could feel the power reigning throughout his own body. With burning blades held before them and an unnatural amount of power flowing through their veins, they would win the battle.

Astaroth cackled, charging toward the Master. He lifted his sword with perfect accuracy and threw an attack toward the Tall Being. At the same moment, his brother jumped up, thrusting his blade toward the Master. The lilac flame swept through the air, cutting through decaying skin. He didn't react…

He didn't move. He didn't fight back. It was as if he had given up knowing that no matter what he did, he would still fail. *He had to let them go.*

Why did he give up so easily? What had he planned that he allowed himself to die so easily?

S could feel his consciousness return to his body as his flaming blade pierced the heart of the one, they once called Master. His blade collided with his brother's, a grand ringing sound echoing through the room. The flames went out as the blades felt the wet innards of the disturber, completing their task.

S and his brother drew their blades from the heart. The Master began to cackle, his smile growing, his emerald eye gleaming as his decay melted into the stone below. Soon, the laughter died out, and all that remained was his attire.

The Master was dead. S looked at his brother, dropping the sword to the ground and running to him. He smiled, embracing his brother with elation. "We did it, Courier! We're free!" Letting go of his brother, he studied his emotions. Both were unable to shake the joy.

"Come on, let's get out of here. I want to see the world... the *real* world." S nodded, stepping toward the stained cloak laying in viscous decay. Rummaging through his pocket, S found the keys.

Opening the door, S took his brother's hand and returned to the void. He smiled, the open door unlocking the endless ways to the void, the endless opportunities of their freedom. S spoke, looking into his brother's empty eyes. "Where should we go first?"

Epilogue

Days had passed since the death of Athreal, and the world was finally at peace. Once the war had finally ended, everyone had the opportunity to rest, and find their friends and loved ones again. Kardama himself had slept through those days, regaining his lost energy after having created the spell, only to wake up to a nearly barren meadow.

Kardama stood atop one of the enormous stalagmites which had emerged from the ground, overlooking the meadows. The colorful grass was stained with the dark decay of thousands of Darlids, and the decay of *every* Broken Soul that once lived.

Alex's body, casted in stone, had been found beneath the conglomeration of rock formations. His dagger was tightly grasped within his fingers, his left arm amputated, and his nose shattered. His statue wasn't perfect, but it would be a symbol for the people.

The statue stood gracefully at the base of the rock formations, overlooking the crowd.

The people that remained- luckily over two thirds that had come to fight- waited patiently in an audience for their king to speak. The words were difficult to create. There was so much death and pain. But this day was to be commemorated. For the bravery of them all.

Kardama sighed and nodded at his scribes who would deliver the messages to the people further back. He spoke, projecting his voice over the valley. "Peace has finally been obtained!" he announced. "Never again will a Broken Soul challenge the fate of this world, for the fate has already been set. A fate of peace. A fate of hope. A fate of love.

"On this day we come here to commemorate the heroes of this world." He looked over his army. They looked so tired, so worn. Many of them had lost loved ones. There was so much pain. "You all are the heroes of this land. All of you played a part in defeating our greatest foe. All of you contributed to the fall of the demon." He heard cheers erupt.

Kardama smiled faintly. *He had lost so many. He didn't have time to spend with each of those that died.*

"But today, we have come here also to remember those who died during this war. They have chosen a better life. Their souls were great. They fought valiantly until the end and brought us closer to our victory. Without them- and all of you- this world would be cursed by the demon.

"And on this day, we will remember the one who saved us all. The one who sacrificed himself to slay the demon. He who despite his losses, and trials, and errors, gave us a head in the battle and saved us from Athreal's reign.

"Today, we remember our savior: Alex Raider."

The Master- the decayed body of Athreal- smiled. His insides felt warm, like a fire had been burning within his heart. He could still feel the points of the blades in his skin despite their removal. He had influenced the children too well. *He wanted them to escape.*

After they had tried to kill him, he dissolved his body; a power given to him by his rage of power centuries ago. He could hear their joy from just two rooms down. They'd disappear with the help of S's magic within moments.

Little did they know that their Master still lived. Little did they know that their torture would never end. Little did they know that in the future, the world would belong to him and there was nothing they could do about that fact. They would never be able to fight Athreal on their own. He would take back what was rightfully his.

His plan was all too cunning for two mere children. He had influenced R too well. He was an expert at lying, even within his mind, and had given R a simple minor inconvenience disguised as his weakness. And it worked perfectly.

Fire itself had no effect on him. After creating enough potions, he had created one which gave him immunity. And though the sharpness of the blades stung, his body was too decayed to break at the mere feel of a point.

Still, after years of torturing them, after all that time training them, it almost felt like he had given up. Like he had thrown away a perfect elixir before its use. But he had his reasons.

He had a feeling that they would be more important in other ways…

He just had to wait.

Acknowledgements

The creation of this book would not be possible without the influence and hard work of others. It is my pleasure to show my appreciation for their help.

First, I would like to thank all those who had read through my book beforehand- even if it was only a short section or two- to help fix my mistakes and give suggestions on my writing. This book would not be the same without everyone who helped me along the way.

I would also like to thank all of my friends and family. They give me so much inspiration and joy every single day. Without their influence on me, this book would have been much different from the direction I took it.

I would like to make a special acknowledgement to Brian A. Flores, who created the fantastic cover art for me.

Finally, I would like to thank you- the reader. My dreams would not be possible without someone picking up this book.

CPSIA information can be obtained
at www.ICGtesting.com
Printed in the USA
BVHW041613080921
616216BV00032B/290